THE KILLER

After a degree in law and a stint as a journalist, Susan Wilkins embarked on a career in television drama. She has written numerous scripts for shows ranging from *Casualty* and *Heartbeat* to *Coronation Street* and *East-Enders*. She created and wrote the London-based detective drama *South of the Border* of which the BBC made two series. *The Killer* is her third novel and completes a trilogy.

Also by Susan Wilkins

The Informant
The Mourner

THE
KILLER

SUSAN
WILKINS

PAN BOOKS

First published 2017 by Macmillan

First published in paperback 2017 by Macmillan

This edition first published 2017 by Pan Books
an imprint of Pan Macmillan
20 New Wharf Road, London N1 9RR
Associated companies throughout the world
www.panmacmillan.com

ISBN 978-1-5098-0435-1

1 3 5 7 9 8 6 4 2

A CIP catalogue record for this book is available from the British Library.

Typeset by Ellipsis, Glasgow
Printed and bound by CPI Group (UK) Ltd, Croydon, CR0 4YY

Visit www.panmacmillan.com to read more about all our books
and to buy them. You will also find features, author interviews and
news of any author events, and you can sign up for e-newsletters
so that you're always first to hear about our new releases.

To Sue Kenyon

PROLOGUE

Sweat trickled down his face. Wiping it away, Yevgeny Koshkin adjusted the aviator shades. He'd lost count of the number of funerals he'd attended. Too many, that's all he knew. And that didn't include the funerals he'd caused, of the men he'd killed. Those he dismissed from his mind. He'd done his job and if the ghosts of his victims haunted him he'd never have admitted it.

The noonday sun was high and blinding and he smiled to himself as he imagined it beating down on the mob of paparazzi and camera crews waiting ten miles away at Chelmsford crematorium. Pretty soon they'd realize that they'd been duped. Joey Phelps, the angel-faced cop killer the tabloids loved to hate, would not be arriving there in a grand horse-drawn hearse, as they'd been led to believe. Instead he'd be laid to rest here, in this forgotten churchyard, surrounded by late summer birdsong rather than the click-clack of prying lenses.

The ancient church was set on a knoll above rich and rolling Essex farmland, a small pond fringed with sedges separating it from a winding lane. Yevgeny stood in the shade of the lychgate. The fresh-faced curate was beside him in surplice and cassock, hands clasping his prayer book, practising his funereal face.

He was the most junior member of the local ministry. Evangelical and ambitious to serve the Lord, he'd interpreted it as God's munificence when a polite Russian with a briefcase full of cash had turned up on his doorstep offering to make a large donation to the church's restoration fund. And money was desperately needed. The boiler was bust, the roof leaked and scaffolding held up the reputedly Saxon tower, giving the building a mysterious and abandoned air.

The curate let his gaze drift upwards to the rooks circling the elderly yew in the far corner of the clumpy, overgrown churchyard. Two fresh graves had been dug; the Russian had arrived early to select the spot. There were to be no headstones, just a planting of bulbs – a carpet of crocuses and narcissi – to bloom in the spring.

If he was honest, the secrecy of the proceedings excited the young cleric; 'total privacy' was the phrase the Russian had used. He should have discussed it with his boss and followed proper procedures, he knew that. So what if the paperwork was sketchy? Modern ministry meant thinking outside the box. He was guessing the departed were illegal immigrants, and the Russian said nothing to disabuse him of this assumption. No one else was about to solve the problem of his crumbling spire and didn't all souls deserve a Christian burial, whether or not they had the right passport? He felt he'd made a compassionate decision as well as a pragmatic one and if necessary he would defend it all the way up to the bishop.

Yevgeny cast a wary professional eye over his surroundings. He had a couple of his own men, including his cousin Mika, discreetly placed in the churchyard, although with the official funeral scheduled to take place miles away he didn't expect any problems. He checked his watch as a plain black Mercedes panel van turned from the lane into the short gravel drive and drew up at the gate. It was right on time. Behind it came a chauffeured four-by-four with dark tinted windows. The

2

Russian gave the curate a nod then stepped forward to open the rear door of the car.

There were two passengers and Kaz Phelps was the first out. She wore black jeans and a tailored jacket, her only concession to the formality of the occasion. Her dark eyes were wary, her face pale and inscrutable. She'd come to bury her little brother, her Joey, the needy, adoring boy who'd grown into a monster. That's what the press had dubbed him and it was hard to disagree. The fact he'd been trying to help her when he died, riddled with bullets on a London street, fuelled the toxic brew of guilt and anger swilling round in her head, though there was no way she'd ever show it.

As far as Yevgeny or anyone else could see, the shock of Joey's death had left her contained and distant. She didn't crack, she didn't even cry. But there were two graves because the Russian had lost a brother too. Tolya had been gunned down in the same foolhardy escapade and Yevgeny had certainly cried – alone, on a Skype call to his elderly mother in Magnitogorsk and cradling his sister, Irina, in his arms.

Since he'd left home at seventeen to join the army, Yevgeny Koshkin had hammered out his own moral code and loyalty was at its heart. He'd served his country, obeyed his officers and, in more recent years, the bosses who'd hired and trusted him. Following orders, he'd killed but he took no pleasure in it. It was just part of a soldier's job. He'd always tried to make it fast and clean. He was a hard man, circumstances had left him with little choice, but he'd resisted the temptation to become cruel.

After years of rootless wandering, following the money and the next job, he'd started to feel the need to settle and England appealed to him. Women, outside his immediate family, had hardly figured in his life. Short-term sexual liaisons had satisfied his needs. As a young man he'd once fancied himself in love with a Chechen nurse; she'd been beaten to death by her own father for fraternizing with the enemy.

When Yevgeny first met Kaz Phelps she'd not long been released from jail. He found it hard to explain the attraction; she was beautiful certainly, but there was something in her physical presence – tough yet sensual – and the sharp watchfulness in her eye, that both unnerved and excited him. However, he'd been working for her brother at the time and any approach would have been unprofessional. Now that Joey was dead and she was staying in his house, under his protection you could say, he hoped that she might start to notice and appreciate his interest.

Offering his hand, he helped her out of the back of the four-by-four. Her palm rested lightly in his for hardly a second yet he felt a pulse of raw energy shoot up his arm. No woman had ever had such a visceral effect on him before. But her eyes skated away from his face and back into the car towards Irina.

The girls – to Yevgeny they were girls – had become firm friends and he was glad. His sister seemed so skittish and young; she'd always been cosseted. To have a comrade, and maybe in time a sister-in-law, like Kaz – someone a couple of years older who really knew the score – was bound to be a steadying influence.

His attention moved across to the four beefy pall-bearers, in black tailcoats and leather gloves, climbing out of the van. Being unfamiliar with the customs of the country, he'd made discreet enquiries and been recommended an East End firm, who boasted a long history of *taking care of things* for clients on the wrong side of the law. Still it surprised him to see that the funeral director accompanying them was female. She wore a top hat, carried a cane and issued her instructions in a soft sing-song voice which Yevgeny strained to hear. It wasn't English, a couple of words sounded vaguely Slavic, but not quite. Then he realized she was speaking Albanian.

As they unloaded the first of the two solid oak caskets from the Mercedes onto silver coffin trolleys, an old Vauxhall Vectra, with a dent in the boot, pulled up behind the four-by-four at the gate. The three remaining mourners had arrived.

Yevgeny was well aware of the strained relationship between Kaz and her mother. He had gone personally to break the news of her son's death to Ellie Phelps. She was a stupid and vindictive woman and, if she made any kind of scene, he was ready to intervene and shut her up. But Ellie stumbled out of the car and had to be rescued and supported by her companion Brian. Whatever medication she was on, prescribed or otherwise, it had rendered her dead-eyed and docile. A black fascinator with a lacy veil had been planted askew on her unwashed hair and she looked flushed in a collarless leather coat too hot for a late summer's day.

Ignoring her mother and Brian, Kaz gave a smile of acknowledgement to the third mourner, Glynis. Yevgeny watched the small, bird-like creature move forward and grasp Kaz's hand. 'So sorry, love. Must be awful for you.'

Kaz's smile soured. 'Fucking cops wouldn't release the bodies for ages.'

'They never give no thought to the families, do they?'

Ellie swayed on the balls of her feet. She seemed to be trying to focus on her daughter. Yevgeny readied himself to step in. A low, keening moan rose from deep in the woman's chest and Kaz edged back, expecting it to be followed by a blow. But Ellie toppled forward into her arms and began to sob. 'My babies, my poor babies! What we gonna do without him, Kaz? What we gonna do?'

Detaching herself from the maternal grasp, Kaz gave no hint of the welter of emotions rippling through her. She was there to bury Joey, quietly, without fuss or fanfare, in an anonymous grave. Would he have approved of such an ending? Probably not. But she didn't care. She glanced at Yevgeny. 'Can we just get this over with?'

He smiled, took her arm and they followed the coffins into the church.

Yevgeny, Kaz and Irina settled in the wooden pews on one side of the aisle, Ellie, Brian and Glynis on the other.

Sensing a tension between the camps the curate pitched straight in. 'I am the resurrection and the life, saith the Lord . . .'

Yevgeny's thoughts drifted back to his homeland. Even in Soviet times his mother had been a religious woman.

'He that believeth in me, though he were dead, yet shall he live . . .'

All his brothers were dead now – Tolya had been the last – and all had suffered violent ends. Only him and Irina were left.

'And whosoever liveth and believeth in me shall never die.'

The language was a little arcane for Yevgeny to grasp completely but the curate's incantatory tone soothed him. In the far recesses of memory he was still a small boy, clinging to his mother's skirt as the priest sailed by in his vestments, censer swinging and billowing smoke. That intense fragrance, frankincense undercut with the sharp resin of fir, wafted through his unconscious and tethered him to the place where he was born. How could he bury his brother without incense? It felt wrong. He neither believed nor disbelieved in God. But he believed in family.

The grass was sun-baked and crackled underfoot as the

mourners picked their way through the untended churchyard and gathered around the open graves. The rooks cawed and the young curate fumbled with the pages of his prayer book.

'Oh holy and most merciful Saviour, deliver us not into the bitter pains of eternal death. Thou knowest, Lord, the secrets of our hearts . . .'

Yevgeny glanced at Kaz standing beside him. Would this woman ever allow him to glimpse the secrets of her heart?

This was what he was wondering, this was what he was hoping for when a flash of light caught his eye. In a single frozen moment he realized it was sunshine glinting off the barrel of a gun, he heard its report and felt the gust of the bullet whooshing between him and Kaz, nicking the lobe of her ear and causing her to yelp.

With his jacket buttoned, denying him instant access to his own holstered weapon, he had only a split second to make a decision. He barged Kaz sideways first, then he went for his gun. But the funeral director had already fired her second shot. It struck him in the temple; he was dead before he even hit the ground. Rolling over, his body came to rest on the mound of soft earth edging his brother's grave.

1

Nicci Armstrong watched from her desk as the men in suits filed out of the boardroom. There were handshakes and pleasantries but it was impossible to tell if the meeting had been a success. She glanced across at Pascale, her researcher. They didn't speak. Both were wondering the same thing: did they still have a job?

Everyone knew the business was in dire financial straits, there had already been redundancies and the small investigations team, led by Nicci, was down to three. The remaining employees, in cybercrime and security, were scattered across the smart open-plan office, beavering away at their desks, but they all knew the score.

Since the firm's inception Simon Blake Associates had sailed pretty close to the wind. Blake himself, in the opinion of many in the security industry, was just too arrogant and now he was getting his comeuppance. SBA's most recent case had led to the high-profile arrest of Robert Hollister, a prominent politician and member of the shadow cabinet. The media had loved it and showered SBA with praise and glossy profiles in the Sunday supplements. But they were the new kids on the block and it soon became obvious that upsetting the establishment came with a hefty price tag.

Nicci kept a surreptitious eye on the boss as he escorted his guests to the lifts. His manner was unctuous, which she found disturbing. An ex-copper, who'd made it to the senior rank of commander in the Met, Simon Blake had dealt with a slew of serious villains and he took no prisoners. But now he'd moved into the private sector he'd become a hostage to fortune and the moneymen had brought him down. The City fixers and twisters, who'd initially backed his enterprise, had decided they didn't like his attitude or priorities. He'd crossed the wrong people so they'd pulled the plug.

Rising from her desk Nicci wandered towards the coffee station in the hope of waylaying him. He was meandering back to his office with a glazed expression.

'Get you a coffee, boss?'

Blake seemed startled but he smiled. 'Yeah, why not?'

The task of assembling mugs and pushing buttons removed the necessity for small talk. Blake gazed across the room and out of the window at the fine late September day beyond. His look was wistful; the view – the towering cityscape of steel and glass and power – was the thing that had sold him on the location.

Nicci shot him a covert glance. He was jiggling the change in his trouser pocket. The aroma of fresh coffee wafted from the machine as it filled their cups.

'How did it go?' She knew it was the question he didn't want to hear, though she hoped he wouldn't evade it.

He sucked his teeth. 'Who can tell? They will bail us out. The loan's agreed in principle. The accountants are being upbeat. But there are stringent conditions. The bottom line is we have to do a lot more with a lot less.'

She handed him the coffee. He stared down at the dark steaming liquid as if in search of inspiration.

'Y'know, Nic, all my years as a serving officer I lived on my salary, had a mortgage but not a penny more of debt. Not even a car loan. Now?' He gave a bleak chuckle. 'Now I'm in hock up to my eyeballs. My future's in hock, my kids' futures. And there's no sodding guarantee they won't turn round in three months and say, "Sorry, target's not met, we're calling it in. Declaring you bankrupt."'

Nicci watched him, noting the moistness in his eyes. She'd worked for him inside the Met and on the outside as a private detective. When she was at her lowest ebb he'd given her a chance. They weren't exactly friends, the bond was in a sense deeper: professional colleagues with shared values. And, whatever else, she owed him.

Tipping a sachet of sugar into her own coffee she cast him a sidelong glance. 'Goes without saying, if there's anything I can do.'

'As a matter of fact there is.' He grinned. 'But you're not going to like it.'

With a dip of the head he invited her to join him in his office. She followed him in and closed the door.

Plonking down in his chair he rested the mug of coffee on a leather coaster. He was a precise man with an organized mind; it was what had made him such a good copper.

Nicci settled on the sofa and waited.

Blake steepled his fingers. 'Here's the situation. The new equity partners will come on board provided we concentrate on the security side of the business. That's where they think the money is. According to the *Sunday Times* Rich List, London's got more resident billionaires than any other city on the planet. Reliable ex-coppers as minders is the brand they want to promote.'

She sniffed. 'No investigations at all then?'

'Depends on whether we can get on the right side of the Police and Crime Commissioners and land a few outsourcing contracts. But that's down to me – and you know how rubbish I am at charming politicians.'

'Don't sell yourself short. You can brown-nose with the best.'

'Yeah, well, I'm going to have to. And we've got cybercrime. That's obviously a growth area and they'll put money into that.'

'So who's going to run the security side with Rory gone? I hope that's not what you're asking me to do.'

Rory McLaren was the former Head of Security; he'd decamped to set up his own firm with his brother, a City boy with excellent connections.

'Rory's the competition now.' Swivelling his chair, Blake sighed. 'And I reckon a few of our clients'll end up going with him.' He hesitated. 'Are you two . . .'

Nicci flashed him a warning look. 'No, and we never were.'

He raised his palms. 'Sorry.'

They sat in silence for a moment, sharp fingers of afternoon sun filtering through the blinds.

Blake gave her a sheepish smile. 'I didn't mean to—'

'It was a casual fuck, Simon. Well, a casual several fucks. He's a buttoned-up lunatic, which is not what I need in my life.'

'No indeed.'

She shook her head, chuckled. 'Look, I don't mean to be so . . . y'know.'

He waved away the apology. 'Hugo's in charge of security for now.'

'As long as you're not lining me up for the job.'

'I still want you in charge of investigations.' He looked at her directly and frowned. 'But the reality is a major part of the work, for defence briefs and the like, depends on checks we do online. It's a research job, Pascale can handle that.'

Nicci sipped her coffee. She noticed his eyes were puffy; sleepless nights haunted by problems he couldn't solve. His back was against the wall.

'So what do you want me to do that I'm not going to like?'

'HNWIs – that's our target market. High Net Worth Individuals.'

'Yeah, I get it. The billionaires.'

'Plus all the multimillionaires too, many of whom hail from the Middle East. They have wives. Sometimes several. And they want those wives protected by female personnel.'

'You want me to become a minder? Take some rich woman shopping and carry her packages?' Nicci exhaled.

She'd been forced out of the only career she'd ever wanted – that of police officer. Being a private detective had always felt a poor substitute. But this?

Blake rubbed his close-cropped scalp, a habitual gesture when he felt tense. 'There is a potential threat both from financially motivated kidnappers as well as terrorists.'

'What, that makes the job more interesting? Taking on terrorists unarmed?'

Blake managed a smile.

Nicci raised her eyebrows. 'The Federation's talking about every officer having a taser. You can't even offer me that.'

'They'll never agree. Training would be too costly.'

'Get real, Simon. If push comes to shove they'll hand them out without the training.'

Blake grinned. 'I'll throw in some pepper spray. And it would only be temporary. Until I can afford to start hiring again.'

They both knew that wouldn't be anytime soon. Still there was no way she could let him down. She shook her head wearily. 'I'll think about it.'

'That's all I ask.'

Returning to her desk, Nicci cast an eye over the investigations section, which she'd come to regard as her domain. Blake was right, most of the day-to-day inquiries could be handled by Pascale. Sharp as a tack, she was also a grafter. Unfortunately no one could say that of the remaining member of the team.

Eddie Lunt was munching his way through a triple-decker chicken BLT as he lounged in his chair. Nicci found his relentlessly smarmy attitude a constant irritant. Nevertheless Eddie had his talents and, more importantly, his contacts, although it had taken her a while to come to terms with these annoying facts.

She sighed. 'Have you come up with any more background on that stuff I asked you?'

He wiped the mayo from his lips. 'I'm on it, boss.'

He insisted on calling her boss even though she told him, about once a week, that she hated it. Stalemate.

She shot him a sceptical look. He responded with his pixie smile. 'Oh, I answered your phone. Some copper's looking for you. Says it's urgent.'

'A copper? Who?'

He waved the sandwich. 'Stonehouse?'

'Stoneham?'

'That's the one. Apparently a gunfight broke out at Joey Phelps's funeral. I checked online. Three dead, according to the Beeb.'

The face of Karen Phelps flashed into Nicci's mind, plus that old familiar stab of fear that heralded bad news. She wasn't exactly a friend either. A target, a pain-in-the-arse and a sometime ally – she'd been all those things, not to mention a shedload of trouble. But in spite of Nicci's best efforts not to care, somehow she did. 'Three dead? They say who?'

Eddie shook his head. 'A woman and two blokes, that's all it said. Number's on the pad. This Stoneham wants you to call ASAP.'

2

Nicci got to Liverpool Street station by four forty-five, just as the early surge of homeward-bound Essex commuters hit the trains. With some gentle pushing and shoving she managed to secure a window seat. The fast train to Chelmsford took thirty-two minutes.

She gazed blankly out of the window as East London's higgledy-piggledy vista of buildings, bridges, rail-tracks and roads rushed by, gradually loosening to include swathes of green. Her mind too was racing.

The phone conversation she'd had with Detective Chief Inspector Cheryl Stoneham had been businesslike; their connection was entirely professional although it had always been friendly.

'Nic, it's been a while. You're a hard woman to track down.'

'I was retired on medical grounds.' Nicci wondered how much Stoneham knew.

'Yeah, I gather.' She knew. There was a respectful pause to acknowledge Nicci's tragedy: the death of her little girl in a road accident. Stoneham was a mother herself so the searing agony of such a loss was all too easy for her to imagine. 'But you're bearing up?'

'Mostly.'

'And you're a private investigator now?'

'It pays the bills.' This was the glib explanation Nicci always gave. It was a polite rebuff.

Stoneham took the hint. 'Well, I've got a shoot-out in a country churchyard. Turned out to be Joey Phelps's funeral. Three dead, two more injured.'

'Including Karen Phelps?'

'She's okay. A bit shaken – though with her it's hard to tell. We've spent the afternoon trying to interview her, but she's being very cagey.'

Relief flooded through Nicci; she didn't want it, but again, there it was. She tried to sound nonchalant. 'Doesn't surprise me.'

'She's pointing the finger at some Russian by the name of Pudovkin. And she says we should talk to you, says that you know all about it. Do you?'

Nicci hesitated. 'I know a bit but . . . it's complicated.'

'It would be. I realize you're not in the job any more. But I'd really appreciate your input.'

It had been a friendly enough request but Nicci knew she didn't have a lot of choice. And with her job prospects getting rockier by the day, it didn't seem sensible to alienate one of the few allies she still had at a senior level in the police.

She walked the short distance from Chelmsford station to New Street and the brutalist-style concrete bunker that housed the headquarters of Essex Police. She gave her name at the desk and Stoneham met her in person when she emerged from the lift.

The DCI was what a casual observer might call a jolly woman – fiftyish, rotund, chatty, with a jokey greeting for everyone. But it was easy to be fooled by her manner; underneath there lurked a whip-smart intellect. She was a leading Senior Investigating Officer in the Serious Crime Directorate run jointly by Essex and Kent police. She'd been invited to apply for promotion and could've probably made it to Chief Constable. But Stoneham was a detective in her blood and bones; climbing the greasy pole of senior management didn't appeal to her.

'Thanks for coming so promptly.'

Nicci shrugged. 'If I can help, I'm only too pleased.'

Stoneham led the way down a short corridor towards her office. 'The Phelps funeral was scheduled for twelve o'clock at the crematorium. Given his violent death, we had officers present, including firearms officers. But it seems the family fooled us and everyone else.' She gave a wry chuckle. 'Well, not quite everyone. Anyway, they changed the venue.'

'I don't know Karen well, but I can see that the prospect of holding her brother's funeral in the middle of a media circus probably wouldn't appeal.'

The office was small and bright with a pleasing view over the city rooftops. Stoneham offered Nicci a chair, closed the door and settled herself behind the desk.

'Our SCD was supposed to be liaising with the Met on Joey Phelps's death. But this shooting obviously changes things. The ACC has asked me to oversee the investigation because of the organized crime element. We're running it from our MIT office in Brentwood, they're nearest to the scene.'

Nicci made a conscious effort to relax. SCD, ACC, MIT – she could feel a sense of elation as Stoneham trotted out all the insider acronyms. The tension around a big police operation was always exciting. The seriousness and importance of the job, this was the buzz she craved. 'Did the Met tell you that Pudovkin was the target Joey was after when he was killed?'

'That name was mentioned. But they're being a bit evasive. Hard to know if it's deliberate or they really are clueless.'

'The politics of the Met is the one thing I don't miss.' Nicci grinned, prompting a sympathetic smile from Stoneham in return.

'We can all be territorial. And with all these cuts – sorry, "reforms" – don't think we haven't got our share of stupid politics.'

The dry common sense of the DCI reminded Nicci of why she'd always liked her. If anyone could unpack this can of worms it was her. But was Nicci there simply to be pumped for information or was Stoneham really prepared to trust her? 'Have you ID'd the three dead?'

Stoneham hesitated, but only for a second, then she slipped her glasses on and consulted the file on her desk. 'So far we've got Yevgeny Koshkin, a Russian businessman, recently granted a business visa. According to his application he's an importer of fine wines. Who knows if that's true? The woman is more interesting. Jumira Bogdani. She's Albanian, operates under several aliases and there's a European arrest warrant out on her. She has connections with various people-trafficking gangs and could be a hired assassin.'

'Did she start the shooting?'

'According to one witness – Glynis Phelps – possibly. Though there's a deal of confusion around the chain of events.'

'You think she could've been hired to carry out a hit?'

'Looks that way. But who was the target and why?'

'The Russian businessman? Koshkin?'

'There are certainly precedents for that. Particularly if he's on the Kremlin's shit list.' The DCI removed her glasses. 'But I'm wondering about Karen Phelps. Is there any reason to think it might be her?'

'She's Joey's sister. Which could be enough.'

'And Joey, for whatever reason, took it into his head to try and murder this Pudovkin. There was a shoot-out and Joey ended up dead. Question is, what was it all about? The Met seem pretty clueless.' The DCI rocked back in her chair, the preliminaries were over, they'd both laid their cards on the table. She laced her fingers and waited.

Nicci knew it was her turn to share. 'The firm I work for, Simon Blake Associates, was hired to look into the death of Helen Warner.'

'The MP who committed suicide?'

'Her partner refused to accept the suicide verdict, that's why she hired us.'

Stoneham frowned. 'I didn't follow the case in detail, but didn't it emerge that Warner was an abuse victim? And Robert Hollister, the Labour bigwig – wasn't he involved?'

'Hollister was a student of Warner's father; he started to have sex with her when she was fourteen. He's been charged. He's out on bail. I don't know the trial date.'

The DCI made a note on her pad. 'What's the connection with Karen Phelps and this Pudovkin?'

'For a number of years Helen Warner was Karen's lawyer.'

Stoneham's brow furrowed as she dredged her memory. 'I think I knew that.'

'If you recall she attended that interview we did together in Southend.'

'Oh yeah. After the sister's boyfriend bought it.'

'When Karen got out of prison, it became a more intimate relationship.'

'That wasn't very professional of Ms Warner.'

Nicci shrugged. 'By the time Warner died they'd gone their separate ways. Karen was relocated by witness protection. But she didn't buy the suicide story either.'

'So is that why she turfed up here in July when Joey broke

out? I caught her lurking round the old family pile when we went looking for him.'

'I'm surprised you didn't nick her.'

'I gave her the benefit of the doubt.' The DCI pursed her lips. 'Looks like I made a mistake.'

'Maybe not. I'm pretty sure she didn't aid or abet her brother. She was obsessed with Helen and finding out what happened. She was very helpful to our investigation.'

Nicci hesitated. The remainder of what she knew was speculation and it wasn't up to her to send a major police investigation off on a wild goose chase. She needed to be careful. But would that best serve the interests of justice? She was torn. Being asked for her input, as Stoneham had phrased it, was seductive. It made her realize just how much she wanted to feel like an insider again.

She gave Stoneham a diffident smile. 'The rest is pure guesswork.'

The hook went in. Stoneham beamed. 'Round here we call it informed hypothesis. It's what makes this job fun.'

Nicci felt a pang of guilt but ploughed on. 'Okay, Viktor Pudovkin is a rich Russian, who lives in London.'

'Oligarch rich?'

'Certainly edging into the billionaires' club.'

'Any connection between him and our dead Russian?'

'Not as far as I know. Anyway, my boss, Simon Blake, talked to an old colleague in MI5 about Pudovkin.'

'So what is he? Spook or dissident?' The DCI chortled. 'Strikes me the Russian community in London is divided into two camps: those working for Putin and those trying to escape him.'

'Spook. Ex-KGB. It's how a lot of them made their money. And Hollister's wife is mates with him, though mates is probably not the right word. The theory is she feared Warner was about to blow the whistle on her husband and, naively, she asked Pudovkin for help.'

'And this spook arranged the apparent suicide of Helen Warner?'

'Yes.'

Stoneham twiddled her pen. 'Karen Phelps knows all this?'

'Yes.'

'And the Met won't touch it with a bargepole?'

'There's no evidence.'

The DCI's eyes lit up. 'So our Kaz, Terry Phelps's little girl, gets the bit between her teeth and asks Joey to help her take out this Pudovkin?'

'No, I don't think it was like that. The point is why Pudovkin decided to—'

The DCI cut her short. 'Really? Joey's gunned down in the attempt, presumably leaving this Russian rather pissed off with the Phelps gang.' She turned over a page in the file and scanned it. 'Tolya Koshkin – presumably related to Yevgeny – was killed with Joey, trying to carry out the hit. This so-called businessman and his brother or cousin or whatever – were they in fact Joey's thugs?'

Nicci wished she'd kept her mouth shut. She'd opened the floodgates to conjecture, which was reckless. 'I know it sounds plausible that she asked him, but remember, Karen's testimony helped send her brother down.'

'I think she did that just to stay out of jail.' The DCI leant forward over the desk. 'Nic, I watched her and her nasty little brother grow up. They're villains to the core. And smarter than their old man by a country mile. Now she may have been helpful to you because it served her purpose. But come on, where's your copper's instinct?'

Nicci shifted in her seat, silently cursing her own stupidity. The jollity was gone and the DCI's unremitting gaze was boring into her. Stoneham had a point and Nicci knew it. Yet it wasn't the whole story, she knew that too.

Stoneham was on a roll. 'Criminals like Phelps don't change, not fundamentally. Okay, you can blame the terrible childhood, the abuse, the drugs. Rehabilitation of offenders? It works with some, but the statistics are not good. When Karen gets angry and frustrated, she'll do what she's always done. You've had a chance to watch her up close. Put your hand on your heart, Nic, and tell me I'm wrong.'

'She says Joey did it to please her, to get her onside again. But she swears she had no knowledge.' The argument sounded weak even to Nicci.

'You believe that?'

Nicci's thoughts skittered back to pain, the knife slicing into her arm on the night she was attacked by a vicious teenage gang. Would she have survived if Karen Phelps, for all her dubious morals and motives, hadn't turned up to save her?

'I believe her desire to put the old life behind her is genuine.'

Stoneham wasn't listening. 'I've got three dead. A stupid young vicar in surgery fighting for his life and the media all over it demanding to know how we let it happen. I haven't got the luxury of another mistake.'

'Can I at least talk to her?'

'I wish you would. You're likely to get more out of her than we can. I'll have one of my lads drive you over to Brentwood. But she's under lock and key, Nic, and she's going to stay that way. She's in breach of her licence and as soon as the probation service can sort out the paperwork and revoke it, she's going back to jail.'

3

Kaz Phelps had spent the afternoon being shunted from inter-view room to cell and back. A police doctor had examined her, placed a dressing on the bloody gash in the lobe of her left ear, and declared her fit to be questioned.

Being locked in a cell was a relief; it gave her time to try and gather her scattered thoughts. She'd missed death or serious injury by a whisker. Yevgeny had shoved her sideways and she'd landed in the patch of sun-baked earth at the edge of Joey's grave, an unnerving experience but one that had saved her life. As she cowered in the dirt, a head shot, which was probably meant for her, felled her protector. Then Yevgeny's cousin had started shooting back.

He and the other minder had gunned down the funeral director and one of the pall-bearers, causing the remaining three to flee. But as the deadly volley of shots had whizzed across the churchyard, the curate had been struck in the chest and Ellie Phelps had run screaming hysterically into the cross-fire.

Mika was ex-military too, from Yevgeny's old unit. He knew his business and what his dead cousin would've expected of him. While he gave first aid to the curate, his companion used a burner to call an ambulance. Ellie had been hit in the arm, Glynis knelt beside her, Brian was hiding under a bush. The

23

minders' next priority was to remove their charges from the scene.

Irina was sobbing over her brother's corpse and had to be dragged bodily from it. Mika hoisted her over his shoulder and trotted towards the car. The other minder hauled Kaz to her feet and looped an arm round her waist. 'Okay? We go now.'

Kaz turned and saw her prostrate mother. 'Hang on!'

'No! No time. We go!' He pulled her after him.

Kaz wrenched herself free. She could hear Ellie gasping and moaning.

Glynis was clasping her hand and crying. 'All right, lovey. It's gonna be all right. Don't you worry.' She lifted her head; her desperate gaze met Kaz's but she didn't speak.

The minder grabbed Kaz's arm. 'The police come. We must go. Now!'

Kaz's head was spinning and her ear stung. She could feel her own blood, wet and sticky on her neck.

She held up her hand to ward him off. 'You go. Take care of Irina. I'm fine. I need to help my mother.'

Ellie had taken a bullet through the upper arm; it had passed through the muscle but missed the bone. Kneeling down beside her, Kaz had ripped a strip of gauze from her mother's ridiculous hat and used it to bind the wound as Glynis cradled her head.

Brian emerged warily from his hiding place. 'Fuck me! She all right?'

Kaz gave him a withering look but no reply. He was a weasel of a man, a cowardly opportunist. Her father had often used him as a punchbag and Kaz could see why.

She'd moved over to the young curate; he was struggling to breathe, blood bubbling up between his lips. Kaz took his hand

and his eyes sought hers. They were full of dread and panic; he spluttered as she stroked his brow.

'Try not to speak. Ambulance is coming. You're gonna be okay.' Did she sound convincing? Probably not. It had seemed surreal – her giving comfort to a dying priest. She'd racked her brains for some sort of prayer. *Our Father, who art in heaven* – but what the hell came after that?

She'd trawled her memory and couldn't come up with anything further so she'd simply gripped his hand. Over the hedge, in the lane next to the church, she'd glimpsed two women on horseback. They'd heard the gunfire, and one of them was speaking urgently into a mobile phone. The horses were steaming as they circled restlessly. The cleric's eyes flickered; he seemed to be drifting off.

Kaz squeezed his hand. 'C'mon, stay with me. Open your eyes. Look at me.'

His eyelids fluttered. He didn't look old enough to be a clergyman. Kaz felt responsible for him. He must've known how dodgy the whole deal was, yet he'd still helped them. Somewhere behind her Kaz could hear her mother whimpering and Glynis's soft voice soothing her. For some unexplained reason, Brian had gone to check his car.

Finally, after what had seemed an age, the wail of a distant siren came drifting over the fields on the summer breeze.

On reflection, Kaz realized that it might've been sensible at that point to slip away but she'd remained to hold the young man's damp palm. By the time he was stretchered to the ambulance by paramedics, two squad cars were pulling up followed by a van of armed police.

The officers who'd interviewed her initially were young and rather over-excited by the whole event. It had been easy enough for Kaz to evade their questions and pretend to be in shock. Indeed, she was in shock. Her ear was missing a chunk and surprisingly painful; it reminded her that she'd had an extremely close brush with death.

However, once they'd pulled up her records and identified her as an ex-offender released on licence, they put her in a cell.

She didn't doubt that Viktor Pudovkin was behind the hit. Who else could it be? Joey had tried to kill him and had damn near succeeded. It must've given the Russian billionaire quite a scare to face an assassin's bullet right outside his own front door. But what he wouldn't have known at the time was that the attack was an act of revenge for the murder of Helen Warner.

The day after Joey and Tolya were gunned down she'd sat with Yevgeny in the sunlit garden in Berkshire and discussed the fallout from her brother's suicidal attempt to please her. Yevgeny knew only too well that if Pudovkin joined up the dots and figured out Joey's motive, he'd come after Kaz. So he'd devised a plan to try and protect her.

'Pudovkin must think is a professional hit, that Joey do it for money. Just money. Not revenge.'

'How you gonna make him think that?'

Yevgeny had thrown open his palms and beamed. 'I go and I tell him.'

'Yeah, right.'

But her dead friend had been as good as his word. Through an intermediary he'd sought an audience with the billionaire. Kaz only had Yevgeny's report of the meeting to rely on. Pudovkin had been courteous, he'd listened and seemingly accepted Yevgeny's tale of two foolish young men, hyped up on coke and paid a tempting sum, by persons unknown, to carry out the hit. Yevgeny came away convinced he'd sold him on the lie.

It was now clear that he'd been wrong. Pudovkin was not as easy to fool as they'd hoped. Yevgeny had been played; lulled into a false sense of security.

Sitting in a police cell, ear throbbing, nerves jangling, Kaz came to the conclusion that the billionaire spook must've somehow known the truth all along; he'd simply waited patiently until Joey Phelps's funeral to exact his revenge.

And with Yevgeny gone she was on her own. When questioned, she'd given the police Pudovkin's name. She saw no reason to hold back. There was a slim chance they might take her seriously, although she doubted it.

Leaning back against the wall, feet up on the hard plastic bunk in her cell, she thought of Irina, wondering if she was okay and wishing she could take her friend in her arms and comfort her.

Irina had been the first electrifying and arousing presence in Kaz's life since Helen. In the short while since meeting, they'd laughed a lot and played around with clothes and make-up and music like a couple of teenagers. Having grown up in the dour industrial surroundings of Magnitogorsk, Irina had revelled in her new life in London. Her brothers had spoilt her, her clothes all had designer labels and she was invited to an endless round of parties and social events.

Kaz had intrigued her although language divided them. And the young Russian wasn't naive; she was well aware of the sexual frisson zinging between her and her new playmate. The fact her devout mother would've been appalled by such western deviance made it all the more delicious. In her new life, Irina wanted money and the freedom to do exactly as she pleased. Teasing and flirting and maybe even sleeping with Kaz Phelps was simply part of the fun.

But the partying had ended abruptly with the murders of

Joey and Tolya. Kaz had been left reeling. In guilt and grief she'd retreated into herself. Yevgeny had become silent and stern and, as Irina relied on him to translate her more complicated conversations with Kaz, communication had dwindled to almost nothing.

Alone in her cell, Kaz regretted this. Now she was worried about Irina. With her brothers gone how would she cope? She had her cousin, Mika, and other Russian friends in London, but would they want to be involved in the complicated fallout from Yevgeny's death? None of them would dare to cross Pudovkin.

As Kaz struggled to get a handle on events, more questions rose up to torment her and they made her head spin. What did Pudovkin know? He had unlimited resources and contacts, it wouldn't have been so hard for him to figure it all out: the connection between her and Helen – that sleazy perve Robert Hollister would've filled him in on that – and the fact his attacker was her brother.

Was the bullet that killed Yevgeny meant for her? She was standing right beside him and it was pure luck that she'd survived. Slowly it began to dawn on her the kind of danger she was in. Being in police custody was hardly going to protect her. She was exposed and alone. An angry Russian billionaire, beyond the reach of the law, had set out to kill her and it was more than likely that he would succeed.

4

The Major Investigation Team office in Brentwood was a hive of activity. They were the lead on 'a brutal gangland slaying', to use the press's well-worn phrase. The media were all over it, begging for sound bites. It was the kind of case that made careers, a fact not lost on the rather young detective inspector in charge of the intelligence cell. The whole team numbered thirty officers, but the intelligence cell was the hub. Made up of two officers and three civilian analysts, they operated from their own private cubbyhole with a digital lock on the door.

Escorting Nicci into an empty meeting room, the DI held out his hand. 'Tom Rivlin.'

She shook it and smiled. 'Nicci Armstrong.'

'SIO says you know Phelps.'

'I was on the team that took down her brother. I dealt with her then, when I was in the job, and subsequently.'

Shirtsleeves rolled up, Rivlin rested his palms lightly on his narrow hips. He had the frame of a runner but Nicci could see that his most winning aspect was his smile.

It produced boyish dimples, offset by a square chin – and he knew exactly how to deploy it. 'Well, the boss wants her licence revoked, which is fine and dandy. Trouble is, that's not going to encourage her to talk to us about who shot up her brother's funeral and why.'

'She knows me. Possibly even trusts me.'

He scanned her with an appraising eye. 'DCI's in charge. It's her show.'

Nicci got the clear impression Rivlin regarded it as his, or at least the intelligence-gathering part of it. And he didn't like the idea of an outsider, even if she was an ex-cop, walking in and stealing his thunder. She'd met his type before: lizard charm concealing calculating ambition.

She jutted her chin. 'It was DCI Stoneham who contacted me and asked for my help.' The tone was bullish; she wasn't in the mood for testosterone-driven games.

'And we're grateful. Phelps has mentioned you briefly. So I guess we could say you're her "reasonably named person".'

He treated her to the smile again, but Nicci had the measure of him.

She shrugged. 'I wouldn't want to break the rules.'

'You know what it's like. I just need to tick the boxes. So what's your preference? Interview room or cell?'

'I'm happy with an interview room. Means your officers can listen in.'

He acknowledged the gesture with a nod. 'I'll set it up. Coffee?'

A DC was summoned to provide refreshments and an escort. Nicci opted for a herbal tea; it was getting late in the day and she decided she probably had enough caffeine zapping round her synapses.

After a ten-minute wait the DC showed her into an interview room. It was the usual small, nondescript box with wall-mounted cameras, a table and two chairs.

Kaz Phelps looked up at her in genuine surprise. 'Fuck me, I never thought they'd actually get you!'

'Nice to see you too.' Nicci took a seat across the table from her. 'What happened to your ear?'

'Thanks to you morons being too pussy to do your job and nick him, some fucking stooge of Pudovkin's tried to blow my fucking head off.'

'I'm sorry about your friend who was killed.'

Kaz glared at her. Then her chin quivered and her eyes started to well up. For an instant it seemed she was about to cry, but she gritted her teeth and swallowed it down. She leant forward, her voice barely audible: 'What the fuck am I gonna do, Nicci? I am truly, I mean well and truly, fucked.'

Nicci reached across the table, putting her hand over Kaz's. The move was impulsive, the way you'd comfort a friend. 'You're in shock. You've had a very traumatic experience.'

'This is what Joey's left me. My life is fucked, thanks to him. He's up there somewhere laughing his fucking socks off.'

'You walked away from him and that life before. You can do it again.'

'How? Talk to your mates? I've told them who's behind this. What the fuck difference does it make? And don't tell me there's no evidence. No one's gone looking.'

'Building a case against someone like Pudovkin—'

'You said yourself, the Met was told to leave well alone.'

'Maybe so. But no one's above the law.'

'What planet you living on? 'Cause it ain't the same one as me.'

Nicci forced a smile. 'Have you had a drink and something to eat?'

'Not hungry.'

'So how can I help you? I've already told the SIO about the possible connection between Helen Warner's death and Pudovkin.'

'Get me back on witness protection.'

'I don't know how easy that's going to be.'

Kaz rubbed the back of her hand across her nose with the air of an aggrieved toddler. 'No one's even told me how my mum is.'

'Your mum was injured?'

'Yeah, in the arm. And the vicar who done the service for us, what's happened to him?'

Nicci glanced at the wall-mounted camera. 'Okay, I'll see what I can—'

She didn't need to finish. The door to the interview room opened and Tom Rivlin strolled in. Sliding his hands into his pockets, he stood between the two women. 'Hello, Karen. I'm DI Rivlin.'

Kaz gave him a scathing look. 'Oh, finally the organ grinder instead of the fucking monkeys.'

'Well, one of the organ grinders.' He smiled. 'I'm sorry you haven't been kept informed. Your mother has a flesh wound in the upper arm. Not life-threatening, but my understanding is they're keeping her under observation for a day or so. The Reverend Taylor is in surgery. His condition is serious.'

Kaz dipped her head and swallowed. Nicci and Rivlin exchanged a covert glance.

'Tell us about the funeral directors you hired, Karen.' The copper seemed to be looming over her.

'I've told you already. Yev did all that. I don't know nothing about it.'

'A name? Or even where they were based?'

'I ain't lying. If I fucking knew anything, I'd tell you, okay!'

Rivlin seemed unruffled. 'Okay, I'll get one of my DCs to bring you both a cup of tea.' More beverages, Nicci thought, but when they were working a big case that's what MIT's subsisted on – round-the-clock caffeine.

He disappeared out of the door. Kaz met Nicci's eye. 'I'm

not lying. Yev sorted it all out. He didn't discuss the ins and outs with me.'

'I know you're not lying. But the funeral directors are key. Whoever Pudovkin sent, they facilitated it. Make that link and we have a case.'

Kaz rocked in her chair. Her gaze was scooting nervously around the room – from the door to the cameras and back. Nicci couldn't recall ever having seen her so agitated. It was understandable in terms of the shock she'd had. But this was Karen Phelps unmasked. Nicci could feel her raw fear.

Kaz shot her a belligerent look. 'Once this lot've got what they can from me, they're gonna revoke my licence and ship me back, aren't they?'

'Is that why you're being evasive?'

'No. I don't fucking know who the funeral directors are.'

Nicci held her gaze. 'And did you really not know what Joey planned to do?'

'I thought he planned to kill me, not Pudovkin.' Kaz was balancing her chair on two legs like a defiant pupil at the back of the class.

'Why do you think he didn't?'

'Joey was a complicated boy.' She brought the chair down onto four legs with a thump. 'He didn't see the world like other people.'

'Psychopaths don't.'

'I ain't an expert on that.'

'But you knew your brother.'

Kaz let her gaze come to rest on Nicci's face. Nicci could read the calculation in her eyes but there was something else: a profound sadness.

She shook her head. 'When we was little, before Natalie came along, it was just him and me. I was about six when I figured how to steal money from me mum's purse, go down the shops, so we could eat.'

'Your mum didn't look after you?'

'Mostly she was out of it. She was a drug addict, married to a gangster who beat the shit out of her.'

'Did social services never get involved?'

'Now and then. But the old man soon saw them off.'

'Very few people would've survived such an upbringing unscathed.'

'Joey hated people feeling sorry for us.'

'Do you?'

'A bit.' This was the most Nicci had ever heard her say about her family. Would she say more? Nicci waited; she knew the importance of leaving space. It was what had made her a good interviewer.

Finally she was rewarded. 'When I was in the nick I went to this therapy group for a while. They wanted us to talk about all the family stuff. And about responsibility. It really pissed me off, these stupid girls who sat there going, "Oh poor me, I had a terrible childhood, so that's why I went out nicking."'

'You saw that as self-pity?'

'I saw it as bullshit. They went nicking to get stuff to buy drugs. And they sat there giving the spiel 'cause they thought it's what the shrinks wanted to hear.'

'Why did they want to take the drugs in the first place?'

'People make stupid choices. Then they look for excuses.'

Nicci sighed. 'Some might say drugs are an escape.'

Kaz gave her a withering look. 'No shit, Sherlock. Don't you want out from time to time? One drink too many? A little holiday from reality? But it's still a choice.'

'Point taken.' Nicci couldn't help smiling.

'I was a stupid kid. They sent me to jail. I got no quarrel

with that. You do what you do and you face the consequences. But I've served my time, Nicci.'

'Technically not until your licence expires.'

'My brother reckoned it was all a game, one with different rules for different people. He just refused to play by the rules set down for slags like us.'

'Sounds like you admire him.'

'I loved him. And I hated him. But he was one clever little fucker.'

'Not clever enough to stop himself from getting killed.'

'Part of him couldn't have given a toss if he lived or died. Death or glory, that was Joey.' She leant forward across the table. 'But I'm not like that. In case you haven't noticed, I'm bricking it. You know what prison's like. Inside, you can arrange a hit for the price of a fucking mobile phone. If they send me back, I'll be found strung up to some shower rail. Just another suicide.'

Nicci was aware of the burning intensity of the other woman's scrutiny. She took a breath. 'As I said before, you're in shock. And I'm sure the prison authorities will take measures—'

'They ain't got the staff or the inclination. I'll be another fucking statistic. I don't wanna guilt-trip you, but you owe me, Nicci.'

'Thought you said we were even.'

'What about Helen? And that mate of hers, the bloke from the Labour Party who went under the tube train? Don't go all cop on me and say this sort of thing doesn't happen in England, 'cause you know full well it does.' Nicci could see the moisture gathering at the corners of the dark eyes. 'Help me. Please. They put me back inside, I'm dead meat.'

5

'Quite a performance. She deserves an Oscar.' Tom Rivlin was waving a tenner at the barman and finally managed to catch his eye. 'Pint of Guinness and . . . ?' He glanced at Nicci.

'Glass of Pinot Grigio, thanks.'

'Make that a large glass, mate.'

Nicci thought of objecting but it had been a long day and she didn't have the energy to be coy. They were in an Irish-themed gastropub in Brentwood High Street, surrounded by gaggles of thirsty office workers and a few of Rivlin's colleagues.

Nicci watched the DI slide an oversized glass of wine along the bar towards her and collect his change. He seemed a rather unlikely Guinness drinker.

As they settled themselves in a quieter corner booth she found herself checking his left hand. No ring. But that didn't mean a thing and, anyway, why was she even looking? She'd decided she didn't like him.

Rivlin had an agenda, that was clear enough. But Nicci knew it wasn't personal. He was possibly a year or two younger than her and he was already a DI. Young, white and male, that was still the main predictor for success in the job. Add to that his energy and drive and it was obvious he was going places.

He took a sip of his beer. 'So what's life like as a private investigator?'

'Frustrating.' She wished he'd dispense with the small talk and get on with it. They were there to trade. But she needed him to make the opening gambit.

He smiled. 'Smart move, some might say. Won't be long before half the job is privatized. We'll have a few noddy cops in uniform as first responders and anything specialist'll be farmed out to outfits like yours.'

'I didn't become a private investigator by choice.'

'Did you not?' He gave her a sceptical look. 'Get into one of these security companies on the ground floor, collect your share options and bonuses. Mate of mine is thinking of it, reckons it'll make him a millionaire.'

Nicci's mind went back to Blake; he'd had the same dream. Now he was struggling to keep his head above water. 'I thought we were here to talk about Karen Phelps, not career opportunities for today's police officer.' There was swingeing sarcasm in her tone, she couldn't help it.

The DI chuckled. 'Sorry. Didn't mean to ruffle your feathers.'

Annoyed that she'd allowed herself to be needled, Nicci twisted the stem of her glass. The bowl was beaded with moisture from the chilled wine. 'I'm guessing you want your firm to retain the lead on this case.'

'That would be nice. But if we're chasing Russian spooks I'll be lucky, won't I? The Met or even the NCA, they'll get it.'

'From my experience of Cheryl Stoneham she's not going to want to hand over the reins to the Met.'

'She's also not going to be happy to let Phelps go.' The smile was teasing. 'That's what you're angling for, isn't it? "You owe me, Nicci." Isn't that what Phelps said to you? Ex-cop beholden to a villain? Bit iffy, some might say.'

His tone was jokey, almost flirtatious, but she knew he was baiting her. She decided to play it straight and ignore his game.

'What if her fears of what might happen to her in prison are not entirely unfounded?'

Rivlin shrugged. 'Come on, let's not be melodramatic. If the threat is real, special arrangements can be made. Our jails are not as lawless as the media would have us think.'

'They're not particularly safe either. The DCI thinks Phelps lied to her, that's why she's pissed off. And she's covering her own arse.'

'She's covering the Chief Constable's arse, which is her job. And my job is to cover hers.'

Nicci couldn't help a wry grin. 'It's easy to see why you're climbing the greasy pole at a rate of knots.'

'Maybe I'm just clever and hard-working.' His eyes were blue but the hair was dark and slightly curly. A Celtic connection perhaps, which might explain his taste in beer. He also exuded pheromones, which Nicci was doing her best to ignore.

She met his gaze. 'Okay, officer, you've got me sussed. You know what I want. What do you want from me?' She took a mouthful of wine.

'An Albanian shooter hired in for the occasion? Someone has gone to trouble and expense. The Met have let me access their inquiries relating to Joey Phelps and I've read everything that's on the system. But you know yourself, stuff gets left out for all kinds of reasons. My job is to gather intelligence, so what I'm in need of is the real inside track.'

'I've already told the DCI what I know. Presumably she's given you the gist.'

'You feel loyalty to the Met, that's understandable.'

Nicci guffawed. 'You're joking!' She wondered what Stoneham had told him about her; maybe nothing. But suddenly it mattered that she was someone more than the cop with a dead kid who went off the rails. She opened her palms. 'Look, whatever you want to know, ask me. I do want to help.'

'Why would some Russian billionaire want to kill a British MP?'

'The best theory we came up with was that he was collecting assets. It wasn't about Helen Warner, he was just using her to get leverage over Robert Hollister.'

'And Hollister could've ended up Home Secretary. Pretty heavy stuff. But you say the Met wouldn't touch it?'

'My understanding is they were told to leave Pudovkin alone.'

Rivlin lounged back in his seat and rubbed his chin. 'So Hollister gets arrested, which means our Russian billionaire has gone to all that trouble for nothing. Then to add insult to injury some gangster tries to kill him.'

'It was a revenge attack because he had Helen Warner killed. Once he finds that out, he's got a plausible motive for the churchyard.'

The DI sipped his drink, wiping froth from his lips with an index finger and thumb. 'Which brings us back to Karen Phelps.'

'I know her a lot better than Stoneham does. Is she a danger to the general public? No.' Nicci leant forward. 'What she is, is your best lead. She blames Pudovkin for the deaths of two of the most important people in her life. I'd let her run and see what happens.'

Rivlin shook his head and grinned. 'You lot in the Met, you're cold-blooded bastards, aren't you?'

'I'm not in the Met any more. But I'll still take that as a compliment.'

'Stoneham's my boss. I go against her, she'll have my balls in the wringer.'

Nicci gave an arch shrug. 'Well, we wouldn't want that.'

'But . . .' The dimples on his cheeks danced. 'It's not actually her call. Revocation of Phelps's licence is down to the probation service. I don't know who's dealing with it. But, with the current reorganization, the local office is in some chaos.'

'The work's being split, isn't it? Eighty per cent to private companies.'

'Preferred bidders just announced. I know someone who works there. They're not a happy crew. Might be worth your while to pay them a call?'

Nicci knew he was dangling a solution under her nose and she knew why. He was a canny bastard and no mistake. All the same, maybe she should go with the flow. Why the hell not?

6

The taxi crawled in a diesel-tainted fug of slow-moving morning traffic down Southampton Row and into Kingsway. The journey from West London had taken an age and, fidgeting in the back, Robert Hollister checked his watch for the umpteenth time. Being late would not create the right impression; he should have taken the tube. During his time in the Shadow Cabinet he'd made a point of using public transport at least once a week or, occasionally in good weather, riding to Westminster on his bicycle. But the purpose of those jaunts had been to be seen and photographed, an ordinary bloke on his way to work, a man with whom the voters could connect. Back then he'd enjoyed being recognized and accosted. Now all he craved was privacy and invisibility.

Since the police had charged him with unlawful sex with a minor, his glittering political career had collapsed around his ears. The party had dumped him without a second thought. Expelled from the Shadow Cabinet the day he was arrested, his constituency party had begun proceedings to deselect him less than a week later. So much for innocent until proven guilty.

What had followed was a thorough and sustained media beasting. His character and reputation had been ripped to shreds. Women he'd fucked half a lifetime ago, secretaries and researchers whose names he couldn't even remember, had slithered out of the swamp to call him a rapist and sell their stories to the *Sun*. Even a high-class hooker who operated on the Westminster beat had claimed him as a client – which was patently ridiculous; he'd never had to pay for it in his life. There was a reason why *Private Eye* had dubbed him 'Rob the Throb' and people, usually women, often commented on his resemblance to a young George Clooney.

Instructing the cabbie to drop him just past Holborn tube he took a deep breath and stepped out onto the pavement. Dark suit, silk tie, leather briefcase, he looked like any other middle-aged lawyer as he turned the corner and strode briskly down Remnant Street and into Lincoln's Inn Fields.

The firm of solicitors who'd represented him initially were high profile and expensive enough but as the weeks had passed, with him hanging in limbo awaiting his trial date, he'd begun to feel they were dragging their heels. Then Henry, an old pal from Oxford, now a tax lawyer worth millions, had advised him to go to Isabel Merrow.

Isabel Merrow QC had been a prosecutor and a very senior lawyer in the CPS. But rumour had it when she was passed over for promotion she got in a snit and took a lucrative job with a leading defence firm. The offices of Smith Khan Caldwell occupied a listed building in a Georgian terrace and Hollister was ushered into a pleasant high-ceilinged conference room, with a partial view of the square, at ten thirty on the dot. He was relieved to have made it on time. Merrow was already seated at the heavy oak table. She got up, offered him her hand and introduced her junior.

Being represented by a woman wouldn't have been Hollister's instinctive choice, but in the circumstances he knew it was a sensible move. Over the years, he'd worked with plenty of female colleagues and that was fine as long as he had the seniority and the power. Women in charge made him feel awkward. Of course nowadays he would never dream of admitting such a bias. But he was a red-blooded male in the prime of life with a healthy sexual appetite; if he encountered an attractive female he'd prefer it to be in the bedroom, not the boardroom. This was normal and natural and what most men thought, if they were honest.

Merrow was in her early fifties, a bit long in the tooth for his taste, but slim, well preserved and elegantly turned out.

She fixed him with an unnervingly direct look. 'Well, Mr Hollister, an unpleasant few weeks for you, I gather.'

As he settled in his chair he presented her with his 'aw shucks' little-boy look; it tended to do the trick with most females. 'What can I say? They were out to get me and they have.'

'And they are . . . ?'

'Hard to say precisely who's behind it. A security firm set up the sting.'

The QC rested her glasses on her nose and peered down at the open file in front of her. 'That would be Simon Blake Associates?'

'Can you believe it: they used an ex-con. Released on licence.' He gave her a confiding smile. 'Karen Phelps? Don't know if you caught the news this morning. But apparently she was involved in a shooting yesterday at her gangster brother's funeral. So you can see the kind of people we're dealing with.'

Merrow nodded. 'Well, she's rather irrelevant at present as the CPS are not proceeding with the charge that you sexually assaulted her. Although she is a witness to your supposed confession.'

Hollister sniggered. 'And who's going to believe someone like her? Anyway, the recording was doctored. We've already got two experts ready to testify to that.'

'Let's talk about the historic charge of unlawful sexual intercourse with a minor. Tell me about your relationship with Helen Warner.'

Hollister frowned, focused his gaze on the table in front of him and took a moment to compose himself. Then he looked up and met the lawyer's eye directly.

'Helen's suicide is the most terrible tragedy and I do blame myself. It's the one thing in this whole sorry mess of which I am undoubtedly guilty.' He blinked several times and wiped his palm across his face.

'Guilty in what way?'

'I'm not a saint, Ms Merrow. I've never pretended to be. And I've not been a faithful husband. Political office puts you in the way of myriad temptations. When I ended my affair with Helen I thought I was doing the right thing for both of us. I never dreamt for one moment that she'd be so upset as to take her own life.'

Hollister dipped his head. The only sound in the room was the tap-tapping as the junior took notes on a laptop.

When Hollister finally raised his gaze he found the QC staring straight at him. Her expression was unreadable. He judged his performance to have been credible; her manner remained frosty, but lawyers were like that. What mattered was whether she would live up to her reputation and get him off.

She sighed and laced her fingers. 'First things first: the facts. How old were you and how old was Helen Warner when you first met?'

With an earnest puckering of the brows he gave the question his full consideration. 'Honest truth is I'm not sure. I went up to Oxford when I was nineteen. Charles Warner, Helen's father, became my tutor in my second year. But you know the system, as an undergraduate you're just one of many. It was only when I became a postgraduate and Charles supervised my thesis that I got to know him better.'

'So how old were you when you met his family?'

'Possibly twenty-two.'

'And Helen was twelve years younger than you, so that would make her ten?'

'I don't really remember her at that age. All I remember is kicking a football round the garden with her little brothers.'

'Helen wasn't a footballer?' The lawyer's tone seemed neutral but was there a hint of irony? Hollister couldn't be sure.

'I think I probably first noticed Helen when my girlfriend, Paige, started to babysit for them.'

'Paige subsequently became your wife?'

'Helen adored Paige. Some years later she was a bridesmaid at our wedding.'

'So you knew Helen Warner as a child and, in spite of her affection for your wife, you had a long-term affair with her as an adult?'

'We were young and back then, you must remember how it was, things were far more laissez-faire. I think we've turned into a nation of puritans.' He gave Merrow a winsome smile; she didn't respond, so he ploughed on. 'You're probably going to ask about all the lesbian stuff. Okay, Helen had a female partner. But she got tied up with feminism at a time when they were peddling the notion that lesbianism was a political choice.'

'So you're saying heterosexuality rather than lesbianism was her secret? That's somewhat unusual.'

He noticed that the lipstick she wore was scarlet though her lips were thin and pursed, turning her mouth into a narrow red gash. Maybe she was a rug-muncher herself? She was a humourless old bag, if that was anything to go by. Hollister tried to remember what Henry had said about her. He might've mentioned a husband.

'I can only say how she was with me. She certainly kept coming back for more.'

The QC removed her glasses. He got the impression she was rather bored.

'Here's the bottom line, Mr Hollister. A politician is accused of historic child sexual abuse. In the current climate, the police and the CPS must be seen to take this seriously. The public interest here is clear and does not operate in our favour. That leaves us with the question of whether there is sufficient evidence to provide a realistic chance of conviction. The victim is dead. The only version of events that we have from her prior to her death is from a private discussion with a senior police officer in which she claimed she was fourteen at the time of the offence. She did not specifically name you, but your identity can arguably be inferred. This is hearsay, however. Is it likely to be admissible? That may depend on the other evidence. And what other evidence is there? A somewhat outlandish recorded confession, which, as you say, can be discredited on forensic grounds. Helen's mother is also dead. Charles Warner's statement is that he had no knowledge of the alleged offence and doubts it took place. Which leaves us with Paige, your estranged wife.'

'So it's down to Paige?'

'The interview the police conducted with her was stopped on medical advice. And I gather she's being treated for severe depression.'

'She took an overdose.'

'Some might call that an unfortunate coincidence, Mr Hollister.' Her cool grey eyes were boring straight into him and something in Robert Hollister snapped. Weeks holed up in that fucking flat, the paps chasing him like hounds, his friends ignoring his calls, his stupid mother sobbing down the phone and now this fucking bitch was laughing at him.

Shoving back his chair he stood up. 'You don't get to judge me. Not at eight-fifty an hour. You want my instructions? Here they are. Helen Warner was sixteen and gave full consent when I first had sex with her. And I've never raped a woman in my life, I've never had to. Now I expect you to do your fucking job.'

Isabel Merrow QC didn't flinch or cower, she didn't even move, although a glint of amusement flickered briefly behind her deadpan gaze. Hollister was steaming. But he read the look and realized he'd been suckered. She'd pushed his buttons to see how he'd react; if he hadn't been so stressed out he'd never have fallen for it.

He took a deep breath and forced a smile. 'Sorry. As you said at the outset, it's been a difficult few weeks.'

She raised her eyebrows. 'Do sit down, Mr Hollister.' He shrugged with boyish contrition and obeyed. Her next remark would be placatory, that's usually what women did. She'd want to make him feel better.

But she simply put her glasses on and glanced at the file. 'If I were prosecuting this case I wouldn't want to lose, makes the whole system look flawed and the papers would scream waste of public money. So if I had doubts – and I would, because there's no sworn statement from Helen – I'd try and shelve it. I'd go for a discontinuance.'

'That would mean no further action, right?'

'No further action unless new evidence comes to light.'

'Can you get me that?'

'It's achievable if the evidence looks weak.'

'It is weak. It's a pack of lies.'

She glossed over this with a chilly smile. 'Only if, as you say, Helen was sixteen and Paige will corroborate that fact.'

'That's all you need, a statement from Paige?' Hollister felt a surge of hope in his gut. This was what he knew, a process he understood. Every legal system ever invented was rigged and all you needed was the right move to play it.

Merrow nodded. Finally she was earning her fee.

Hollister drummed his index finger on the solid oak table. 'Right. You'll have it by Monday.'

7

The office of the local probation service occupied a two-tone brick building, fronted by a patch of parched grass, on a residential street in Laindon. The door was propped open and two removal men were struggling to get a desk through it.

Nicci had spent a sleepless night wondering whether she was doing the right thing. Her motives were mixed, to say the least, though she was having a hard time admitting that to herself. Blake had been hassling her with texts and finally, in the late evening, she'd called to update him.

'Thing is, Simon, being helpful to Stoneham and her team is not going to do us any harm. We get a rep with them it could lead to business further down the line.'

'Sounds worth a punt.' His mood seemed lighter, the result, probably, of several large whiskies. 'Is this your way of telling me you won't be helping out on the security side?'

'No. I told you, you can rely on me. I'll babysit your HNWIs, whatever's necessary.' She didn't mean her tone to be quite so tetchy. 'Just give me a day to sort out this stuff in Essex, okay?'

'Fine. Listen, I'm sorry.'

'Stop apologizing. I'll have to spend my time in some seriously posh shops. It's not that much of a hardship.'

He'd chuckled. 'Goodnight, Nic.'

She'd lain awake, her brain buzzing. Karen Phelps and her

guilt trip; Nicci hated being under any sort of obligation to her, but she was. And Stoneham? She hadn't told Blake the whole truth. It wasn't the DCI she was hoping to impress, it was Tom Rivlin. He was playing her and she realized that. Did he even know her history? He might've heard the gossip. And the last thing she wanted was to be seen as some lonely basket case, forced out of the job for being an alchy. She'd sipped the wine he'd bought her in the pub and left half the glass un-drunk. He knew he was good-looking and he used it like a girl. She hated blokes like that. He was a complete tosser; this was the conclusion she'd come to at around five a.m., when at long last she'd drifted into a fitful slumber.

She waited for about a quarter of an hour in the reception area together with two of the probation services' clients. One was clearly a junkie – he avoided all eye contact – the other, a stocky youth, gnawed his fingernails and glared at her.

A tall, slightly stooped figure with greying hair appeared in the doorway. He bore an uncanny resemblance to Tom Rivlin. He smiled. 'Nicci? I'm Steve O'Connor. Come on through.'

He held open a set of swing doors and she followed him down the corridor.

'Tom mentioned you were with the Met.' There was a defin-ite Irish lilt in the voice.

'Used to be.'

'I worked in Camden back in the day, before it became so trendy.'

His office was tiny and crammed with cardboard cartons of files. He dismissed them with a flick of the hand. 'They're still trying to computerize something or other. More bloody sys-tems that don't work. Let me clear you a seat.'

He removed some documents from a chair and placed it in front of the desk for her.

'Thanks for agreeing to see me. Looks like you're very busy.'

'I figure there's a choice.' He settled behind the desk. 'You either drive yourself mad trying to keep up, or you work at the pace you can manage. The targets we've been set are nonsense – I'm just hoping for a decent redundancy package.'

'You're not in favour of the reforms?'

He simply chortled and shook his head.

'Tom said you're a fair-minded man.'

'Did he now? Well, he's my sister's boy, so he has to say that.'

'He didn't mention you were related.'

'He gets his good looks from our side of the family, can't you tell?'

Nicci smiled and met his eye. Rivlin and his uncle shared the same twinkly teasing charm. But her mood this morning was prim and in control of all unruly emotions. She decided she could easily end up disliking the whole clan, or at least the men.

Steve O'Connor opened the file on his desk and picked up his glasses. 'Okay, Karen Phelps. She was being looked after by our colleagues north of the border. But in July she emailed them and said she was spending the summer down here to further her artistic studies. Is that correct?'

'Broadly speaking.' Nicci felt uncomfortable. There was a moral line and she was skating perilously close to it.

'The file was passed to us because her previous known permanent address, her mother's, is in our area.' He was gazing at her expectantly over the top of his glasses.

Nicci gave him a smile. 'During her time in prison she took full advantage of the educational opportunities on offer. Her family background was grim. After her release she gave evidence in court, which led to the conviction of her brother. I worked on the case. Her testimony was vital.'

O'Connor nodded. 'Her previous probation officer seemed pretty convinced she'd kicked the drug habit. That's one of the conditions of her licence.'

'She has. And she doesn't drink. She has turned her life around.' Nicci sat back in her chair and waited. If she was reading O'Connor correctly then the detached professional stance was probably her best bet with him. The easy-going manner, she judged, was a bit of an act. He was a career public servant, an old-school probation officer, and making the right decision mattered to him.

He tilted his head and gave her a searching look. 'If you'll forgive the personal question, why did you leave the police?'

His enquiry hung in the air for a moment. It confirmed Nicci's assessment of him: he wanted to know what sort of ex-copper he was dealing with. Had her cooperation simply been bought?

'My nine-year-old daughter was killed in a road traffic accident.'

He frowned. 'I'm so sorry. I really had no idea.'

'No reason you should.' The shift in his sympathy was palpable. She'd gone from being an unknown quantity to instantly trustworthy. But she found his pity annoying. That look, the saccharine words, she'd had a bellyful since Sophie's death. So much for the detached approach, now she had to suppress her irritation. 'Look, Karen Phelps's brother was a nasty psychopath. He broke out of jail and she had every reason to believe he wanted to kill her.'

'Because her testimony sent him down?'

'Exactly. He was involved with some Russian gangsters and, for whatever reason, they tried to murder a Russian businessman. Joey Phelps and one of his mates got themselves killed in the process.' She was playing fast and loose with the truth, but somehow that had ceased to matter. 'DCI Stoneham is assuming Karen had some involvement with this. I disagree. I don't think she did.'

'Now Tom's lot are investigating a shooting at this brother's funeral?'

'The funeral was going to be a media circus. The Phelps family changed the venue to avoid this. As a result, the police were in the wrong place and ended up looking very stupid.'

'So DCI Stoneham's angry and she's taking it out on Phelps?'

Nicci reined herself in. Had she gone a bit too far? 'It's not for me to comment on that. I'm saying if the police have a prima facie case that Karen Phelps aided and abetted her brother then they need to make it. In the meantime, she's entitled to be released. Her mother was injured and is in hospital. She herself narrowly avoided being a victim.'

'Why are you going to all this trouble for her?'

Good question, she thought. She was on slippery terrain, but following that copper's instinct that Stoneham had reminded her of. At least, she hoped that's what she was doing.

'Joey Phelps murdered two colleagues of mine, both police officers working undercover. I know how dangerous he was and the risk Karen took when she decided to testify. This current situation was caused entirely by her brother and his criminality. I don't think it's fair that she should be dragged down by him.'

'You'll vouch for her then?'

'Isn't that what I'm doing?'

The probation officer nodded slowly. Annoyingly his smile made Nicci think about his nephew even more.

8

Brian Mason, feet up on the opulent peach sofa, can of premium lager in his hand, was waiting for the two thirty at Haydock Park to begin. The horses were being lined up at the starting gate and the 4K HD 65-inch screen, which occupied half the wall facing him, showed every flare of the nostrils and twitch of the rump in perfect resolution. He'd always been a betting man and regarded himself as a good judge of horseflesh. Nowadays there wasn't even the need to go to the bookies. He could enjoy it all in the considerable comfort of his own home with a telly and a phone.

Turning his head away from the screen slightly to take a sip of ice-cool beer, he suddenly became aware of a figure standing stock-still in the doorway, watching him. It was Kaz Phelps.

'Blimey. How did you get in?'

She held up a front-door key. 'Mum gave me this. I just been down the hospital to see her.'

'She all right? When's she coming home?'

Kaz strolled into the room. 'She's a bit pissed off with you, Bri. You ran out on her.'

'There was no point in us all getting nicked. I thought it was best to lie low.'

Kaz glanced at the massive screen. The horses were under starter's orders. 'You got ten minutes to pack your gear and get out.'

'Excuse me?' He laughed and took a sip of beer. 'I think you'll find your mum'd have something to say about that.'

'Really?' The starting gate flew up, the horses were off and in the same instant Kaz's right foot struck the can of lager, booting it clean out of Brian's hand. It landed on the carpet, fizzing spilt beer.

She loomed over him. 'I've had a rough couple of days. I'm not in a good mood. Don't push me, Bri.'

Struggling to sit up, he spluttered, 'You can't fucking come in here and chuck me out! You grassed up your own brother. You ain't part of this family no more. Ellie fucking hates you.'

'She's a fickle woman, my mother. Her precious boy is gone and she's scared shitless. But she's also a pragmatist and she knows what a useless prick you are.'

'Useless? I looked after your dad. Two years he was in that wheelchair after his stroke. I washed him, fed him, wiped his arse.'

'My heart bleeds. Joey hired a couple of nurses to do all that.'

'They wasn't here 24/7. You was in the nick, you don't know what it was like.'

Kaz placed her hands on her hips. 'I don't wanna argue with you. But we both need to get real. Joey's gone and everything's changed.'

'I wanna talk to Ellie.' He managed finally to scramble to his feet and face her. But she was taller and the energy pulsing off her was unnervingly threatening.

'She don't wanna talk to you. She's coming home this afternoon and she wants you gone.'

'I don't believe you.'

Kaz folded her arms. 'Oh come on, Bri. You've lived pretty high on the hog for the last few years. But when the shooting started and Mum really needed you, you bottled it. You only got yourself to blame.'

'This ain't fair.'

Kaz took a step towards him, fixed him with an icy stare. 'That's life. What you gonna do about it?'

He didn't reply. With a sullen glare, he scooted around her and disappeared out of the door. She could hear him climbing the stairs.

She leant over, picked up the can of lager and carried it through to the kitchen. Her torn ear was throbbing; she'd spent an uncomfortable night sleeping in a police cell. But then this morning, out of the blue, some spotty-faced uniform had appeared and told her she was free to go. He'd handed her a card with a phone number – the probation service; she had forty-eight hours to contact them and make an appointment to see her new offender manager.

As she emptied the remains of the beer down the sink and chucked the can in the bin, she looked around her. Being back in this house, the place where she grew up, the scene of so many difficult memories, felt decidedly odd. But with the afternoon sun flooding through the kitchen window it seemed benign enough now. She didn't have a plan, but she needed a bolthole, a place to hide and think; this was as good as any.

Returning to the sitting room with a cloth, she turned off the television and swabbed the scum and remaining beer from the soggy carpet.

She'd arrived at Basildon Hospital shortly after midday and had found her mother tucked up in a corner bed, eyes glazed, looking lost and abandoned. The nursing staff had greeted the appearance of a relative with enthusiasm. They needed the bed, insisted she was ready to be discharged, the doctors had signed her off; all that remained was to order her medication and arrange transport.

Mother and daughter had faced each other with wariness on both sides. Then Ellie had started to cry. 'What's going on, Kaz? I don't understand none of it.'

'Joey's legacy, I think that's what I'd call it.'

'Why do they wanna kill us? We ain't done nothing.'

Kaz smiled to herself – was the naivety real or feigned? 'Come on, Mum. You was married to the old man for long enough. You know how it works.'

'I never asked him about business and he never told me. Your dad took care of things, that's all I knew.'

Kaz perched on the bedside chair. 'Then Joey stepped into his shoes, right?'

'I know you think I'm a stupid woman. And maybe I am. But I done my best for all three of you. Terry was never an easy bloke.'

'Amen to that.'

Ellie gazed up at her daughter. Her eyes were shiny and moist, reminding Kaz of a frightened lapdog. 'What we gonna do now?'

'We? Where d'you get *we* from?'

As fear turned to desperation in her mother's face, Kaz had wondered if she could ever feel anything more than contempt for this woman.

Then Ellie's small, pudgy hand had emerged from under the covers and clutched her daughter's arm. 'I know I said some stuff to you that I shouldn't've. But, well, families fall out, it's natural.' A tear spilled from the lapdog eyes. 'In the end, family's all we got, innit?'

Kaz returned to the kitchen and rinsed the cloth out in the sink. Then she went to the foot of the stairs and listened. There was a sound – a soft clonk, then another – of furniture being moved. Mounting the stairs silently, two at a time, she crept down the hallway to the master bedroom.

The door was ajar and through it she could glimpse Brian, on his knees and hunched over, in the far corner of the room. Her mother's dressing table was at an angle and a section of carpet behind it had been pulled back. Brian had a claw hammer in his hand and he was carefully levering up the floorboards.

Kaz crossed the room in four swift strides, grasped him from behind by the shoulders and threw him sideways.

He raised the hammer to strike her. 'You fucking bitch!'

She kicked it out of his hand and socked him under the jaw. All her pent-up fury and grief flew into the blow and it left Brian reeling on his back on the floor.

Kaz grabbed the hammer. Seeing the rage in her eyes, he held his arms across his face to protect himself. 'Na, please, don't! Don't!'

Staring down at him, she became aware of her own thumping heartbeat as the events of the last twenty-four hours cascaded through her brain. The image of Yevgeny, his skull cracked open, his vacant gaze, haunted her, fuelling a murderous wrath. She wanted revenge – for him, for Joey, for Helen, for all of it.

Brian had the look of a scared rodent and vermin should be exterminated, there was no dispute in her mind about that. Her brother wouldn't have hesitated. She raised the hammer, watched Brian flinch, heard him whimper. And suddenly the pain of it all flooded through her and tears were prickling her eyes. She wasn't Joey and she didn't ever want to be.

Taking a step back, she lowered the weapon. 'Get the fuck out of here before I change my mind.'

Scrabbling to his feet, Brian glanced at the exposed cavity under the floorboards. 'You said get your gear. That's all I was doing.'

She glared at him. '*Your* gear? I don't think so.'

He scuttled towards the door, then, judging himself to be at a safe distance, he turned and gave her a sour smile. 'Never realized you'd turn out to be such a chip off the old block. Your old man'd be proud, you know that?'

9

Nicci Armstrong stood at the vast plate-glass window and gazed at the westward sweep of the Thames glistening in the afternoon sun. She was in a penthouse apartment at Chelsea Harbour owned by a Hong Kong-based hedge fund manager who used the place on his occasional visits to London, about twice a year.

Simon Blake Associates had the security contract for the building, which included managing the concierge service and ensuring the cleaners did their job. The apartments, many of which stood empty for a good part of the year, were supposed to be cleaned once a week. But an irate owner from Shanghai had arrived to install her daughter at University College and had discovered dust on her kitchen worktops. Threats were issued, Blake had come down to apologize to the client personally. Further inquiries had revealed that Hugo, SBA's acting head of security, had been skiving off. When an explanation was demanded of him, Hugo called in sick; Blake concluded he'd already got another job.

Nicci had been on her way back from Essex when a hassled Blake had phoned her and asked if she'd help sort out the mess left by Hugo. So she was checking the flats one by one to assess how recently they'd been cleaned.

She had her phone in her hand. A text from Tom Rivlin had just popped up informing her that Karen Phelps had been released. She texted back: *Hows Stoneham taking it?* His reply buzzed back a minute later: *Dont worry. I'll talk her round.*

Nicci put her phone in her bag and returned to the view out of the window. She'd been imagining what it would be like to live in such a place. It made her own flat feel like a broom cupboard. She was not a woman much given to envy, certainly not of the material kind. She sometimes gazed wistfully at families with kids of the age Sophie would've been. But to be surrounded by such wealth suddenly felt uncomfortable. Did the people who owned it really deserve to have so much to spare and so much to waste?

She shook the thought out of her head; little in her life, particularly in recent years, had been fair. But jealousy and resentment were toxins. If you let them poison your mind, life became a misery. She knew this and she knew that, for her, staying on an even keel was a daily task and one she had to work at.

Once she'd finished checking the penthouse she took the lift back down to the ground floor. The manager of the cleaning company had just arrived and was waiting for her. In his forties, with doleful brown eyes and hunched shoulders, he put Nicci in mind of a whipped dog.

She offered him a handshake. 'Nicci Armstrong, from SBA.'

He took her hand awkwardly, his palm damp. 'Samir Naseer. I'm so sorry, Ms Armstrong. As I explained to Hugo—'

'Hugo has moved on. You need to explain to me.' The cop in her had been expecting a shifty gangmaster with a bunch of illegal immigrants in his employ. Naseer looked like a stressed-out businessman with too many problems on his plate.

'I apologize. There really is no excuse.' He gave her a sheepish smile. 'We pay above the minimum wage to attract better staff. But reliability is always a problem. I realize we are in breach of our contract with you.'

'The flats I've checked don't actually look that bad.' Nicci had been through half a dozen. They were unlived in, the air a little stale, some were furnished, others completely empty. And they were all cleaner than her own place. She sighed. 'But a client has complained so we're obliged to take that seriously.'

He nodded. 'Of course.'

They stood silently for a moment in the spacious marble-floored foyer. Nicci felt at a loss. Naseer wasn't in the wrong, as far as she could see, any more than she was. Yet they were both being called upon to account for their perceived shortcomings. This wasn't a world she was used to, the world of power and money. But her job now was to provide a service and not to argue.

Naseer bowed his head. 'The client is always right.'

Fuck that, was Nicci's immediate thought, although she managed to hold back from saying it.

She took a business card from her bag. 'Get some industrial-sized cans of air freshener, Mr Naseer.' She handed him the card. 'Ask the concierge to call you when he knows any of the owners are expected. Go in and spray the flat before they arrive. And call me if you have problems.'

He inclined his head and smiled, his features softening. 'You are very understanding.'

The phone in her bag buzzed and she gave him a nod. 'Excuse me.'

Stepping aside, she took the phone out. Rivlin again. She adopted a polite but disinterested tone. 'Tom, how's it going?'

'I've got a piece of intel that I was hoping you might interpret for me.'

'If I can.'

'Yevgeny Koshkin has cropped up in a trawl of some surveillance photos taken last week by the intelligence unit of the Met's Serious and Organized Crime Command.'

'Doing what?'

'Entering premises under surveillance: old industrial machine shop, which has been turned into a skunk factory. It's thought to be controlled by a Turkish gang, the Kemals. Ever hear of them?'

Nicci took a breath as her mind hurtled back to a dark alley in Tottenham and her encounter with these nasty, vicious, misogynistic drug dealers. She'd always feared that night would return to haunt her. Now it had.

10

Once Brian had left, slamming the front door behind him, Kaz used his abandoned claw hammer to lever up two more floorboards. Stashed in the gap between the joists she found a bundle of cash wrapped in a Tesco's carrier bag. The plastic was filmed with dust and cobwebs, suggesting it had been there for a while, but the fifty-pound notes inside were crisp and pristine. Kaz sat on the bed and counted them out: twenty-five grand – quite a haul. No wonder Brian had been anxious to get his paws on it.

Returning to the kitchen with the money, Kaz made herself a cup of tea. She stacked the notes in a neat pile on the granite worktop. Her brother's legacy was far from simple. On the one hand, it was thanks to him that she had a Russian billionaire after her. Pudovkin had already eliminated Joey, Tolya and Yevgeny, and he wanted her dead too. But on the other hand, her brother had left assets; knowing him, he'd have squirrelled stuff like this away in numerous secret locations. Joey Phelps had been a major-league drug dealer as well as a savvy businessman and the cash she'd unearthed was probably only the tip of the iceberg.

She sipped her tea and considered her situation. For whatever reason, the cops had let her go. So the immediate threat of being trapped in a jail cell, unable to escape her pursuers, had been lifted. But she was far from home free.

Nicci Armstrong had turned out to be a tosser. But it'd been a moronic idea to even think the ex-cop would do anything to help her. She was typical of the breed and her weasel words didn't cut any ice with Kaz. They always reverted to type, she should've known better. What she needed now was to be in a position to defend herself. No one else was going to do it for her. She also had to protect Irina, who may well be another loose end as far as Pudovkin was concerned.

As soon as she'd been released from custody Kaz had phoned Irina, but she wasn't picking up. She'd gone to ground with her phone switched off. Kaz assumed she was with Mika. He worked for Yevgeny, but how good would he be at keeping Irina safe and how long could his loyalty be relied upon without a boss to pay his wages? It all came back to money. Only money, serious money, was going to insulate Kaz and her friend from harm.

Her brooding was interrupted by the faint crunching of tyres on the gravel drive outside. Anxiety was keeping her senses sharp and that was good, it would help her survive. As she strode briskly through the hall to investigate, she made a mental note: the electric gate needed repairing. Peering through the spyhole in the front door she watched a minicab pull up. As the back window slid into her sightline she saw her mother's tight, apprehensive face. Ellie Phelps had arrived home.

Kaz opened the front door and stepped out to greet her. The taxi driver was helping her out of the back of the cab. 'All right, love? Nice and easy.' Ellie huffed and moaned, but he was patient with her.

Turning to Kaz, he grinned. 'Don't remember me, do you?'

She frowned; it took her a moment to get him in focus. He was about her own age, tawny skin, broad-shouldered and well-muscled, one side of his head razored to the latest cut. His dark eyes twinkled. 'We was in the same class for a bit.'

'I never paid much attention at school.'

Supporting Ellie's weight with one arm, he offered Kaz his other hand to shake. 'Darius Johnson. Everyone called me Woggie back then.'

Kaz accepted the firm handshake. 'Don't expect they do that no more.'

'Nah, they don't. Not twice anyway.' As he chuckled, Kaz caught a glimpse of steel behind the smile. Then he turned his attention to Ellie. 'Let's get you inside, eh? She was saying she feels very shaky. Probably the meds. I do the hospital run a lot. They discharge people far too soon.'

Leaning heavily on Darius's strong arm, Ellie was shepherded into the sitting room and installed on one of the large sofas. She gave him a weak smile. 'Thanks, lovey.'

'No problem, Mrs P. Happy to help.'

Kaz extracted a note from her jeans pocket. 'What do we owe you, Darius?'

He waved the money away. 'No sweat. I seen the news. Your brother's funeral, all that stuff.' He shook his head sadly, then gave Kaz a speculative look. 'I was never in Joey's league, but we know people in common, if you get my drift. I do other things besides minicabbing. Work the doors on some of the clubs round here.' He pulled a business card from his shirt pocket. 'You ever need help with any bits and bobs, ask around, you'll find I got a good rep.'

Taking the card, she returned the smile. 'I'll bear that in mind.'

'Right, I'm off.' He gave Ellie a mock salute. 'Get well soon, Mrs P.'

Kaz escorted him out and double-locked the front door

behind him. She turned the card over in her hand and pondered. One side had his name printed on it with a phone number, email and website. The other side had a picture of him in headphones grooving over a set of turntables and the slogan: *DJ and the Essex crew.* She racked her brains; could she even remember him?

Schooldays seemed a ghostly, disconnected memory; a time she didn't want to revisit. The boys in her class had never registered on her radar; they were scrawny, spotty and silly. In common with most of the other girls she'd only ever deigned to notice the boys who were older. She did vaguely recall that there were several black and mixed-race kids, who were generally bullied and racially abused by their white peers. But by then she'd tuned out; she was never part of the schoolyard gang. She'd been forced to join the adult world far too soon. Looking back wistfully she almost wished that she did remember Darius Johnson. But then, when she thought about it, she wished most of her teenage years had been different.

However, he remembered her and that gave her an odd sense of reassurance. It made her realize she wasn't entirely alone, there were other resources, other useful individuals out there that she could call upon if she chose to. She wasn't restricted to her brother's former employees and business contacts. The Phelps name still carried clout with the likes of Darius Johnson. Her brother and father may be dead and gone, but her family's fearsome reputation lived on and she was the beneficiary. This was also Joey's legacy to her.

11

Nicci had agreed to meet Tom Rivlin; she'd found it hard to refuse, though she was unsure what she would say. It was five o'clock and the pavements, pubs and cafes of Soho were teeming. Along Old Compton Street tourists meandered, gaggles of thirsty office workers made a beeline for the bars, loungers and liggers drifted, waiting to see who or what would turn up. It was the last place she'd have picked, but then she was a Londoner.

She found Rivlin sitting at a kerbside table outside Bar Italia in Frith Street. He was wearing sunglasses, sipping a small espresso and enjoying looking cool. Nicci had to smile.

'You look like a man who's skiving.'

He shifted the shades up onto his forehead and gave her a lazy grin. 'Had to attend a joint briefing with the Met, so technically I'm doing a double shift. Plus you're my new chis. So what can I get you – I'm on expenses.'

'Just a green tea.' She took the chair opposite. He caught the waiter's eye and placed the order.

'This is such a great little hang-out. A DI from SOCD I palled up with told me about it. You ever been here before?'

He seemed so smug that Nicci couldn't resist the temptation to tease. 'Not for about ten years.'

'Aah, don't burst my bubble.' Rivlin chuckled. 'I thought I

was hanging with the hipsters here. Now you're pulling rank and going all London and snobby on me.'

'I'm sorry.'

'You should be.' His look was very direct. He was playing her again and she knew it. But it didn't stop the fluttery feeling in her lower belly. Annoyance came to her aid. However good-looking he was, she wasn't about to be the chump.

'The coffee is supposed to be very good.' She checked her watch, making it clear to him that she had other places to be.

'Seriously, thanks for coming.' He was hanging on to the eye contact, still trying to reel her in.

The waiter placed a glass cup of water on the table in front of her. She concentrated on that, lifting the teabag out of the saucer and dunking it. 'The Kemals, then.' She sighed. 'Really not much I can tell you. I'm sure you'll get more from SCD7.'

'Yevgeny Koshkin was talking to them only days before the shooting. Why?'

Nicci focused on her tea and tried not to sound evasive. 'What do my former colleagues say?'

'They gave me quite a lot of background: powerful North London gang, part of the so-called Turkish mafia, well-connected back in Turkey, established heroin, cocaine and people-traffickers. Older brother, Asil, he's the brains and boss; younger brother, Sadik, is the enforcer. But a skunk factory is not really part of their usual business model. They're smugglers, they move things.'

'Perhaps they were going to move something for the Russian. All these gangsters do business with each other.'

'Then why visit the skunk factory?'

Nicci had an inkling of where Rivlin might be headed, but she continued on the evasive tack. 'If the Kemals didn't want it, maybe he planned to buy it?'

Rivlin smiled and took a small Moleskine notebook out of his inside pocket. 'I've got a theory I want to run by you.' He thumbed through the pages. 'The National Crime Agency has been trying to recover assets from Joey Phelps's little empire for more than a year. Not much joy so far. But one of their assumptions is that Phelps had a large slice of the cannabis trade in North London, particularly skunk. So I'm thinking, what if the Kemals simply moved in and took over the operation when Joey went down in . . . when was it, May? North London's their backyard. To them, Joey Phelps was an Essex wide boy, muscling in.'

Nicci was watching him closely; his intensity was compelling. His long, lean fingers stroked the notebook as he unravelled the puzzle; he was being a proper detective and she envied that.

He tapped the notebook on the edge of the metal table. 'It explains why a bunch of traffickers would suddenly end up with a skunk factory and it explains why Yevgeny Koshkin knew where it was and went round there. I think he was hoping to reclaim Joey's property. Maybe he was doing it for Karen Phelps?'

She took a breath. There was no way she wanted to get embroiled in this. 'It's a promising theory.'

'It's also a motive for the churchyard killings. Let's say the Russian was trying to heavy them but the Kemals weren't about to roll over. It's what most gangland murders are about: turf.'

Nicci sipped her tea and gave him a tepid smile. She'd spent a hot and hassled tube journey across town panicking about the Kemals. As soon as Rivlin had mentioned them on the phone her brain had scrambled into overdrive. The fucking Kemals! It was a mess she should've never got involved in. But then nor should Karen Phelps for that matter.

She thought about Viktor Pudovkin and Kaz's firm belief that he was the one behind the shootings. Did she buy the notion of the Kemals as alternative suspects? It made a lot more sense than Pudovkin.

Rivlin opened the notebook again, glanced at a page. 'Then we've got Jumira Bogdani, our dead Albanian shooter. She's quite a piece of work. I've talked to the Dutch police and they've got her as a key player in a Turkish people-smuggling ring they busted back in 2011. She slipped the net. But the leading members of the gang did go down and, guess what, one of them turns out to be a cousin of the Kemal brothers.'

Nicci shrugged. 'I don't know what you need me for. Looks like you're well on the way to cracking it.'

'Well, we've got the bare bones to start building a case, but it's early days. Thing I wanted to ask you was, do you think Karen Phelps knows the Kemals?'

'Possibly.' Nicci would have preferred to lie outright, but she decided not to risk it.

'Well, she's never going to talk to me. But you could ask her about them.'

'C'mon, giving you background information's one thing—'

'I just want the information to get fed back, see how she reacts. From her point of view, it could be good news. Means Koshkin was the target, not her. The Kemals probably don't even know about her.'

Nicci knew for a fact that wasn't true, though she said nothing. She could've splurged out the whole sorry story of that night in Tottenham, the night Kaz Phelps would have got shot if Nicci and her former colleague, Rory, an ex-Army major, hadn't turned up to save her. It was a chance for Nicci to 'fess up and get herself back on the right side of the law. After all, it was Rory who'd done all the shooting.

But Rivlin's attitude irked her. He'd referred to her as his chis, his informant, and it was becoming apparent that it wasn't entirely a joke. She wondered if he'd told DCI Stoneham that he was using her in this way. She'd spoken to them as colleagues and out of a desire to help. Now an invisible line had been crossed. He was placing her firmly on the outside, handling her exactly as you would a chis – keeping it friendly, charming her, but with a calculated purpose. Before she knew it, she'd be on the register. It left her feeling uncomfortable and also unclean.

Tom Rivlin treated her to his twinkly Irish smile. 'It was your idea. Let her go and let her run, you said. See where she leads us.'

'How come I've ended up as the go-between in all this?'

'C'mon, Nicci – by rights she should be back in jail. But you pleaded her case and I had a word in the right ear.'

'Uncle Steve, you mean?'

'This is the quid pro quo, surely you understand that. How else do you think I got Stoneham to sign off on it?'

Nicci stood up. 'I thought you might've had the balls to act on your own initiative. Clearly I was wrong.'

'You're misunderstanding this whole situation—'

'Am I? Run back to the boss and tell her I'm a former police officer and a private investigator. I'm not anyone's fucking chis!'

Spinning on her heel she stalked off.

'Nicci, hang on. Please!'

His voice drifted after her but she didn't give him a backward glance. Dodging pedestrians and vehicles she strode onwards, driven by anger. How dare they try to use her as if she was some ex-con to be manipulated? Covert human intelligence source! It was an insult and it left her seething. She didn't pause for breath until she reached Charing Cross Road.

12

Kaz stared at her phone. It was the third text from Nicci Armstrong in half an hour. She'd also had two calls from the ex-cop which she'd refused. Clearly she needed to ditch this phone and the SIM; one more item to add to her to-do list.

Ellie was dozing on the sofa. Her breathing was heavy and regular, punctuated by the occasional snuffle as she surfaced for a moment then sank back into slumber. Kaz had opened a can of tomato soup from the cupboard, heated the contents and spooned it into her mother's mouth. The patient had been grateful and compliant. Neither had spoken much but the process had left Kaz feeling odd. Ellie's physical frailty was unsettling. She wanted to remain detached but the smell of her mother's unwashed hair and damp skin spiralled her back into long-forgotten memories.

Sitting on the opposite sofa, watching Ellie sleep, she'd replayed some of the highlights of their relationship in her mind. The venom of their last real encounter before Joey died still permeated everything. The purity of Ellie's hatred of her daughter on that day had cut like a knife.

Throughout Kaz's childhood, Ellie's preference for her beloved son had simply been a fact of life. Her two daughters were sometimes useful, mostly an annoyance and, in Kaz's case as she grew up, a source of jealousy. But when Kaz testified in court against her brother the already tenuous maternal bond had been severed irrevocably – or so it felt at the time. The last thing Kaz had ever expected or wanted was to find herself back in this house feeding soup to her sick mother.

She scrolled through Nicci's latest text: *Need to speak. URGENTLY. Plse call.* She had no idea what the ex-cop could want and she certainly didn't care. She'd asked her for help and been refused. The prison authorities would protect her, that's what Nicci had said, although they both knew it was bollocks. As she clicked the phone off and tossed it aside she became aware of Ellie's crinkled, piggy eyes blinking at her.

'How you feeling?'

'Ropey.' Ellie's voice was barely a croak.

'Does it hurt, the arm?'

'Yeah.'

Kaz stood up. 'I'll get you some more painkillers.'

'Did Bri say anything before he left?'

'Not really. Tried to help himself to twenty-five grand stashed under the floorboards in your bedroom.'

'Bastard.' Ellie seemed to have found a new object for her rancour. 'I can't believe he just drove off and left us. What a bastard!'

Kaz shrugged. 'Fancy a cup of tea?'

'What you gonna do now?'

'Make a cup of tea.'

'Nah, I don't mean that, stupid.' Ellie used her good arm to ease herself up into a sitting position. 'I mean how you gonna sort this out?'

Kaz folded her arms and faced her mother. 'Dunno. You got any ideas?'

A look of alarm spread across the poor woman's features. 'I don't even fucking know what it's about. Joey upset someone?'

'Joey tried to kill them, got shot in the process.'

Ellie's chin quivered, tears welling up. 'I don't understand none of it. Joey wasn't . . . I mean, he must've had his reasons. He wasn't bad.'

Kaz watched her mother struggling to reconcile her fantasies with reality. 'Depends what counts as bad. He liked killing people. When I first got out the nick I tried to persuade him it was a ridiculous risk, he should stop and focus on the business. He didn't take my advice.'

'He was always wilful. But he was a good son.'

'Unlike me.' Kaz wanted to sound neutral, but she couldn't keep the bitterness out of her voice. 'You never thought I was a good daughter, did you?'

Her mother blinked at her a couple times. She looked more like a frightened child. 'All he wanted was the two of you working together. He loved you, Kaz.'

'Then he should've listened to me.'

Ellie's gaze veered off. She wasn't ready to tarnish the memory of her golden boy by agreeing to that.

Kaz shoved her hands in her pockets. She'd spent most of her life trying to escape the burden that came with Joey's love. And even in death he'd succeeded in trapping her with an act of love. He'd gone out to kill for her, to prove a point. And in doing so he'd turned her into a target.

She shook her head wearily. 'I'll put the kettle on and get them painkillers.'

'Hang on, love.'

Kaz stopped in her tracks. It had been a while since her mother had used that or any other term of endearment.

'I need to say this.' Ellie took a breath. 'I been wrong about a lot of things. Late in the day to admit it, I know. Your dad . . .' Her voice trailed off and she couldn't hold her daughter's eye.

The knot in Kaz's belly twisted, bile rose in her throat. She swallowed it down. 'We don't need to talk about him, Mum. Probably better if we don't.'

Ellie raised a beseeching hand. 'I should've . . . I know I should've . . . I tried to . . . but he . . .' Her voice faded to a whisper. 'I knew it was wrong.'

It was a shocking admission and at first Kaz wasn't even sure what her mother was admitting. She stared at her blankly for a moment. Ellie's small, watery eyes turned away. She pursed her lips, dipped her head. Was this what shame looked like? Or was she begging because she was desperate, because she was shit-scared and Kaz was all she had left?

Her insides were churning but Kaz was determined to remain detached. She wasn't about to be suckered by some half-arsed apology fifteen years too late. Her tone was matter-of-fact. 'You was out of your box on pills most of the time. He used to come to my room to tuck me in. That's how it started.'

Slowly Ellie raised her head. Kaz noticed that underneath the dye-job her roots were nearly white. 'I shoulda stood up to him. I was just too scared.'

Kaz's thoughts skittered back to the kitchen in their old place in Basildon – Ellie leaning over the sink, sobbing and spitting blood, one eye socket so swollen and disfigured she couldn't see – and suddenly her mother's agony felt so real Kaz could even taste the blood. The knot in her belly tightened and pain ripped up through her torso. But she fought it. Then the anger came to her rescue.

Ellie was a user, she always had been, and Kaz was way too smart to fall for a number like this. With Joey gone, her mother would say or do whatever it took to get Kaz onside. But it was all lies and bullshit, nothing more.

Staring down at her, Kaz refused to feel anything but scorn.

Ellie raised her eyes and gave her daughter a sour smile. 'Blokes, eh! They're not worth a fucking candle, any of 'em.'

'You're the one who married him.' Her shoulders felt rigid and she was close to tears, but Kaz forced herself to turn away and head for the kitchen. 'I'm gonna go and make that tea.'

13

By the time Tom Rivlin got to Chelmsford the press conference was nearly over. With the announcement of Reverend Taylor's death, interest in the case had rocketed and it was standing-room only, even though the venue had been moved to the County Council Chamber. Edging through a side door, Rivlin counted half a dozen television news crews from all the main domestic broadcasters, plus international stringers, a horde of print journalists, bloggers, photographers and radio reporters.

The atmosphere was subdued, punctuated by the rapid-fire click-clack of camera shutters. Cheryl Stoneham sat behind a jumble of microphones on the dais at the front, flanked by the uniformed District Commander and a sharply suited, shaven-headed man in a dog collar.

The Bishop was addressing the room in a sombre tone: '. . . and our thoughts and prayers are with Justin Taylor's family at this terrible time. Especially his wife, Charlotte, and their baby daughter, Emily . . .' He seemed about to continue, then he simply shook his head abruptly, as if to erase the horror, and wiped his nose and mouth with his palm.

DCI Stoneham glanced at him and waited a moment. Then she turned to face the microphones. 'Thank you, Bishop. Okay, I'll take one more question from the floor.'

A forest of competing arms flew up and Stoneham pointed

at random. An eager young woman jumped to her feet. 'Did Reverend Taylor know he was burying Joey Phelps?'

Stoneham shook her head. 'No. He was duped. By professional criminals.'

'Will action be taken against the Phelps family?'

The Bishop flapped his hand, his chin quivering. 'Justin was an open-hearted young man, totally dedicated to his ministry. He would not have judged the Phelps family – or any other grieving family, for that matter—'

Sensing a chink in the official line, a tabloid hack dived in. 'Wouldn't he have thought it all a bit odd, Bishop? Shouldn't he have smelled a rat? Referred it up? To yourself, perhaps? Did any money change hands?'

Colour rose in the clergyman's cheeks. He was already overwrought and this was the last straw. The police had questioned him at some length as to why proper procedures were not followed. He seemed about to deliver a riposte, but Stoneham laid a discreetly restraining hand on his forearm and took control.

'This is both a tragic and complex case involving organized crime. Four people died in this murderous shooting. And our absolute priority is to bring those responsible to justice. So I'm going to thank you for your attention, ladies and gentlemen. There will be another press briefing tomorrow at . . . twelve noon?' She glanced at the Press Officer for confirmation. 'Yes, twelve o'clock.'

The room erupted in noise and shuffle. Cameras were demounted from tripods and kit was packed. As Tom Rivlin threaded his way around those heaving and shifting equipment he cast an appraising eye over the milling hacks. He noticed several well-known faces among them – reporters who featured regularly on the national television news – and it gave him a buzz. The news editors were deploying their big guns. This wasn't another domestic or the fallout from a bar-room brawl. Stoneham had said it: this was a complex case involving organized crime. She might be fronting it, but he was the one who had the story they were all dying to hear. He was entitled to feel a little smug.

He approached the boss, who was standing in a corner delivering soothing words to the traumatized Bishop. Rivlin hung back and watched them shake hands. He got the impression that the priest was giving the DCI a blessing, which struck him as faintly amusing. Ritual over, the Bishop turned and left.

Stoneham picked up her sheaf of papers and gave him a wry look. 'Right, I hope you've got something better for me than a wing and a prayer.'

'Looks like you could use a drink, boss. My shout.'

The DCI sighed. 'Why not? My old man'll just have to put up with takeaway again tonight.'

Weaving through the press pack and out into the evening sunshine they headed for the Riverside Inn, far enough away, they judged, to avoid any thirsty reporters.

Rivlin was a sportsman and a fast walker but he wisely let Stoneham set the pace. She was overweight, menopausal and her smart, mid-heel court shoes – part of the press conference outfit – meant she could only totter along. He liked her and he worried for her; she was a woman of huge capabilities who took care of everything and everyone but herself.

She cast him a sideways glance. 'You reckon the Kemals are our prime suspects then?'

'I think so. We can connect them to Koshkin, we can connect them to the Albanian shooter, plus they have a motive. Met aren't going to be happy to give us the lead. They've got a small surveillance operation ongoing, for the people-trafficking and the drugs, but it hasn't yielded enough evidence so far to mount a prosecution.'

'Nothing on the funeral directors' van yet?'

'We're assuming they came out of East London towards Essex. I've got three officers trawling CCTV for potential vans in likely locations, then we're running the index numbers through the ANPR database. But it's a lot of footage to view and there are a lot of vans out there.'

'How was Nicci?'

'She's fine. Happy to cooperate.' Rivlin didn't regard this as a lie. The DCI had enough on her plate. The spat with Nicci was his problem. He should have handled her with more care. It was a minor issue and he'd put it on the back burner until he could find a way to sort it out.

As the DCI paused to get her breath and cross the road, she tilted her head and considered him. Some of her junior officers thought she had second sight; it was spooky the things she picked up on. 'I told you she was medically discharged, didn't I?'

'She's an alchy, yeah. Though I noticed she still drinks.'

Stoneham shook her head. 'Her daughter was killed in an RTA. That might cause anyone to take a drink or two. Before that, she was a bloody good cop.'

Rivlin read the rebuke in her tone immediately. He was also shocked. 'No, boss, you didn't mention that.'

'If your theory is right and we're looking at a feud between what remains of Joey Phelps's crew and the Kemals, then Karen Phelps could be key. That's the only reason she's still out there.'

'I appreciate that.' Rivlin was thinking about Nicci. A dead kid? She'd given no hint of that. His self-congratulatory mood was dissolving into vague unease.

'You want me to talk to Nicci again?' Stoneham gave him a mildly quizzical look.

'No, it's all fine.' He met her eye; he knew she was on to him. 'Though I think she may be a bit offended by the notion that she's acting as our chis.'

Stoneham chuckled; his discomfort, the whole scenario had suddenly fallen into place. 'You actually said that to her?'

'I was . . . y'know, being jokey.'

'Thomas, you are a silly boy. I've told you before: don't play with women unless you mean it.'

'Don't know what you mean, boss.' When she used that tone it pissed him off royally. He wasn't her teenage son.

'She's a professional and a former colleague – treat her as such.'

'I thought I was.' He sounded petulant.

The traffic had slowed to a crawl; holding up her hand imperiously, Stoneham stepped out into the road. Rivlin followed her across and they entered the Riverside Inn.

He was annoyed, mainly with himself. He was ambitious, he liked to win and it wouldn't be too many years before he had Stoneham's job. The thing holding him back was his in-ability to read people accurately. He'd waded through the psychology books, he'd done courses and tried to study human behaviour at every opportunity. Men were easier but women usually defeated him – a cliché but true. He wished he could take a peek at the world through his boss's eyes, if only for five minutes.

He knew he was regarded as arrogant. It was the comment that kept coming up in his performance reviews, though he couldn't see why. How could he be arrogant when it felt as though he was always playing catch-up? Self-improvement was his religion, that was why he ran. Once he had a goal, there was no stopping him.

It hadn't always been that way. At school he'd messed up; in the end he had to go through clearing and settle for a geography degree, having failed to get the grades to study law. Most of his mates from the running club had gone into the business world or retail. But he didn't want to be a supermarket manager. He wanted his life to be about something more than just making money. Lurking deep inside there was still the boyish yen to be a hero, to fight the good fight. So he'd joined the police.

He followed Stoneham through the oak-beamed interior of the pub to the bar.

She turned and smiled at him. 'Don't get upset, Tom. You can't expect to always second-guess how people are going to react. But I wouldn't mind betting that Nicci Armstrong knows more about Kaz Phelps and the Kemals than she's letting on. Wouldn't you agree?'

As usual, the DCI had put her finger on it. 'Maybe that's why she got so arsey with me?'

'We're the lucky ones. We've got the rules to guide us and procedures to follow. She got hung out to dry. How do you hold on to your moral compass in the world she finds herself in?' Stoneham rested one elbow on the bar, reached down and pulled off her left shoe. 'Ouch! I hate these bloody things.'

'I was only trying to make her like me. And trust me.' His brow was furrowed. He hated having to make excuses, to explain, especially to Stoneham. But she should've briefed him properly. A dead kid, no wonder she was so reactive. Okay, he'd played Nicci all wrong but it wasn't entirely his fault. He realized Stoneham was scanning him.

'I'll have a G and T, a large one.'

He gave her a curt nod and concentrated on getting the barman's attention.

Cheryl Stoneham rubbed her sore foot. Rivlin was clever and analytical in his approach, which was good. But he also had a tendency to bulldoze everything in his path. Stoneham had nothing against his aspirations; he was her protégé and she genuinely wanted him to succeed. But he had an emotional blind spot and sometimes a little tug on the reins was required to get him to take stock and think things through.

Nicci Armstrong had sussed him out all too easily. But if she'd gone off in a huff that suggested she wasn't totally immune to his charms. Stoneham had no wish to exploit the poor woman's vulnerabilities, but on the other hand she was SIO on a multiple homicide. Nicci was their route, probably their only route, to Karen Phelps. Stoneham knew she couldn't afford to be soft.

Rivlin plonked a fizzing highball glass of gin, ice and tonic on the bar in front of her. She lifted it to her lips and took a refreshing draught. The first sip was always the best. 'So . . .' she smiled at him. 'Just call her. And apologize.'

14

Walking briskly through Covent Garden, Nicci's temper had cooled; she'd hopped on a bus in High Holborn and returned to the office. She often worked late. The peace and quiet of the deserted building soothed her, while the evidence of other people – the abandoned coffee cups, the drift of sweet wrappers on Eddie's desk – made it somehow more homely than her empty flat.

She'd tried to contact Karen Phelps but her texts had been ignored and her calls had gone to voicemail. If the hit really was the work of the Kemals, Phelps needed to know. Thanks to Nicci's intervention, she'd been released from police custody and was probably lying low, afraid that Pudovkin would have another crack at her. Trouble was, Nicci had no idea where she might be hiding.

Nicci had spent upwards of an hour dealing with emails and the neat line of Post-its that Pascale had left across the bottom of her computer screen. None of it was urgent and most of it wasn't even interesting. The meeting with Rivlin had left her dispirited and dissatisfied. Life as a DS in the Met hadn't been a bowl of cherries, but she'd been out of it long enough for memory to start playing its tricks. If things had been different, she mused, maybe she'd have been promoted to DI herself by this time. Rivlin was smart but she knew deep down she was a better copper. It was all too easy to slip into reverie and regret about what might have been.

Outside, twilight had turned to darkness with an orange glow leeching up from the streets to the rooftops. Nicci's stomach was telling her she needed to eat. She clicked her computer into sleep mode and started to pack up her things.

A movement across the other side of the room alerted her to a presence. She assumed it was the security guard doing his rounds. When she took a second look she saw it was Simon Blake. He raised a hand in salute and Nicci watched him weave around the desks towards her. He was obviously drunk.

'Still here, Nic? Reckon you're my most hardworking employee.' His words weren't exactly slurred but the slow delivery suggested a man holding on to himself – just. He plonked down in an adjacent chair.

'You look like you've had a skinful.'

He gave his head a vehement shake. 'I hate getting drunk.'

'Yeah, looks like it.'

'S'true. But sometimes the occasion calls for it. It's all part of the game.'

'What game?' Nicci was reflecting that in all the years she'd known him, she'd never seen him pissed, not even slightly. Simon Blake liked to be in control, always.

He frowned with concern. 'Why are you still here, Nic? It's no life. I worry about you.'

'I'm fine.'

'We are going to sort this out. I promise.'

'Sort what out?'

Reaching over impulsively, he grabbed her hand. 'I do worry about you. If I lost one of my three, don't know what I'd do.'

She eased herself from his grasp. 'You need to go home, Simon.'

He flopped back in the chair. 'Sorry. I'm pissed.'

'How about I call you a cab?'

His alcohol-fuddled brain seemed to be skittering between random thoughts. 'That Russian, he's a canny bastard.'

'What Russian?'

'Thinks he can play us.'

'Who're you talking about? Pudovkin?'

'They're all the same.'

'The same as Pudovkin?'

'Think they can just buy their way in. That it's all for sale.' He gave a sour laugh. 'And I'll tell you a secret, Nic – it is. Welcome to London, money-laundering capital of the world. Let's all bow our knee and tug our forelock to our new masters.'

'Who the hell have you been talking to?'

'Hush hush, can't possibly say. It's all bollocks, of course. I don't know who the fuck we think we're protecting.'

'Someone's been talking to you about Viktor Pudovkin? So what's that bastard up to now?'

'Should've nicked him for the murder of Helen Warner.' He wagged his finger at her. 'They should've done it.'

'I know.'

'I was still in the job, I'd've done it. Lean on Hollister and his barmy wife hard enough, they'd've coughed.'

'I agree.'

'Now look where we are.' His chin quivered. He seemed close to tears.

'Where are we, Simon?'

'Fucked. It was bad enough before. Now we're well and truly, every which way, fucked!'

She knew the booze was talking. Even so, she found his

drunken despair hard to witness. Simon Blake was one of the few men she truly respected and admired.

He wiped his nose with his fingers and shot her an anxious glance. 'I go home like this, Heather'll kill me. I could sleep in my office, couldn't I?'

'Have you called her? She'll be worried.'

'Sent a text. Earlier.'

Nicci held out her hand. 'Give me your phone.'

He rummaged in his jacket pocket and handed it over. 'Tell her I'm sorry. I didn't mean to let her down. I didn't mean to let you down.'

'You haven't. You're just drunk.'

His head rolled sideways. 'Probably not drunk enough.'

Nicci scrolled through his contacts until she found Heather's name. She sighed then pressed the call button. It rang twice before a fretful voice came on the line. 'Where the hell are you? I waited at the station for an hour.'

'It's Nicci Armstrong, Heather. He's okay. We're at the office and he's drunk.'

'Nicci – oh.' If she was surprised, she hardly showed it. 'He sent a text that was complete nonsense.'

'That figures. I don't know where he's been. But I was working late and he turned up here.'

'Oh.' Now embarrassment had crept into her voice. 'I'm sorry you've been bothered with all this.'

'It's not a bother.' Nicci reflected that Heather and her husband were very similar: both polite and contained people, who gave nothing away. It made Blake's drunken ramblings all the more shocking. There was an awkward pause.

'I'll get a sitter for the boys then I'll drive in and collect him.'

'Okay. Listen, Heather, I know he's been under a lot of

pressure lately. Only today we discovered Hugo's gone AWOL, so it's hardly surprising that—'

'He was going to have a drink with Colin. Do you know if that's what he did?' Her tone was brusque.

'Colin?'

'Colin McCain. He and Colin were at Hendon together.'

'I've no idea.' Nicci had never heard of any Colin McCain. A former colleague in the Met? She glanced across at Blake; his eyes were closed, chin slumped on his chest. 'Want me to ask him?'

'No, no. It's probably going to take me over an hour to get there. Is that all right?'

'Yeah, I'll keep an eye on him.'

'Thanks, Nicci. I'm sure we both appreciate it.'

Nicci had no chance to respond; Heather Blake was gone. Clicking the phone off she stared at her slumbering boss. So what had this former colleague been telling him? And what the hell was going on?

15

Settling down to sleep once again in her childhood bedroom produced uncomfortable feelings in Kaz. The room had been redecorated by Ellie, in various shades of pink, to celebrate Kaz's release from prison two years earlier. It was girly and frilly, a pre-teen boudoir stuffed with cuddly toys and odd-looking gonks; only now did it dawn on Kaz that maybe this was her mother's attempt to airbrush the past.

Throughout the evening they'd hardly spoken. Kaz had turned on the television and they'd watched a property show in which a smug couple with more money than sense argued about whether they wanted a penthouse overlooking the Thames or a renovated farmhouse in the Cotswolds. All concerned seemed very pleased with themselves. Kaz let the succession of luxurious images wash over her while Ellie dozed.

Was she being too hard on her mother? Could shame and regret have brought on a change of heart? Kaz doubted it. Ellie's neediness ruled her actions, it always had. She was not so much selfish as incapable of recognizing anyone else's needs but her own.

As a small boy, Joey had dubbed her 'the old bat'; he knew how to play her even then. He and Kaz would giggle together over his latest ruse to wangle even more cash out of her. But once he'd grown up, Joey morphed into the dutiful son who took care of everything. The house was stuffed to the gunnels with sumptuous soft furnishings and furniture, every kitchen gadget on the market, the electronic wizardry to play music in every room and watch telly in the bath. Joey had provided all this together with a generous monthly allowance. Her husband had certainly disappointed her, but Ellie got all the trappings of luxury she'd ever desired from her loving son. It left Kaz wondering who had really been manipulating who in the end.

Having lined up the gonks on the windowsill, Kaz slipped under the soft fat duvet. What she needed more than anything was rest. The days running up to the funeral, the bloody gun battle and the police grilling had left her shattered. On top of all this had come Ellie's pathetic attempt at contrition, which had brought to the surface a slew of memories and feelings she'd been trying for so many years to ignore. Her lacerated ear was throbbing, her body felt heavy and her mind leaden with a weight she could hardly bear.

Somehow she'd found the energy to tuck Ellie up in her own room with more painkillers and a hot drink. All she wanted now was sleep. As she closed her eyes an image swam through her brain of the gonks staring at her, a definite malevolence in their black felt eyes. But she was bone-weary and within moments she was fast asleep.

When she came to the first thing to hit her was the smell. She sat up abruptly; the room was dark but filled with an acrid fug that immediately made her cough. As she took a breath a sharp pain pierced her lungs and she gasped. Her next breath only made it worse. She clasped her palm reflexively over her mouth and half jumped, half tumbled out of bed.

Struggling to see, eyes stinging and watering, she felt a deep rumbling quivering up through the whole house.

The smoke seeping under the door swirled around the room and every breath she was forced to take disorientated her more.

Grasping the handle, she managed to wrench open the door and that was when the heat smacked into her in a savage whooshing wave. The stairs were ablaze, a crackling inferno with flames leaping from the ground floor up the stairwell and licking the walls and ceiling. Her mother's room was along the landing, closer to the fire, and its door was already blazing.

With the last ounce of her strength Kaz put her shoulder against her own door and forced it shut. She stumbled towards the window, but her face was scorched, her lungs paralysed. Falling to her knees, she tried to crawl. It was too dark to see the gonks up on the windowsill yet she knew they were laughing at her. It was her last thought. As she reached up to grab the sill, her head spun and a searing blackness rose up to engulf her.

16

Although it was late, Robert Hollister was buzzing and it wasn't just the whisky. The morning's meeting with his new lawyer had brought a sense of purpose back into his life. Isabel Merrow QC was a frosty bitch but she was respected and connected. Turning hopeless defence briefs into acquittals was her speciality. She could find the weak spot in any case, deftly prise it open and in would flood the magic elixir known in legal parlance as 'reasonable doubt'.

The police had failed to get a coherent statement out of Paige Hollister and that was the flaw in their case. Fifteen minutes into the interview she'd started to scream and rant, saying she'd been set up and lashing out at anyone who came near her. She'd had to be restrained, sedated and sectioned.

But Hollister knew his wife; it was all an act. Behind her flips into hysterics there was always calculation. It was Paige who'd got him into this mess. She'd miscalculated badly when she went to Pudovkin and told him about Helen Warner; the old Russian spook didn't hesitate. He'd spent years in the KGB and was a senior officer in the FSB, which replaced it. He knew the information Paige had given him was gold dust and that once he'd helped Hollister, by removing Helen from the scene, the politician would be in his pocket forever.

Once Paige realized the seriousness of her blunder she panicked and made a rather melodramatic suicide attempt, after which she was transferred to an exclusive private clinic for which Viktor Pudovkin, as a concerned friend, was footing the bill. This had succeeded in shutting her up, which was everyone's priority at the time.

Hollister himself, released on police bail, had gone to ground in a rented mansion-block flat near Hammersmith Bridge. The location was supposed to be secret but one of his former policy advisors ratted him out and for the first couple of weeks the place had been besieged by paps. But gradually things had quietened down, his fall from grace was no longer a hot item on the news agenda and he was able to get out for walks. He'd wander along the towpath, mostly after dark. The rest of the time he spent on social media. He never posted, he simply watched enviously as the Westminster circus rolled along on its merry way, leaving him behind.

To say he was bitter was an understatement. Suppressed fury was devouring him. He was the victim of malign fate; he'd done nothing wrong yet his life had been ripped apart. The accusations concerning Helen Warner were simply ridiculous. She may have been around fourteen when he'd first fucked her, but he could hardly be blamed. As a girl she'd been a precocious little minx who'd had a complete crush on him. When he and Paige had invited her to join them in a threesome, she didn't say no. She was an adventurous kid, up for anything. No one forced her.

In his view, society had become far too prissy about these things. In many cultures around the world girls were married with their first kid at fourteen. Unfortunately, the Jimmy Savile case had caused political correctness to go into overdrive. The man was obviously a creep; Hollister had met him at a fundraiser for some charity or other, and he'd thought so at the time. Interfering with kids in hospital was clearly beyond the pale. But as a result all kinds of perfectly normal sexual behaviour had become suspect.

When he was at Oxford, more than twenty years ago, he'd had plenty of mates who were having sex with teenage girls. With their thigh-high skirts and their boobs in your face, they were broadcasting an unambiguous message and no one asked to see their birth certificates. Maybe, as a good-looking bloke with his pick of the pack, he'd shagged more than most. But you got your leg over whenever you could, everyone did, and no one was expecting to be prosecuted all these years later for what even the girls accepted was part of the culture.

Hollister sat brooding over his whisky. Most evenings he got through at least half a bottle. He'd spent a frustrating afternoon trying to get Viktor Pudovkin on the phone. The billionaire finally returned his call explaining he was airborne, returning from a business lunch in Munich. Hollister imagined himself sitting beside the Russian in one of the plush leather armchairs in his Gulfstream jet. Private air travel had always appealed to him. In his darker moments, mourning the loss of his political career, he'd comforted himself with the notion that there was a silver lining. Once criminal charges had been dropped, he could forget about the voters and the unions and all the left-wing bleeding hearts he'd spent years wooing, and turn his attention to making some serious money.

Pudovkin spoke German and English fluently, in addition to his native tongue, and his tone had been brisk. 'So, Robert, what can I do for you?'

'The lawyer says I need Paige to make a statement.'

'Then ask her. She's your wife.'

Hollister wondered if Pudovkin was being deliberately obtuse. Several days before his arrest he'd informed Paige that he intended to divorce her. After what she'd done, what did the stupid bitch expect? True to form she'd freaked and since then had refused to speak to him.

'Viktor, you know the situation. I need you to explain to her how important this is. To all of us.'

There was a hollow silence, followed by a metallic click. Had he hung up or had the connection simply dropped out?

A few seconds passed, then the Russian came back on the line. 'And how are the boys?'

'Fine.' His two teenage sons were practically grown-up. Boarding school had been their choice. He texted them a couple of times a week and occasionally got a reply. His youngest child, five-year-old Phoebe, was currently in Scotland being cared for by Paige's parents. The thought of her brought a lump to Hollister's throat. He missed his little daughter, even though she'd been a mistake, the result of a drunken holiday shag. Paige, having omitted to mention she'd come off the pill, had used the pregnancy to get him back onside after an earlier bust-up.

'And little Phoebe?'

'Yeah, fine. But listen, Viktor—'

'Robert, there is only so much I can do. You have to talk to Paige yourself.'

'Things haven't quite worked out as you planned, so now you're hanging me out to dry too, is that it?' Hollister regretted this as soon as he'd said it. The only reason he could afford that bitch Merrow's fees was because Pudovkin was picking up the tab for that as well. He shoved his fist in his mouth and bit down on the knuckle to stop himself from saying more.

He heard the Russian sigh. 'Now is not the time to discuss this. We'll have lunch. We'll talk.'

'When?'

'One of my PAs will call you.'

Hollister took a breath and reined in his temper. Much as he hated the situation he needed the rich fucker and he couldn't afford to let his rage rule him. 'I'm sorry. I don't mean to sound impatient. I know you're a busy man.'

'I am never too busy for my friends. Patience is hard, Robert, I understand this. But your current difficulties will be resolved. Have a little faith.'

As soon as he'd ended the call, Hollister had opened a fresh bottle of whisky. The clinic treating Paige was in Gloucestershire. The train was out of the question; if he was going to tackle her himself he'd need a chauffeured car. He could go at the weekend. Scrolling through the contacts on his phone he found the number of the hire company. Having to make these practical arrangements himself was another irksome reminder of everything he'd lost. He'd talked to some snotty cow who'd informed him they had nothing available until Tuesday. He wanted to scream: Do you fucking know who I am! But she undoubtedly did: he was someone who'd been relegated to the D list.

Still he was determined not to be downhearted. The meeting with the lawyer had brought him hope. Politics was an excellent training ground for life's disappointments. It had taught him how to roll with the punches, get up and fight back. And what Merrow had given him was the means to do that. So he filled his glass, ordered in a takeaway and spent the evening gazing vacantly out at the softly illuminated ironwork of the Victorian suspension bridge whilst keeping an eye on the political shenanigans – who was briefing against who – on social media.

It was some time after midnight when he saw pictures of the fire. The blaze had been filmed by a neighbour and uploaded. The building was crackling away merrily and part of the roof collapsed in a thunderous whoosh of flames, sparks leaping high into the night sky.

Hollister poured himself another drink and watched. It was mesmerizing, the elemental power of the fire. The footage was already trending on Twitter before anyone posted the location. But information began to filter through. It was Essex apparently, a substantial house several miles from Billericay. Then a local blogger broke the news that the house belonged to the family of the dead gangster Joey Phelps and the whole thing went viral.

Staring at the screen of his iPad, Hollister's expression turned from disbelief to total delight. Joey Phelps was the psychopath brother of the bitch who'd suckered him, the miserable slag who'd set him up, leading to his arrest. When they'd first discovered who was involved – her and a bunch of sleazy private investigators – Pudovkin had urged restraint. But he'd also promised to sort things out. *Have a little faith.* That's what he'd said on the phone. Now it was all starting to make sense to Hollister.

Phelps was the gangster who'd tried to assassinate Pudovkin. Could it have actually been some kind of stupid revenge attack for Warner? There was no way the Russian would let that go. He was a dangerous bastard and no mistake. Didn't these moronic lowlifes realize that? Well, they did now. Pudovkin had simply been biding his time. And it was perfect. Was the bitch in the house when Pudovkin's people set the fire? Hollister hoped so. He imagined her roasting in the flames.

Chuckling to himself, he raised his glass in a toast. 'Here's to you, Karen Phelps. Now you really can go fuck yourself!'

17

Was it the blood rushing to her head or the fresh air that revived her? It felt as though she was upside down, or the top half of her was. Head, shoulders, arms were all hanging down and swaying. Then she could see the ground, the rough gravel drive below her. And people and flashing lights. The searing heat was receding. Her legs were being firmly held. She was being carried. The fireman got to the bottom of the ladder and gently eased her off his shoulder into waiting arms. She was lifted onto a stretcher.

Kaz started to cough then retched. Someone was holding her hand, a paramedic, though she could hardly see him, her eyes were so sore. 'Just let it come up, love. Spit out whatever you can.'

He put a supporting arm under her shoulder and raised her up so she could lean over the side of the stretcher trolley. She wanted to puke but her throat felt so raw and constricted. Every breath, every swallow was painful. She spat and a small trickle of sticky black saliva snaked down her chin. The paramedic wiped it away.

'I'm going to give you some oxygen. That'll help.'

Kaz struggled to speak but no sound emerged. She tried to cough again, managing only a hoarse rasp. The paramedic leant forward to listen. Her head was thumping but she willed herself to focus. 'My mum . . . my mum—'

'Don't worry. They've already got her out. She's on her way to hospital. Was there anyone else in the house?'

Kaz shook her head and sank back on the stretcher. The paramedic fitted a mask over her face and she felt the cool, cleansing oxygen flowing up her nose and down into her grateful lungs.

She didn't recall much about the ambulance ride to hospital. All she was aware of was an excruciating headache. But she was alive. For the second time in two days she'd cheated death.

In A&E many hands bustled around her. She heard soothing words, felt the prick of a needle in her arm as they inserted a cannula. They cut off her blackened T-shirt and knickers, listened to her chest, looked down her throat, wiped her body down from top to toe. She didn't complain; she bore the pain of these intrusions stoically. Finally, the poking and prodding ceased. Dressed in a clean hospital gown, with a nebulizer fitted over her nose and mouth, she was transferred to a ward.

When she awoke again bright sunshine was seeping through the chinks in the blinds and she had a raging thirst. A nurse gave her water, which she drank through a straw. It was the most refreshing drink she'd ever had. But they insisted she put the nebulizer back on; it was delivering the medication that she needed. They only removed it again to feed her porridge, which tasted surprisingly good. Kaz took the spoon and managed to finish the bowl by herself.

Sitting up, she saw she was in a bay of eight beds, occupied mostly by older women, who were variously dozing and breakfasting. The woman in the next bed was in her fifties, her bleached hair forming a messy halo over dark roots. She gave Kaz a broad smile.

'How you feeling, lovey?'

The words, the familiar Essex accent, the bad dye-job, made

Kaz immediately think of Ellie. What had happened to her mother? Where was she? Here in the hospital, in another ward?

Finding the buzzer hanging from a length of flex at the side of the bed, Kaz summoned the nurse. But they could tell her nothing. With the mask of the nebulizer back on her face, she was instructed to rest.

Lying back on the pillows Kaz did a mental inventory of her condition. Her head still ached but not as badly as before. It had shifted from acute to bearable. Her breathing had eased considerably, throat and chest were quite sore, but again, it was bearable. The nebulizer was doing its job. She had a burn on her right hand, which had been dressed, and the rest of her skin felt tight and quite tender, as if she'd been out in the sun. Running a hand through her hair, she found it rough and brittle. Considering she'd been rescued, unconscious, from a burning building, she concluded that she'd been extremely lucky.

But how had the house caught fire in the first place? Somehow it just didn't feel like a random accident. She needed some answers but there was no one to ask. The medical staff were going about their business, her neighbours in the bay were chatting, one of them offered to lend her a magazine. She didn't want to read about beauty tips or the love life of some soap star, she wanted information.

Impatiently pulling back the covers, she swung her legs over the side of the bed. Despite a slight giddiness, she managed to stand up. Wobbly at first, she made her way slowly to the toilet. Looking at herself in the mirror she got a shock. Her face was quite red but shiny with some spray-on balm. Her hair was frizzled and a little singed at the front. A flash of memory returned: the wall of blistering heat that hit her when she'd opened the bedroom door.

She managed to pee, then exited the bathroom and headed for the nurses' station. A smiling charge nurse waylaid her. 'You all right, love?'

'I need to talk to someone about what happened.' Her voice was croaky but it worked.

'You're Karen, aren't you? I believe you've got visitors. Arrived a couple of minutes ago.'

He took her gently by the elbow and shepherded her back towards her bed. Glynis Phelps was standing at the end of it with an anxious frown on her face. 'Oh, Kaz!' Tears welled up in her eyes. 'My God, look at you. I just found out. We come straight down here. Are you all right?'

'Surviving. You seen Mum?'

'I asked about her. They said she's been transferred to the Burns Unit at Chelmsford.'

Glynis stepped forward and enveloped her in a cautious hug. It was only then that Kaz realized she was not alone. A young woman was standing slightly apart; she'd been gazing out of the window. As she turned back Kaz recognized her sister, Natalie. And Natalie was holding a child, a toddler about eighteen months old.

Kaz peered at them. She couldn't believe it. How long had it been? 'Nat?'

Natalie gave her an apologetic smile. 'Sorry I didn't make it to the funeral.'

'Bloody good job you didn't.'

'Yeah, I heard what happened.'

Natalie seemed nervous; she couldn't hold her sister's gaze. She transferred the baby onto her other hip. 'I was gonna come. Then the sitter let me down at the last minute. I should introduce you. This is Finlay. Finlay, meet your Auntie Kaz.'

Kaz smiled at the child but her brain was reeling. The last

time she'd seen her sister was nearly two years before at another funeral: their father's. Natalie had been in rehab back then, a nervous junkie on the fragile road to recovery. And there had certainly been no sign of any pregnancy.

The little boy was a restless bundle of energy fidgeting in his mother's arms. But for a moment he turned and met Kaz's eye. His hair was white blonde, his face angelic with two piercing blue eyes. Kaz simply stared: that family resemblance, he reminded her so much of Joey at the same age. And she realized that, in spite of all the grief he'd caused her, she missed her brother desperately. His death had left a void in her that could never be filled. Anger dissolved into desolate sorrow and the tears began to flow. She couldn't stop them.

Glynis gathered Kaz gently in her arms. 'It's all right, lovey. It's the shock. You've had a terrible experience. It's just the shock.'

18

Nicci Armstrong strolled into the office shortly before ten. She felt justified; by the time Heather Blake had turned up to retrieve her drunken husband, it had been pretty late. There was no sign of him this morning. His office door stood open. Nicci greeted Alicia on reception, headed for the coffee station and poured herself a mug.

She'd received two missed calls, a voicemail and a text from Tom Rivlin, all of which she was ignoring. The voicemail, sent the previous evening, sounded awkward; eating humble pie wasn't his style. Still it amused her to hear him try. And it served him right. If she didn't reply then the next call, she calculated, would be from Cheryl Stoneham. That one she would answer, giving some vague excuse about how busy she'd been. But the point would've been made. They'd have got the message.

As she approached the investigations section she noticed that Eddie Lunt was at his desk and Pascale was peering over his shoulder. They were watching a clip on YouTube. It looked like a fire.

Eddie immediately swivelled his chair. 'Think you might wanna see this, boss.'

Nicci dumped her bag on the adjacent desk. 'What is it?'

'Big blaze at this place in Billericay last night. Turns out it belongs to your mate Karen Phelps's mum.'

'What? Shit! Anyone hurt?'

'Two rescued. No other casualties.'

Was that where she'd gone after the police released her? Nicci had some vague memory of the Phelps's family home in Essex; she couldn't remember its exact location. But after her testimony against Joey and the subsequent rift with her family, would Karen have gone back there? Surely not.

Eddie clicked on Twitter. 'This lot are going bananas. That shoot-out at Joey Phelps's funeral, then this hardly a day later – bit of a coincidence. Speculation is it's a gang war. Cops are keeping schtum.'

Nicci's head was in a spin. The Kemals! She'd tried to warn Karen, but her calls had been ignored, just as she'd been ignoring Rivlin's. She grabbed her bag, pulled out her phone and brought up Tom Rivlin's last text. It had been sent at seven a.m. She'd only skimmed it before, but now she read it: *Developments this end. Really need to talk to you. Tom.*

'Shit!'

She clicked on his number and called it. After a single ring it went to voicemail. Putting her hands on her hips she shook her head and cursed her own stupidity. Karen should've been warned about the Kemals. Nicci had been given the information but she'd failed to pass it on. She was too preoccupied with playing cat and mouse with Tom Rivlin and too concerned with how the police were treating her. Pascale and Eddie were looking at her expectantly. She wanted to scream in sheer frustration.

Pascale came to her rescue. 'Want me to check the local A&E, see if I can find her?'

'Yeah, good idea.'

She turned to Eddie and was about to speak when Alicia came hurrying over. 'Nicci, we've got a bit of a situation.'

'What kind of situation?' She couldn't keep the annoyance out of her voice.

'Simon has a ten o'clock. And there's no sign of him. They're here and they don't look too happy.'

'Well, apologize. Tell them he's sick, there's been an emergency. We'll have to reschedule.'

'It's a new client. And he's really important. Some sort of sheikh, I think.' Alicia shrugged apologetically.

Nicci glanced towards the reception area. A tall young man was pacing restlessly and checking his phone, another was standing nearby, hands folded in front of him. He was stocky and looked like the minder.

'What the hell am I suppose to do about it?'

'Well, you're sort of Simon's number two, aren't you? And now Hugo's gone . . .' Her voice trailed off and she gave Nicci a hopeful look.

Eddie Lunt got up from his desk, hitched his trousers over his considerable paunch and smiled. 'Tell you what, boss, why don't I go down to Billericay and find out what's going on. I know a couple of news boys on Radio Essex, I can get the low-down on this fire while you sort out his nibs.'

Nicci glanced at Eddie. She didn't expect him to be helpful and it always seemed to take her by surprise when he was.

He gave her his pixie grin. 'Not like I've got anything better to do, is it? And if this place goes tits up we're all out of a job anyway.'

Nicci nodded, although the pointedness of his last remark was irritating. He was right of course. They couldn't afford to alienate a new client.

She turned to Alicia. 'What is it? A security job?'

'Yes, I think so.' Alicia handed her a file.

Opening it, Nicci found a note written in Simon's neat,

almost feminine handwriting. Turki bin Qassim? Presumably that was the client's name.

Eddie scooped his leather jacket from his chair and headed out. 'I'll keep you posted, boss.'

Nicci frowned. 'You sure he's a sheikh? What do I call him?'

Alicia shrugged again.

Walking across the office to the reception area, Nicci opted for a neutral approach. She held out her hand.

'I'm Nicci Armstrong. I'm so sorry you've been kept waiting. Unfortunately, Mr Blake is unwell.'

He was young – hardly more than mid-twenties was Nicci's guess – a spare frame with a sculpted Van Dyke beard, dark open-necked shirt and an immaculate grey suit. Accepting the handshake, he inclined his head. 'Turki bin Qassim bin Faleh Al Thani.' He had the languid confidence of a man accustomed to privilege.

'I'm pleased to meet you, your, erm, royal highness—'

His features broke into an amused grin. 'Mr Qassim is fine, Ms Armstrong. I don't stand on ceremony. As an Al Thani I am of course distantly related to the Emir of Qatar, but then there are several thousand of us.'

Nicci gave him an appraising look. He had the swagger and style of a male model with the dark curly hair expertly coiffed into precisely the right amount of disarray. His English was perfect, the accent mid-Atlantic. It was her first real encounter with one of Blake's HNWIs but if the company was to survive she needed to get used to it.

She painted on a smile. 'Coffee?'

'Thank you. Mr Karim recommended you. He said he'd found you very reliable.'

Who was Mr Karim? Nicci had no clue. But then she'd never worked in the security side of the business before.

'Mr Karim is extremely generous.' Nicci hoped she sounded convincing.

But the young Qatari simply laughed. 'Karim, generous? That's a novel idea.'

19

Getting out of his car DI Tom Rivlin gazed at the water-doused wreck that had been the Phelps home. It looked eerie and forbidding even in the morning sunshine. The trees surrounding it had been reduced to stark carbonized stumps. Black ossified chips were all that was left of the thick ivy, which had covered the perimeter wall. The area had been cordoned off with red-and-white Fire and Rescue Service barrier tape. Rivlin showed his warrant card to the uniformed police officer standing outside the gate.

The fire investigators in forensic suits were already on site. They were carefully scanning the area where the front door had been with a portable hydrocarbon detector. Rivlin had seen these electronic sniffers used before and knew their usefulness.

Holding out his ID he approached the fire officer in charge. 'Morning. Tom Rivlin.'

'Ken Jones.' They shook hands. Jones was taking a break outside the cordon. His hood was pushed back and he was cradling a takeaway coffee that someone had fetched him. He looked weary. Rivlin guessed he'd been there most of the night.

The firefighter shook his head. 'This was a right stubborn bastard. We thought at one point it might take the neighbouring properties with it.'

'I gather you got the occupants out.'

'Yeah. Two women. They were very lucky. It was after midnight. The mother managed to open her window and shout for help. Fortunately, one of the neighbours was walking his dog. So we got here pretty quick. But getting it under control was another matter. Two gas canisters on the back patio exploded.'

'Like the ones you'd use on a barbeque?'

'Well, you might. Or they could've been placed deliberately. Whole thing looked wrong from the outset. That's why I'm still here. I should've gone off shift, but I want to know what started this bastard.'

'You think it was arson?'

'You hear that clicking?' Jones pointed to the fire investigator, who was meticulously scoping what was left of a charred doorframe with a probe. The probe was connected to the detector, which was emitting a rapid staccato click. 'The sniffer's picking up accelerant vapours all round the front door. Faster the click, the higher the level.'

'What do you think the accelerant was? Petrol?'

'That would be my guess. We're going to have to get samples to the lab and tested before we can say anything for certain though.'

'But we're probably looking at arson?'

'On a provisional assessment, yes.'

Rivlin held out his hand to shake. 'Thanks, Ken. I need to let my team know.'

The firefighter gave him a curt nod. 'Whoever did this, they're evil sods. Could've been very nasty.'

'There'll probably be quite a lot of press interest. So we'll send some more officers to secure the site.'

He didn't need to say more. Jones's professionalism was written all over him. 'I'll tell my lads to keep their mouths shut.'

Rivlin smiled. 'Thanks.'

As he picked his way around the black puddles of sludge it was hard not to feel excited. Only two days after the shooting and the Phelps's house gets torched? It had to be connected. The case was opening up. Someone had got impatient and for any criminal that was usually a fatal mistake.

20

In the two years since they last met, Kaz had made several attempts to keep in touch with her sister but once she'd been accepted onto the witness protection scheme she'd effectively lost contact with her family. She'd spent more than a few sleepless nights worrying about Natalie because, despite several expensive bouts of rehab, her baby sister had been a serious junkie.

However, the girl before her now looked bright-eyed and clear-skinned. The listless waif Kaz remembered had morphed into a young mother, rather tense but alert, eyes never straying far from her child. Finlay was an inquisitive and energetic toddler. He was into everything, rushing headlong in any direction; he had no fear. So to distract him Glynis took him off on a small investigative tour of the ward.

Left alone, the sisters faced one another awkwardly – Natalie nervous and shy, Kaz still teary-eyed. 'It's so good to see you, Nat.'

'Yeah, good to see you too.' Natalie stepped forward and managed a clumsy hug. 'You all right? Don't wanna hurt you.'

'Nah, it's fine. Skin's a bit sore in places, but I think I was lucky. The worse thing was the smoke.'

'I'd've been bricking it.'

Kaz chuckled. 'You think I wasn't?'

'I couldn't believe it when Glynis phoned me this morning.

How did it happen? Some kind of accident?' She sounded hopeful.

'I doubt it.'

'What the fuck's going on, Kaz?' Natalie frowned and shook her head. 'At the funeral, now this. Is it 'cause of Joey?'

'Yeah, but, nuts as it sounds, he was only trying to help me.'

'You know who's behind it then?'

'Maybe. But don't worry, they ain't after the family. Only me.'

'What you gonna do?'

'I've no fucking idea.'

'Can't the police protect you?'

'You're joking! All they want is to revoke my licence and send me back to jail.'

Kaz drew a tissue from the box on the bedside locker and carefully wiped her face. Her sister had turned up, which was something. But the gulf between them felt enormous. She forced a smile. 'Well, Finlay's certainly a surprise. I never even knew you was pregnant.'

'I didn't realize myself 'til quite late on. Took ages for me to show.'

'Who's the dad? Not Jez, surely?'

At the mention of her murdered boyfriend Natalie flinched.

'Sorry, didn't mean to . . .' Reaching out impulsively, Kaz brushed her sister's arm and felt her stiffen. It was hardly surprising. Without the drugs deadening her mind Natalie would've had plenty of time to reflect on what had happened to Jez. She knew it was Joey who'd killed him, chucked him off a balcony like a bag of garbage. Did she hold her sister responsible too? Kaz wasn't sure. An aura of resentment pulsed around Natalie but she wasn't giving anything away.

'No, Jez ain't the dad. Just as well really.'

'I know I should've stopped him, Nat.'

'How was you gonna do that?' Her chin quivered and she clenched her jaw. 'No one could control Joey. Not even you.'

They stood for a moment in silence and it struck Kaz that the woman facing her was a complete stranger. Their shared childhood, the family bond, was irrelevant.

Natalie folded her arms defensively. 'It was a casual thing. Someone I met when I was in rehab. I never wanted him involved.'

There was finality in her tone. She wasn't about to say more. Whoever Finlay's father was, he was summarily dismissed.

Kaz shrugged. 'You've managed this all on your own then. What about Mum? Didn't she help?'

'Sort of, but you know what she's like. I was at home for a bit. But listening to her crap, day in day out, her and Brian, nearly drove me round the bend. So I called Doctor Iqbal.'

'The bloke that ran the rehab place – Wood something?'

'Woodcote Hall. Yeah.' For a moment her expression turned wistful. 'He sorted it all out for me. I went to this really nice place up in the Lake District. It was a special clinic for if you was a drug addict and got pregnant. That's where Finlay was born. We stayed up there for about another nine months. It was great. I learnt how to look after him properly. I had a lot of support. Then I got in touch with Glynis and she helped me find a place in Southend.'

As Kaz scanned her sister's face she could see that having a baby was maybe the best thing that could've happened to her. 'And you've stayed clean?'

'Yeah. I go to NA, which helps. And I know that what I'm doing every day is for him. I didn't want it to be like when we were kids. That's why I stayed up north for so long. I wanted to be sure I was strong enough. I didn't want to be tempted.'

'Sounds expensive though. Who paid for it? Not Mum?'

Natalie's gaze skated away out of the window. 'Doctor Iqbal got some charity to pay.'

Kaz sighed. 'I just wish I'd known, babes. Maybe I could've helped.'

Natalie continued to stare out of the window, her narrow shoulders hunched. 'You done the right thing, Kaz. You walked away.'

'It wasn't what I wanted.'

Natalie turned and gave her sister a wintery smile. 'When the fuck did either of us ever get what we wanted?'

21

Eddie Lunt was waiting for Nicci at Billericay station. Parked up opposite the entrance, he was two bites into his lunch – a shish kebab in pitta bread – when a trickle of passengers started to appear from the London train, which had just pulled in. Eddie managed a third bite then, catching sight of Nicci clicking through the ticket barrier, he carefully wrapped the remainder of the food in its foil packet and slipped it in the glove compartment.

Nicci walked over to the Honda Accord and opened the passenger door. She was wearing her customary scowl and made no attempt at a greeting. 'What have you got then?'

Eddie beamed and reflected, not for the first time, that Nicci Armstrong was a hard woman to like. 'Fire was arson; Karen's in Basildon Hospital – I've got the name of the ward; the mother's gone to the Burns Unit at Chelmsford; cops are linking the fire to the shooting at the funeral, although they're denying that to the press.'

Settling into the passenger seat Nicci recollected herself. 'Sorry, didn't mean to be quite so . . .' She forced a smile. 'That's a good morning's work.'

'Thank you, boss.' He inclined his head. 'So did we get the new security contract?'

Nicci nodded. Her meeting with Turki bin Qassim had been polite and surprisingly straightforward. He wanted a minder for his wife, who had recently come from Qatar to the UK to join him. If she went out alone and required an escort it would usually only be during the day. Mr Qassim was perfectly happy with the rates Simon had quoted in his introductory letter and the fact that initially Nicci, a former police officer, would be doing the work herself. The agreement had been sealed with a handshake and paperwork was to follow.

Eddie started the engine. 'Let's hope Simon's grateful. He should be.'

'You ever heard him mention a former colleague called Colin McCain?'

'The spook?'

Nicci shot him a ferocious glance. How the hell did he know that when she'd never even heard the name before last night?

Eddie slipped the car into gear. 'So where we headed? You want to look at the house first? Not much to see really. Or go to the hospital?'

'The hospital. I thought McCain was in the Met. How do you know he's a spook?'

'He's cropped up from time to time.'

'What on earth does that mean?' Nicci was trying hard not to sound impatient.

'Long story short, boss: McCain was with Special Branch back in the day. Then police corruption became his speciality. That didn't make him too many friends inside the Met. So he jumped ship to Thames House. Now he's a back channel between the two organizations. I don't know his official title or role. But he crops up in all sorts of interesting situations. My guess is he's a fixer.'

'What sort of fixer?'

'Stuff goes pear-shaped, the wrong information gets out, he

fixes it. He's a source for a lot of people in the media. Tries to manipulate the news agenda.'

The Honda wasn't that new; it had a throaty diesel engine and Eddie was a cautious driver. He cruised through Billericay well within the speed limit and they headed south towards Basildon. Nicci fidgeted beside him. She was keyed up and irritated. She felt like a juggler trying to keep all the different plates spinning: Karen Phelps, the Kemals, Tom Rivlin, Simon Blake and his drunken revelations. And somewhere in the shadows behind it all, Viktor Pudovkin. Her brain was churning it all over and the more she tried to think things through, the worse she felt.

'And Simon's buddies with this McCain?'

'I gather. Though he's never spoken about it to me.' Eddie shot her a speculative look. 'So what's your interest?'

'Simon met him for a drink. I was wondering if it was significant.'

'You could ask him.'

'I doubt he'd tell me.'

A restless night had left Nicci both weary and wired. She exhaled. 'Do you ever wonder what the fuck you're doing and why?'

He chuckled. 'Meaning of life, that sort of thing? Nah, far as I can see there is no meaning.'

'Doesn't that depress you?'

'Well, that's a choice, innit?'

'A choice?' She glanced at him. Was he taking the piss? He had an odd sense of humour. 'How is it a choice?'

He seemed perfectly serious. 'Everyone decides for themselves how to look at things. Stuff happens, but it's up to you what you make of it.'

'So some moron, with dodgy brakes on his lorry, kills my

little girl – ' the bitterness and anger erupted without warning, Nicci could feel its sour sting like bile in her throat – 'and I'm supposed to think, "Oh well, that's life. Stuff happens. Move on."'

Eddie didn't reply. He kept his eyes on the road.

Immediately she regretted her outburst. Baring her soul to Eddie Fucking Lunt had not been her intention. It was a sure sign the stress was catching up with her.

They travelled on in silence for several minutes. Finally, Eddie spoke. 'Thing is, boss, whether or not you blame yourself, that's a choice. And deciding if you can forgive yourself, that's a choice too.'

Nicci glared at him. He'd pissed her off since the day they first met with his criminal record as a phone hacker, not to mention his questionable attitude to breaking the law, and now he was presuming to give her advice. Well, Eddie Lunt's trite self-help philosophy was something she could certainly do without. She shot him a malevolent look. 'So all the scams you've pulled over the years, all the times you've broken the law, is that what you do? Just say: Oh well, never mind. I'll forgive myself. You're a fucking hypocrite, Eddie.'

He inclined his head and shrugged. 'Well, maybe so.'

22

Tom Rivlin checked in at the nurses' station. He showed his warrant card and confirmed that they had Karen Phelps. The staff nurse asked him if he wouldn't mind waiting; the consultant was doing her rounds. She pointed through to one of the bays and Rivlin caught a glimpse of Phelps with a cluster of doctors around her bed.

He turned his attention to the staff nurse, who seemed inclined to linger. She was small and neat, lovely almond eyes, partly oriental. He'd been out with several nurses over the years and had colleagues married to nurses; somehow cops and nurses often made a good match. He wondered idly what this one would be like between the sheets. She was smiling, rather coyly, which suggested that if he asked for her number she wouldn't refuse. But he was only filling time.

He'd relayed to Stoneham the fire officer's provisional assessment and now the priority was to get Karen Phelps onside. If Nicci Armstrong wasn't prepared to help then he'd just have to manage it on his own. There was also the issue of whether or not Phelps was in danger. But he couldn't really address that until she started talking to him.

'I know the information's probably confidential – ' he treated the staff nurse to his best smile – 'but what's the story with Karen? How soon do you think they'll discharge her?'

'We're waiting for the results of some tests to assess her

lung function. If the consultant's happy with those and her heart's not affected, could be as soon as tomorrow. We need the beds.' Her tone was serious and confidential, one professional talking to another; she obviously knew about nurses and cops too.

'Has she had any visitors?'

'Two women, both family. One of them with a small child.'

Those almond eyes were gazing at him expectantly, hopefully, and Rivlin had to admit he was tempted. But the timing wasn't good. This was the biggest case to come his way since he'd been promoted to DI. He wasn't taking any chances, which is why he wanted to make a connection with Phelps himself instead of relying on one of his team. He gave the staff nurse a wistful look. No, sadly he didn't have time for it.

The consultant, a rather serious-looking lady, came out of the bay, issuing instructions to one of the gaggle trotting behind her. She swept past Rivlin.

He smiled at the staff nurse. 'Okay if I go in now?'

She nodded; she'd felt the frisson, seen the look in his eye, but somehow she'd blown it. He probably had a girlfriend. Unlikely a bloke like him would be single.

Karen Phelps was sitting on the side of the bed, facing away from him and gazing out of the window. The hospital gown was gaping at the back, revealing the sweeping curve of her naked spine. Rivlin hesitated. He found her vulnerability unexpectedly moving and didn't want her to be startled. But some kind of sixth sense alerted her and she turned abruptly to look at him.

'Hello, Karen. Remember me? DI Rivlin.' He smiled.

'I was wondering when you lot'd show up.'

'How you feeling?'

'The fuck you care.' She coughed. Dry and rasping, it

121

sounded painful. 'You still trying to revoke my licence and send me back to jail?'

'Nope.' He slipped his hands into his trouser pockets. 'But I think that we can both agree that your brother has left you in a very tricky situation.'

She fixed him with a hard, piercing stare. 'Oh. So the fire wasn't an accident.'

'The fire investigators are examining the site now, but they've found accelerant vapours, so, yes, we're probably looking at arson.'

Even though she'd already come to that conclusion herself, hearing the official confirmation sent a jolt right through her. But there was no way she'd show it. She got up and faced him, back to the window, with folded arms.

'Murder and arson, eh?' The tone was mocking. 'You crack this one and you're gonna be up that greasy pole like a rat up a drain.'

He smiled. 'I need your help in this investigation, that's true. But you also need mine, Karen. I'm not the enemy.'

'What are you then? My new best friend? So let's see you prove it. Put me back on witness protection with a new ID.'

'I'm afraid that's not my call.'

'There's a surprise. In that case, you got nothing to offer. I'll take care of myself, thanks very much, and you can fuck off.'

He tilted his head and, although his hair was dark and curly, the eyes were blue. For a split second his look put her in mind of Joey, whose ghost seemed to be everywhere, ganging up on her, taunting her for not trusting him. Rely on a cop? How her brother would've laughed. Kaz could feel a cold rage rising inside her. No, there was no way she'd let this tosser use her.

Rivlin sighed. 'Listen, why don't we—'

The anger gave her a surge of energy and she put her hands on her hips. 'You deaf or something? I said fuck off!' The voice was still croaky but loud enough to make all the other patients in the bay stop and turn to look. 'If I've done something wrong, then nick me. If not, fuck off! I don't wanna talk to you.'

'Okay.' He raised his palms in a placatory gesture. 'Calm down—'

Calm down? She was icily calm and, taking a deep breath, she found more volume. 'Don't patronize me. Just FUCK OFF!'

The staff nurse appeared round the corner with a concerned look, having heard the rumpus. Rivlin turned to her apologetically. 'It's okay, I'm going.'

Kaz took a step forward. 'And don't fucking come back.'

All the women in the bay were glaring at him. He was some invading male on their territory and they instinctively took Kaz's side because she was one of them. Rivlin could feel his colour and embarrassment rising. As he turned away, he couldn't meet the staff nurse's eye. His previous notion of seducing her had evaporated. He'd clearly misjudged Phelps's reaction and he felt a fool. Now he wanted to get out as quickly as possible. But in his haste he walked straight into Nicci Armstrong, who was coming round the corner with a short, fat bloke in tow.

For a frozen moment they stared at each other. Nicci smiled. Rivlin huffed. 'Maybe you can talk some sense into her.'

Standing at the end of her bed, holding her ground, Kaz's glowering look turned to annoyance as she saw Nicci. 'Oh, what the fuck!'

Rivlin wagged his finger. 'If you won't listen to me, Karen, then listen to her. She definitely is your friend. My boss did want to lock you up. She's the one who persuaded the probation service to give you the benefit of the doubt. You owe her.'

23

Asil Kemal was struggling to contain his annoyance. He was standing in his pleasant sitting room in Muswell Hill trying to talk sense into his beloved son, Tevfik. The boy was supposed to be revising for his resits. He'd completed the first year of a Business Administration course at London Metropolitan University, which he'd managed to fail. Still he didn't seem at all bothered and Asil had caught him, lounging on the sofa, watching American football instead of working.

Of his three daughters, two had already graduated and one was in her final year. But, if Asil was honest with himself, he had to admit that his youngest, the precious son he'd waited so long for, was a big disappointment to him. The boy was indolent, arrogant and, even though he'd been brought up bilingual, too lazy to speak Turkish. He also kept saying he wanted to be a DJ, which was clearly absurd.

It had taken Kemal grit, ruthlessness and hard work to get from the poor mountain village where he was born to this affluent London suburb. The enterprises and assets he controlled with his brother, Sadik, were now 25 per cent legitimate and, if he managed to carry through his current five-year business plan, he hoped to raise that figure to 50 per cent. But what was the purpose of it all if his son couldn't pick up the reins?

He made this point yet again to Tevfik, as he had done on numerous previous occasions.

In return, he got a surly look. 'Baba, I don't need to go to uni to take over the business.'

'If I had had such a chance, a proper education, you think I would've done the things I've had to do? Taken the risks we take?'

'I like risk.'

'You wouldn't like going to jail.'

'You didn't go to uni. Why should I?'

'But I studied! Every spare moment. I studied and I worked.'

The boy picked up the remote from the coffee table and began to channel-hop.

'You listen to me when I speak to you, Tevfik.' The tone of voice was resigned; it carried no real threat and the boy knew it.

'I am listening.' He gave his father an innocent look even though his attention was on a re-run of *Jackass*, which was making him giggle.

The door to the sitting room opened and Sadik Kemal walked in. He scanned the all-too-familiar scene: father and son at loggerheads. Tevfik was a spoilt brat in his uncle's view and Sadik had no patience with him. Asil had been in his late forties when his son was born; he'd overindulged the boy from day one and was now suffering the consequences. Sadik's own sons were still small – eight and ten years old – but he guided them with a firm hand and had privately resolved that, in spite of his loyalty to Asil, they would inherit the firm, not Tevfik.

Asil glanced across at his half-brother and shook his head wearily. There was a twenty-year age gap between the two men. Several inches shorter, Asil's spare frame and glasses gave him the appearance of an accountant and rivals had often been fooled by his manner; he looked nothing like a gangster. But a combination of relentless ambition and strategic thinking had turned him into the dominant player in the web of Turkish gangs trafficking heroin and cocaine into the UK.

With a sigh he abandoned the battle with his son and strolled out of the room and across the hall to his study. Sadik followed. He'd only been fourteen when he first joined his brother's early forays from Istanbul across Europe, smuggling large consignments of drugs. Asil had started out as a foot soldier working for a Turkish-based cousin but he was too ambitious and way too smart to remain anyone's subordinate. Competitors were dispatched with cold-blooded efficiency until Asil established a solid foothold in North London.

As Sadik grew and filled out he became the new firm's indispensable enforcer and together the brothers proved a lethal combination. Now, after twenty-five years in the business, they were serious players in the UK's illegal drugs industry. Asil had fashioned a network of alliances that took in Turkish and Albanian gangs in the Netherlands and Germany, commanded the fealty of younger London street gangs and snaked back to Istanbul. He'd anticipated the surge of European-bound migrants and got into the people-smuggling business early on. Now, through his chain of kebab shops and a London-wide taxi business, he funnelled the illicit profits into a burgeoning commercial property portfolio.

Sinking into his padded leather chair he drummed his fingers on the oak desk and glanced up at his brother.

'Can we do anything?' He had a hard look in his eye and he wasn't talking about his son.

'It's not the Met. This is Essex cops. They're running the investigation.'

'It's the fucking Met taking pictures of me every time I step outside my own door.'

'Sure, they carry out the surveillance, but for Essex.'

Asil gave him a baleful look.

Sadik shrugged. 'That's what they tell me.'

'How much we pay to keep these bastards off our backs? Too fucking much.'

'I speak to some more people, see what can be done.'

Asil's gaze darted up towards the ceiling and the light fitting. 'And get this place, the office, everything swept for bugs again.'

'They got nothing. They sniff around. Make it look like they do something.'

'How come the finger is pointing at us? That's what I want to know?'

Sadik shook his head. 'No way it's Bogdani. He's so pissed they shot his daughter he refused payment. He done the fire job for free.'

'And still made a mess of it. He's a fucking gypsy. He's got no control over his own people.'

Sadik took a gold cigarette lighter from his pocket and started to turn it over rhythmically between thumb and forefinger. He waited. Asil was a worrier. It was a process he had to go through and Sadik was used to it. The more successful they'd become, the more he worried.

Asil opened a hand-carved ivory box, took out a Sobranie Black Russian and tamped it on the desk. He was a man of rituals and his brother knew them all. As he placed the gold filter between his lips, Sadik sparked the lighter and offered the flame.

Asil Kemal sighed and leant forward to light his cigarette. 'Okay, I want this matter concluded. And I don't want no more fuck-ups.'

Sadik bowed his head.

'The Russian was business, but this bitch—' Asil took a long pull on the cigarette and it seemed to calm him. 'She held a fucking gun to my head, Sadik. This bitch I want dead.'

'I told you. You should've left it to me in the first place.'

Asil met his brother's eye and the hint of criticism in the tone didn't escape him. Since the incident, there had been a shift, barely discernible, but nevertheless a lessening in the deference his younger brother showed him. Did Sadik think he was past it?

Kaz Phelps had come storming into his office looking for her whore of a friend and waving a gun. He'd fronted it out. A fighter his whole life, his nerve had never cracked. But then he'd found himself lying face down in that alley, volleys of automatic fire ricocheting off the walls, and suddenly it had felt like the end. Convinced he was about to die, he'd crapped himself. And that's how Sadik had found him. It turned out that Phelps had backup, which was how she got away. But she'd humiliated him, robbed him of his self-esteem, his manhood and maybe even his brother's respect. It had become a matter of honour. In spite of the police interest, there was no way he could let this go.

A thin grey-blue coil of smoke curled up from the tip of his Sobranie. 'I warned her. Make sure she knows I keep my promise.'

'Oh she will know, brother. She will have plenty of time to regret what she's done.' Sadik was already relishing the prospect. 'And when I've finished with her, she'll be begging me to kill her.'

24

Kaz Phelps settled back against the pillows and frowned at her visitors. The staff nurse had insisted she put the nebulizer back on. It was an effective way of calming her down and shutting her up.

Eddie Lunt found a couple of chairs, one of which he handed to Nicci.

She sat down at the side of the bed. 'Steve O'Connor. That's the name of your probation officer, right?'

Kaz thought back to the slip of paper she'd been given by the police when they'd released her. It seemed like an age ago. She simply nodded.

'I went to see him yesterday morning first thing. Put it to him that you were not a danger to the public. He obviously believed me.' Nicci smiled ruefully. 'Though if you'd been in a police cell last night you probably wouldn't have ended up here. So maybe it wasn't such a favour after all.'

Kaz slipped the nebulizer off. 'I wouldn't have been any safer back in the nick. They'd've got to me somehow.' She hesitated; her earlier desperation in the police interview room after the shooting had left her embarrassed. Never show weakness was the motto she lived by. 'Thanks anyway.'

Acknowledging this with a nod, Nicci scanned the patient. Before, she'd looked scared. Now she seemed brooding and wary. Understandable. Her life had been threatened twice in as many days. She'd been through the mill. Nicci wanted to reach out, but the aura around Kaz made it clear that physical contact wouldn't be welcome.

'You still thinking this is Pudovkin?'

The dark eyes met Nicci's. 'Don't you? Joey tried to kill him and he knows why.'

'What about the Kemals?'

This produced a disdainful huff from Kaz, which caused her to cough. Eddie got up and poured her a beaker of water.

Watching Kaz drink, Nicci shifted in her chair. 'Thing is, Karen, the police can connect the shooter at Joey's funeral to them.' She waited for this to sink in.

'Well, I'm not scared of the fucking Kemals.' It sounded like bravado and Nicci took it as such.

'Maybe you should be. When you went to rescue Yasmin you held a gun to Asil Kemal's head. You think they're the sort to let that go?'

'Then why shoot Yevgeny?' She took another sip of water.

'Could be they were aiming at you and he got in the way?'

Kaz's memory of events was a jumble: the bullet lacerating her ear, Yevgeny shoving her sideways out of harm's way. She hadn't had time to process any of it. Could it really have been the Kemals? It had never occurred to her.

'It was your fucking bug-up-his-arse mate Rory who shot at the Kemals. Not me.'

Nicci glanced at Eddie. 'Probably best not to mention that to Simon.'

'Wasn't going to, boss.' He'd already surmised that the connection between her and their erstwhile colleague was decidedly dodgy. That's why they were here. The former cop wasn't as squeaky clean as she made out. He grinned. 'In my experience, these ex-army hard cases often do turn out to be nutters.'

It sounded supportive but Nicci suspected he was taking the piss.

Kaz's gaze had drifted towards the window as she mulled it over. 'Eddie's right. He was the nutter. Once I'd got Yasmin I just wanted to get out of there. It wasn't me that tried to kill Kemal.'

'What if they don't see it that way?'

Kaz let the nebulizer settle back on her face. Viktor Pudovkin was a Russian billionaire that the law couldn't touch. But the Kemals were grubby little gangsters and she'd dealt with their sort her whole life. Maybe Nicci was right. As the thought percolated she began to feel slightly less beleaguered.

Nicci watched her. Edgy with impatience, she was forcing herself to wait. Kaz needed time but, in a fast-moving investigation like this, it was the one thing they didn't have. And Nicci did feel part of the investigation. Her default mode was still that of a police officer. She couldn't help it. Rivlin slipped into her mind; was she doing this to impress him? She dismissed the thought.

Having taken a couple of cleansing breaths, Kaz pulled the nebulizer off again. 'What's-his-face, your slimy cop mate—'

'Rivlin? He's not my mate.'

'Well, he reckons the fire was arson.'

Nicci tossed her head and sighed. She'd guessed as much, but this compounded her guilt. 'Then there's only one way you'll be safe: when the police nick the Kemals.'

'Well, yeah.' Kaz kicked back the sheets, her growing anger and frustration palpable.

'You've got to cooperate, Karen. Tell them everything you know.'

'Like what? What do I fucking know? What do you think I know?'

Nicci hesitated, but only for a moment. She wanted to be gentle but she didn't have that luxury.

'The police have surveillance photos of your recently deceased Russian friend entering premises in North London, an old clothing factory, now being used to grow cannabis.'

'So?' It sounded to Kaz like the place she'd visited with Joey, but she couldn't be sure. The thunk of the low oscillating fans over a vast sea of luscious plants skipped briefly into her mind. Joey had been so proud when he'd showed off the place to her.

'What was he doing there?'

'How should I know?'

'He was Joey's enforcer, wasn't he?'

'That's crap.' Kaz folded her arms defensively. 'Yev was just a friend.'

'Don't bullshit me, Karen. He was helping Joey evade the law. And the police think he was trying to get Joey's assets back from the Kemals. Wasn't it his brother that was killed with Joey?'

'So this is still about Joey? I testified against him. Sent my own fucking brother down. Now he's dead. Isn't that enough?'

Sunk in the mound of pillows, dark hair a straggly mess, Kaz clenched her jaw to resist the tears. Observing this, Nicci sighed.

'Rivlin's not stupid and he's not going to go away.'

Kaz glared at her. 'Is this why those bastards won't put me back on witness protection? Because they want the Kemals and I'm the bait?'

In spite of being hurt and over-emotional she'd cut through to the heart of the matter and Nicci felt a stab of conscience. *Let her run and see what happens.* It was the argument Nicci herself had used to put pressure on Rivlin.

The ex-cop shook her head. 'You've got to offer them something.'

'That's a two-way street. Look around. You see any uniforms here to keep an eye on me?'

'I'll talk to Stoneham. She's the DCI in charge.'

Kaz turned away and the tone was bitter. 'Yeah, right. You'll have a word, 'cause you're all in the same club. Why should I trust any of you?'

Why indeed? That was Nicci's immediate thought and she was summoning up the energy to defend herself when Eddie Lunt leaned forward in his chair. 'You should trust her because she doesn't need to be here. Doesn't need to be doing any of this. You're in a hole, mate. She's trying to help you.'

The laugh was acerbic and brought on another coughing fit. 'I'm not in a very trusting mood right now.'

'Course you're not. You feel like shit and you're still trying to figure out what the bloody hell's going on. But you need to think strategically. You can't ignore the cops because they won't ignore you. You need an ally. As ex-coppers go, she ain't that bad – and she's on your side.'

Kaz looked at Eddie. He shrugged. She had to admit, if only to herself, that he was stating the obvious.

'You want to know the truth, Karen?' Nicci stood up. 'I'm here because I feel guilty. The police told me about the Kemals yesterday and I should've warned you.'

The dark eyes scanned her.

'You ignored my calls. But I should've tracked you down. I'm sorry.'

Kaz shook her head wearily. It was all starting to make sense. 'The fucking Kemals! Can you believe it? I should've shot those bastards when I had the chance.'

Nicci leant over, put a hand on Kaz's shoulder. 'Listen. I will talk to the police. I'll get a uniformed officer here or, failing that, a private security guard from our own firm.'

'Another ex-squaddie with an itchy trigger finger? Isn't that what got me into this mess?' Nicci shot her an acid look and got a grin in return. 'It's a joke, Nicci.'

'Yeah, very amusing.'

The staff nurse appeared at the end of the bed. She'd been keeping a careful eye on things after Kaz's earlier outburst. The stream of visitors in and out of the bay and the disruption generated by Kaz's presence didn't please her. She also disapproved of the way Kaz had spoken to a police officer. Whatever the girl had suffered there was no excuse for bad behaviour in her book. Checking Kaz's notes she fixed her with an imperious look. 'I think you've had enough excitement for one day. You really need to rest.'

Nicci took the hint. 'We're just going.' She gave Eddie the nod and he got up.

'Try to keep the nebulizer on.' The instruction was accompanied by the nurse's tight professional smile.

Kaz complied and allowed herself to be settled back on the pillows.

Nicci ran her fingertips lightly over the sheet. 'Sit tight and we'll get back to you. Okay?'

Kaz nodded. As the nurse took her pulse she watched them walk away, Nicci and her short, fat sidekick. They were like chalk and cheese, and Kaz knew which of the two she preferred. Eddie Lunt had a far more realistic view of the world than the ex-cop. He understood the kind of weakness and pressures that could land you on the wrong side of the law.

Nicci had always been prickly and buttoned up, hiding everything behind a professional facade. It was only by chance that Kaz had discovered why Nicci had left the police. The death of her daughter in a road accident must've been completely devastating, but Kaz had never heard her mention it. Nicci sat on everything, including her private grief.

Even though she was still in her twenties, the shadow of death, often violent death, had been a presence in Kaz's life ever since she could remember. She'd grown up knowing people who killed people: her father and then her brother, Joey. And she'd been forced, in self-defence, to step over that line herself. Her cousin Sean had raped her repeatedly as a teenager. But when he'd tried it again more recently, he'd got a bullet through his brain. Kaz didn't regret her actions in any way. She'd simply done what she had to in order to protect herself.

The world and the family that had shaped her had violence at its core. So the fact that possibly two attempts had been made on her own life didn't feel as outlandish to her as it might have. She had very little sense of religion or faith but her underlying philosophy was fatalistic. If your number was up then there was nothing to be done about it. But, since you were unlikely to know in advance, you should fight until your dying breath, which she had every intention of doing.

She feared more for others than for herself. Irina had hardly been out of her thoughts. She wanted her friend to stay safe. But that didn't stop the need, the longing to be with her.

The staff nurse made a note on her clipboard, gave Kaz another professional smile and walked away. Kaz knew the woman didn't approve of her. But she was a Phelps, she'd been disapproved of her whole life. Teachers, social workers and the police themselves; there'd been plenty, like the nurse, who'd sat in judgement. Kaz had grown a thick skin at an early age. But privately she'd always longed to escape the taint of her tribe.

Ironically the death of Joey had brought the family back

into her life and now she felt responsible for them. Her mother, Ellie, was a woman ill-equipped to survive in the world without a man to protect her. But the men were all dead, if you didn't count Brian. And Natalie had a baby son, which had come as a total surprise to Kaz.

She'd walked away, cut herself off; it had been what she'd wanted. But the notion of a new generation was producing a welter of contradictory emotions in her. As soon as she saw Finlay her maternal instincts were aroused. He was so young and innocent and new. She wanted him to have a chance, not to grow up in the vicious cauldron of parental selfishness and neglect that had shaped her and Natalie and Joey. And although her sister seemed to be coping, there was no disguising the fact she was a recovering drug addict. If things got tough would she succumb to temptation? Kaz knew only too well what that feeling was like: the itch at the edge of consciousness, the desire for just one more fix.

The life she'd been leading on witness protection as an art student in Glasgow seemed very far away now. Maybe that escape into anonymity had always been a dream. She'd hardly picked up her sketchbook since she'd been back home. And Essex was home, there was no getting away from that. Even with the house a burnt-out wreck she was back where she belonged. There were people who needed her and she couldn't let them down. But first there was the question of the Kemals – and Nicci was probably right: it was this vicious bunch of scumbags who were out to kill her.

25

Sadik Kemal decided to take his wife shopping. He had his driver drop them at the back of Selfridges and they walked round to the side entrance. They were due to fly out to Turkey the following week for a cousin's wedding and Elif didn't want to go empty-handed. She always made a point of finding special gifts for Sadik's mother and his married sisters. She was also on the lookout for a couple of new outfits for herself.

In the perfume department they were waylaid by a sales assistant enticing Elif into trying the latest offering by a famous clothes designer Sadik had never heard of. As the sales assistant sprayed scent onto a strip of card and waggled it to help the fragrance settle, Sadik waited patiently and let his gaze rove around the store. But it wasn't the merchandise that interested him, it was the customers.

What he was looking for was some kind of recognition, a face he'd noticed before. He hadn't been entirely candid with his brother; he knew the Met had them both under surveillance, although he doubted they had a full team on him. The cutbacks were biting – his sources kept telling him that – and, unless there was good reason, the usual five-man operation had been scaled back to three. Sadik concluded that now it was a joint investigation, with Essex taking the lead, they'd probably be even more reluctant to commit resources.

Taking the escalator up to the second floor they wandered

into the womenswear department. Elif made a beeline for the Whistles concession. She was a small woman, elfin as her name suggested, a seemingly fragile figure beside her husband's muscle and bulk.

Sadik had been advised by his brother to go back to Turkey to find a wife. But Elif was second generation, a London girl who'd been managing a hairdresser's in Tottenham when Sadik first set eyes on her. He'd led such an unsettled life since his earliest years, always moving on, following Asil's orders, wary of everyone he met. He never felt he belonged in London or indeed anywhere else until he met Elif. She was already past thirty and not considered marriageable, which helped persuade her respectable parents to accept a man they suspected of being a thug.

But Elif knew her own mind. She wanted an impressive house, her own business and an escape from the parental home and the pity of her married peers. She sensed in Sadik the raw hunger for acceptance behind the impenetrable facade. It wasn't a love-match but they understood each other perfectly. She gave him two sons and the confidence to believe himself as good as his brother. He gave her a chain of hair salons and a large detached house in East Finchley, which was the envy of her extended family and friends. She never interrogated him about his business; he ran a taxi firm for his brother and she decided that was all she and her family ever needed to know.

Elif pulled a blue, silky dress from the rack and held it in front of her. 'Well?'

He nodded and smiled. He didn't need to be there. And she wondered why he was. She had a raft of credit cards in her purse and plenty of confidence in her own taste.

She noticed the restlessness in his eye. Sadik was a man of

secrets but that had never bothered her. She closed her ears to the gossip that swirled her way from time to time. And if she wondered, in the privacy of her own mind, whether the law would ever catch up with him, she didn't worry unduly. The house, the hairdressing business, it was all in her name. It was the price of her acquiescence and discretion, and Sadik had been happy to pay it.

'Try it on.'

'I think I will. You want to hang around? Or maybe get a coffee?'

'Yeah. A coffee. Maybe make some calls.'

She patted the sleeve of his expensive leather jacket. 'Good idea. I'll catch up with you later.'

The hooded eyes considered her for a moment. He had certainly made a better choice than his brother, whose wife was both stupid and had a tendency to nag. Asil lost his temper from time to time and hit her. But the great thing about Elif was that violence was never necessary. She always read his mood and understood his needs; to his mind, that made her the perfect wife.

Even before he reached the escalator she had plucked two more dresses from the rack and was heading for the changing rooms without a backward glance.

He rode the escalator to the top floor. It was mid-afternoon but there was no lull in the shoppers' appetite to browse and buy. He scanned each floor as he passed; plenty of people were milling about. Craning his head, he gazed down through the open shaft surrounding the moving stairway. A young man in a rugby shirt was riding upwards from the floor below. His hands were in his jeans pockets, he looked completely bored and he was wearing an ear bud with a wire trailing to a phone in his back pocket.

Sadik smiled to himself. He'd already clocked him in the perfume department, staring intently at some macho eau de cologne. He made a mental note: number one.

On the top floor Sadik meandered among the lighting, keeping a wary eye on number one, who wandered through the furniture section. Then, turning on his heel abruptly, Sadik executed a U-turn and headed into the coffee shop. He stopped at the counter to consider the array of cakes and pastries and out of the corner of his eye caught sight of number one following. The young man appeared to be mumbling to himself but stopped short when he saw Sadik smile and look directly at him. He knew he was blown and he walked briskly away.

Sadik chuckled. Looking at his watch he saw he had plenty of time. He liked playing cat and mouse with the cops. He ordered himself a black Americano, sat down and waited for number two to show up.

A woman with a backpack joined the queue at the counter. She had a dykey haircut and also seemed intent on listening to music from her phone. Whilst she had her back to him Sadik got up and, abandoning his coffee, slipped through a side door to the toilets. He strode down a short corridor, which brought him back to the shop floor. Doubling round, he returned to the entrance to the cafe. The dyke was standing there, anxiously scanning. Their eyes met and she immediately turned away. As he walked past he gave her a sardonic grin. Two down, one to go.

Returning to the second floor, Sadik found his wife. Loaded down with several bags, she was browsing among the shoes. 'I couldn't decide between the blue or the green, so I got both.'

'Good idea. Something has come up. I need to go.'

'I can get a taxi. It's no problem.' Her smile was serene and detached.

He nodded. She really was the best sort of wife. She offered him her cheek, which he brushed with his lips. As he walked away he caught sight of a solid-looking bloke in his thirties. He had a ladies' knee-high boot in his meaty fist and was intent on examining it. Number three?

Sadik took the down escalator two steps at a time. He glanced back and the bloke was following. When he reached the ground floor he stopped abruptly at the sunglasses display, forcing number three to execute a sideways feint into jewellery. Sadik tried on a few frames as he tracked his pursuer with his peripheral vision. He wanted to give him time to settle before making his move.

From behind the jewellery counter an enthusiastic young sales assistant came to Sadik's aid. She engaged the bloke in conversation and he was forced to respond. While his attention was on the sales assistant, Sadik scooted round behind the racks of sunglasses and headed for the main doors. Out on Oxford Street he threaded rapidly through the crowds and darted down Duke Street. A quick glance over his shoulder revealed a sea of meandering faces but no sign of number three.

On the corner of Edwards Mews he hailed a cab. Settling down in the back he told the driver to drop him at Baker Street tube. It was a busy station and though he was pretty sure he'd lost the tail it paid to be cautious. He'd take the Jubilee Line to Finchley Road, giving him a couple of stops to do a final check, and his pick-up would be waiting. It was a clean vehicle, hired that very afternoon. He never used stolen cars; that was plain stupid.

Glancing at his watch he decided he was still in good time. The M25 would be busy but that didn't matter. Once he got to Basildon he wanted to do a proper recce of the hospital himself. Their contact there, a hospital security guard, would provide them with uniforms and that should make the snatch straightforward. But these types were not always reliable and Asil insisted that in all their operations they erred on the side of caution. It's what had kept them out of jail.

As the cab cruised round Manchester Square, Sadik imagined the look on Kaz Phelps's face when they spirited her away. She was a smart girl, she'd have no illusions. She'd know what was coming. And that would intensify his pleasure.

26

Tom Rivlin didn't hang about at the hospital. He had little toleration of failure or weakness in others and he hated it in himself. The fact that Nicci Armstrong had witnessed the fiasco with Karen Phelps made it ten times worse. He went straight back to Brentwood where the incident room was ticking over quietly: actions were being followed up, calls answered, leads chased. The hum of quiet industry reassured him. This was what he was good at.

As he sifted through the reports on his desk he tried to put Phelps out of his mind. His job was to gather and collate intelligence. If he had a responsibility to her, he'd discharged it. Her refusal to cooperate or even listen to him made it impossible for him to help her. But her attitude told him one thing: she wasn't simply an innocent victim caught in the crossfire. When gangsters fell out the results were usually bloody. And this was clearly an argument between what remained of Joey Phelps's firm and the Kemals.

Rivlin's main problem was what to tell the boss. The fact he'd failed to make any headway with Phelps was the last thing he wanted to admit to Cheryl Stoneham. But he couldn't lie. She'd sniff him out in a nanosecond. He was pondering the best approach, how to achieve some sort of middle way, when a phone behind him rang. One of the new DCs he didn't really know, who'd been brought in to beef up the investigation, answered it.

She swivelled her chair, cradling the receiver in her hand. 'DCI wants a word, sir.'

Rivlin stared at her. Maybe the rumours were right and Stoneham did have second sight. He got up and took the phone.

'Rivlin.'

'I've been ringing you on your mobile.'

'Sorry, boss. Battery's on the blink.'

The truth was, as he left the hospital, he'd switched it off. He shouldn't have, but he needed time out and to avoid exactly this: interrogation by Stoneham.

'You sound a bit down in the mouth, Tom. What's up?'

'Frustrated, more like. I went to see Karen Phelps in hospital.'

'I gather.'

He felt his hackles rising. Bloody Nicci, she hadn't wasted any time. She'd gone running straight to Stoneham.

Rivlin took a breath. 'She's obviously in shock and it's making her quite reactive. I think we'll get her to cooperate eventually, though.'

'When do we expect to hear from the fire service?'

'The official report will take a few days. But as I said before, they reckon it's arson.'

'And they're convinced about that?'

'I went down this morning, talked to the fire officer myself.'

There was a moment of silence as the DCI pondered. She sighed. 'We can't wait for their report. These two incidents so close together mean that we have to construe them as attempts on Karen Phelps's life.'

'I agree, boss. But if she won't even talk to us—'

'I've spoken to Nicci Armstrong and she thinks Phelps will agree to some form of police protection. And we can't afford to be negligent in this regard, Tom.'

The rebuke was mild but it was there and he felt its sting. Bloody Nicci Armstrong.

'I was about to—'

'It's an exceptional situation and I think the fact that a former officer of Nicci's calibre is prepared to work with us on this is something we should be taking full advantage of. I don't blame you for not being able to manage Phelps on your own. She doesn't like the police and she's a complete handful. If the probation service had agreed to revoke her licence, we wouldn't even be in this situation.'

Rivlin had to rein in his emotions. That was Nicci's fault too. She'd suckered him. He wondered if Stoneham had got wind of his involvement in that. He could always argue it was simply a coincidence that Steve O'Connor was his uncle.

'What do you want me to do now?' He sounded pathetic even to himself.

'Get in touch with Nicci and work with her.'

'I don't think she likes me, boss.'

'Use your charm.' Stoneham's voice was weary. 'If we're going to put a proper protection team around Phelps it'll be expensive so I'll have to get it signed off.' There was a pause and a sigh. 'It's four thirty now. I don't know how long it's going to take me to organize it.'

'I'll go back to the hospital myself if you like and cover.'

'That's not exactly a good use of your time.'

'Getting Phelps to talk is the breakthrough we need. Gives me another chance to try and get her onside.'

'Yeah, you're right. Good idea.'

The feeling that he'd managed to redeem himself a notch fuelled his confidence.

'If our theory is correct, boss, and this is the Kemals, then two failed attempts in as many days is going to give them pause for thought. It's very unlikely they'll try anything else immediately. As long as we get something in place in the next couple of days I think we'll be covered.'

Stoneham considered this for a moment. 'If the hospital discharge her we'll need a safe house. I need to run this by the Assistant Chief; I'd rather not do it on the phone and he's at an ACPO seminar in Manchester.'

'Look, I'll talk to hospital security and make sure they keep an eye on Phelps tonight.'

'It would certainly make things easier if I could tackle him face-to-face tomorrow, because he's not going to like the cost.'

'Don't worry. I'll see to it something's sorted out for tonight.'

'Okay, well, I'll leave it with you.' She sounded relieved. Rivlin appreciated the burden she carried but he also knew that taking some of it upon himself would earn him brownie points.

'And you'll get in touch with Nicci?'

'I will, boss.'

'For what it's worth, I get the impression that she does like you. Keep me updated.'

'Of course.'

Rivlin put the phone down and headed for the coffee machine. The whole discussion had gone much better than he'd expected. He felt he was back in the driving seat. As to the innuendo about Nicci – Stoneham's tone implied it – she was definitely not his type. No way. Nor was he about to rely on some flaky ex-cop, discharged on medical grounds, to do his job for him. He'd phone her and he'd be polite, but there was no way she was going to call the shots.

27

Sadik Kemal arrived at Basildon Hospital shortly after seven p.m. He brought a driver and Riza, a young man he was training up from a street gang in Wood Green. A similar age to Tevfik, Riza had all the qualities his nephew lacked. He was quiet and focused; he obeyed orders without demur.

They stopped at Thurrock services for a burger. A heavy downpour had slowed traffic to a crawl and they waited for it to pass over and the congestion to ease before continuing on the A13 to Basildon. Ignoring the signs directing them to the multistorey car park, the white transit van peeled off to the left and followed the service road that looped around the jumble of old and new buildings at the back of the hospital. They pulled up at a side door where their contact was waiting.

The security guard was Somali and he looked extremely anxious.

Sadik got out of the van. 'You Jaafi?'

The guard nodded. He owed the Kemals six thousand dollars, which was the only reason he was standing there. They'd trafficked him into the country four years ago and after months in detention he'd finally been granted asylum, but the debt remained.

Taking his arm, Sadik smiled. 'Don't look so worried, my friend. You do this small service for us tonight and we wipe the slate clean. You should be happy.'

'The police have been here.' Jaafi blurted it out, his apprehension overcoming his fear of the gangster.

'What d'you mean?'

'They come to the office. A detective inspector. And he give us special instructions to watch this woman. My boss is not happy. He don't have enough men. On the night shift only three guards for the whole hospital.'

Riza got out of the van and came to stand behind Sadik. He folded his arms and gave the Somali a menacing stare.

The Turk rubbed his chin then a smile spread across his features. 'Well, this is all to the good. I think we help your boss out.'

'I don't understand.' Jaafi frowned. 'You want to talk to her, why you don't make a visit in the day?'

'Have you got the uniforms?'

'Yes.'

'Then you don't need to worry about nothing else.' Sadik started to propel the Somali towards the door. 'What time's the night shift start?'

'Eight o'clock.'

Sadik tapped the radio clipped to the guard's belt. 'You call your boss. You say you got it covered. You'll keep an eye on her.'

'But what if—'

'Six thousand dollars, my friend. That's a lot of money. You still got family back home?'

Jaafi nodded. His shoulders were hunched and the blue uniform shirt was baggy on his spare lanky frame.

'Then think of them. Think what the extra money you send home can do for them. Forget about this woman, she ain't nothing to you.'

28

In spite of her protestations that it wasn't necessary, Eddie Lunt drove Nicci home. After they'd left Basildon Hospital they went to Chelmsford. She'd judged it was best to tackle Cheryl Stoneham in person. Leaving Eddie in a coffee shop near the market, she'd had to wait nearly three-quarters of an hour to get an audience with the DCI.

Behind the jokey, jolly facade, Stoneham looked harassed. 'Sorry for keeping you waiting, Nic. Liaison meeting with your old lot to agree a joint strategy.'

'Are they being difficult?'

'Not particularly. Nowadays it's all about budgets. Who's paying for what. That's what I spend most of my time on, not chasing villains.'

Nicci had duly commiserated and they'd shared a bit of banter about the up-themselves attitudes of the Met, but Nicci knew Stoneham wouldn't be fooled. What she was asking the DCI to do would involve spending even more of the police's over-stretched budget. Although Stoneham didn't share Nicci's view of Karen Phelps as a victim, she had to concede that, if her life was in danger, she was entitled to police protection. Also, facing a press conference with another dead body to explain was not a prospect Stoneham relished. They both knew this was the bottom line, but Nicci had been too polite to mention it.

It was early evening by the time she and Eddie had headed back to London, but at least Nicci was reassured that Kaz Phelps was in no immediate danger.

Traffic had been sluggish and Nicci had dozed until a sharp thundery shower had hit them on the A12 around Gidea Park. Slouched in the passenger seat she'd reflected that this was probably the most amount of time she'd spent on her own with Eddie. He hadn't interrogated her about the meeting with Stoneham, which was a relief. He'd simply asked if she minded a bit of Classic FM. They'd travelled without conversation to the soft strains of Brahms and then Liszt. Nicci had been expecting some cringeworthy joke involving cockney rhyming slang but Eddie kept his thoughts to himself as the music washed over them.

He dropped her right outside the door and she was putting the kettle on and considering what to microwave when her phone rang. She saw from the screen that it was Tom Rivlin. Stoneham had obviously been on his case, which amused her. She let the phone ring a couple of times before answering.

'Hi, Tom.' The tone was as disinterested as she could manage, though there was a tension in her lower belly. They hadn't spoken since she'd given him a piece of her mind.

'Yeah, er, hi. Sorry to bother you.' He sounded apprehensive, which pleased her. 'I've just had a call from the sister in charge of Karen Phelps's ward. They're a bit worried. She seems to have disappeared. I was wondering if you had any idea of her whereabouts?'

29

The loose gravel on the path was sharp and lacerated her bare feet as she ran but she made it round the corner of what looked like the hospital's boiler house. In a welcome patch of inky darkness, away from the orange glow of the sodium lamps, Kaz Phelps squatted, back against the wall, and got her breath. She didn't dare look. The young one was fast and he was after her.

She'd been in the bathroom, cleaning her teeth, when the two security guards, pushing an A&E trolley, had wandered into her bay. The slimy cop, Rivlin, had been round earlier. Kaz had clocked him talking to one of the nurses, who'd relayed the message that extra security had been arranged. At least Nicci had kept her word.

Presuming the guards were there to protect her, Kaz had emerged from the bathroom and was wandering back to her bed when a shiver ran down her spine. Her subconscious knew before she did: something wasn't right. He was standing with his back towards her, solid muscle, grey hair slicked back, chatting to the healthcare assistant who was dispensing evening drinks. He'd turned his head slightly and that's when Kaz had glimpsed his profile. It'd hit her like a punch in the gut. Although he was wearing the hospital's security uniform it was definitely Sadik Kemal.

Backing away, Kaz had slipped through the swing doors

into the corridor. Then she ran. Visiting hours were over and there were few people or staff about. The hospital was hunkering down for the night. Next to naked, with the flimsy gown gaping at the back and flapping round her knees, she'd hurtled down the corridor. Her thoughts were in a spin. The fucking Kemals! Dressed up as security. Who was going to help her? And who could she even trust?

Spotting a sign for the fire exit, she'd glanced over her shoulder – and that's when she'd seen him coming. The other, younger guard who'd been with Kemal was sprinting down the corridor after her.

Her lungs had begun to smart with every breath but she'd slammed into the fire exit door, kicking it open. It led out into the darkness and a metal staircase. Two floors below a gravel path snaked away to a concrete service road. It had seemed like her only escape route.

Holed up in the shadow of the boiler house Kaz started to realize that leaving the building was probably a mistake. She pulled a piece of grit from the sole of her bleeding foot as she struggled to calm her ragged breathing. Her lungs were still sore from smoke inhalation and she glanced around, trying to get her bearings. She seemed to have come out at the back of the hospital, an area of loading bays, ramps and scrubby grass bathed in pools of light from a row of street lamps that followed the loop of the service road. It was eerie and deserted, no one to call upon for help and no witnesses. She needed to get round to the front of the building, to the A&E department where there were bound to be people about.

The fire door slammed, followed by the clatter of boots on the staircase. Her pulse raced; she should've kept running. Now, as soon as she broke cover, he'd see her. But staying put wasn't an option either.

He appeared on the gravel path. She cowered into her dark bolthole and he ran past her down to the concrete road. He was young and fit; the chase had hardly winded him. The fire door banged again and Sadik Kemal trotted down the staircase, talking into his phone.

As he passed her hiding place Kaz caught a snippet of his conversation: '. . . and keep your fucking eyes open! Bitch can't have got far.'

A white transit van cruised into view on the service road. It stopped beside the young guard, who was standing, hands on hips, scanning the back of the hospital. Getting out of the van, the driver handed him a torch. As its piercing beam arced across brickwork illuminating the unlit flank of the building, Sadik joined them, issuing instructions that Kaz couldn't hear. If she was going to make a break for it, she needed to do it now. Once they started to search the nooks and crannies with the torch she'd be exposed and trapped.

They were possibly a hundred metres away from her. As they moved forward to begin a systematic search she leapt up and propelled herself in a diagonal line towards the road. Clocking her immediately, Sadik shouted at the driver, who jumped into the van and started it up.

Kaz didn't look back. She ran. Fear and pure adrenaline drove her screaming body on. She hit the concrete roadway and pounded along it, reasoning it would lead her out of the nether regions of the site to the main entrance. She could hear the van behind her; she heard it brake to pick up her pursuers.

Every muscle and sinew straining, she knew she was running for her life. The roar of the engine told her that the vehicle was closing fast, but up ahead she saw the red-and-white traffic barrier. Could she make it that far? Every breath was agonizing. The rough concrete was tearing her feet but terror helped her drive on through the pain. Scooting round the barrier, her heart soared. The van was forced to stop; the young guard sprang from the vehicle to raise the traffic arm. But she was now precious seconds ahead.

As she rounded a corner, the front of the building came into view. She could make out the lights of A&E. She made a beeline for it, darting between cars parked on the taxi rank.

Suddenly a figure stepped out from behind one of the cabs and grabbed her. She struggled to free herself but the chase had drained her of the last ounce of strength. Dizzy and gasping for air she heard a soothing voice in her ear. 'Kaz, it's okay! It's me.'

She was lifted bodily and deposited in the back of a minicab. He jumped in beside her and pulled the sliding door shut. Out of the tinted side window she caught a glimpse of the white transit van driving past. Sadik Kemal was staring straight ahead. They hadn't seen her. She turned to look at her rescuer for the first time and realized it was the taxi driver who'd brought her mother home from the hospital.

He was keeping a wary eye on the retreating transit through the front window. Turning back, he gave her a grin. 'Bastards, eh? Don't worry, you're safe now.'

She hardly knew him but relief flooded through her. Cowering in the back of his taxi, heart thumping, it took several minutes for her body to catch up with the fact she'd escaped. With lungs still screaming, her mouth gaped wide as she gasped for air.

He took her hand and his touch was gentle. 'Just breathe. Nice and slow. You're going to be okay. They've gone.'

Kaz did as she was told and gradually each rasping inhalation became marginally less painful.

Unscrewing the top he handed her a plastic bottle of water. 'Here you go. Drink it slowly.'

She couldn't help spluttering as she gulped down the cool soothing liquid.

'Slowly, mate!'

Finally she managed to focus on his face and the name came to her: Darius Johnson. The schoolmate she couldn't remember had saved her from Sadik Kemal. He was a boy she'd grown up with, he'd known Joey, and in spite of her inbuilt wariness Kaz knew instinctively she could trust him.

30

Staring at the bubbling hot lasagne she'd just microwaved, Nicci decided she'd lost her appetite. She dumped the carton of food in the sink, where it hissed and sizzled, and poured herself a glass of wine.

Karen Phelps had disappeared. If she had a mobile phone it'd almost certainly have been destroyed in the fire, along with everything else. This left Nicci with no means of trying to contact her, nor could the police track her location. Rivlin had dispatched officers to the hospital to search for Phelps, but he seemed to be taking the view that in order to avoid further questioning she could simply have decided to discharge herself. In Nicci's opinion, that was very unlikely. His offhand attitude during their phone conversation had irritated her too. It sounded as though, having failed to get any proper security in place, he was looking for a way to cover his arse.

Nicci was annoyed with him but she was more annoyed with herself. If Karen had been left unprotected it was because the police hadn't regarded it as an urgent priority. And that was her fault. She'd been evasive and withheld information. Another piss-poor judgement call on her part! Taking a slug of wine, she steeled herself. She had to call him back and come clean. Clicking on his number, she wondered if he'd even pick up. She was considering what to do if he didn't – there was really only one other option: call Stoneham – when he came on the line. 'Nicci, hi.' The tone was terse and from the background noise, he was driving.

'Look, I should've told you this before: Karen had a run-in with the Kemals not long before her brother was killed.'

'A run-in? What sort of run-in?' He sounded distant. The hands-free mic crackled.

'I never really got the whole story. But the Kemals got hold of a friend of hers, beat her up pretty badly. Karen got mad and went to rescue her. And she did it by threatening the Kemals with a gun.' There was silence on the other end of the line, just the soft road hum and the click-clack of an indicator.

'You're right. You really should've told us that.' His voice was remote, his reaction impossible to read.

'I'm sorry. It was complicated. I knew Stoneham wanted to revoke her licence and well—'

'What the fuck were you thinking, Nicci?' His anger seemed to erupt from nowhere. 'I don't know what your agenda is here—'

'I don't have an agenda.'

More silence on the line and the quiet thrum of the engine. Then finally, 'I'm arriving at the hospital now.'

'Do you want me to come down?'

'Why on earth would I want that?' He was back to cold and disinterested.

'I thought maybe—'

'My officers will find her. We don't need outside help.'

Nicci could feel tears prickling her eyelids. 'I'm sorry, Tom. I should've thought this through.'

'Are you and Phelps involved in some kind of affair? Is that what this is about? You're trying to protect your lover?' He spat the last word. *Lover.* It sounded sordid. Nicci felt as though she'd been sucker-punched.

'No. Don't be ridiculous. My connection with Karen Phelps has only ever been professional. Cheryl Stoneham asked for my help and I've done my level best to give it.'

'In which case, as a former police officer, knowing she was in breach of her licence – I mean, running around with a bloody gun! – you should've informed the authorities before any of this happened.'

He was right of course and she felt wretched. 'I know that.'

'But instead you went to see Steve and told him a pack of lies. And I helped you! I bloody helped you. I tell you, I can hardly get my head round this.' Now he had full possession of the moral high ground there was no mistaking the hint of triumphalism in his voice.

'I didn't lie to Steve. I told him she wasn't a danger to the public. Which is true.'

'Four people are dead, Nicci. A house has been torched, putting two more in hospital. And all this could've been avoided.'

Nicci wanted to argue. It wasn't that simple; he hadn't been there and he didn't know Karen Phelps.

'Now she's disappeared and we don't even know—'

Clicking her phone off she hurled it at the sofa. She refused to listen to any more of his rant. It bounced and fell on the floor. She ignored it. Whatever recriminations he'd flung at her, they were trivial compared to the burden of guilt she was loading on herself. If the Kemals had got hold of Karen it was because she'd made a mistake. And her brain skittered back to a similar situation when her poor judgement had led to a colleague ending up in the hands of Joey Phelps. DC Mal Bradley had been beaten to death, and that still haunted her. Flopping down on the sofa she put her face in her hands and wept.

31

Curled up on the back seat of Darius Johnson's taxi, his jacket wrapped around her, Kaz Phelps watched the dark country lanes slip by. They'd left the A127 and were cutting northwards past Herongate. She'd recognized the occasional landmark until the road disappeared into black tunnels of overarching trees that formed part of Warley Woods. She felt as though she were disappearing into the safety of a subterranean forest. The darkness embraced her and she wasn't scared.

As the shock of her ordeal subsided she became aware of the pain in her torn and bleeding feet. Hard running across gravel and concrete had lacerated the soles, leaving them raw and bloody. But she'd escaped. She'd outrun that vicious bastard, Sadik Kemal, not to mention his sidekick. As the adrenaline high had begun to ebb, her body had started to shake. She buried her face in the fleecy lining of the jacket. It had a vaguely male miasma overlaid with the sharp scent of eau de cologne.

Darius drove. He occasionally glanced over his shoulder to check she was okay. They didn't speak. He'd been there, understood the danger she was in and he had acted. There seemed no need for Kaz to provide him with any explanation. He'd simply told her that he had a place where she could hide. And she'd accepted his word. She wondered vaguely if she should be suspicious of his motives, but she lacked the energy. Lulled by the steady rumble of the diesel engine, she fell asleep.

Occasional splashes of street lighting rippled through the interior of the cab but exhaustion had engulfed her and she didn't stir. Her brain was in playback mode and she was reliving the chase. But in her dream, Sadik's face soon morphed into another, even meaner individual who seemed to be wagging an accusing finger. Was it her cousin, Sean? The gun was in her hand and she knew she had to shoot, and she wanted to shoot. But the trigger was so tight. She squeezed as hard as she could but it wouldn't budge. And he started to laugh at her.

The taxi slowed and swung into a gateway. Darius got out and the clunk of the door woke Kaz. She sat up and watched Darius opening a wide, five-bar gate. He climbed back into his seat and turned to smile at her.

'How you doing?'

'Where are we?'

'Place belongs to a friend of mine.'

The taxi rolled slowly forward along a short gravel drive. The house was long and low, with a high-pitched, red-tiled roof and gabled windows. Originally an old farmhouse, it was flanked by outbuildings and a wooden barn. A security light came on as the taxi pulled up. Kaz didn't know the place but she recognized where she was: this was the rural Essex of City money, horses with paddocks and posh multimillion-pound conversions.

The front door opened and a man and woman stood framed in the warmth and welcome of the interior. Kaz couldn't really see their faces; she was half-naked and bleeding and suddenly felt very self-conscious.

As Darius opened the door for her, the man trotted down the steps. He was beaming from ear to ear. He looked familiar but her brain struggled to place him.

'Kaz!' He held out his arms. 'We was at the crematorium, all waiting like a bunch of lemons. Poor old Joe, what a shock, eh?'

Peering at him, Kaz took in the close-cropped blond hair, the broad shoulders. He reminded her so much of her brother. But then she realized, it should be the other way round. She stared in disbelief.

'Paul?'

He slapped his rock-hard abdomen. 'I know, I'm getting a bit flabby. But ten years is a long time, babes.'

Babes. Joey had always called her babes. But, as with so many things, he'd only been copying Paul. Five years older, Paul Ackroyd had been a mentor and friend to the teenage Joey. And for nine all too brief months, when she was sixteen, Kaz Phelps had been madly in love with him.

32

Rivlin scanned the ward but the staff nurse who'd taken his fancy had gone. The sister on night duty was short and stout, her bleached hair drawn back in a tight bun. He forced himself to focus on what she was saying.

'Two chaps from hospital security came to transfer her to a private room. I think she saw them and ran. She's a criminal, I gather.'

Rivlin frowned. 'And these two men, they were definitely hospital security?'

'Of course. They all wear a uniform.'

'Lanyards round their necks with proper ID?'

The sister glared at him but her eyes flickered. Rivlin concluded from this and her defensive tone that she hadn't checked. 'They said they were acting under police instructions, transferring her to the private wing. I had no reason to doubt them.'

'I'm sure she wasn't the easiest patient. You were probably glad to get shot of her.'

The sister bristled. 'I only came on at eight. She wasn't a problem as far as I was concerned.'

Rivlin studied the round chubby face; she looked weary and stressed. She had a long shift ahead of her, several wards to cover, and it wasn't even midnight yet. He gave her an encouraging smile. 'Thank you, Sister. You've been very helpful.'

He wasn't lying. She had been helpful. What she'd told him was that, if this was the Kemals, they were resourceful and organized. Sending two men to kidnap Karen Phelps was a bold act. They'd already tried to kill her but now they wanted to take her. Factoring in the new information that Nicci Armstrong had given him, it looked like they had a serious grudge. Which was all to the good. Drug dealers at their level were almost impossible to catch. Their business plan was watertight; only the foot soldiers were ever exposed. But when things got personal like this it was a game-changer.

When he'd first got the call from the hospital it had sent Rivlin into a spin. He'd assured Stoneham that Phelps was protected. Now, as he strode down the corridor, he realized that this unexpected turn of events could also be the breakthrough they needed. It all depended on how he played it and if he could convince Stoneham of that fact. The Met had been targeting the Kemals for years and got nowhere. Essex wasn't their turf. They were off-piste, but only because they were after Karen Phelps.

By the time he got back to the security office the uniforms had completed their search of the hospital. Phelps was nowhere to be found. A couple of his DCs had arrived and, having connected up their laptops, were busily downloading the footage from the hospital's security cameras.

Rivlin turned his attention to the Somali security guard who was sitting in the corner, looking tense. Earlier in the evening they'd exchanged a few words when Rivlin had popped in to ask them to keep a special eye on Karen Phelps.

Perching on the edge of the desk, Rivlin leant over and fixed the young Somali with a piercing look. 'You going to tell me what's going on, Jaafi?'

'I don't know nothing.'

'Yeah you do.'

Staring into his lap, Jaafi twisted the narrow leather thong on his wrist. He looked completely wretched.

The cop patted his shoulder. 'Come on, mate. What did they ask you to do? Get them uniforms?'

'I don't know nothing.'

'They tell you to say that?'

'I'm a good man. I work hard. Extra shifts whenever the boss ask me. I make no trouble.'

Rivlin leant back, folding his arms. He knew the story, it was commonplace: a desperate journey from a war-torn, lawless place. They were about the same age. *There but for the grace . . .* 'I bet it was bloody horrible getting here, wasn't it?'

The ebony eyes met his. 'Three months in detention but I get asylum. I got papers, I'm not illegal.'

'Look, I don't want to mess things up for you.' Rivlin sighed. 'I got no interest in that. So what do you say we help each other out, eh?'

Jaafi wiped the back of his fist across his nose. He'd had to make a lot of tricky decisions in his life, weighing up the risks. And he'd been very lucky, so far. 'Six thousand dollar I owe them.'

'The traffickers?'

'Turks. You say no to them, you fucked.'

'I can believe that.' Rivlin smiled, encouraging him to go on.

'They come with a white van.'

'Transit van?'

Jaafi nodded. 'Two men and a driver. They want uniforms so they can take this woman away. They say she's bad, she dishonour them.'

'Did they get her?'

'I don't know. They tell me, stay in the office.'

'Well done, mate.' Rivlin squeezed his shoulder. 'Okay, one of my officers is going to show you some pictures – mugshots. You need to tell us if you recognize any of the men.'

'You don't send me back to detention?'

'You're just a witness. You were intimidated. And you told me the truth. That's how we do things here.'

A solitary tear rolled down the Somali's cheek. He brushed it away.

The DC scrolling through the security footage turned her head towards Rivlin. 'Take a look at this, boss. The taxi rank in front of the hospital.'

Rivlin came to look over her shoulder as she rewound and replayed.

On the screen, a figure appeared round the corner running wildly towards the camera. Behind her, a white transit appeared. The runner ducked sideways and disappeared between the cabs. The van cruised towards the front of A&E. The DC froze the frame and selected a different clip.

'From the time code, this follows directly on. The van drove round the front of the hospital, it didn't stop. I think they missed her.'

'Check it again, we need to be sure.'

As the DC rewound the footage, Rivlin paced. There was a confidence, an audacity even, about this kidnap attempt. Dishonour, that was the word they'd used to the security guard. He turned to the other DC. 'Have you got those surveillance shots the Met sent?'

'Yeah, I think so.' The DC opened up a file on his iPad and handed it to Rivlin. The DI swiped through a series of photos. The first few were distance shots, taken on the street. Then he got to a close-up outside a restaurant.

Holding the iPad up in front of Jaafi, Rivlin's tone was deliberately casual. 'Recognize him?'

There was no hesitation. 'He was the boss. He threaten me.'

'Sure?'

The young Somali nodded. 'Sure.'

Rivlin's spirits soared. Sadik Kemal had come for Phelps in person. A crack in the impenetrable facade had opened up.

The first DC swivelled her chair. 'I've tracked the van until it left the hospital site. No stops, no one got in or out. I think she escaped.'

Rivlin smiled to himself. He was glad Karen Phelps had got away. Not least because that would help him square things with Stoneham. But if Sadik Kemal continued to pursue Phelps, it was game on. Nicci Armstrong had been right: Phelps was the bait to draw the Kemals out. By exposing themselves in this way, they were finally offering the police an opportunity to nail them. And Tom Rivlin was the officer in pole position to do it.

33

They'd wrapped Kaz in a soft feather-and-down duvet and sat her on the sofa. A woman – was she Paul's partner? – had brought a bowl of warm salted water and was bathing her feet. Kaz struggled to focus. The woman's hair was dark and lustrous, her touch gentle as she used her hand to scoop up the water and sluice it over Kaz's lacerated feet.

Somewhere off to the right, Paul handed Darius a beer and they chinked bottles. 'Well done, mate.' He perched on the arm of the sofa and smiled down at Kaz. 'I was hoping to see you at the funeral. Quite a few of the old crew turned out. No one knew you'd changed the venue.'

Kaz gazed up at him. Paul Ackroyd. She could hardly believe it. Everything seemed to have slowed to a dreamlike pace, then her head started to spin.

His voice became disembodied. 'Understandable. Filth were all over the place, taking photos. Bloody cheek of it. They got no respect.' He seemed very far away.

Kaz leaned back on the sofa; she'd been shivering but now she felt hot, impossibly hot and feverish. As she tried to push the duvet off herself she felt the woman's cool hand on her brow. They were speaking to her but she couldn't make out the words. Closing her eyes, she knew she was going, but she couldn't stop herself from falling into a dead faint.

She surfaced briefly as she was lifted. Paul was strong, a big solid man like her brother. He carried her with ease. When he laid her down she felt the welcome chill of crisp sheets. Words drifted into her consciousness: the voice was female, with an accent. 'You safe now . . . You sleep.'

And she slept. A dreamless slumber. She finally awoke to slivers of daylight rippling through the gap between the heavy drapes and the wall. Was it early morning? It was impossible to tell. As she tried to sit up, pain shot from her hamstrings to her lower back. She'd pulled a muscle or two.

The room was sizeable with pale walls and a half-open door leading to an en suite bathroom. The ceiling beams belonged to the original farmhouse but the floor was smoothly sanded, the furnishings sleek and modern. Kaz eased back the covers and swung her legs over the side of the bed. The soles of her feet were sore but she managed to hobble across the room to the bathroom. Settling on the loo, she took her time having a pee. Her brain was still foggy and she was trying to identify the fragrance emanating from the scent sticks above the washbasin when she heard the outer door of the room open.

Emerging from the en suite she came face to face with the woman, who was carrying a tray.

Almost as tall as Kaz, the dark hair pulled back, she gave her guest a warm smile. 'I brought some breakfast, if you fancy it. I'm Rafaella, Paul's wife.' Paul had a wife? Well, after ten years, why wouldn't he? Kaz watched her set the tray down on the bedside table. And there was no denying it, she was gorgeous.

'Thank you.' Kaz felt awkward and broken. Her head was swirling with questions but she didn't know where to begin.

Rafaella seemed to sense this. 'You must feel very confused.'

'Yeah.'

'Paul, he's so impatient. He wants to talk to you, but I tell him, no, let the poor girl sleep.' Her English was good but with a heavy accent. Spanish or Italian, maybe? She gave Kaz a sad smile. 'I really liked Joey, y'know. He was fun.'

'You knew him?'

'Oh yeah. I was working in the bar when him and Paul first come to Ibiza.' She pronounced Ibiza like a Spaniard.

Kaz sat on the bed. The years she'd spent in prison had cut a big chunk out of her life. Joey had taken over the firm after her father's stroke, but she knew very little of how he'd accomplished that. 'I never even knew they were in touch, Joey and Paul.'

Rafaella moved over to the window and indicated the curtains. 'You mind?'

Kaz shook her head. Rafaella drew back one of the curtains and sunshine flooded the room.

'Take some coffee, eat. Plenty of time to catch up.' She gave Kaz another smile and left, closing the door gently behind her.

The breakfast tray was like the room, elegant and immaculately arranged. But the aroma from the cafetière threw Kaz back into memories of her Russian friends. Yevgeny and Irina had both loved good coffee. Staying with them in the weeks before Joey's funeral, they had sat in the sunlit kitchen in Berkshire drinking endless cups. But now Yevgeny was dead and Irina had gone to ground. Kaz felt their loss like a lead weight in her belly. But she would find Irina. Now she knew who was responsible for the shootings, there was no need for Irina to hide.

Getting to her feet again, she made her way over to the window. Her body ached, her feet were sensitive but the more she moved the easier it became. She found herself gazing out over a vista of undulating farmland. Fields of stubble from the recent harvest, divided by neat hedgerows, rising to a small copse of trees on the far hill. Several other properties were visible in the distance, substantial houses with land. Whatever else Paul Ackroyd had been up to in recent years he'd made some serious money.

Returning to the bed she poured coffee into the large bone china breakfast cup. There was a jug of warm frothed milk, croissants, butter and jam, and a white linen napkin. She propped herself up on the mountain of pillows and started to eat.

The croissant was delicious. She found she was hungry. As she brushed the crumbs from her fingers with the starched napkin she heard footsteps in the hall, a man's voice and a child's giggle, followed by a tap on the door.

'Yeah, come in.'

The door opened, Paul filled the doorway and in his arms he was holding a little girl, about four years old, with a mop of coppery curls. 'Got someone here who's dying to meet you. This is Lacey.'

He put the child down and she trotted over to the bed. Beaming at Kaz, she held out a folded sheet of paper. 'We made a card.'

'Wow. Thank you.' Kaz looked at the front, a bright felt-tip picture of the house. Inside, 'welcome to our home' was written in an adult hand with 'Lacey' underneath in large carefully formed letters.

'I can write my name.'

Kaz gazed at the little girl, who was brimming with smiles and confidence. 'I can see that. You're really clever, aren't you?'

'Gets it from her mother, not me.' He stroked the soft curls. 'Go and see if Mummy needs any help while I have a chat to Auntie Kaz.'

Lacey turned on her heel and scampered out. Rafaella's

voice could be heard shepherding the child down the stairs.

Paul pulled up a chair. Left alone with him, Kaz felt uncomfortable. She was still wearing the hospital gown. 'You have a lovely family.'

'I been very lucky.'

An awkward silence descended as he sat down and they looked at each other. The last time Kaz had seen him he was nineteen. Ten years on and he was bigger and broader, but it was muscle, not flab. She remembered her father's fury when he'd found out about them. Terry Phelps had ignored her pleas, knocked her aside and then kicked the shit out of Paul. She doubted that would be possible now.

But his grey eyes were the same, vigilant and camouflaged by the easy smile. 'How you feeling? I said to Rafaella maybe we should get a doctor to come and have a look at you. We got a private bloke, he's very good.'

'No, I think I'm all right.'

'I was worried last night. But you're looking a lot better this morning. Darius is a good lad; he does bits and pieces for me. When I heard about the fire I told him to keep an eye on things at the hospital. Though if I'd guessed those bastards were gonna try anything else . . . Anyway, you're safe now.'

Kaz raked her hand through her hair. It felt dry and brittle. She knew she looked a fright. 'After what the old man did to you, I'm surprised you'd wanna help me.'

Paul chuckled. 'He was a complete bastard, your dad, no two ways about it. But he taught me a lot.'

'They set you up. To get rid of you. You know that, don't you?'

He shrugged. 'I served two and a half of a five. Toughened me up, I reckon. When I got out I was planning to pay him a visit. But then Joe came looking for me and I realized he hated the old bastard worse than I did. We always got on, me and your brother. Then a couple months later, Terry had his stroke.'

'Joey never told me you two were back in contact.'

'Lot of water under the bridge. I was running things in Ibiza when you got out. And I'd just got married.' He gave her a sheepish look. 'Joe thought you might be a bit miffed. He wanted to break it to you gently.'

Kaz laughed. 'Ten years is a long time. A lot of water under the bridge for me too.' She wondered what he'd make of her relationship with Helen. Would he be shocked? 'And anyway, we was only kids back then.'

'Yeah.' He relaxed visibly.

'She's really lovely, Rafaella.'

He grinned. 'She is. Done me good, having her and Lacey to focus on.'

'Looks like you done all right for yourself.'

'Business is pretty good.' He interlinked his fingers and gave her a wary look. 'Joey got a bit lairy . . . well, you know that. All the killing. Macho stuff, just plain stupid. I told him it had to stop and, truth to tell, we fell out over it.'

'I told him too. That's why I ended up testifying against him.'

'Don't reckon you had a lot of choice, mate. But I don't think he held it against you. He was full of contradictions, your brother.'

Kaz felt a sudden constriction in her throat. Even though Joey was gone, he still haunted her. She swallowed hard to stop them but the tears welled and ran down her face. 'Thing is, Paul, he was killed because of me. He was trying to help me.'

Paul got up, came and sat on the bed. He took her hand. 'I didn't know that. But it don't surprise me. I went to see him in the nick. All he talked about was you.'

'It's my fault he's dead.'

He drew her into his arms and the relief she felt was over-whelming. 'No, it ain't, babes. Joey was Joey. He went his own way, no matter what. But he loved you.'

She felt his hand stroking her hair. It was so soothing and seductive; the years that divided them fell away. It had been a long time since a man had held her like this. All her recent relationships had been with women. But that didn't seem to matter now. Gay or straight, she'd always regarded these categories as meaningless. She wanted him to love her again, to love her and keep her safe. If only she could rest here, cradled in his strong arms, forever.

34

Nicci Armstrong had spent the entire weekend holed up in her flat. September was drawing to a close and London had become drab and drizzly and autumnal. She was trying to cut down on her alcohol consumption – she only allowed herself a glass of wine in the evening now – and for most of the two days she'd watched movies and pigged out on chocolate. So what if she turned into a fat blob? Tom Rivlin wouldn't have looked twice at her anyway, and that was before she'd pissed him off by withholding vital information about Karen Phelps.

She tried not to think about what had happened to Karen. Having learnt that it was the Kemals who were after her she could have decided to make herself scarce. If they had taken her, then it was down to Essex police and the Met to find her. There was little that Nicci could do.

Monday morning found Nicci in a sober but sullen mood, heading into town on the bus. She had a job, for the time being, and all she could do was get on with it. If the death of her daughter had taught her anything it was how to soldier on. One foot in front of the other. Don't think about anything too much. Survival was a choice and Nicci knew that.

At the offices of Simon Blake Associates everything seemed normal. Alicia was on reception, the cyber geeks were at their desks, Pascale gave her a smile and asked if she'd had a good weekend. Eddie had his feet up and was reading the *Sun*.

Nicci noticed that Blake's door was closed. She went and tapped on it and received a peremptory instruction to come in.

Blake was at his desk wearing a solemn face and a serious suit. She hadn't seen or heard from him since the previous Thursday evening when he was taken home drunk by his wife.

'Morning.' He looked up at her over his glasses and his stern expression suggested that the slew of questions she wanted to ask would not be well received.

'Morning.'

'Thank you for sorting out this new security contract.' He held up the document he'd been perusing. 'Turki bin Qassim could turn out to be a valuable client.'

'Who is he, apart from rich?' Nicci found it hard to keep the sarcasm out of her voice.

Blake simply blinked at her. If anything, he had a hunted look and that made Nicci feel bad for being adolescent about the whole thing. After all, they were in the security business and all the individual clients were rich.

She forced a smile. 'We were recommended by a Mr Karim. Do you know him?'

Blake's gaze was inscrutable. 'By repute.'

Pulling off his glasses he rubbed the crease between his brows; there was hesitancy in his manner. Maybe he did want to confide in her? It was on the tip of her tongue to ask about McCain. Was he a spook, as Eddie Lunt had suggested?

'Simon, I don't mean to be arsey. I only want to help—'

The offer seemed to galvanize him, but he brushed it aside. 'Heather says I should apologize to you for my gross behaviour, and I do.'

'I don't need apologies. I'd rather you just told me what the hell was going on.'

'And when there's something you should know, I will.' The

tone was harsh and brooked no argument. He was stepping back into boss mode.

His gaze – an aloof glare – held hers for a moment, then he replaced his glasses and looked down at the contract. 'Turki bin Qassim buys property. For himself and members of the Qatari ruling family. He's related in some way to the Al Thanis. He could put a lot of business our way if he likes us.'

The rebuke stung, but Nicci was determined not to react. The fact he was being such a testosterone-driven knob fuelled her concern. This wasn't the Simon Blake she knew.

Rising from the desk, he buttoned his jacket. 'Anyway, I thought I'd come over with you this morning and introduce myself.'

Nicci said nothing. She'd been presuming that her new career as a rich woman's minder would start today. She simply nodded and followed him out of the room.

Blake was anxious to impress their new client so they took a taxi to Mayfair and got out in Mount Street. The Qassims' house was a five-storey red-brick mansion. Steps led up to a portico with two standard bay trees in tubs either side of the double front door.

Staring up at it for a moment, Blake became uncharacteristically hesitant.

Nicci gave him a caustic look. 'What are we supposed to do? Use the tradesmen's entrance?'

'Probably, but what the hell.'

He walked confidently up the steps and pressed the polished brass bell.

The door was opened by a maid with rudimentary English, who kept them waiting in the hall. A sweeping staircase wound up the centre of the house in a spiral. On a marble-topped table, which matched the chequered marble floor, sat an enormous vase of roses and lilies. Nicci found the scent oppressive. Her former in-laws had insisted on a wreath of lilies on Sophie's coffin. Ever since then, Nicci had hated the flower.

After five minutes Turki bin Qassim came up from the basement, in sports kit, dabbing sweat from his face with a towel. 'Good morning. Mr Blake, I presume?'

The ex-cop inclined his head and held out his hand to shake. 'Good morning, sir. I think you already know Ms Armstrong.'

'Of course.' Qassim gave her a languid smile. 'My wife is sleeping. Still a little jet-lagged, I think.'

Blake tried to look concerned. 'I wanted to come over and introduce myself and to say that, if you wish to discuss any aspect of your wife's security, I am of course always available.'

'Good to know, Mr Blake. I don't anticipate any problems. London is such a convenient and comfortable city. I enjoy spending time here.'

Qassim turned his attention to Nicci. 'I don't know what Ayisha's plans are today. The maid will make you some coffee and you can wait in the kitchen.'

'Thank you, Mr Qassim.' Nicci had already decided that she wasn't calling him sir.

He inclined his head. 'If you'll excuse me.' The conversation was obviously over and he disappeared down the stairs to the basement.

Nicci and Blake exchanged looks. Blake shrugged. 'Seems a reasonable bloke.'

For the next six hours, as she sat on a stool or paced around the pristine kitchen, Nicci thought of a lot of names for him but reasonable bloke wasn't one of them. She wasn't used to this kind of boredom.

The maid was young and rather nervous. She didn't respond

to Nicci's attempts at conversation. To entertain herself, Nicci surfed the Net on her phone, wandered around the ground-floor rooms, all palatial and formal, sent an email to her mother, which she'd been meaning to do for ages, and watched the hands travel all too slowly round the kitchen clock.

In the back of her mind she continued to brood about the disappearance of Karen Phelps. The more she thought about it, the more frustrated she felt. Simply doing nothing was not an acceptable option. In desperation she called Eddie Lunt.

She heard the front door slam and watched Turki bin Qassim through the window as he slipped into the back seat of a chauffeured black Mercedes. She ventured into the vast basement, discovering the gym, a fifteen-metre pool, a Jacuzzi and sauna.

The maid prepared her a sandwich for lunch and didn't appear to understand when she asked if Mrs Qassim was up yet. Shortly afterwards a delivery arrived from an exclusive Mayfair restaurant: a lunch hamper, which the maid carried upstairs.

Around four o'clock Turki bin Qassim returned. He came into the kitchen and frowned. 'Oh, Ms Armstrong, Ayisha won't be needing you today. You can go home.'

Nicci had to make a supreme effort not to show him how pissed off she was.

The maid appeared and hovered. He addressed her without making eye contact. 'A glass of iced water.'

She scurried to the fridge. Qassim turned back to Nicci as if he was surprised to still see her.

She fixed him with a direct stare. 'Will your wife require a bodyguard tomorrow, Mr Qassim?'

He accepted a glass of iced water from the maid, again without any eye contact, and took a sip. 'Yes, be here at nine.

And it's more convenient if staff use the side entrance. The maid will let you in.'

'It would be even more convenient if I had the door code.'

He seemed to consider this. 'Okay, she can show you.'

'Does she have a name?'

'Maria, is it?' He gave the girl a quizzical glance. 'The Filipino ones we usually call Maria.'

Nicci had already located the side gate. She gave him a nod, turned on her heel and walked out. The young maid trotted after her and tapped the entry code into the gate lock.

Simply stepping into the street felt like liberation to Nicci. Her brain squirmed with dark fantasies. Maybe she'd get lucky and some random terrorist would nab him or, better than that, perhaps his car would break down and he'd be exposed to the indignity of travelling on the tube.

She'd had days in her life when she'd felt wretched and she'd been on lengthy stakeouts where she'd got extremely bored. But those two feelings had never come together at work before. She couldn't quite fathom why the experience had riled her so. She'd had plenty of shitty jobs in her youth. As she strode down Mount Street, past the elegant shops, she wondered whether she could even do this. But, even though he was being snotty with her, she'd made a promise to Blake to help keep SBA afloat, and she wasn't about to break her word just because some smarmy rich git thought he could treat her like a servant.

35

Two DCs on the surveillance team had worked all day Saturday and into Sunday to complete the analysis of the ANPR footage. They tracked both the white transit filmed on CCTV at the hospital and also any dark panel vans in the area at the time of the funeral. According to a witness, Glynis Phelps, this had been the type of vehicle used as a covered hearse by the funeral directors. Tom Rivlin, who had worked most of the weekend himself, had them email a copy of their report for him to study on the Sunday evening.

The white transit had been easy enough for them to trace, but it had been dumped and torched the same night on some wasteland near Epping Forest. The van was a rental and, first thing Monday morning, Rivlin dispatched a DC to question the hire company and chase the paperwork, though he wasn't hopeful of the outcome. The Kemals were far too savvy to leave any evidence that could be linked to them. Rivlin's guess was that the van would've been hired by a stooge using forged documents.

Identifying the funeral directors' vehicle had involved a far more detailed analysis, combining CCTV footage with ANPR data on all main approach roads leading to the church at around the time of the funeral. The country lanes in the immediate vicinity didn't contain any cameras and the volume of traffic on the A12 that Wednesday morning had been heavy.

But they'd finally managed to narrow it down to a plain black Mercedes panel van, which entered the area shortly before noon and hit the A12 again at speed and driving erratically a little over an hour later. The vehicle was registered to a firm of funeral directors who had premises off Lea Bridge Road in Walthamstow.

Rivlin took all the intelligence gathered to the Monday-morning briefing. He'd lined up the home address of the sole proprietor of the firm, Mrs Sheila Mabey, whose website billed her as 'a caring lady funeral director with a reputation for her sensitive handling of clients' needs at a difficult time'. Rivlin proposed a dawn raid with armed backup to put the fear of God in Mrs Mabey and persuade her to cooperate.

DCI Stoneham leant forward in her chair and steepled her fingers. She'd said nothing to Rivlin so far about the failure to protect Karen Phelps at the hospital.

'Armed backup, Tom? For a lady funeral director? Really?' The sarcasm was unmistakable. He'd been expecting some kind of comeback and here it was. A rap over the knuckles in front of the whole team. They were all watching goggle-eyed, and some would be privately pleased that golden balls – a nickname he didn't appreciate – had fallen from grace.

'A precaution, boss. Mrs Mabey could just be a front. We don't know what we'll be walking into.'

Of course he was right to be cautious; he was also sure that, ordinarily, Stoneham would've agreed. But that wasn't really what this was about. The DCI turned to her left. There were over a dozen officers sitting round the conference table, including a new face.

Stoneham gave the young woman a smile. 'This is probably a good time to introduce DS Amy Raheem from the Met. She's going to be embedded with us and handle liaison with the Met for the duration of this investigation.'

All eyes turned to focus on the interloper. Raheem lounged in her chair, legs crossed, a blank but attentive expression on her face. She didn't return Stoneham's smile and gave no sign of being at all bothered by the sudden scrutiny of a dozen strangers. Rivlin had noticed her wandering through the office earlier. Glossy brown hair swept up into a bun and a cropped suit jacket over tight denim jeans, she looked on the young side for a DS.

Stoneham's gimlet eye moved back to Rivlin. 'Where's this funeral director live?'

'Walthamstow. Two doors down from the funeral parlour. Area looks a bit scuzzy on streetview.'

The DCI looked at Raheem. 'Your turf, Amy. What do you think?'

The dark eyes surveyed the room and then settled on Rivlin. 'If the DI's intel suggests we should go mob-handed, it's obviously his call. I can request TSG support.'

Rivlin had a sinking feeling. Stoneham must be really pissed if she was prepared to use some hotshot from the Met to give him a public spanking. It felt unjust, but he knew he had to suck it up.

Raheem's attention switched back to Stoneham. 'I'd be inclined to look the place over first, ma'am. We may be able to glean the intelligence we need from a straightforward conversation. But if Mrs Mabey doesn't want to cooperate, we can always waterboard her later.'

It took several seconds for the joke to register. Smiles and sniggers rolled round the table and Rivlin's humiliation was complete. He managed a rictus grin and a shrug. But the tension in the room was broken.

Stoneham chuckled. 'Okay, Amy will inform the Met that we're on the plot and may need backup. But let's talk to Mrs Mabey first. Take a search warrant. If she's basically legit, that should be enough to make her pliable. If she isn't, then we'll know.' The DCI's gaze skated past Rivlin to another DI. 'Mark, you organize.'

'Yes, boss.'

As the meeting broke up, Rivlin reflected that it could've been worse. It was his initiative but he'd been cut out of the loop. He gathered up his papers with one eye on Raheem, who was having words with the deputy SIO. He wasn't sure whether to be grateful for her joke or to resent it. She'd been canny enough to read the DCI's tetchy mood and roll with it. That was usually his trick. She was attractive but had ball-breaker written all over her; he resolved to give her a wide berth.

As he wandered down the corridor, trying not to feel too sorry for himself, a voice assailed him.

'Tom, a word!'

It was Stoneham, collecting a coffee from the hot drinks machine. She beckoned him. As he approached he noticed the coffee was black. If she was on another diet that could also explain why he'd got it in the neck.

She started to walk and he fell into step beside her. 'Good work for tracking down the funeral director so quickly.' He had to admire her technique; she'd made her point, she was moving on. It was seamless.

'Thanks, boss.'

'You made a judgement at the hospital and I accepted it. Turns out we were both wrong.'

'It was a bad call. My fault. I'm sorry.' But he was damned if he'd take the rap alone. 'Part of the problem was Nicci Armstrong didn't tell us the whole story.'

'You're blaming this on her?'

'I'm not blaming anyone. Apparently Phelps has got history with the Kemals. This is a personal grudge. I only found that out later on Friday night when Nicci phoned me.'

'Why the hell didn't she tell us that before?'

'She was protecting Phelps, didn't want her licence to be revoked.' Even as he said it he felt like a snitch. If he'd thought there would be some pleasure in getting one up on the sainted Nicci, he was wrong.

Stoneham stopped and sipped her coffee. Then she shook her head wearily. 'This is a mess. We have to find Phelps before the Kemals do.'

'I know.'

'What about Glynis Phelps?'

'I had her place checked on Saturday. We tracked down the sister too – lives in Southend – nothing.'

The DCI stared into the middle distance, planning her next move. Any anger with him had passed; he didn't want to feel relieved, but he did. Punishment and forgiveness; it took him back to childhood.

She fixed him with a quizzical frown. 'And you've got a security guard at the hospital who ID'd Sadik Kemal?'

'Yeah, but I wouldn't want to stand him up in court.'

'Still, it's grounds enough for us to go and kick Sadik's door down and see what we can find. Raheem can talk to her bosses.'

'Wouldn't it be better if you did that yourself?'

Stoneham smiled. 'I'm playing the game, Tom. You know what the Met's like, they won't give you anything until they know what's in it for them.'

'I don't want to be partisan, but we should be the ones who nail the Kemals.'

'And we will. A gangster with a grudge ceases to be a businessman. He starts to make mistakes. He's after Phelps – that's our opportunity. So you know what your priority is?'

'Yeah. Find Karen Phelps. Get her testimony.'

'And soon.'

36

She'd never been one for lying in bed, even when she was really ill. By midday on Saturday Kaz'd kicked off the duvet and was prowling the room. Rafaella provided her with underwear, soft bedsocks, trackie bottoms and a sweatshirt, and invited her to join them downstairs for lunch.

The farmhouse kitchen was spacious and sunny; they'd eaten at the long wooden table, then Kaz had been co-opted as Lacey's new playmate. Kaz could draw and the little girl found that thrilling. She demanded a horse and Kaz rapidly sketched an outline that looked exactly like a horse. Lacey squealed with pleasure.

Paul had leaned back in his chair, beaming and sharing his daughter's delight. 'Blimey, I never knew you could do all this.'

'There's a lot about me you don't know.'

The afternoon had been spent creating a menagerie of animals with Kaz encouraging Lacey to make her own drawings. By six o'clock they'd both run out of energy. Rafaella took the little girl upstairs for her bath and Kaz fell asleep on the sofa.

She knew that sleep was her healer and, having found a safe place, she needed to rest. There were questions, too many questions, but they would have to wait. Back in her room she'd slept from early Saturday evening to late on Sunday morning. When she finally woke, the soreness in her lungs caused by smoke inhalation had subsided; she was left with a phlegmy cough, which felt like the aftermath of a chest cold.

Brunch was served, again at the large kitchen table. Rafaella smiled a lot and said very little. Kaz had become used to the unobtrusive presence of Paul's wife. How much did she know about his past? It was impossible to tell. All Kaz got from her was kindness and solicitous attention to her every need; this left Kaz with a vaguely guilty feeling.

In the afternoon the two women basked on the terrace in a brief burst of late September sun while Paul played football on the lawn with his daughter. Watching him with Lacey was a pleasure. Kaz's memories of him were of a strutting boy; both she and Joey had been mesmerized. She could still recall the first time he took her for a spin on his silver Kawasaki Ninja. She was probably only fifteen. It was at night and they did a ton on the M25. Joey had been so jealous.

Back then it would have been impossible to imagine Paul playing with a child. He was tough, streetwise, a dealer and, to a teenage girl, impossibly cool. But in truth that boy was a distant echo, part of her confused and painful adolescence. Kaz hadn't really thought about him for years. Now she couldn't stop thinking about him. The what-ifs crowded her mind. What if the old man hadn't intervened?

Terry's incestuous interest in his daughter had made him ultra possessive. No one looked twice at Kaz Phelps, not if they valued their own skin. But Paul had dared. What if he hadn't gone to jail? She had certainly loved him back then with all the intense passion of teenage romance. Could she have ever turned into Rafaella? Could she have been the wife and mother, the mistress of this beautiful house, living a safe, care-free existence with a man to take care of her?

On Monday morning Rafaella took Lacey to nursery. Kaz

watched from the kitchen window as she carefully strapped the little girl into her car seat. The BMW X3 turned out of the driveway and disappeared down the country lane. Paul closed the five-bar gate behind it and gave Kaz a wave as he strolled back towards the house. It was the first time they'd been left alone together.

Kaz was loading the breakfast plates and cutlery into the dishwasher when he returned to the kitchen. Just for a moment she toyed with the fantasy that this was her house and her husband.

'Hey, you don't have to do that. You're a guest.'

Forced to let the dream dissolve, Kaz smiled. 'You've both been so kind. Least I can do is help out.'

He picked up the kettle and filled it at the sink. 'How about I make us a fresh coffee and we can talk some business. Rafa goes to the gym after she drops Lacey off. So we got all morning.'

Kaz wasn't sure what kind of proposition she'd been expecting or even hoping for from Paul – but *talking business*? Part of her was disappointed.

He made a cafetière of coffee, placed it on a tray with ceramic mugs and a jug of milk and invited her to join him in his den. Situated at the back of the house, with French doors on to the garden, part study, part chill-out space, it was a very masculine room.

She settled herself in one corner of the leather sofa and watched him pour the coffee. Refusing milk, she took the steaming mug and waited.

He seemed restless, opening the French doors, adjusting the blinds. Was he nervous? He gave that impression. He was a married man but they were alone now. Did he still have feelings for her?

Pulling the swivel chair out from behind the glass desk, he finally sat down. 'Rafa's great. She's a brilliant wife and mother. But I don't involve her in the business. She's a Spaniard, grew up in a sleepy little town where her dad was the baker. She don't understand the life I've led or our kind of background.'

'Does she know you've been in prison?'

'Oh yeah. I haven't lied to her. And she's known for years that I was once involved with Joey's sister.'

He said this in such a matter-of-fact way, referring to Joey's sister as if she were another person, a stranger who existed only in the past. Even so, Kaz found herself wanting to reach out and touch him, to see what it would feel like after all these years. Instead she folded her fingers round her mug of coffee.

'Don't she mind me being here?'

'Not at all.' He met her eye. Maybe he did still want her, but his gaze didn't show it. 'Look, Joey filled me in. When I visited him in the nick.'

'Filled you in about what?'

'Told me that nowadays you're batting for the other side. I got no problem with that. Makes things easier, really.'

Kaz gave him a wry smile. So he knew. And part of her was glad. It provided a safety net for both of them. All the same, somewhere inside she felt a stab of regret. 'It wasn't a particularly conscious choice. I fell madly in love with a woman.'

'The important thing is, did she love you back?'

'Maybe. For a while. But she's dead.'

'I'm sorry to hear that, babes. That's tough.'

'She was murdered. By the rich Russian that Joey tried to kill.'

Paul took a moment to absorb this; he gave a low whistle. 'Fuck me! So that's what it was all about.'

Kaz found herself struggling to hold back the tears. Helen

Warner was always there, a gentle presence in the deep recesses of her mind. It was the one thing she had that consoled her. Her teenage passion for Paul had been all-consuming at the time, and then as now he'd been her rescuer. But those feelings couldn't compare to the desire and craving she'd felt for Helen. The idea of herself in Rafaella's shoes was a comforting daydream, but that's not who she was; she'd always be an outsider and she knew it.

Realizing that Paul was watching her, she brushed the back of her hand across her face. 'Take no notice. It all gets to me from time to time.'

'Understandable, mate.' He frowned with concern but he was twisting the signet ring on his little finger. She could sense his impatience; he'd never been any good at the emotional stuff. He had his own agenda and he was just waiting.

She took a slug of coffee and put on a serious face. 'You wanted to talk business.'

He opened his palms and leant forward in his chair. He had the look of a salesman, glad to finally make his pitch. 'I'd never have all this if it weren't for Joey. And I want to do right by him. But he was a difficult bloke to work with at times, you know that.'

Kaz could feel the tension in him and, if it wasn't about his feelings for an old flame, she began to wonder what else he was trying to hide. Wariness was her default setting. People always disappointed you – that was her experience – especially the ones you trusted. She decided to sit back and see what happened.

'As you know, I was running things out in Ibiza when Joey got nicked. It was a tight operation, people on holiday want party drugs and we was making a mint.'

'You'd said before the two of you had fallen out.'

'Nah, not completely.' His eyes slid off to one side; he couldn't hold her gaze. 'We had a bit of a disagreement, that's all. He was one clever fucker, your little brother. The Internet, what it meant for business – he understood all that. A market without rules, that's what he called it. Buy what you like, sell what you like. Particularly drugs. And no old bill breathing down your neck.'

'Pity he didn't stick to business; he'd never have landed in jail.'

'That's what I told him. But Joey had a taste for the rough stuff. Liked to get his hands dirty. It gave him a buzz like nothing else. I seen it and I knew in the end that'd get us in trouble.'

Kaz found herself wondering what he wasn't telling her. A bit of a disagreement, or was it much more than that? It would certainly explain why Joey had never spoken to her about any partnership with Paul. She continued to smile. 'I wish I'd known you was involved. We could've joined forces.'

'Maybe it ain't too late for that.' He met her gaze, but there was the nervousness again.

'How d'you mean?'

'I used to watch him. He'd get out his laptop and show me how he'd squirrel it all away. We made a shitload out of the drugs. I lost track. But that was the tip of the iceberg. You can do all sorts on the Net. I always remember, years ago, your old man saying, "No one robs banks any more, too fucking hard." Thanks to the Net, now it's too fucking easy.'

Kaz scanned his face. Why on earth would an apparently successful man like him want to join forces with her?

'It's a generous offer, Paul. But if you're into all that you don't need me.'

He frowned. 'There's millions out there. Carefully stashed

away. Joey meant for you and your sister to have it. He told me as much. That's what I was gonna tell you at the funeral.' *Now they were getting to the nub of it.*

'Yeah, but where?'

'Offshore accounts. British Virgin Islands, probably. "Give it to the Virgins to look after," that was his joke. He set up a network of companies, untraceable.'

Kaz laughed. 'You think if I could get my hands on Joey's money I'd be sitting round in this country, waiting for every scumbag with a beef to have a pop at me?'

'Joey was a meticulous planner, he always had a back door.'

'If he had, he never told me about it.'

'Thing is, babes, he probably did. He would've made sure you had the information to access it somehow.'

'Maybe he told Natalie.'

'I don't think so. I've popped round to see her a couple of times. Y'know, make sure she's all right. But she's a bit flaky, your sister. Too many drugs over the years. Joe's much more likely to have left the information somewhere for you. You just haven't found it yet.'

'I don't even know what I'd be looking for.'

'That's why I think we should join forces. I reckon if we work together, we can figure it out.'

He was looking at her earnestly, hopefully. She was in his lovely home, he'd saved her from the Kemals, supposedly made sure Darius was at the hospital to keep an eye on her. But it was all beginning to make sense. Paul had worked with or for her brother. They'd fallen out. Paul probably felt he'd been shafted and, knowing Joey, that could well be true. What Paul wanted now was to get his hands on Joey's money – and he planned to use Kaz in order to do it.

He was as full of charm as he'd ever been, but she was being set up. And she'd nearly fallen for it.

Still she managed to smile serenely. 'Sounds like a plan. Let's do it.'

37

Eddie Lunt, armed with a large bouquet of flowers, wandered round the hospital. Nicci had phoned him. She was tied up with this stupid security job but she was fretting about Karen Phelps, so she'd dispatched Eddie to see what he could find out.

Working for an ex-cop was no bother to Eddie. He'd found over the years that most of them were amenable. A couple of pints or a free lunch usually got you the information you wanted. Then he encountered Nicci Armstrong and the former DS had taken against him from the off. It didn't seem to matter to her that he'd served his time; he was a criminal and that stuck in her craw. As far as he was concerned he'd only been doing his job. Phone hacking had been an accepted practice in the newspaper business for years, everyone knew about it. But when the shit hit the fan the bosses got away with it and blokes like him took the fall. It was the way of the world; he felt no resentment.

He started with the ward where he and Nicci had visited Karen. Posing as a visitor, he got short shrift from the shrewish sister, who informed him Phelps had been discharged and any queries about her whereabouts should be addressed to the police.

Meandering around for a bit, he waited for a shift change and trailed two student nurses and a nursing assistant to the canteen. Pretending to peruse the menu board, he watched the three young women. They were lively, gossipy girls, teasing each other as they queued for the salad bar. He opted for shepherd's pie, paid for his food and selected a table next to the young nurses.

Unfurling his cutlery from its napkin he tuned in: their discussion was about boyfriends and their myriad failings.

'He's lying, it's obvious.' The first girl had a confident manner, the self-appointed leader of the trio.

'Yeah, but if I say that to him he'll dump me.' The second girl looked hardly eighteen to Eddie, beautiful and anxious to please. Her two mates obviously considered her naive.

'He's gonna dump you anyway, soon as he gets it on with her.'

'He might not.'

'He will!' they cried in unison.

'He will.' All three turned in surprise to stare at Eddie. He beamed. 'I know I'm an old fart who should mind my own business, but look at you. You're a lovely girl. You shouldn't let any bloke give you the run-around. I'd give him a dose of his own medicine.'

'That's what I said.' The first girl smiled in vindication.

Eddie held out his bunch of flowers. 'Here, have these to cheer you up.'

The eighteen-year-old gave him a suspicious what-kind-of-perve-are-you look. As if in answer, Eddie shrugged. 'I'm a reporter. On a job. Came to visit this girl who was in a fire. But she's done a bunk.'

A salvo of looks flew between the girls. Recognition followed by hesitation. Eddie pretended to be oblivious. He chuckled. 'Could be quite a story. I shouldn't tell you this, but

I reckon something's happened to her and the cops are trying to cover their arses.'

He took a large forkful of shepherd's pie, chewed it thoughtfully and waited.

It took about thirty seconds. Glances flashed between the young nurses. 'Do you work for a paper or the telly?'

'Oh, I shouldn't say, love. Forget it. I shouldn't be talking about this.'

But they'd swallowed the bait. Eddie watched out of the corner of his eye as two of them shot silent exhortations at the third to egg her on.

Finally Eddie's patience was rewarded. It was the nursing assistant with the unfaithful boyfriend. 'I was on duty when she disappeared. But Sister told us not to say anything. One of the senior managers came down and gave her a right telling off. We all heard it.'

'Really?' Eddie tried to sound surprised. Ten minutes later he'd extracted the whole story: the security guards who'd come to transfer Phelps to the private wing, her flight, them chasing her out of a fire door at the back of the hospital, the confusion and subsequent realization they were imposters, the appearance of managers then the police. Red faces all round.

Having cleaned his plate, he thanked them and presented them with the flowers. 'Of course, I can't say anything for certain. But we are the largest-circulation tabloid in the UK, so watch this space, as they say.'

They assured him they would and dissolved into collective giggles as he left the canteen.

Eddie soon located the fire door that Karen Phelps must've used. He peered through the reinforced glass at the metal stairway and gravel path leading to the concrete service road beyond. He was reluctant to open the door as it would probably trigger an alarm. Instead he headed for the main entrance and set off on a recce around the back of the building.

It would've been dark and there were several avenues of escape Phelps could've chosen. But did she escape? There had been no mention in the media of a kidnap or a police search. If she'd been taken by the Kemals, it would've been impossible for the police to keep that under wraps for the whole weekend. Eddie concluded that somehow she'd got away.

He wandered from the flank of the building to the front and saw the A&E department. Running from her pursuers in the dark, this would have been the beacon of light and help that she would have seen once she rounded the corner of the building.

There was an ambulance bay directly in front of A&E and then further along, close to the main hospital entrance, a taxi rank.

Eddie strolled along the column of parked taxis. Two drivers were leaning on the side of the front cab, chatting and smoking. They were both dumpy with beer bellies and balding pates, one older, the other younger; they could even be father and son.

Eddie gave them a comradely nod. 'All right, lads.'

The elder of the two ditched his fag. 'Where you wanna go, pal?'

Opening his wallet, Eddie fished out a twenty-pound note. The old techniques were often the best and he usually opened the bidding with a score. 'Looking for information.'

They eyed him suspiciously. 'Oh yeah?'

'Friday night. Bit of a rumpus, I hear.'

Dad was the spokesman. 'Some kind of trouble kicks off at A&E most weekends. It's the booze.'

'This was a bit different. A girl. A patient. Being chased.'

The cabbies exchanged looks.

'You press? You ain't local.'

'Nah, mate. I'm from the fucking *Guardian*.'

They all three laughed. Dad pulled out a packet of Marlboro Reds and sparked up with a chrome Zippo.

He sucked down a lungful of smoke, exhaled through the nose and gave Eddie a speculative look. 'Tell you what, pal, you make that a ton and I'll tell you who picked the girl up and where you can find him.'

38

Nicci Armstrong got back to the office around five o'clock. She could've simply headed home, but she didn't trust her mood. One single day working as a minder for some rich bitch who couldn't even be arsed to get out of bed had offended her more than she'd expected. Being alone in her flat with a bottle didn't feel like a sensible plan. She needed distraction.

As she emerged from the lift she read a text from Eddie. It was cryptic: *Could be on to s/thing. will keep u posted.* Walking into reception, she raised her eyes from the phone and was nonplussed to see Tom Rivlin getting up from the sofa and beaming at her.

The feelings of the next thirty seconds pitched her back into adolescent panic. Her stomach lurched and she flushed red from her neck to the roots of her hair. Or it felt as if she did. She covered this by scowling and looking down at her phone.

Ignoring him, she continued to walk in the direction of the open-plan office and he fell into step beside her. 'Nicci, look, I owe you an apology. Can we talk?'

Having taken a couple of deep breaths to calm herself, she managed to stop and face him. 'You can't find her, can you?'

'I was out of order and I'm an arsehole.'

'Self-knowledge is a marvellous thing.' The sarcasm helped her regain her composure.

'Stoneham says you're a good detective and I need your

help.' She knew he was trying to be appealing to hook her. But he did have an unnervingly gorgeous smile. 'The Kemals tried to take Karen. We're pretty certain she got away. She's gone to ground. We've looked in all the obvious places.'

'I doubt she'd put her family at risk if the Kemals are after her.'

'We've got her sister and her cousin, Glynis, under surveillance in case she turns up or the Kemals get any ideas.'

'That's a bit stable door and horse, isn't it?'

He sighed. 'Let me buy you a drink – dinner, maybe. We put our heads together and see if we can come up with a way forward on this. I know you want to help her.'

'Don't guilt-trip me, Rivlin.'

He tilted his head; the eyes were possibly more seductive than the smile. 'You know what Stoneham wrote on my last review? "He needs to be a less reactive and more strategic thinker." I was reactive. I am reactive, it's the Celtic blood. I know your dealings with Phelps have been complex.'

'In a totally professional context.'

'In a totally professional context, obviously.'

She met his gaze directly, but only for a moment. 'There's a pub down on Gray's Inn Road – the Blue Lion. I'll meet you there in half an hour. I've got a few things I need to do.'

'And will you have dinner with me?'

She needed to escape and marshal her unruly desires. 'I'll help you, okay. You don't need to do the full charm offensive.'

'I'd like to have dinner with you because . . . well, because I'd like to have dinner with you.' He seemed rather boyish and abashed which only made it worse for Nicci.

'I'll think about it. See you in the pub.'

She turned and stalked away across the office without a backward glance.

Pascale had been watching from the investigations section with wide-eyed intrigue. 'Who is that luscious man?'

'Some cop who needs information.'

'I volunteer – I'll help him with his inquiries.' She followed this with a lascivious *err-hum* deep in her throat.

'Oh, for fuck's sake, Pascale! You're worse than a bloke.' Nicci wanted to cry or scream or both. She was way too old to be having these kinds of mad feelings. Especially for a man who was just trying to use her.

Pascale raised her palms and her eyebrows and mouthed: *Sorry!*

Nicci dumped her bag on the desk with some force and exhaled. 'No, I'm the one should apologize. Bad day.'

Pascale slipped her pen behind her ear where it habitually rested between two neat cornrows. Her brown eyes twinkled with amusement. 'You need to sleep with him, girl. Now. Tonight. Before you blow a fuse.'

39

The clothes Rafaella lent her – Chloé jeans, a silk top – fitted perfectly; they were a similar height and build. Kaz considered herself in the full-length mirror. A whiff of Chanel and she could almost be Rafaella, the expensively dressed wife of a successful businessman.

It had crossed her mind that the resemblance between her and Paul's wife might not be coincidence. Attraction was an odd thing and it worked at such a subconscious level. When Paul Ackroyd had met a girl in a bar in Ibiza and fallen for her, had he still been pining for his lost first love? Kaz smiled at her own vanity; it would suit her ego to believe that. But now Paul was the one who thought he could play her to get his hands on Joey's hidden stash, so it was reasonable, even necessary, for her to find a way to pull his strings. The fact that he was a married man and she was gay may have seemingly ruled out reigniting their romance. He was relying purely on charm to get her onside but, as she gazed at her own image in the mirror, it occurred to Kaz that lust might be the way to beat him at his own game.

Darius Johnson arrived to drive her in his minicab. Paul was insistent that she should be properly protected even on a short trip to the hospital to visit her mother.

Kaz had not seen Darius since he plucked her out of harm's way and hid her in his taxi on the night she was running from

Sadik Kemal. He greeted her with a shy smile but she immediately pulled him into a hug and squeezed him tight. She'd modified her behaviour into something slightly more girly, but that was for Paul's benefit, not Darius's.

'Thanks, mate. I owe you. Big time.'

He seemed embarrassed. 'I just, y'know, wanna help out.'

Releasing him, Kaz smiled. 'Well you did. You were fucking brilliant.'

Paul slapped Darius on the back. 'Take care of her today. Keep an eye out.'

'Don't worry. I'm on the case.'

As Kaz climbed into the front of the MPV beside Darius she glanced over at the back seat and the tinted windows. It was the cover provided by those windows, coupled with Darius's quick thinking, that had saved her.

He started the vehicle up and with a wave from Paul they set off through the maze of leafy lanes. Kaz sat back for a bit and simply enjoyed the ride. It was good to be out, to escape the confines of the farmhouse; somehow she felt more comfortable with Darius than the Ackroyds. He had an easy presence and a quiet manner; he was undoubtedly tough without being macho or aggressive. She had a lot to think about and the drive offered her some much-needed headspace.

They were cruising along the A12 when she finally turned to him. 'I'm gonna 'fess up. Truth is, I don't remember you from school. I wish I did.'

He chuckled. 'I was a miserable, skinny little runt back then. It ain't so surprising.'

'You and Paul seem pretty tight?'

It was obviously Darius's job to keep a close eye on her and report back to Paul. But he took his eyes off the road long enough to give her a direct look.

'Nah, not really. He gives me stuff to do from time to time. Deliveries. Y'know. But I don't work for him.'

They drove in silence for several moments while Kaz digested this.

'Yeah, but he's paying you for today?'

'I'm freelance though, work for who I want to.'

Kaz glanced across at him. This was interesting. He was making it pretty clear that he had no loyalty to Paul. Either that or he was trying to sucker her into trusting him. Darius Johnson, her self-effacing saviour in Paul's presence, was cannier than he looked.

He reached into his shirt pocket and pulled out a business card. 'Cops have been asking loads of questions, but I've avoided them. I've kept away from the hospital. But this afternoon this bloke came looking for me – Eddie. Says you know him and his boss is a friend of yours.'

Kaz took the card. 'What did you tell him?'

'Nothing. And I've told no one else about him.' He shot her another direct glance. 'That includes Paul.'

She turned the card over in her hand. On one side a smart company logo, on the other: *Eddie Lunt. Simon Blake Associates*, followed by an email address and several phone numbers.

'What else did he say?'

'He mentioned a Nicci? Said she's worried about you. Will you just call them. They won't tell the cops.'

Kaz sniggered. 'Not much. Eddie's all right. But Nicci was a cop.'

'You don't trust her?'

'Oh, I dunno.' She leant back on the headrest and sighed. 'Joey always insisted there was two sides: them and us. I used to think that was ridiculous. I didn't want to be put in a box like that.'

'Sounds like you've changed your mind.'

'I was a stupid kid who deserved to get nicked. But I've served my time. As far as the cops are concerned though, I'm a villain. People are trying to kill me, but to them I'm still a villain.'

'They should've protected you.'

'Yeah, but 'cause of my dad, 'cause of my brother, I'm on the wrong side of the line. Don't matter what I do, that's how they see it. They only want to use me.'

Darius kept his eyes on the road ahead. 'So now you think Joey was right?'

'I think I have to take care of myself. No one else is going to.'

'Well, you got my help if you want it.'

She'd had Paul's pitch, now this was his. The myth of Joey's money was a magnet. But did these blokes think that because she was female she'd be an easy mark? Well, they were wrong about that.

She shrugged. 'I'll bear that in mind.'

They skirted the suburbs of Chelmsford and arrived at the hospital around seven p.m. The outpatient clinics were over for the day and most visitors had left, so it was easy for Darius to find a slot in the car park.

As he backed into the space, he turned to her. 'Have you considered that the old bill might have someone keeping an eye on your mum?'

Kaz lifted the large Mulberry handbag she'd borrowed from Rafaella on to her lap.

'Why d'you think I've got this?' She pulled a pair of heavy-rimmed black spectacles out of the bag and put them on.

He switched the engine off. 'You got something to cover your hair?'

Rummaging in the bag, she produced a long silk scarf and arranged it loosely around her head.

They both got out of the cab. She looped the bag over her arm and posed. 'What d'you think?'

He grinned. 'Makes you look about forty.'

'You don't think it's too obviously a disguise?'

'Depends how sharp they are.'

Sighing, she peered anxiously at her reflection in the wing mirror. She did look faintly ridiculous. 'Aaww, fuck it! Let's just do it.'

Kaz strode imperiously into the hospital with Darius at her side. They followed the signs, which eventually led them down the main corridor to the Burns Unit and its specialist ITU. There was an entryphone on the door. Kaz pressed the button and put on her poshest voice. 'I've come to see Mrs Phelps. I rang up. I'm Mrs Ackroyd, her sister-in-law.'

They were buzzed in. A charge nurse in blue surgical scrubs emerged from behind the desk to meet them. He was thin and balding with a polite, professional smile.

'Mrs Ackroyd? We spoke on the phone.'

Kaz slipped seamlessly into the part. 'Yes. Is it all right if my driver waits out here?'

'That's fine. As I said on the phone, Ellie has already had some surgery. She's in a side room – for security reasons, while the police investigate the fire.' He led her down the corridor. 'And she's partially sedated.'

A young female PC was seated outside the door. She got up as they approached. Kaz met the cop's eye firmly as the charge nurse addressed her. 'This is Mrs Phelps's sister-in-law.'

The PC simply smiled at Kaz and opened the door for them.

The ease with which her mad impersonation had worked

buoyed Kaz; it all seemed like a surreal joke. But stepping into the room, she came down to earth with a jolt when she saw her mother.

Ellie was lost in a sea of tubes and drips and leads connecting her to an array of machines around the bed. Her face was covered in white gauze with small slits for the eyes, giving her the appearance of an already mummified corpse.

Kaz must've gasped because the charge nurse gave her a concerned look. 'Sit down next to her and talk to her.' He turned to the patient and removed the nebulizer covering her nose and mouth. 'You've got a visitor, Ellie. Your sister-in-law. Let's take this off for a moment.' He removed the mask and turned to Kaz. 'The pain relief makes her drowsy, but she can understand you. Ten minutes?'

Kaz nodded dumbly. He left the room, quietly closing the door behind him. Kaz dumped the bag and the glasses and pulled off the scarf. She felt a panic rising in her throat. Was her mother going to die? Ellie wasn't a small woman but even her stout frame looked frail and overwhelmed. She'd been shot at the funeral and then this.

On the night of the fire it had been Ellie who'd shouted for help, but her bedroom had been much closer to the flames as they roared up the stairwell. Kaz herself may have escaped the inferno relatively unscathed, but clearly her mother had not. Tears of rage and impotence began welling in Kaz's eyes.

Then a barely audible voice came from behind the gauze. 'Who is it? 'Cause I ain't got a sister-in-law.'

There was a chair. Kaz moved it next to the bed, careful not to disturb any of the medical paraphernalia. She sat down. She wanted to take Ellie's hand but that too was covered in gauze.

She leant forward. 'It's me, Mum. It's Kaz.'

'Kaz? Oh Kaz! I was worried you didn't get out.'

'I got out. You shouted for help and they came. You saved us both.'

'I been asking and asking about you, but no one knew.' The voice was a rasping whisper, the fingers on the hand flexed. Kaz reached out and gently touched the very tips.

'I'm okay, Mum.'

Ellie seemed to drift; without the nebulizer, her breathing was laboured. 'I been so worried about you.'

Kaz scanned her. Machines to monitor and help keep her alive. The charge nurse had mentioned that she'd had some surgery. It was clear that her mother was extremely poorly.

'You don't have to worry no more.'

'I been so worried.'

Had she? Kaz's default setting was to distrust everything Ellie said, and over the years she'd had good reason. But seeing her mother like this had a visceral impact and she couldn't stop the flood of fear that rushed through her. Ellie's pain seared her as if the raw scorched flesh were her own. Gulping down the tears, Kaz was overwhelmed by a desperate desire to save her.

'Don't worry. I'm here now and I'm gonna take care of things.'

'You're a good girl.'

That had never been Ellie's opinion of her daughter and they both knew it. But none of that mattered now.

'You need to rest and get well, 'cause me and Nat, we need you, Mum.'

'I been so worried.' The voice was barely a whisper.

'Sssh. It's gonna be okay.'

The rigidity and tension in Ellie's body finally ebbed and she seemed to relax. Her breathing slowed and behind the narrow slits in the gauze her eyes closed and she dozed. Kaz had no idea how to pray, so instead she sat quietly watching over her for the rest of the allotted ten minutes.

She'd tried to walk away and put her life on a different course. But fate seemed to have other ideas for her. No one got to choose where they were born or who their parents were. The cards were dealt and you played the hand you were given.

Joey was dead and her mother might be about to join him. But she had a sister and a new nephew. And if Ellie did recover she'd need a safe place to go and recuperate. Then there were the Kemals, the scumbags who'd done this to Ellie and who'd tried twice now to put Kaz in the ground.

If her childhood had taught Kaz Phelps anything, it was how to survive and how to hate. These were the talents she could rely on. She'd done her level best to go straight and this was where she'd wound up: on the run from both the police and a bunch of murderous gangsters. The priority now was to protect herself and her family from any further harm. Sadly, Joey had been proved right. There were two sides and you didn't get to swap. Not really. She wondered if her brother was looking down on her now; he'd surely be smirking. Who you were was determined by where you were born and the family you came from. Didn't matter how far you ran. That was the truth, and in the end there was no escaping it.

40

Nicci spent the best part of half an hour nursing a white wine spritzer. Small, ladylike sips. She felt virtuous; for her this had to be some kind of record, but the real boost it gave her was a sense of control, something she needed more than the buzz. She'd made Rivlin wait for forty-five minutes before joining him in the Blue Lion. The pub was standing-room only, loud and chock-full of office workers. But he'd secured a quiet table at the back.

Already a couple of pints ahead of her, the alcohol had loosened him. His brow was damp, his long fingers mobile as he spoke. 'Thing is, Nicci, Stoneham knows you and she trusts you.'

Was this still true? She didn't think so, especially since the DCI had heard of her intervention on Phelps's behalf with the probation service. But they were in a hole and she could imagine Rivlin being instructed by his boss in no uncertain terms to sort it out. That's why he was here.

He took a sip of Guinness and wiped his lip. 'It goes without saying that all this is in confidence.'

'Obviously.'

Her face was serious but inside she was smirking. Having to come to her cap in hand like this must really be pissing him off, although you wouldn't think so. He was slick and trying, albeit subtly now, to reel her in – the direct, rather seductive look in his eye, the boyish tilt of the head – and Nicci had to admit that it was tempting. She also knew she had to take care of herself. Pascale's jibe about sleeping with him was all very well, but he'd dump her flat once she'd served her purpose, and she was determined not to end up a hostage to fortune.

In spite of that, she couldn't help being drawn in by his confiding manner. 'We've tracked down the firm of funeral directors. East End business, quite small. Some colleagues from the Met are interviewing the woman that owns it. And I've also got a witness who can place Sadik Kemal at Basildon Hospital at the relevant time, so we're going to bring him in.'

'Wow! He went after Karen himself?' This was news and Nicci didn't conceal her excitement. 'That was a bit reckless.' It was more than that, it could turn out to be the breakthrough they needed.

Rivlin simply nodded. 'You were right. You said you thought it was a personal grudge, so it makes sense.'

'Will you have enough to charge him?'

'Maybe attempted kidnap. But that's not really what we want and my guess is the CPS won't rate the evidence. We'll certainly hold him for the full thirty-six.'

'That'll give Karen some respite.'

'On the other hand, it could wind Asil Kemal up even more. He might commission another hit.'

Nicci pondered this. 'Well, I haven't managed to get in touch with her yet, but I've got a line on someone who may know where she is.'

'Feel like sharing?'

He'd included her, made her feel like an insider again. She admired his skill but wasn't about to succumb that easily. He'd have to work harder than that.

She gave him a wry smile. 'If you think that a direct

approach from the police is going to be the best way to force this contact to give her up and persuade her to cooperate?'

He leant back in his chair and sighed. 'Okay, you win. I think we both know the answer to that.'

'And you're going to need her to testify against Kemal on the kidnap attempt.'

'If she thought he was going down, why wouldn't she?'

'Tom, she knows these people. They've got a long reach and even longer memories.'

'We could offer to put her back on witness protection?'

'She's still going to need some persuading.'

They sat in silence for several moments, the hubbub of the pub reverberating around them. It gave Nicci a chance to observe him. His gaze darted about, sharp as a tack, taking everything in. He was a watcher and that told her he was probably a good detective. She already knew he was smart, not to mention manipulative. But he looked weary, dark shadows under his eyes; he was under a lot of pressure. That didn't stop her envying him. How she would love his job: a DI running the intel cell on a major investigation involving organized crime. The long hours and the stress wouldn't bother her. She'd never truly appreciated how much she'd loved the job until they booted her out.

Rivlin drained his glass. 'Fancy another?'

Nicci shook her head. 'I should go.'

'Why won't you have dinner with me?' His look was petulant; he didn't like to be refused. 'Look, I've worked all weekend, I've had a bollocking from the boss. I know you think I'm an arrogant tosser. And it's true, I am an arrogant tosser. But I'm hungry. And I eat too many meals alone. We don't need to talk about the fucking Kemals or Phelps or any of it. I just want to escape for a couple of hours and enjoy some agreeable company. I promise to be on my best behaviour.'

Halfway through his diatribe, Nicci started to smile. Okay, she knew she was being played. But Pascale was right: sod the consequences, she needed to do this.

She gave him an arch look. 'Italian or Greek? There's a very good Italian at the top of Essex Road not that far from where I live.'

He met her eye and grinned. 'Italian.'

41

The disguise held and Kaz Phelps left Broomfield Hospital at a quarter to eight without being recognized. She and Darius walked back to the car park in silence. As they'd left the Burns Unit he'd enquired if she was okay and she'd replied with a simple nod. But her pale, devastated face told another story.

Getting into the taxi she finally spoke. 'I need to go and see my sister. She lives in Southend.'

Darius started the engine. 'You got an address?'

'Not yet.'

Kaz's head was in a complete spin. Seeing her mother in such a state had given rise to a welter of conflicting emotions. And her sister was possibly the only person who would understand.

Natalie had her own place, that much she knew. But where exactly? Paul Ackroyd had said he'd visited her so she could ask him. That would be the easy option, but she hesitated. He was trying to use her. She glanced at Darius. The neon glow of the car park lights strafed his face. He'd tried to distance himself but she was still pretty sure he was keeping tabs on her for Paul.

Getting out her temporary phone – a prepaid burner that Paul'd given her – she used directory enquiries to find Glynis's number.

Glynis Phelps had been married to her cousin, Sean. They'd

never been friends exactly, but their shared history meant they'd always be allies.

By the time the cab left the hospital site and turned on to the main road, Glynis was on the phone.

'Kaz! What's going on? Are you okay?'

'Yeah. But I just seen Mum. She's not in a good way.'

'I know. Me and Natalie went over yesterday.'

'She never said.'

'It's the drugs. She don't remember much. She asked about you. But I didn't know what to tell her. Hospital said you discharged yourself. We didn't know where you was.'

'It's complicated. I'm gonna come over and explain. But first I gotta talk to Natalie. Can you text me her address?'

'Course. Y'know, I've had the old bill round looking for you. But don't worry, I fobbed them off.'

Kaz's stomach lurched. In her anxiety to sidestep Paul it hadn't occurred to her that the police would've questioned Glynis. Were they also monitoring her cousin's calls? Possibly. But it was too late now.

'You're a rock, Glyn. I'll get back to you, promise.'

'Take care, lovey. I'll text you now.'

Clicking the phone off, Kaz cursed her own stupidity. It should've been a simple matter, getting her sister's address, but she hadn't thought it through. Her brain was in a scramble and she needed to get a grip. This was the kind of elementary mistake she couldn't afford.

Making an effort to focus her thoughts, she stared out blankly at the eerie suburban road of detached houses picked out in hazy pools of lamplight. She'd always liked Chelmsford but the autumnal mist creeping across the river meadows gave the homes they were passing a spectral air and this fuelled her rising paranoia. Still, paranoia had its uses; it was a mindset that kept you safe. Joey's problem had always been that he was too blasé about these sorts of details, an error Kaz wouldn't repeat.

After a couple of minutes the phone buzzed with an incoming text. Kaz opened it and read out the postcode and house number to Darius, who tapped it into his satnav. Then, sliding the back casing off the phone, she removed the SIM. Would the police really be listening in to every call? She doubted they had the resources. Anyway, she didn't plan on staying long at her sister's. Even if they were on the case, she'd be in and out before they turned up.

The cab joined the A12 at a roundabout and as it accelerated up the slip road on to the dual carriageway she wound the window down, threw the phone out into the darkness and followed it with the SIM. From now on she'd take proper care.

Darius looked across at her. Leaving the urban fringes behind for the blackness of the open road, he could only glimpse her face when it was thrown into relief by the oncoming headlights. She was understandably upset and, he suspected, in shock. He'd learnt from the charge nurse that Ellie had suffered over 30 per cent burns. He wanted to offer words of comfort but settled for a conversational tone. 'She's your cousin?'

'What?'

'The one you called.'

'Oh. Yeah. Sort of cousin-in-law.'

'She's married to Sean? Paul's mentioned him, but I never met him. I hear he's in Spain.'

'I heard that too.'

'Couldn't he help you?'

'No.' The tone was curt and dismissive. She turned away.

'Sorry. I didn't mean to piss you off.'

After a moment he heard her sigh. 'You haven't. I just don't need twenty questions right now.'

'Sorry.'

They relapsed into silence and didn't speak again until they reached the outskirts of Southend.

Coming out of her reverie, Kaz turned to him. 'You any good at finding out stuff?'

'I don't know. Try me.'

'There's someone I need to find. Her name's Irina Koshkin. Her brother was shot at the funeral.'

'You've no idea where she is?'

'Her brother had a place in Berkshire, but she ain't there. I checked. I think she could be in London. She's got a cousin too, called Mika. My guess is she's staying with him.'

'You got a mobile number?'

'Her phone's been turned off.'

Darius puffed out his cheeks. 'I know a bloke who tracks people down. I'll talk to him.'

Kaz nodded her thanks. Her train of thought had already moved on.

The satnav led them to a sixties semi on the eastern edge of the town towards Shoebury. It was neat with a small garden and two tubs of pansies either side of the front door. This was not at all the kind of place Kaz had been expecting. In her previous life as a junkie, Natalie had lived in a squalid tower-block flat from which she rarely emerged. The notion of her sister as a gardener, tending her pots, struck Kaz as incongruous but also hopeful.

The cab parked a few doors down and she glanced at Darius. He smiled. 'I'll wait here.'

'Thanks. I don't plan on staying long.'

As she walked up the short front path the security light

over the porch came on. She rang the doorbell and heard the singsong chime echo through the house. The curtain in the living room window shifted and several minutes later a shadow appeared behind the frosted glass door.

Natalie opened the door. Gripping a towelling bathrobe tightly round her, she presented her sister with an irritated frown. 'Fucking hell, Kaz. You all right?'

'Yeah. But Mum isn't.'

'I know.'

As she stepped over the threshold, Natalie pulled her into a hug. Kaz clutched her sister's narrow frame. She'd come here intending to be strong. She was the big sister, that was her job. But something inside simply cracked and she couldn't hold on to the tears of rage and desperation any longer. They flooded out, her head dipped down on her sister's shoulder and she sobbed. Natalie stroked the back of her head. 'It's okay.'

'It fucking isn't!'

'Sssh, babes.'

Raising her head, Kaz swept her palm across her face. 'I'm sorry. I hope I haven't woken the baby.'

'It's fine. Come in the kitchen, I got some tissues.'

Natalie closed the front door and led the way down the hall.

The décor was plain; magnolia walls, a beige carpet. The place had a well-ordered homely feel. A baby stroller was tucked away in the recess under the stairs. Kaz followed her sister into the compact tidy kitchen, accepted a handful of tissues and blew her nose.

'Looks like you're ready for bed.'

Natalie gave her a faint smile. 'Not exactly.'

At that moment the door to the sitting room opened.

Kaz turned. 'Oh, sorry . . .'

The girl who stepped out into the hall was probably about

Natalie's age, elegant, with a mane of jet-black hair; she had on a tight leather bustier, a rhinestone-studded thong and little else. Kaz did a double take and her gaze flew back to her sister. It was only then she noticed that Natalie, like her friend, was wearing full make-up plus a sprinkling of glitter on her cheek-bones.

Natalie grinned. 'Your face, Kaz! This is my mate, Ling, we met at NA – she's my sponsor. Monday nights she joins me on my show.'

'Your show?'

'I got a show on the Net. I'm a cam girl.'

'What? You mean porn?'

'Well, sort of. I've built up a pretty good following. We strip off, dance around a bit. But really it's like a little club.'

'What sort of club?'

'I work through this site. Blokes want to fantasize they got a relationship with you. They make offers of how much they'll pay for you to do certain stuff. You only do what you're com-fortable with. I usually work four nights a week, once Finlay's tucked up in bed.'

'And it pays?'

'Oh yeah. How do you think I afford the rent on this place? I couldn't have gone back home to live with Mum.'

Kaz shook her head in horror. 'If I'd've known you was doing something like this . . .'

Natalie laughed and turned to Ling. 'She thinks she's cool. But she's such a fucking old woman, my sister.'

'Nat, it's porn.'

'It's acting. I'm my own boss. And actually we have a really good laugh.'

Ling tossed her hair and giggled. 'She's very talented.'

Natalie had let her bathrobe fall open and Kaz saw that she was wearing a tight corset fringed with lace and a thong.

Slumping down on one of the kitchen chairs, Kaz leant her elbows on the table and put her face in her hands. Her brain was desperately playing catch-up. Seeing Ellie, now this – the events of the last few days had finally caught up with her. She was a physical and emotional wreck.

On the way to Southend she'd been hatching some kind of grand plan to take care of her baby sister, to make up for all the neglect of the past. But clearly Natalie didn't need her help. She'd grown up, she was a mother and she could stand on her own two feet.

She patted Kaz's shoulder. 'You've had a rough time, mate. Fancy a nice cup of tea? Then we can discuss what we're gonna do about Mum.'

42

The restaurant was buzzy, the food delicious, they shared an excellent bottle of Montepulciano and by the time they got to the coffee Nicci realized that she was happy without being completely drunk. Tom Rivlin was an entertaining companion when he chose to be and they avoided any discussion of the job.

He amused her with a convoluted tale of his various efforts to become an athlete. When he first went to uni his ambition had been to play American football, but he was too willowy for a linebacker and, although he could run and tried to be a wide receiver, he turned out to be rubbish at catching the ball. Turning his attention to the triathlon, he'd made some headway. He could swim well enough and run, but had a tendency to muck things up by falling off his bike.

The stories he recounted of his youthful self were both funny and self-deprecating, which didn't exactly go with the reputation for arrogance. Moreover, his portrait of himself as a failed sportsman was belied by his physical appearance; he was lean and lithe as an athlete and Nicci concluded he must work hard at keeping fit.

Sitting back, she began to forget about the job and Stoneham and Karen Phelps and the web of favours and obligations that tied her to her old life as a police officer. She was just a woman in a restaurant, sitting across the table from a very attractive bloke who wanted to please her.

He talked with his hands; they were constantly in motion, fingers splayed or scooping the air to make a point – he couldn't keep them still. And she found herself smiling and laughing, sipping the wine, savouring the piquancy of the pasta sauce. It was what people did when they went out for a meal. You could even call it a date.

For a long time after Sophie's death she'd shut herself away. Divorced, bereaved, the last thing she'd wanted was to socialize. Time hadn't really healed the pain of her loss but it had muted it to a dull ache. It was loneliness that'd finally dragged her from her redoubt.

She'd gone out a couple of times with a cop from Hackney; he was good company. Then they'd slept together and it didn't work. He was awkward, uncomfortable in his own skin, embarrassed in the act. He was also a chain smoker and Nicci got the feeling he just wanted to get it over with so he could move on to the cigarette. She liked him but concluded that she didn't have the energy to take on the sexual education of a repressed middle-aged man.

For a while she'd returned to Rory. But her erstwhile colleague at SBA was an accident that should never have happened. The sex was proficient, occasionally passionate, but the man himself was a seething cauldron of stifled needs with an unstable temper. Nicci didn't much fancy the role of emotional carer to his damaged war veteran. So when he left the firm, she'd used it as an excuse to cut the connection.

But where had all this left her? Wasn't she yet another thirty-something woman with her own indelible scars, a desire for sex and companionship but little toleration for the flaws of potential partners? In idle moments she'd surfed a few dating websites but concluded that joining the desperate shagfest they seemed to promise really would drive her to despair.

Now she found herself wondering if a man like Tom Rivlin would even look twice at her if he didn't have an ulterior motive for wooing her. She doubted it. Still, to indulge in the fantasy, if only for a few hours, was pleasant enough.

He topped up their glasses with the last of the wine. 'All I've done is talk. You must be fed up with the sound of my voice.'

'It's restful.'

He gave her a quizzical look, only too well aware that sarcasm was her default setting.

'I read this article in a magazine about how women hate it when blokes take them out and then talk non-stop about themselves.'

Nicci laughed. 'At least you're not mad about football. Triathlons are quite interesting.'

'Quite interesting? That's a bit scathing. Right, now it's your turn. I'm going to shut up.'

'I don't think you could do that if you tried.'

'Oh, a challenge!'

He folded his arms and grinned.

Nicci shook her head and sighed. 'Don't torment me, Rivlin. I'm out of practice with all this male/female teasey games stuff.'

'Then tell me something about yourself you wouldn't ordinarily reveal.'

She took a sip of wine. 'I don't think you want to go down that road.'

'What was she called, your daughter?'

Nicci's gaze slammed into his. He'd caught her off guard well and truly. But his look was serious and full of concern.

She hesitated, but only for a second. 'Sophie.'

'That's lovely.'

She didn't know where to look or what to say. She'd been

having a good time, but now she felt intruded upon, invaded almost.

He reached out across the table. 'Hope you don't mind me asking.'

'Why the fuck are you asking?' She withdrew her hand.

'Because she's obviously such a big part of your life. If I'm going to know anything about you, apart from trivialities, I need to know about her.'

'Let's stick to trivialities. It's safer.'

'I can see I've upset you. I'm sorry.'

Nicci swallowed hard. She was damned if she'd cry. She drained her glass and set it down. 'Thank you for a nice meal. I'm going to let you pay because I'm sure you can put it on expenses: *Dinner with new chis*.' She got up and plonked her napkin on the table. 'Give my regards to Stoneham.'

He tilted his head and sighed. 'Nicci, don't do this. If I've been insensitive, I'm truly sorry.'

'It's me. Sometimes I can't . . .' She had to take a deep breath to steady herself.

Getting up, he beckoned the waiter. 'At least let me get you a cab.'

She allowed him to take her arm and shepherd her towards the cloakroom. While she collected her jacket, he settled the bill. She heard him asking the maître d' to call them a cab.

Determined to take care of herself, she pulled her jacket around her. 'No, I don't need a cab. I'll walk. It's not far.'

'Five minutes, madam.' The maître d' gave her a superior smile. He probably thought she was drunk.

Nicci ignored him and pushed open the door. Stepping out onto the pavement, she walked into a sharp breeze. There was a dampness in the air and the chill of approaching autumn. Nicci found the shock of it refreshing and took a couple of deep breaths. She hadn't been drinking that much lately, so maybe the wine had tipped her over the edge, loosened her emotions.

Rivlin came out of the restaurant behind her. 'Nicci, don't just walk off . . .'

She pivoted on her heel to face him. It was hard for her to say precisely what happened next. Did he touch her shoulder first, or did she put her arm round his neck? It seemed to all happen at once. She turned her face upwards – they kissed. Neither one hesitated or held back. She felt his arms close around her back as he pulled her towards him. He tasted of wine and she realized she'd spent the entire meal wanting exactly this. She could feel his energy and the rawness of his desire. It surged through her.

Some lads came strolling by and barracked them with a friendly cacophony of lewd comments and suggestive grunts. But neither of them took any notice. They continued to kiss until a black cab pulled up kerbside. Only then, when Rivlin finally released her, did Nicci notice that it was starting to rain.

43

'Talk to the old bill. Use them. I would.' Natalie placed a small ceramic cup of camomile tea on the table in front of Kaz.

'All they wanna do is revoke my licence. Put me back inside.' Picking up the tea, Kaz wrinkled her nose. 'What is this?'

'Camomile. It's great for chilling you out. I drink it all the time.'

Ling had returned to the sitting room to continue the show and she could be heard chatting and laughing against a musical backdrop.

Kaz gave her sister a baleful glance. 'She get you into all this?'

'Not really. I had some mates who'd done it before.'

'Yeah. Junkies.'

Natalie sighed. 'You've had a rough time so I'm gonna ignore the fact you're being completely snotty.'

'Doesn't it bother you, having a whole bunch of sleazebags out there wanking themselves off at the sight of you?'

'That's up to them. I don't see it. I'm a recovering addict, Kaz. I got a baby to support. I got no qualifications. I don't wanna live on benefits. I just wanna pay my bills and concentrate on keeping myself clean and sober, one day at a time.'

The voice was calm and contained but there was a fierce determination in her little sister's eye that Kaz had never seen before. She was only twenty. At that age Kaz had been in jail and still struggling. She found Natalie's maturity astonishing.

She gave her sister a ghostly smile. 'I never thought rehab worked, but it clearly has for you.'

'Rehab gives you a starting point, space and support. In the end you have to make the choice to save yourself. You of all people should know that.'

Sitting in an unfamiliar kitchen, drinking an odd herbal brew while her baby sister stood there like a lap dancer on her tea break, struck Kaz as bizarre. But then why had she come and what did she expect to find?

Taking a sip of tea, she frowned. 'Do you think Mum's gonna die?'

'Probably not. I talked to the doctor. He seemed quite optimistic. But it's gonna be a long haul. She's gonna need looking after and then somewhere to live. I don't place much faith in Brian.'

'I booted him out.'

'Good for you.' Natalie cradled the ceramic cup in both palms. She had a sad, faraway look. 'Problem is, Joey always took care of everything for her. That's what she's used to.'

'Joey had the money to do it. Push comes to shove, that's what it comes down to.'

Natalie shrugged. 'Is the house in her name or his? Was it even insured?'

'Don't know. But he was canny about all the business stuff. My guess is it's in her name.'

Natalie seemed about to speak, then she hesitated, took another sip of tea.

Kaz gave her a direct look. 'What?'

There was a deep crease in Natalie's brow. Under the bright kitchen lights, the glitter and the make-up made her features seem hard. She put down the cup and folded her arms. She appeared to be struggling with something.

Kaz watched her. 'Nat?'

A sigh, long and drawn out, was followed by a sorrowful shake of the head. Natalie turned to her. 'I got something I wanna give you.'

Before Kaz could question her further she disappeared into the hall and up the stairs. Music leaked through from the sitting room, a popular disco track from the eighties. Kaz let her gaze rove round the kitchen. There was a calendar stuck on the fridge with a magnet, the days and details of her sister's life.

On Mondays, Wednesdays and Thursdays there was a clown-face sticker. Finlay's nursery days? Under each one was a time and the initials NA. On Friday evening it said NA social with an exclamation mark. Narcotics Anonymous. Kaz had attended a few of their meetings herself, but never regularly. Then on Wednesday at two p.m. there was a scribbled note: L and T at gym. Ling and another friend maybe? Staring at the calendar, Kaz realized these were the bare bones of a life she knew nothing about.

She was pondering this when Natalie returned carrying a white padded envelope, A4 size, which she laid gingerly on the table. It was sealed and blank, slightly crumpled with dog-eared corners as though it had been shoved away somewhere in a drawer.

It was impossible to read the expression on Natalie's face. The eyes were wary with more of the hunted look Kaz associated with the old Natalie.

'What is it?' Kaz turned it over: no inscription of any sort.

Pulling the bathrobe round her tightly, Natalie settled in the opposite chair. 'Doctor Iqbal gave it to me. When he arranged for me to go to the clinic where I had Finlay.' She hesitated. 'It came from Joey.'

'Why haven't you opened it?'

She shook her head, batting the question away. 'You might be able to make some use of it?'

'What's inside? Money?'

'I've no idea. And I don't wanna know.' There was no mistaking the bitterness in Natalie's tone.

'Joey must have been in prison by then. Did he know you was pregnant?'

Kaz started to pull at the tag to open the envelope but Natalie grabbed her wrist. 'No! Just take it.'

Putting the envelope down, Kaz leant back in her chair. 'What the fuck, Nat? Joey found out you was pregnant, maybe Iqbal told him, so he wanted to help. Why have you got a problem with that? Because he killed Jez? He was still your brother.'

As soon as she said it, Kaz knew the answer. It slammed into her like a bolt.

There was a tremor in Natalie's hand as she stroked her cheek with her ring finger, gently rubbing away the glitter. Beneath the make-up she was pale.

Kaz swallowed hard as the realization sank in. 'Finlay's his, isn't he? He's Joey's baby.'

Natalie fixed her with a glassy-eyed stare. 'I want nothing from him.'

'Jesus, Nat. When did this happen? When you was at Woodcote Hall? Did he rape you?'

A morbid smile crept over her sister's features. 'Did you ever say no to Joey? Did you even try? Did anyone?'

Kaz put a hand over her mouth. She felt sick. It was so obvious – those piercing blue eyes, the blond hair – Finlay was the image of her dead brother.

Natalie shook her head. 'Joey had to be in control. You'd pissed him off royally. Having it off with some copper, is what he said.'

'He got that all wrong.'

Natalie's lip curled. 'He wanted to be sure I really loved him. That's what he told me.'

'Babes, I am so sorry.' Kaz could feel the tears running down her cheek.

'Don't be. Take the envelope and whatever's in it and fuck off and let me get on with my life.'

44

Stepping in from the misty chill of an autumn morning, an hour and a half before sunrise, a smiling Tom Rivlin joined the Met briefing for the planned raid on Sadik Kemal. Someone handed him a coffee and DS Amy Raheem introduced him to the Project Team from SCD7.

Raheem was brisk. 'You look happy. Does that mean you're off Stoneham's shit list?'

Rivlin grinned. 'Yeah, well, she's a fair boss. She's never pissed for long.' He didn't mention that the real source of his sunny mood at such an ungodly hour was the night he'd spent in Nicci Armstrong's bed.

He'd had his share of sexual encounters over the years, some more casual than others. But Nicci was a revelation. She was a woman with formidable defences and knowing even a little of her history he could understand why. When the barricades came down, a different person emerged. Once she'd made up her mind to let go, there'd been no holding back.

At first they'd both been shy and tentative but then it had turned into the most exciting sex he'd had since his first proper girlfriend. The wistful feeling left by that teenage romance had never gone away; they'd left home to go to different universities and agreed that it was better to move on. But that first taste of a desire that was more than lust had never left him. He'd used the word love on several occasions because he knew women liked to hear it. But did he really know what it meant? Connecting his emotions to appropriate words had always been an uphill struggle.

Riding in the back of a cab to his pre-dawn rendezvous with Raheem's team he'd tried to compose a text to Nicci. *Thank you* seemed a bit inadequate. *I had a great time* made him sound like a teenager. She'd probably gone back to sleep anyway and he didn't want to wake her. He scrolled through the range of emojis on his phone and decided not to go down that route. Eventually he gave up and slipped the phone back in his pocket. After he'd slept with a woman he usually waited a couple of days before calling her. He didn't want to seem uncool or creepy. But somehow, in this instance, that just didn't feel right.

He tried to distract himself by thinking about the job. Taking Sadik Kemal off the streets was possible because of his hard work and Stoneham was recognizing this by relenting from her previous stance and choosing him to go on the raid. Even if they couldn't hold the Turk for long, they could seize his computers, tablets and phones and take the house apart, which might give them something useful.

But as he struggled to focus, running through his mental checklist, he found his father's image floating into his head. And Nicci: his senses were still full of the taste and smell of her. Impulsively he pulled out his phone again, searched for an appropriate website, ordered a dozen red roses and sent them to her without a card at her office address. Over the top, maybe, but this was his dad's secret weapon and flowers had always brought a smile to his mother's face.

An hour later, sitting in the back of a police van crammed with burly suited-and-booted coppers, sweating in his stab vest, Rivlin began to regret this impetuous gesture. She'd hate it, she'd be embarrassed, she'd think he was a complete plonker.

With dawn breaking, the police convoy drew up outside a substantial detached Edwardian property in East Finchley. The heavy mob went in first. The oak front door came off its hinges after three swings of the ram. A couple of Dobermans, more yap and bared teeth than anything else, had to be contained and restrained. Sadik Kemal was led out in a tracksuit, hands cuffed, looking moderately pissed off.

Raheem came out of the house to where Rivlin was waiting politely beside one of the vans. 'Boss says come and join the party.'

Rivlin nodded his thanks and they began to walk back. 'Did Kemal say anything?'

'Possibly a curse word in Turkish. But make the most of this – he'll have an alibi by breakfast and his lawyers'll be threatening to sue for wrongful arrest before lunch.'

'We've got him on the back foot, though. It was a mistake, him going after Karen Phelps in person, and he knows it. We might get lucky and find the hospital security uniforms.'

Raheem shrugged. 'Last time we turned his brother over he got five grand compensation and a new front door.'

Rivlin smiled. 'Look at it this way: that won't have even covered his lawyers' bill. So we're still disrupting their operations.'

45

Most of the time, Paige Hollister was bored. She hadn't had a decent glass of wine in weeks and was subsisting on twenty Marlboros a day that she was bribing some care assistant to fetch for her. The old Jacobean manor, where she'd been incarcerated, was not far from Tewkesbury. Set above what the website called idyllic water meadows, it retained the air of a country house hotel, which it had formerly been. Now it housed – warehoused was more accurate, in Paige's view – rich reprobates whose addictions or mental health problems made them a social embarrassment.

The rooms were comfortable, the largely foreign staff a cross between care assistants and servants, and there was a team of medical professionals on hand 24/7 to deal with any kind of crisis. Paige had opted for equine-assisted therapy. She'd done some three-day eventing as a teenager and spending time in a field of horses seemed preferable to sitting in group therapy listening to a bunch of crazy plutocrats bitch and moan.

She'd managed for years on Xanax, but they'd taken her stash and prescribed a new regime of SNRIs, the administration of which was strictly controlled. The private American healthcare company that ran the place was well aware they were operating in a litigious world and if any of their charges came to harm they'd be slapped with an enormous lawsuit. As a result, every nook and cranny was covered by CCTV. It was impossible to even go to the loo without being under surveillance. But in spite of the many annoyances and restrictions on her freedom, Paige had to admit she was feeling better.

The howling fury that had nearly torn her apart when the police took her in for questioning after Robert's arrest had been labelled *a psychotic episode*. All Paige remembered was a murderous anger at being put in a room and bombarded with questions. She'd kicked off all right and that had soon put an end to their nonsense.

Since then she'd had plenty of time to reflect on her situation. She was missing Phoebe. Her parents sent pictures every day: ice-cream treats, an outing to the beach. But even in a few short weeks she'd begun to notice her daughter changing. The child needed to be back home and in school. She needed her life back, they both did.

Robert had not been in contact since his arrest. He seemed to blame her for his predicament, which was absurd. She'd been trying to save him from the consequences of his own folly. As a loyal wife, that was her job. And she might've succeeded if he hadn't been driven by an overwhelming compulsion to shag any slut who looked twice at him.

Early on in their relationship she'd sought some maternal advice on what to do about her fiancé's roving eye. Her mother had dismissed her concerns – men were like that. What mattered was the woman they married and came home to. It had taken Paige another ten years to realize this wasn't a viewpoint most women would share. Her own father was loving and kind, a man who'd kept his infidelities discreet and never allowed them to impinge on family life. And he adored the grandchildren. She wished Robert could be more like him.

Helen Warner occasionally strayed into her consciousness,

but she refused to feel any guilt. Helen's death was unfortunate. The woman had been a hypocrite, who, in spite of all the feminist claptrap she spouted, still used sex to get ahead. Even as a kid she'd played Robert, teased him, and Paige had been forced to watch. She had no regrets about discussing the threat Helen was posing to Robert and his career with Viktor Pudovkin. It was a ruthless world; Helen had made it plain that she was out to destroy Robert, and Paige couldn't be blamed for what happened as a consequence.

Although it was many years since she'd been on horseback, Paige had soon become proficient enough to be allowed out of the field on longer rides with a couple of other inmates and a groom in attendance. Her daily excursions had become the thing she looked forward to; it broke up the tedium of the day.

It was a chilly morning for late September but the lanes and hedgerows were starting to explode with autumn colour. As usual, they ended with a canter across the field behind the manor house. She'd been given no notice of Robert's visit. They clattered into the stable yard at the end of their ride and there he was. He was a total bastard who was threatening to divorce her, but even so the unexpected sight of him sent a rush of adrenaline through her whole body. He was standing, hands in pockets, chatting to one of the management team.

As she was helped off her horse, he came over wearing his I've-been-a-bad-boy-but-I'm-sorry smile.

She pulled off her helmet. 'Thought they'd put you in jail. Or is that just me?'

'I'm on bail.'

'Lucky old you. Can I get bail?'

'I would've come before, but—'

'That's such a cliché, Robert. Remember that little PR girl you used to fuck, wasn't she always warning you about clichés?'

'She was a colleague. I never slept with her.'

Paige shot him a cynical look. Same old lies, same boyish grin. But lying was his default setting, it was what had made him such a successful politician.

'Have you seen the boys? Alex sent me a text saying he's got a bad cold.'

'I'm in contact most days, but I hardly think they're going to thank me if I turn up at the school and embarrass them.'

Paige had to agree. Both her sons had dealt with their father's disgrace in a silent and manly way. Being away at school was the best thing for them and she was glad now that she'd stood out against sending them to some crap comprehensive so the party managers could demonstrate that their rising star was on message.

As they strolled from the stables back to the main house she remained silent. Was she glad to see him? Relieved even? She'd never admit it. He'd come with some kind of agenda, but she wasn't going to make it easy for him. She led him to the sitting room, where coffee was served. They each took a cup and then found a secluded corner in the conservatory.

Paige glanced up at one of the unobtrusive wall-mounted cameras. 'I don't know if the place is wired for sound, but they certainly get everything on camera.'

Robert looked up too and the presence of the camera seemed to inspire him. He sat down on a cane sofa and placed his face in his hands. 'I do know I've been an absolute fool.'

She took a chair opposite and settled back to watch his performance with a sardonic eye. His mea culpas were always well rehearsed. She said nothing.

'You know how much I've missed you, Paige?' He wiped a tear from the corner of his eye.

After all these weeks, he'd finally turned up. But what was

his game? The tears were real enough but this was a ritual they'd played out many times: his contrition, followed by a declaration of love. He needed her back onside – but why? She'd been almost certain that this time he really was dumping her. Speaking to Pudovkin, seeking his help to deal with the threat posed by Helen Warner, had been a calculated risk on her part. And when Robert had first found out what she'd done, he'd gone ballistic. It had turned into one of their classic rows and the memory was still bitter.

Now she simply smiled. 'You've changed your tune.'

'Darling, I was angry. You put me in a very difficult position. But you know I love you.'

'I put you . . . ? I saved you, you ungrateful bastard! That sly bitch was planning to go to the media. They'd have crucified you, but I found a way out. It was a risk worth taking.'

'Did you really not know what he'd do to her?'

She met his eye. This was ridiculous. Did he expect guilt? Was he so weak that she was supposed to carry the burden of all this?

'What the fuck do you care about Helen Warner? She was out to destroy you.'

'Pudovkin would've had me in his pocket.'

'You'd've still been in office and still had a career.'

'And say we win the election next year? What did you think was going to happen then? The man's ex-KGB, Paige! I love my country. Why on earth would I want to be a stooge for the Kremlin?'

His tone was peevish, but what she found more annoying was his naivety. He was the politician, how could he be so ignorant of how the world worked?

She fixed him with a disdainful glare. 'It wouldn't have come to that. Are you seriously telling me that once we made it to Number Ten there wouldn't have been ways and people to deal with a man like Viktor?'

Hollister shook his head wearily. 'Well, it's all gone tits-up, so I'm not going to argue the point now. The end result is' – he threw out his palms – 'it looks like I'm going to jail.'

'The lawyers have told you that?'

'More or less.'

'Can't they do anything?'

Hollister slumped back in his chair. 'Probably only serve a couple of years. Open prison, won't be too bad. I'll write my memoirs.'

'You're a bit young for that.'

He reached out and brushed her hand; the earnest look he gave her was one of his best, with a lick of hair tumbling over his forehead. 'I've disappointed you, my darling, and I'm so sorry. I've disappointed everyone. That fatal flaw.' His eyes glistened with tears. 'Got me in the end.'

Paige felt a lump in her throat. Seeing him defeated brought her no pleasure. She had a sudden desire to take him in her arms, stroke his hair and soothe him. He reminded her of one of his own sons, trying to be brave after taking a tumble off their skateboard. The hurt was obvious. And it ripped into her.

His gaze met hers; his dark eyes were pleading and his chin quivered. 'I just need you to forgive me. I was too ashamed to come before.'

'Oh, Robbie!' She got up and went to him, she couldn't help it. He pulled her onto his lap, enveloped her in a hug and squeezed her tight. Then, burying his face in her shoulder, he began to sob.

She kissed his hair, soft and glossy as ever. Stroked his damp forehead. He was such a beautiful man; he wasn't perfect, nowhere near, but he'd chosen her. He'd married her.

'Sssh, my sweet boy!'

'I'm lost without you.'

'I'm here. I'm always here, you know that.'

'I don't care about the career, I don't even care about going to prison. As long as I've got you and the kids.'

'Sssh! We'll get through this.'

'Will we?' He looked up at her, face streaked with tears and snot, like a lost child.

And Paige smiled down at him. She was his mother, his protector, his saviour. The bond between them was eternal, that was something a stupid little dyke like Helen Warner could never hope to understand. Marriage was a sacred vow. He was her life.

Pulling a tissue from her pocket, she wiped his face. 'There must be something the lawyers can do. Maybe you should get a new lawyer?'

'I have. A woman Henry recommended. Supposed to be really smart.'

'Well, what does she say?'

'The evidence is stacked against me. And you know what the media's like: they want blood.'

'Surely she can come up with something? If she's that smart.'

Robert Hollister gave his head a sorrowful shake. 'The only thing that might make a difference is if we could say Helen was sixteen when I first had sex with her.'

'So why don't you say that? She's not here to contradict you.'

'Me saying it is not enough.' His teary eyes sought hers. 'There has to be evidence to back me up.'

'What about if I said it?'

He tilted his head and his gaze drifted off across the room. 'I don't know if that would work.'

'It's worth a try, surely. Now that I'm better, I could make a statement to the police.'

'But you'd be lying. Perverting the course of justice, that's what they call it.'

'Who would know? And how would they prove it?'

His eyes brimmed with tears. 'You'd do that for me?'

'Of course I would.'

With a ghost of a smile he raised her hand to his lips and kissed her fingers. 'I don't deserve you.'

As she rested her head on his shoulder, he glanced at his watch. Mission accomplished; he'd be back in town by lunchtime.

46

Kaz Phelps remembered little of the journey back from her sister's. It was late, the country lanes full of inky black foreboding. Darius had dropped her off at the Ackroyds' house and, refusing Rafaella's offer of a hot drink, she'd gone straight to her room.

The image of Joey forcing himself on their baby sister was burning in her brain and she could find no way to expunge it. The fact that it was her fault made it all the harder to bear. She should've known that by challenging her brother she'd been putting Natalie at risk of some twisted reprisal. No wonder her sister hadn't turned up to his funeral. Kaz had thought it odd at the time. Then all hell had broken loose. It was only a week ago, but it seemed like an age.

She'd tossed the white padded envelope on the bed and stared at it. It felt like bundles of cash. The nausea was still churning in her gut and her head was in a spin. She thought about her small nephew, an innocent child. But with Joey's malevolent genes, what were Finlay's chances of a decent life? Would Natalie succeed in bringing him up free of the taint of the Phelps family? She was a recovering addict, scraping a living as a cam girl. The odds didn't look good.

Natalie had made it clear that she didn't want Joey's money or Kaz's help. But what good was that going to do? Grabbing the envelope, Kaz had ripped back the tab and tipped the contents onto the bed: three bundles of banknotes, vacuum-packed in plastic, and a small rectangular envelope. The notes were fifties, each bundle only a few centimetres thick. The envelope was blank. Kaz had torn it open. Inside she'd found a small dove-grey business card and a key. The card looked classy. The inscription, in a fine oblique font, read: Jonathan Sullivan LLB. There was an email address and a mobile phone number. Kaz had turned the card over in her fingers in search of any message, but the reverse was blank. The key was silvered metal, small and flat, maybe some kind of locker key?

She'd scooped up one of the bundles. It broke a memory of her father, who'd always dealt in cash and carried a fat roll of twenties in his trouser pocket. The fifty-pound note was slightly larger. On the back, it had two old blokes in wigs instead of the usual one and it matched the stash she'd found under the floorboards in her mother's bedroom.

Picking furiously at the seal on one of the bundles, she'd managed to peel back the plastic on the compacted banknotes. It was a hefty wedge, a lot of money. She'd tried to count it, but her tormented mind refused to focus. Eventually she'd given up.

Collapsing on the bed, she'd fallen asleep fully clothed. Her dreams were tense with menace. She was running from a man whose face she couldn't see. She felt the heat and bulk of him overwhelming her and she gagged on his acrid breath. Escape was impossible; her mouth was being stuffed, lungs filling with a thick tarry sludge and she was suffocating.

She awoke with a gasp and had to take several breaths to convince herself she was still alive. It was daylight. Getting up, she looked out of the window to discover a grey morning. The fields were sombre and a heavy slate sky was threatening rain.

After a long, cleansing shower she dressed herself in her

borrowed clothes and ventured downstairs. Rafaella was loading the dishwasher and Paul was sitting at the breakfast bar perusing his iPad.

He jumped to his feet, wreathed in smiles. 'All right, mate? You was late last night. Did you have a good kip?'

'Not bad.'

Rafaella painted on a smile. 'You look better. Some breakfast?'

Kaz was fairly sure she looked worse, hollow-eyed and pale. 'Just a coffee, thanks.'

Paul turned one of the bar stools round for her. 'Nah, you gotta eat, babes. Rafa bakes her own bread. Bit of butter and jam, it's ace.'

He was fussing around her, couldn't keep still, and Kaz got the impression he'd been waiting for her to come downstairs.

She sat on the stool he was offering. 'Maybe one slice then. I'm not that hungry.'

'Tough day yesterday.' He frowned. 'How was your mum?'

'Not too good. I think she'll be in hospital for a while.'

Paul shook his head with concern. He was making all the right noises, but Kaz couldn't help feeling suspicious. Had Darius reported back to him? Did he know she'd seen Natalie? Did they see her with the padded envelope last night? She'd taken pains to hide it under her sweatshirt.

He faced her, hands on hips, a restless energy pulsing off him. 'So what's on the agenda today and how can I help?'

Rafaella put a restraining hand on his arm. 'Let her be, Paul. She seen her poor mother, now she don't need no hassle.'

'Yeah, sorry.' He beamed and turned away.

Kaz watched him prowl the room as Rafaella made coffee and cut bread. Before taking her shower, she'd finally managed to count Joey's money. In the shrink-wrapped bundle she'd already opened there were two hundred notes, all fifties, which added up to ten grand. The other two packets looked identical, so thirty thousand pounds in total. A sizeable chunk of cash, and it had made Kaz think of the words Paul had used before: *the tip of the iceberg.* Had Joey Phelps died a rich man? Paul seemed to think so and it could well be true.

As she sipped her coffee, Paul patrolled the room and fidgeted with his phone. He'd never been a patient bloke – bags of energy but little self-restraint – and, in that respect, he hadn't changed. Kaz noticed Rafaella glancing at him, trying to subdue him with a look.

But he wanted answers and he didn't want to wait. He wanted to lean on her, Kaz could feel it. She wondered how insistent he would become. When would kindness and cajoling turn to arm-twisting? He was convinced that she could lead him to Joey's money and, with the card in her pocket, maybe she could. Who was Jonathan Sullivan LLB? A lawyer? Was he the clue, the contact that Paul was looking for? Should she share this information with him?

It would be all too easy, she decided, to be suckered by the Ackroyds' solicitude. But Paul was no different to her brother when you scratched the surface; both were ruthless gangsters who took what they wanted. And maybe they had been business partners who'd fallen out, but did that make Paul more entitled than her to whatever assets were out there? Kaz decided not.

Having survived one of the worst weeks of her life, she was in no mood to trust anyone. So she accepted a slice of home-made bread and jam from Rafaella with a smile while keeping a wary eye on Paul.

His phone chirped with an incoming text. Paul scanned it

and shook his head ruefully. It looked like he was having a bad day.

But turning to Kaz he managed a grin. 'Rafa's right. I don't wanna hassle you. I just gotta pop out. Bit of business. But when I get back, maybe we can make some plans. 'Cause, y'know, your mum's gonna need somewhere when she gets out of hospital.'

'Fine.' She gave him a reassuring smile.

Finishing her breakfast, she watched from the window as the BMW X5 roared out of the drive. He didn't stop to shut the gate.

Rafaella shook her head and chuckled. 'Men! So impatient.'

As she disappeared out of the kitchen door to close the gate behind him, Kaz made a split-second decision. Picking up the house phone, she quickly scrolled through the address book, found a number for the local taxi firm and ordered a cab.

Then she headed upstairs to her room. She got out the down jacket Rafaella had lent her, stuffed the three bundles of cash in the inside pockets, put on her trainers and waited.

Fifteen minutes later a taxi pulled up in the lane outside and hooted. Kaz trotted down the stairs. A puzzled Rafaella emerged from the laundry room with a basket of damp washing.

Kaz gave her a big smile. 'Listen, I'm gonna go round and see my cousin, Glynis.'

'But you don't need to go by cab. Paul will take you. He'll be back any minute.'

'Nah, I don't wanna be a bother. You two have been running round after me enough.'

'But is it safe? Paul will not be happy with me if I let you—'

'I'll be fine. Don't worry.' Kaz pulled her into a quick hug. 'You done enough, Rafa.' She paused for a moment; gazing into those dark Spanish eyes she could see why Paul had fallen for this woman. A cascade of conflicting feelings surged through her: did she want Rafaella or did she simply want to be her? She smiled wistfully. 'He's a lucky bastard. I'll see you later, okay.'

'But—'

Kaz was out of the front door before she could raise further objections.

Crunching down the gravel drive, opening and closing the five-bar gate, Kaz felt a rising sense of elation. Now she had some serious money in her pocket, it gave her what she needed: options and a real chance to escape all her pursuers, not just the police and the Kemals but also Paul and Rafaella. She wasn't sure where she was headed, but she knew one thing for certain: she wasn't coming back.

47

Nicci Armstrong wandered into the offices of SBA shortly before midday. She was in an amiable mood despite having spent over two hours sitting in the Qassims' kitchen, waiting for her charge to appear. Turki bin Qassim had been there when she'd arrived at nine a.m. and had said that his wife definitely wanted to go shopping.

After he'd retreated to his study, Nicci had worked her way through a pot of coffee prepared by the maid. This time she'd had the foresight to bring her iPad with her. She'd surfed the Net for a while, but her thoughts kept drifting back to Tom Rivlin. It hadn't been her intention to sleep with him. The situation had sort of evolved, she wasn't quite sure how. Had she been drunk? Well, tipsy enough to loosen her inhibitions. But she'd still been in control. Was it something she'd wanted to happen? Definitely. If she was honest, she'd wanted it more or less the first time she met him.

He was far shyer than his arrogance had led her to believe. To begin with, he'd been polite, asking her several times, as he unbuttoned her shirt, if this was okay. She'd replied by dragging him into the bedroom and shoving him on the bed. After that, they'd both relaxed and giggled a lot. His playfulness surprised her – even more so when it turned to full-blown passion. It had felt so easy just to allow herself to be swept up in the moment; it had been a very long time since anything this exciting had happened to her.

But when she awoke in the morning he was gone. And as she stood in the shower, washing the smell of him from her skin, she knew that she needed to rein in her expectations or she could end up getting seriously hurt. It had been a one-night stand following a pleasant dinner, a dinner that, for Rivlin, would've had a purely professional purpose.

She wasn't his type, of that she was fairly certain. She imagined him with someone younger and unscathed: a gym bunny, bright-eyed and bushy-tailed, who could run a marathon and had a good sense of humour. Nicci had been through the emotional wringer; a vitriolic divorce and a dead child had squeezed the optimism out of her. She felt old and used up before her time. Rivlin clearly liked sex as much as the next man, but he also had a certain pragmatism about him. She couldn't see him embarking on a relationship with a woman like her, a lonely woman hollowed out by grief.

When Turki bin Qassim eventually wandered into the kitchen, he'd seemed surprised that Nicci was still there. He had informed her, in his usual off-hand manner, that Ayisha had changed her mind. Nicci couldn't be bothered to be annoyed. She'd simply headed back to the office.

Walking into the reception area at SBA the first thing she saw was an enormous bouquet of red roses sitting on the end of Alicia's desk. She gave the receptionist a nod. 'Nice. New boyfriend?'

'You tell me. They're for you.'

This stopped Nicci in her tracks. She stared at the flowers: a dozen tight scarlet buds nestling in green leaves and wrapped in cellophane with a matching bow. It was absurd. What kind of bloke sent roses nowadays?

'Is there a card?'

Alicia shook her head.

Pascale drifted over from the coffee station and gave Nicci a teasing nudge. 'I guess you took my advice.'

Nicci scowled. She hated her private life being exposed. 'Just put them somewhere, Alicia. Maybe in the conference room? I got no space on my desk.'

Pascale and Alicia exchanged looks, which Nicci ignored. She was striding quickly away to the safety of her own corner when she heard Blake's voice.

'Nic, you got a minute?' He was standing in his office doorway.

Turning, she headed his way. She couldn't help noticing he looked weary and worn down. He gave her a tepid smile as she followed him into the office. Sprawled in the leather armchair, right ankle balanced on his left knee, was a bald-headed bloke with a beard. All he needed was a ring in his ear and he would've looked like a pirate. He got up.

Blake made the introductions. 'Nicci Armstrong. Craig Naylor, our new head of security.'

A second surprise of the morning and she'd only been there five minutes.

Naylor offered a firm handshake and a smile. 'I'm wondering if our paths might've crossed back in the day. I was a DS and also a Federation rep for ten years.'

Nicci looked him up and down; the suit, the manner, the handshake; he reminded her of most of the old-school, middle-rank, can't-be-arsed detectives she'd ever met.

'Maybe.'

'Didn't have the beard when I was in the job. Once I retired I thought, well, why not?' He chuckled as he stroked his chin, but the eyes remained chilly.

Nicci glanced at Blake. He seemed decidedly uncomfortable, jiggling the change in his trouser pocket. She wondered what was going on. This new appointment hadn't even been mentioned; it was, to say the least, precipitous.

Naylor, in contrast, was totally at ease. 'We've been going through the client list. Simon tells me you've been helping out, looking after Turki bin Qassim's wife.'

'I've been to the house, hung around. But I haven't actually met her yet. She hasn't come out of her room.'

'What do you make of him?'

'Treats me like the hired help, which I guess is what I am.'

Naylor gave her a wry smile. 'Yeah, Simon said you're not keen on security work.'

'I don't mind the work. I'm not so keen on some of the clients.'

'HNWIs can be tricky. Nice to meet you, Nicci. I'm sure we'll work well together.'

The dismissal was abrupt. Nicci glanced at Blake, who avoided her gaze and continued to stare out of the window. She walked out of the office and crossed the open-plan room towards her own workstation. Her easy mood had evaporated. What the hell was going on?

Eddie Lunt was lounging at his desk, sipping coffee from his outsized thermal mug. 'Met the new gaffer then?'

Nicci shot him a look. 'Head of security.'

Eddie shrugged.

'What is going on, Eddie?' It annoyed her that he always seemed to know far more than her.

'Hasn't Simon talked to you?'

'Clearly not.'

He took another slug of coffee and Nicci noticed that his usual cheerful demeanour was missing.

Naylor's attitude was certainly confident and he hadn't shown Blake the deference she would've expected. 'You saying he's not just head of security, he's more than that?'

Eddie inhaled and placed his mug on the desk in front of him. 'I'm not saying anything. It's not my place—'

'But what?'

'Well, after he rocked up this morning, I done a bit of digging. Contact of mine knows a lot of ex-cops in the security business. He reckons Naylor used to be a bodyguard for an old friend of ours.'

'Who?'

'Viktor Pudovkin.'

Their eyes met. A shiver of dread ran up Nicci's spine. 'Does Simon know this?'

'I can't believe he doesn't.'

48

The taxi had dropped Kaz at Chelmsford station. She boarded a London-bound train, settled in a window seat and, as she watched the swathes of Essex countryside flashing by, she considered her situation. Since her brother's funeral she'd been shot at, burnt out of her family home and almost kidnapped by a scummy Turkish gangster who seemed to want to teach her some kind of lesson. However, the lesson she'd learnt was that she only had herself to rely on – more so now than ever. Everyone else had their own agenda and the safest policy was to trust no one.

As trees and fields gave way to bricks and flyovers she wondered what she should do next. For the first time in the long and difficult weeks since Joey's death she was completely alone and free. She'd escaped them all and that filled her with a sense of euphoria. Even the knowledge that she was being hunted couldn't puncture her mood. The police were still looking for her. The Kemals were unlikely to give up, and now Paul Ackroyd would probably be joining her list of pursuers. But as the train sped her on her way, none of that seemed to matter. She had no firm plan but she realized that could work to her advantage. The more random her behaviour, the less likely it was that any of them would catch up with her.

The train pulled into Stratford station, the last stop before Liverpool Street, and Kaz found herself gazing out at the vast edifice of the Westfield shopping centre as it slid into view with its tantalizing electronic billboards and the Olympic Park beyond. Seized by an impulse, she jumped up from her seat, grabbed her jacket and slipped through the sliding doors just as they were closing. She walked along the platform, up the stairs and crossed the bridge into this retail mecca. Built whilst she was in jail, she'd never visited the place before. But with money in her pocket, the first thing she wanted was to feel comfortable in her own skin again, not a ragamuffin in borrowed threads.

She spent the next two hours blitzing her way from one upmarket boutique to the next. She bought jeans from Armani, underwear from Calvin Klein, several shirts from a snotty shop assistant who looked her up and down as if she were a tramp, a cashmere jumper, an eight-hundred-quid leather jacket, a pair of snaky ankle boots and Ray-Bans with tortoiseshell frames. With a small suitcase on wheels to carry her new wardrobe and a canvas satchel from Fossil, she finally stopped for a cappuccino.

Scanning the sea of passing faces, she felt safely anonymous. London was home to every tribe and ethnicity. Odd snatches of incomprehensible languages drifted her way as she relaxed and let the human shoal wash around and past her.

Taking the dove-grey business card from her pocket, she considered her next move. Finding a public telephone proved a challenge, but with some advice from the information desk she eventually tracked one down to a hidden nook on a wall next to the toilets.

Inserting a fifty-pence coin – it was all the change she had – she dialled the number on the card and waited. It rang three times.

'Yeah, hello.' The tone was brisk.

'Is that Jonathan Sullivan?'

'Yep, who's this?'

'Karen Phelps.'

There was a deafening silence on the line.

'I'm Joey's sister.'

'Yeah, I know who you are. Listen,' he sighed, the annoyance in his voice unmistakable, 'we can't talk on the phone. You must know that.'

'Can we meet?'

Another long pause.

'You in London?'

'I can be.'

'Okay,' he huffed. 'Say tomorrow morning, ten a.m. at Liverpool Street station, outside the ticket office.'

'How will I—'

'I'll recognize you.'

The line went dead; he'd hung up. Kaz glanced around her. Two women loaded with shopping bags wandered into the nearby toilets; they seemed harmless enough, but at the sight of them her buoyant mood crashed. Somehow they filled her with an eerie sense of foreboding. Here she was, lost in a sea of strangers, and men were trying to kill her. This contact of Joey's, who the hell was he? It was obvious she'd taken him by surprise. Would he even turn up, or was the arrangement a brush-off? Worse still, had she been set up? Would she be standing outside the ticket office with a target on her back?

Although she fought it, she could feel herself spiralling into paranoia. The elation of her escape was gone. Her brother may have left her a lifeline but it was tenuous, to say the least. And if this lawyer had expected a call from anyone, it would've been Natalie. But, he knew who she was, which was something.

Struggling to pull herself together, Kaz meandered around

but the crowds and the shops brimming with glittery goods had begun to oppress her. All of a sudden she was bone-weary. She felt like a refugee, banished from her own land, forced to keep moving, but with no safe haven in sight.

She'd thought about finding a hotel when she was on the train. But that carried risks. The problem was, could she do it and remain under the radar? There was only one way to find out.

Squaring her shoulders, she strolled into the foyer of the Holiday Inn with as much insouciance as she could muster. She chose it because it was there, right in the shopping centre, and it was big, which improved her chances of anonymity.

The receptionist was a fresh-faced young man with a goatee beard and a wide professional smile. 'Can I help you, madam?'

'I'd like a room. Two nights.' Kaz lifted the Ray-Bans and rested them on top of her head. Her hair was still singed from the fire, but she hoped that with her new purchases she looked like any well-heeled tourist.

'We have both standard and executive rooms available.'

'What do I get for executive?'

'Basically a king-sized bed. Free Wi-Fi, flat-screen TV and twenty-four-hour room service are all standard.'

'Okay, the executive. I'll be paying cash.'

'Absolutely fine, madam. Provided you can show us some ID. Either a passport or credit card.'

He blinked at her, the smile fixed in place. Kaz delved into her satchel. This was the moment of truth. She knew they'd ask her for ID so she had to take the risk. She pulled out a credit card.

The receptionist took it and glanced at it. 'Rafaella – that's my sister's name.'

Kaz met his gaze directly. 'My mother was Spanish.'

What would he do next? It was only a confirmation of her ID, so in theory there was no need for him to put it through the system or ask for a PIN. But what if it was the hotel's policy to check?

He grinned and simply handed the card back. '*Lindo nombre.*'

Kaz smiled. 'Sadly, I never learnt to speak it. My dad was a bit funny about all that.'

He shrugged and glanced at his screen. 'Two nights will be two hundred and ninety pounds.'

Reaching into the pocket of her brand-new jeans, Kaz extracted a small wedge of folded notes. She peeled off six fifties. The receptionist took the money, gave her change, a receipt and a magnetized key card.

'Room 91, third floor. Do you need help with any luggage?'

'No thanks.'

'The lifts are over there. Enjoy your stay, Mrs Ackroyd.'

As she slipped the Ray-Bans back on her nose it felt, at least in that moment, as though she really was Mrs Ackroyd. For a second time the impersonation had worked. And as she walked to the lifts she wondered idly if it was more than just a mask to hide behind. It was a different form of escape, one which enabled her to stop thinking about who she really was: Kaz Phelps, a miserable slag on the run, alone, friendless and hunted.

49

After the excitement of the dawn raid, Tom Rivlin had spent the rest of the morning hanging around. Sadik Kemal was arrested and taken to Paddington Green police station for interrogation. It was the Met's show; a Project Team from SCD7 had been targeting the Kemals for nearly a year and they had the lead. But, on top of that, the National Crime Agency had elbowed its way into the operation; they were investigating the Kemals' wider connections with the Turkish Mafia. Two slickly suited senior officers from their Organized Crime Command had vied with the Met for first crack at questioning the suspect. After a bit of horse-trading, the Met had won.

Amy Raheem got Rivlin into the interrogation suite to witness the proceedings. He stood at the back, watching the bank of monitors over the shoulders of his seated colleagues.

Raheem's boss, a grizzled DCI addressed by everyone as Mac, sat in the centre. It was his gameplan that the two officers conducting the first round of questioning followed. Not that it got them very far.

Sadik Kemal lounged back in his chair, his high-priced brief at his side, and he answered every question put to him with a languid, 'No comment.'

After about half an hour he finally said something different: 'I gotta piss.'

A fifteen-minute break was called, during which the two

OCC suits persuaded Mac to let them have a go. No one, at that point, seemed about to acknowledge Essex's interest in the proceedings.

Rivlin wandered down the corridor to the coffee machine with Raheem. He couldn't stop yawning. Turning out before dawn, not to mention very little sleep, was beginning to take its toll.

Raheem gave him a sidelong glance. 'Bet you're glad you came.'

'I should phone Stoneham, keep her in the loop.'

Raheem nodded and left him to it. What he really wanted was to check his phone for any message from Nicci. But there was none. He knew those stupid flowers had been a mistake. He sent a quick text to Stoneham: '*Nothing to report.*'

The second round of questioning by the OCC suits proved as futile as the first. Sadik Kemal savoured his coffee, considered his fingernails and continued to wearily repeat: 'no comment' in the appropriate places.

A lunch break was called. All the officers involved adjourned to a meeting room to discuss the impasse. Burgers were ordered in. Rivlin sat at the back once again, quietly consuming his. Raheem sat beside him eating a healthy home-made salad.

As the discussion maundered on, Rivlin tuned out. He thought about Nicci and what he should do next. If he called her, would she interpret that as pushy? Flowers, calls, he didn't want to come over like a stalker. Possibly a text was better – short, less margin for error. But he needed to come up with something cool and pithy. He was considering this when he heard his name spoken.

It was Mac: 'Anything that Essex would like to offer, DI Rivlin?'

All eyes turned towards him. He saw Raheem smirking. She knew that he hadn't been paying attention.

Setting his burger down and dusting off his fingers with a napkin he bought himself a few seconds. 'Er, well, we think that the Kemals' weak spot is that this would appear to be a personal vendetta against Karen Phelps.'

'Why are you assuming it's personal as opposed to rival crime syndicates falling out over turf or goods?' It was the younger of the two OCC suits; he'd removed his jacket, loosened his tie and was wearing a sullen look.

Rivlin shrugged. 'Sadik took the risk of going after her himself.'

'Isn't that just his arrogance? Proves nothing. Their first attempt they hired in an Albanian shooter.'

Rivlin met the OCC officer's eye. They were about the same age and Rivlin wondered if he should be aiming for an NCA job and a smarter suit instead of vegetating in Essex. The OCC guy was clearly frustrated by the failure of their own round of questioning and was looking for a ruck. Ordinarily, Rivlin would have obliged, but he was tired and his heart wasn't in it.

He simply smiled. 'You could be right.'

Mac had been watching the standoff with interest. He rapped the table with his index finger. 'Okay, Rivlin. The offence we've nicked him for happened on your patch. You're up next. You and DS Raheem.'

Rivlin only had time to collect a file from his briefcase before following Raheem into the interview room. Names and time were stated for the record and Tom Rivlin finally found himself eyeball to eyeball with Sadik Kemal.

'What happened in Tottenham, Mr Kemal?'

The Turk gave him a surly look. 'No comment.'

Rivlin was only too aware of all the hidden faces watching the monitors, judging his performance.

'I'm not talking this week. I'm talking about back in the summer. Karen Phelps really made a fool of you and your brother, didn't she?'

'No comment.'

'As you may know, the Phelps family are from Essex and we've had quite a few dealings with them over the years. Terry Phelps; Joey, his son, recently deceased. But I tell you something, Mr Kemal, Karen is the one to watch, always has been.'

The Turk's eyes bored into Rivlin and the look was one of total disdain. Most of the criminals Rivlin had interviewed in the past tended to crumble or become self-pitying once they were cornered. But Kemal was in a different league.

Rivlin held his gaze and ploughed on. 'She was a junkie as a kid, she's done jail time, but she's clever and tough, turned her life around and went to college. For my money, she's smarter than Joey.'

The lawyer cleared his throat. 'And what is your question in relation to the alleged offence, Inspector?'

Leaning back in his chair, Rivlin took his time. 'Well, it's a bit vague really. I was wondering if you know what she's doing now?'

'No comment.'

'What do you think she's up to? Doesn't it worry you?'

'No comment.'

'You see, Mr Kemal, we've tried on several occasions, since the shooting at her brother's funeral, to offer her police protection. But she's not interested. You have to ask yourself why, don't you?'

The look of boredom had disappeared. The Turk fixed Rivlin with a hard stare. It felt for a moment as if he was actually about to reply to this. Then he gritted his teeth. 'No comment.'

'She obviously believes she can take care of herself. She doesn't need us. And let's face it, she's right. There she was, in a hospital bed, and you still couldn't get her. Two big tough blokes chasing an injured, barefoot girl and you blew it.'

Sadik's lip curled. 'No comment.'

'I think we can agree that you've underestimated her, can't we?'

The Turk inhaled and snorted out. 'No comment.'

Resting his elbows on the table, Rivlin smiled. 'You see, I think she's out there biding her time. Just because she's a woman, you see her as weak – and that's a lethal mistake on your part. Three cracks you've had at her. She's beaten you every time. But she's got to be pretty angry, wouldn't you say?'

Sadik Kemal was leaning back in his chair, but his body had become rigid. An electric tension had replaced the previous atmosphere of languor in the room.

Rivlin leant forward and glared at the gangster. 'You've failed, Mr Kemal. Miserably. And you know what, you're the target now. You, your wife, your kids, your brother and his family. You won't have to go looking for Karen Phelps. All you'll have to do is look over your shoulder. She'll be coming for you.'

Without warning, the Turk erupted from his seat, kicking away the chair. Face contorted with fury, he slammed his fist on the table in front of Rivlin. 'That fucking bitch! I see her in hell if she lays one fucking finger on my kids! I tear her fucking liver out and feed it to my dogs!'

He picked up his chair and smashed it against the wall. The door flew open and uniformed officers piled in. Kemal was restrained and dragged off to the cells shouting: 'Fucking bitch! I fucking kill her! She is fucking dead, I slit her fucking throat myself!'

As the commotion subsided, Raheem turned to Rivlin and grinned. 'Well done. One nil to Essex, I reckon.'

50

Sitting towards the rear of the coffee shop with her back to the wall, Kaz had a good view of all comers. She was off the grid, she'd eluded both the cops and her pursuers, but the flip side of her freedom was a growing sense of emptiness and longing. Her sister didn't want to know her. Everyone else simply wanted to use or abuse her. She wondered what Irina was doing at that moment. It had always felt to Kaz as though there was a special bond between them, but maybe that was just an illusion. Irina had made no attempt to contact her. She must've seen the news, heard about the fire. Or maybe not?

Since the brief telephone call to Joey's supposed lawyer, Kaz's mood had become bleak. The exhilaration of escape had evaporated and all she could do was brood. They wanted her dead, that's all she really knew. These men, their anger, their cruelty demanded that she be punished, tortured – probably for their pleasure – then killed. How was anyone supposed to deal with that sort of hatred? What else could she do but run? Relying on the police to protect her felt way too risky. Was she scared? Foolish not to be. But giving in to fear wasn't an option either. So where did that leave her? Was this what her future would be like – an anonymous fugitive, hiding in a sea of strangers? Money had helped her get away but now what?

She watched the steady drift of afternoon shoppers coming and going; drinking, eating cake, some weary, others gleefully examining their purchases. It made her nostalgic for a mundane life full of ordinary pleasures. But had her life ever been like that? In one way or another she'd always been on the run from someone or something – or herself. Even during her time as an art student in Glasgow, she'd been on the witness protection scheme and hiding behind a false identity. It crossed her mind that she could score some drugs and find respite in chemical oblivion, or simply get drunk. But she knew if she went down that road again she truly would be damned.

Her thoughts skittered back to the hospital: the panic when she recognized Sadik Kemal and the rush of adrenaline as she ran from him. These bastards had tried to shoot her, burn her, kidnap her. Okay, she'd upset their macho pride – she'd had to, to protect a friend – but did that give them the right to hunt her down like this? Even at a distance, she could sense their enmity and the boundless anger that fuelled it. Her father had been a man like that: never forget, never back down, always a destroyer.

All she'd wanted to do was bury her brother and get on with her life. A week had gone by since she'd stood at his graveside with Irina, with Yevgeny – people who'd become her friends. But that was history. Now she was alone and on the run, and it was all down to the Kemals.

She thought of her mother. Seeing Ellie in such distress had stirred something visceral in Kaz. The desire to protect her, in spite of all their past discord, was there and impossible to ignore. And Natalie, struggling with a child born of incest. Kaz could only imagine how that felt.

But as the arguments and resentment continued to spin in her brain, Kaz gradually became aware of a fizzing fury in the pit of her stomach. And it was rising. These slags had left her no option; she had to find a way to fight back. She was a

Phelps after all and the ghost of Joey haunted her. His voice, his laughter – she had few waking moments when they weren't lurking somewhere in her mind. He'd always wanted her back in the family firm and for her to accept who she really was. Why had she wasted so much energy resisting him? To impress a lover? A posh bitch who'd dumped her, and was now dead.

Staring into space, she was ruminating on this when she noticed the nervous, bird-like figure of Glynis Phelps hovering in the doorway of the cafe. Raising her hand, Kaz waved. Seeing her, Glynis smiled and tottered over on her ridiculously high heels. They were cousins by marriage and couldn't be more different but, in her current predicament, Kaz knew the only person she could rely on was Glynis.

She got up and drew her tiny cousin into a hug. 'Thanks for coming, Glyn.'

'I've had that Paul Ackroyd banging on me door, so I knew you'd done a flit.'

'Sorry about that.'

'I don't trust him, Kaz. He's a lairy bugger.'

'I don't trust him either. Let me get you a coffee.'

'Black, please. I'm trying to cut down.'

Kaz smiled at the petite figure settling in a chair. 'Cut down? There's nothing of you as it is.'

Glynis shot her an anxious look. 'I couldn't stand it if I became obese. Your heart, cancer, diabetes – it increases your risk of all them things.'

Deciding not to argue the point, Kaz went to queue at the counter. Glancing back, she watched her cousin take out a compact and check her make-up. She put the compact away, then took it out to check again. Glynis was a rattling bag of nerves, engaged in a constant battle to get through each day. She'd never been a confident woman and the years she'd spent as the punchbag of a brutal husband hadn't helped. Kaz had dispatched Sean, saving them both from his violence; it was the secret they shared and the bond between them.

Presenting Glynis with her coffee, Kaz sat down in the opposite chair. Glynis reached out and stroked her arm.

'Lovely jacket. Feel that leather, so soft.'

Kaz smiled. 'I lost everything in the fire. So I been doing a bit of shopping.'

'You look much better.'

'Hair's a bit frizzy, but I'm getting there.'

'You said on the phone you needed some help.' Glynis fiddled obsessively with the rings on her fingers, twisting, repositioning; her hands were never still.

'I don't like to involve you, but I'm in a fix.'

In spite of her cousin's edginess, Kaz found comfort in her company. They'd never been friends. Their conversations had always been awkward. But Glynis had a good heart.

She shot Kaz a nervous glance. 'So you went to see Natalie?'

'Yeah. Last night. Thanks for the address.'

'Was she okay?'

Kaz sighed, she'd been hoping to skirt round the subject of her sister without saying too much. 'Yeah.'

Glynis sipped her coffee. 'I'm guessing she told you about the boy.' For all her neuroses, she was sharp as a tack.

'She tell you that?'

'She didn't have to. I phoned her this morning. She was in a right old stew. I'm worried about her, Kaz.'

'She more or less told me to get lost.'

'Well, she would, wouldn't she?'

'Would she? Why?' Kaz frowned. She was thinking about Jez, the boyfriend of Natalie's that Joey threw off a balcony. But she decided not to mention that.

''Cause she's ashamed and she thinks everyone's gonna judge her. Especially you.'

'Me? What, she thinks I don't know what my brother was like? The whole thing makes me feel sick.'

'Exactly.'

'Yeah, but that don't mean—'

'You think the look on your face don't give you away? Just now, soon as I mentioned her, you was uncomfortable.'

'Oh come on, Glyn. That don't mean nothing.'

'You sure about that?'

'Okay, I was shocked. And yeah, she would've clocked that from my face.'

'Be honest. You was disgusted.'

'Not with her! For fuck's sake, what am I being accused of here?'

Kaz glared belligerently across the table. But Glynis held her ground.

'I'm not accusing you. I'm only trying to make you see.'

'See what? What the fuck am I not seeing?'

'How it really is for her.'

The two women stared at each other. Kaz got the impression that Glynis had been bottling this up for some time.

'She loves that kiddie so much, Kaz. She's desperate to protect him. But she's ashamed, so ashamed, and she's got nowhere to go with that. It eats away at her.'

'Has she told Mum that he's Joey's?'

'Whadda you think?' An unexpectedly cynical smile crept over Glynis's timid features.

Kaz exhaled. 'Look, I'm not stupid. I get it. She's pushing everyone away because she don't trust them not to judge her. But as far as I'm concerned, she's got nothing to be ashamed of. I know Joey. And I know he did it 'cause of me, 'cause I pissed him off. Anyone should feel guilty, it's me.'

'You need to tell her that.'

'I will. When I get the chance.'

They sat in silence for a full minute. Kaz stared into space. She was beginning to think that getting in touch with Glynis had been a mistake. It was a measure of her desperation.

Glynis twisted a heavy gold signet ring round and round. Eventually she sighed. 'You going back on witness protection?'

'No one's offering that choice. It's jail or run.'

'How you gonna manage?'

'I'll manage. But I need you to keep me posted. About Mum. And about Natalie.'

'Thought that might be the case.' Glynis reached into her large handbag and brought out a small plastic carrier. 'I stopped off at different shops and got you a couple of burners. Paid cash. No way they can be traced back to you.'

Brightening, Kaz peered in the bag at the two prepaid phones. 'You're brilliant, Glyn. Thanks.'

'Being married to Sean all them years, I picked up a few tricks.'

'More than a few.' Kaz grinned.

Glynis stopped fidgeting long enough to give her a warm smile in return. 'I wish you luck, babes. And don't worry, I'll keep an eye on them for you.'

'That sounds like you don't expect to see me again any time soon.'

Glynis shrugged. 'Well, what you gonna do? It's like before – you have to walk away, you got no choice.'

The force of this hit Kaz squarely in the gut. There was no criticism in her cousin's voice, just resignation, and it filled Kaz with even more guilt. She should've been there when Finlay was born, not poncing around at art college. And if she'd had the least inkling she would've been. But her sister hadn't trusted her enough to confide in her.

'I wanted to be there for Natalie. I still do.'

'I know.'

'You don't believe me, do you?'

'Yeah, I do.'

'It's not going to be like before. If only I could turn back the clock—' Could it have been different? That question had tormented Kaz ever since she learnt of her brother's death. If only she could've persuaded him to change.

'You'll go bonkers if you think like that.'

As the anger rose in her, Kaz could feel the energy and suddenly the way forward seemed crystal clear.

'Maybe. But I'm not walking away this time. Not from any of you. All I'm doing is laying low. If we don't take care of each other, who the fuck else is going to, eh? I want you to tell Natalie that. And Mum too, once she comes round enough to hear it.'

'Okay. If that's what you want.' Glynis blinked as her heavily mascaraed eyes welled up.

'I want to put this family back together, Glyn. That's what I want. For Finlay and for all of us. Dad's gone, Joey's gone, Sean's gone. We got a chance to make things different.'

51

Viktor Pudovkin loved to take tea at the Dorchester; it appealed to the unrepentant Anglophile in him. The white linen, the tiered cake stands, the tinkling of silver spoons in bone china cups were, in his view, small but significant hallmarks of civilization, part of what made life in London so pleasant. He drank Earl Grey with a sliver of lemon; milk in tea struck him as an eccentricity too far. But he adored the little fruit scones loaded with raspberry jam and clotted cream. His wife said they were bad for him, all that fat and sugar. But a man needed a few small treats in his life.

And, as he explained to her, it was more than personal indulgence. A tea table tucked away behind a colonnade in the Promenade bar was also the perfect venue for business meetings, particularly with Arab associates. These days most of London's best hotels belonged to owners from the Middle East, and the Russian had found that dealing with them on what they considered their turf tended to make things easier.

He always made a point of arriving early; partly to see who was about and to sniff out the deals that might be going down, but also so he could enjoy his tea and scones in peace.

Eating alone might not suit everyone, but Pudovkin, who spent his life going out to lunch and dinner, regarded it as valuable time out, an opportunity to reflect and plan. His life had become somewhat stressful of late. A shift in the balance of power back home in Moscow was not operating in his favour, in fact quite the opposite. And then there was the assassination attempt, which might or might not be connected. He was worried.

For the last twenty years he'd been a lucky man, astute certainly, but in the chaos following the collapse of the Soviet Union everything had been up for grabs. Like many others, Pudovkin had enriched himself at the state's expense. But he wasn't an egomaniac like some. When the inevitable backlash came, he'd managed to escape Putin's campaign against the oligarchs because he knew exactly how to make himself useful to his old comrade.

Recently, however, siren voices had been whispering in the President's ear, telling him that Pudovkin preferred his life in London, that he was simply too rich and that his connections with MI6 and the CIA were suspect. Pudovkin talked to these people, of course he did. It was how the game was played, always had been even back in his KGB and FSB days. Back channels were important, Putin knew that. But he was surrounded by jealous and greedy people and, in Pudovkin's absence, it was all too easy for them to cast doubt on his loyalty.

Spreading the last dollop of clotted cream on his scone, Pudovkin popped it in his mouth and savoured it. He could go back to Moscow and spend months paying court to the President and his coterie, but spending the winter there didn't appeal and anyway, he had a better idea. He planned to prove his loyalty to the motherland once and for all, as well as demonstrating how useful, indeed vital, it was for him to remain in London.

From his vantage point, Pudovkin kept a close eye on the comings and goings and was pleased when he noticed the maître d' escorting an old friend to a nearby table. He raised his hand in greeting and Ahmad Karim strolled over. His current passport was Lebanese, he had several other names and his origins were lost in the mists of time – even the FSB had never ferreted them out. But Ahmad Karim, investor and crook, was an A-list fixer and over the years Pudovkin had found him a valuable asset.

Rising to his feet, the Russian – a good six foot three in his silk socks – towered over the Arab but they still managed a manly hug.

'You're looking fit, my friend.'

The little man patted his paunch. 'Aww, I'm not so sure about that.'

Standing in Karim's wake, hands in pockets, shoulders squared, was a young man who easily matched Pudovkin in height. The Russian looked him up and down. He exuded the casual arrogance of many of his generation of wealthy young Arabs; he had a preppy tilt to the chin, so educated in America was the Russian's guess.

Karim turned to his companion. 'This is Viktor Pudovkin, an old friend of mine. May I present Turki bin Qassim.'

Handshakes were exchanged. The young man's eyes were sharp behind the languid smile and the accent was indeed transatlantic. 'Mr Pudovkin needs no introduction.'

Karim beamed. He loved parading his connections. 'Turki is the son of another old friend of mine in Qatar, and a member of the Al Thani family.'

Pudovkin inclined his head; the hook was in and he was intrigued. 'Can I offer you both some tea?'

Qassim raised his palm with a teasing smirk. 'Oh but I've been advised against drinking tea in London with Russians.'

Pudovkin laughed out loud, although the joke annoyed him. How many times had he heard it? The Litvinenko case was indeed a bad joke. It was a stupid and totally unnecessary move – he'd said so at the time – to dispose of anyone using radioactive polonium. Such a ridiculous piece of melodrama had upset the usually tolerant Brits and soured relations between London and Moscow.

Karim was chuckling merrily too. 'Another time, Viktor. Turki and I have some matters to discuss. You understand.'

They retreated to their own table and Pudovkin sat down. He wondered why the young Qatari had wanted to rattle his cage. Because he could? Was he part of the Al Thani inner circle, or was Karim simply boasting? The Russian pulled out his phone and sent a text to one of his PAs to have the young Arab checked out. He might be a useful addition to the list and a potential target for his new project.

Robert Hollister was invariably late for their appointments and usually arrived with a flurry of excuses about urgent parliamentary business. Although he no longer had that pretext, Pudovkin presumed his behaviour was unlikely to have changed and he'd factored that in. A disgraced politician, currently under indictment, was about as useful as a fart in the wind, but he'd put a lot of time and effort into the Hollisters, particularly the wife, and he remained hopeful of recouping on his investment.

When Robert Hollister finally appeared, a full half an hour late, he was wreathed in smiles and apologies.

'Viktor, I'm so sorry. I've been down to Tewkesbury to see Paige. Coming back, accident on the M4, hell of a tailback.'

Pudovkin travelled by helicopter or private jet; he rarely encountered such problems. He offered his hand to shake. 'How is she?'

'Better, I think.'

Inviting his guest to sit, Pudovkin signalled to the waiter.

'Some Earl Grey, Robert?'

'God, no. Smells like a pimp's aftershave. How do you drink it? Coffee.' He glanced up at the waiter. 'A cappuccino. But don't dump a load of chocolate on the top.'

'And a fresh pot of tea.'

Dipping his head, the waiter withdrew; the Russian folded his hands in his lap and smiled. Hollister looked wired; he crossed and recrossed his legs several times, unable to sit still. His eyes were bloodshot and pouchy.

'Actually, she's not better. Not really. She's completely fucking nuts, Viktor – you do realize that, don't you?'

'So you're still planning to divorce her?'

'Yes, of course. But not immediately. I took your advice and I've persuaded her to make a statement to the police confirming that Helen Warner was sixteen when I first slept with her.'

'What do the lawyers say? Will that be enough?'

'I just talked to Merrow on the phone. With that she's pretty sure she can get a discontinuance. That means the CPS drops the charges.'

'Congratulations! We should be drinking champagne.'

'Coffee's fine. I've got a cracking headache.'

'But things are "a bit more chipper", isn't that the English expression?'

Hollister found it hard to conceal his disdain. 'Not where I come from, mate.'

In fact, he'd been forced to take the train; the private car hire firm had cancelled on him at the last moment, though he wasn't about to admit that to his host. The journey had been awful, that was no lie. He'd spent it drinking whisky, and trying to avoid the gaze of two old biddies across the aisle – travelling in first was no guarantee nowadays – who were clearly gossiping about him.

The Russian had initially suggested lunch, but when some minion called to arrange it he discovered he'd been demoted to tea. To say he was pissed off was an understatement. He was fighting with every ounce of intellect and cunning he possessed to drag himself out of this shit show. His career had crashed and burned, and the smug bastard was sitting there drinking tea as if he'd had no hand in it.

'So what are your plans?' Pudovkin didn't even sound interested.

'Move to Brussels.'

'That sounds sensible.'

'I've got to say, Viktor, I think you owe me.' He was trying to remain calm and reasonable but Pudovkin's attitude was infuriating.

The Russian frowned. 'How do you come to that conclusion? I've paid your legal fees—'

'I know.'

'And for Paige's treatment.'

'And we're grateful. Obviously. But a few hundred grand tops – that's small change to you.'

Pudovkin opened his palms and smiled. 'I have some contacts in Brussels and if I can—'

'I've got my own contacts.'

The Russian stared at him. He continued to smile but the slate-grey eyes were devoid of sympathy. Hollister knew he was taking a considerable risk, yet there was part of him that simply didn't care.

'Here's the deal, Viktor. Thanks to my stupid wife, you were able to blackmail me—'

Pudovkin glanced around. 'I'd be careful, my friend.'

'Or what? I end up in the river too?'

The Russian simply steepled his fingers and stared. The

look was hard and direct. Hollister imagined facing him in some FSB interrogation cell. Had he been a torturer? Probably.

Helen Warner had been disposed of, neatly, professionally, and it had been dressed up to look like suicide. The quid pro quo had been that once Hollister was in government he would owe the Russian. Who knows what form the payback would've taken? It had never come to that.

Meeting his gaze resolutely, Hollister managed a smile. 'The fire, that was a nice touch. But I gather the bitch survived. And her mother.'

'What fire?'

'Oh come on, don't be coy. The gangster that tried to gun you down on your own doorstep—'

Pudovkin's lip curled. He still thought about that day. The deadly volley of bullets had missed his head by a whisker. He'd had a few close calls in his career, but what chiefly upset him about that incident was the distress it had caused his small son. Sasha, previously a happy boy, had been petrified. Now he'd started to bed-wet. What was the point of all his wealth and his London life if his children weren't safe?

Hollister scanned the old spook but it was impossible to read him. 'His name was Joey Phelps. The bitch that set me up was his sister.'

'And your point is . . . ?'

'You said you were going to sort it out. I presumed you had.'

'You presumed wrong.' Pudovkin glanced at the Daniels Co-axial Chronograph on his wrist. 'I'm afraid we're going to have to wrap this up, Robert. I have an appointment at five.'

'I'm planning to join a hedge fund partnership. I want you to stake me.'

The Russian chuckled. 'You're an interesting man. Smart,

certainly. But like most Westerners you're arrogant, you think everyone should live by your rules. You bluster and bully, but you have nothing to back it up. You have a soft underbelly.'

'You're the one who's going soft if you're letting Karen Phelps walk away.'

'Nowadays I'm a businessman. Profit is my motive.'

'Come on, Viktor. We both know that's not true. What are your friends back home going to think when they hear a couple of cheap gangsters made a fool of you? Can you afford to look that weak?'

The Russian sighed. Could it be that the hit really was some kind of freelance action by an English gangster? It was a reassuring notion certainly. 'Why do you want this stupid girl dead?'

'Because I wouldn't be sitting here now if she hadn't set me up.'

'I've seen a lot of killing in this world. Revenge is never good for the soul.'

'I'm an atheist. I don't believe in the soul. You wanted to buy me, turn me into an asset.'

'That was when you were in a position to be useful.'

'I can still be useful. Once the charges are dropped, I shall be doing some unofficial consulting for an old friend of mine at the European Central Bank.'

Pudovkin sighed again. 'How much do you want?'

'Ten million.'

'Five million. Dollars.'

'And the other matter?'

'You want it to look like an accident?'

'I couldn't give a shit. I just want it done.'

52

Nicci Armstrong had spent a frustrating day hanging around the office, trying to find an opportunity to have a private word with Blake. Naylor had moved in and was busy interviewing new security personnel. A steady stream of meatheads in off-the-peg suits came and went. Blake disappeared, supposedly for a lunch meeting, and didn't come back. With major undisclosed changes in progress, the investigations section felt like a besieged enclave. There was paperwork to be followed up, a couple of routine investigations on defence briefs to go out, but not much else. Were they about to be phased out or restructured or rationalized – whatever the latest management jargon was for cut?

At five o'clock Nicci decided to throw in the towel. She turned to Pascale and Eddie. 'I've had enough of this. Fancy a drink? My shout.'

They were early enough to bag a corner table in the Blue Lion. Eddie offered to go to the bar and Nicci supplied him with the cash.

Pascale gave her an appraising look. 'What d'you think, boss? Should I be looking for a new job?'

'Short answer: I've no idea.'

In the late afternoon Nicci had received a text from Tom Rivlin: *Kemal to be released, any word on Phelps?* After a night of passion, this was what he had to say to her. In which case, why had he sent flowers? Guilt maybe? Or embarrassment? Her ex-husband had always turned up with a bunch of flowers when he'd done something to piss her off. Rivlin appeared to want to forget the fact they'd slept together; it was an aberration, a drunken mistake. Now they were back to business as usual. It left Nicci feeling desolate inside. But better to be let down now than later.

Eddie returned with a tray of drinks: a pint for himself and a bottle of white wine with two glasses.

Nicci glared at him. 'Bloody hell, Eddie. You trying to get us drunk?'

'Cheaper this way. Trying to save you money.' He dumped a handful of change in her palm.

The three of them sat gloomily sipping their drinks, each in their own headspace. Nicci scanned her companions. Pascale would get something else, no trouble. She spoke several languages, her IT skills were top notch and she was easy on the eye. Any employer would regard her as an asset.

Eddie Lunt was a different proposition. But he was resourceful, that's what Blake always said about him, and that covered a multitude of sins. It was all too obvious that the least employable of the three of them was Nicci herself. An ex-cop, retired on medical grounds, she'd be joining the army of discarded officers cast onto the scrapheap before their time by the drastic cuts in the police service. She'd be lucky to land a security job in a supermarket.

Finishing her drink, Pascale made her excuses and left. She had a new boyfriend and a cooked meal to go home to. Nicci stared at the third of a bottle of wine remaining and topped up her glass. Suddenly the purchase of a whole bottle seemed a sensible idea. Eddie was quietly demolishing his second packet of cheese and onion crisps. He offered them to her. She shook her head.

He folded the foil crisp packet neatly into a square and tucked it under his glass. 'Got a bit of a confession to make, boss.'

Nicci's heart sank. The last thing she needed was fallout from some illegal escapade of Eddie's.

She gave him a glowering look. 'What?'

'Simon's private phone, I got his number and put it on a tracker. I been following him all day.'

'What the fuck, Eddie! Snooping on your own boss? Is nothing sacred to you?'

'I just thought, well, what if he's in a fix but is too proud to say?'

Nicci took a slug of wine. 'That sounds like an excuse for you to indulge in your usual schtick.'

'Only trying to help.'

Nicci glared at him, wondering, not for the first time, what she'd done to deserve this malevolent pixie. Ethics mattered. If the ends simply justified the means in every case, then where did that leave you? How you treated people and respect for the law were values to be cherished.

Eddie was watching her and waiting. She knew he thought she was naive. And he was probably right. She wondered idly where all the certainties in her life had gone. How did things get so fucked up? How did she end up having casual sex with a man who was never going to fall for someone like her?

She shrugged. 'Okay, so tell me. Where did he go?'

'According to the diary, he had a lunch appointment. But he ended up in a sandwich shop.'

'I'm surprised you didn't go down there, hide behind the chiller cabinet and take photos.'

Sarcasm washed over him. His piggy eyes twinkled.

'It gets better. The sandwich shop was an ordinary branch of Pret on the corner of Vauxhall Bridge. Across the road from Vauxhall Cross.'

'The MI6 building.'

'Exactly. I'm thinking he met his old chum Colin McCain.'

'But you said McCain's MI5. That's Thames House, the other side of the river on Millbank. Surely they'd meet over there?'

'Not if they were hooking up with someone else. He was only in the sandwich shop three minutes. Comes out onto the bridge, phone disappears off the grid. Comes back on two hours later.'

'He turned it off.'

'Probably. But why? Looks like a security protocol to me.'

Nicci stared at him, dumbfounded. 'You saying he went inside?'

'Could have.'

'Just because he turned his phone off on Vauxhall Bridge doesn't mean he was having a meeting with MI6.'

'Then why go there?'

'All sorts of reasons.'

'Maybe he's feeding them information.'

'But hang on, Eddie. You need special security clearance to get in there. You wouldn't have that if you were an informant. They'd come to you.'

'Maybe Blake's been recruited by the Secret Intelligence Service?'

Nicci huffed. 'Now you're being completely ridiculous. You've spent too much time dreaming up lurid stories for the tabloids.'

'We know something's going down. How would you explain his behaviour?'

'He's a copper, it's in his DNA. What you see is what you get. No way he's playing at being some hole-in-the-wall spook.'

'Then at the very least he's helping them.'

'Helping them do what?'

Eddie grinned. 'That's what we need to figure out.'

53

Moving around, never standing in one spot for more than a couple of minutes, she kept the entrance to the ticket office under surveillance for a good half hour before the appointed time. Kaz Phelps was taking no chances.

She'd spent a restless night in her king-sized hotel bed. Chain on the door plus a chair jammed under the handle; it had felt safe enough. All that had disturbed her were her dreams. The meeting with her cousin Glynis had set in motion a cascade of mad schemes from elaborate revenge scenarios to moving the whole family to Australia. But whatever she did next would depend on the man she was meeting. Kaz wasn't even that convinced he'd turn up.

By ten thirty the incoming stream of commuters at Liverpool Street station had started to thin. The concourse was still busy; gaggles of travellers with backpacks and suitcases were queuing for the Stansted Express. Kaz wondered why the lawyer had picked this as a rendezvous. Maybe he was coming in from Essex himself?

As the station clock ticked forward to ten thirty-one, Kaz strolled casually forward and positioned herself directly outside the entrance to the ticket office. A cleaner with a cart was picking up litter and sweeping. People strode by, heading for the entrance to the underground. Kaz was on full alert, eyes rapidly scanning the sea of passers-by. She thought she had all possible avenues of approach covered and so jumped out of her skin when she felt a hand come to rest on her shoulder.

Spinning round, she found herself face to face with a man of medium height. He was somehow older than she'd expected, mid-forties, a furrowed brow, a crew cut of salt-and-pepper grey hair and a dark blue Goretex anorak over his suit.

'Morning. Hope you haven't been waiting long.' He offered a leather-gloved hand to shake. 'Jonathan Sullivan.'

'Karen Phelps.'

'I thought we'd take a taxi.'

Without a backward glance he headed for the escalator, expecting Kaz to follow. He carried a small backpack, a bit of a paunch round his middle, and didn't seem particularly threatening. Walking briskly, he blended in with the City's worker bees, just part of the swarm of anonymous run-of-the-mill employees who were scurrying to and fro.

He held the door open for her and they jumped into a black cab on Bishopsgate. Sullivan gave the cabbie an address in Knightsbridge and settled back in his seat without further comment.

Kaz scrutinized his profile as she waited for him to speak. A wet shave had left a tiny nick on his jawline; apart from that his appearance was pristine. He remained oblivious to her inspection and simply stared out of the window.

'Where are we going?'

Turning, he seemed surprised she'd spoken. 'Presumably you've got the key?'

She nodded.

'That's where we're going first.'

She was none the wiser.

The traffic was sluggish. It was a damp morning, overcast with a hint of October chill. The taxi driver chose a route along the Embankment then cut up to Sloane Square. Kaz gradually got used to her silent companion. There was no tension in his presence. He gazed out at the passing streets and displayed no impatience at the slow pace of the journey. She decided to play it his way, not that she had much choice.

The cab finally pulled up in a side turning off Brompton Road. Having paid the driver, Sullivan crossed the street to a stone-clad building with a heavy oak door. A brass plaque beside it read: *West London Safe Deposit Centre.* He pressed the bell and the door clicked open.

In contrast to the drab exterior, the foyer was bright and modern with an impersonal, corporate air. Sullivan handed Kaz a key card and she swiped through the entry barrier after him. There followed a short wait on a low-slung leather sofa until a security guard appeared and led them down a flight of stairs to the vaults. Having passed through a full-body scanner, Sullivan placed his index finger on the fingerprint reader and then tapped a ten-digit number into the keypad.

He turned to Kaz. 'If you decide to keep the box, they'll need your print.'

She nodded. The guard invited her to pass through the body scanner too. He then led them through a reinforced steel door into the strongroom, which was lined from floor to ceiling with banks of gunmetal-grey safety deposit boxes. Each box had a number and from that Kaz calculated there must be several hundred, all identical, each with two keyholes in the middle.

The security guard walked along, running his eye over the numbers. He came to a halt at 139. Placing his key in the right-hand slot, he turned to Sullivan.

Sullivan beckoned Kaz. 'Now it's your turn. Got the key?'

Removing the key she'd found in Natalie's envelope from

her jeans pocket, Kaz inserted it in the left-hand slot. Surprisingly enough it fitted. Both keys were turned simultaneously and the long metal drawer slid out. The security guard carried it over to the table, set it down and retreated to the doorway.

Kaz stared at the box. It was oblong, maybe a couple of feet long and a foot or so wide with a hinged lid on the top. She shot the lawyer an enquiring look. His face was inscrutable. He took several steps back, turned away and folded his hands in front of him.

So this was what Joey had left them. Feeling slightly nervous, Kaz lifted the lid. The box was hardly six inches deep and contained three bubble-lined manila envelopes, A4 size and firmly wedged in place. More cash?

She eased the top envelope out and peered cautiously inside. The security guard had positioned himself far enough away to give her privacy. Sullivan's gaze was focused on the bank of boxes on the opposite wall.

The envelope contained a sheaf of legal-looking documents. Kaz decided to take them away to read at her leisure. She placed the envelope on the table beside the box.

The second envelope was, as she'd guessed, stuffed with vacuum-packed bundles of cash. The one she examined looked to be similar to the three packs she already had, each of which contained ten grand. She counted six packs in the envelope. It would probably be safer to leave them where they were, provided Sullivan supplied her with the necessary key card and codes to access the place on her own.

The third envelope was stuck in the bottom of the box. It took some effort for her to prise it out. The contents felt hard and, as she extracted the package, Kaz was aware of a tightening in her stomach muscles. She guessed what it was even before she looked. Glancing inside confirmed it.

Wrapped in clingfilm was the SIG P220 semi-automatic pistol; *one of the most reliable handguns you can get* – that's how her brother had described it when he first gave it to her. She hadn't wanted it, but he'd insisted. And it had sat in her kitchen drawer until her cousin had come calling and she'd shot him dead. This was the gun that had saved her. Her fingerprints were probably still on the grip or the trigger.

Checking that Sullivan and the security guard were looking the other way, Kaz transferred the SIG, the suppressor and the cartridge clips into her shoulder bag. As she zipped it up, a long-forgotten feeling flooded through her. She felt energized and confident – but it was more than that. Now she had a weapon, a serious weapon that she knew how to use, and this gave her the protection she desperately needed. It also gave her power. When she'd got out of bed in her rented hotel room she'd been a lonely fugitive with only her wits to protect her. Now her status had changed. She was still on the run, but she'd turned into what the police might describe as armed and dangerous.

54

When her alarm had gone off at seven, Nicci Armstrong had ignored it and turned over. The previous evening she'd left several phone messages for Simon Blake and received no reply. Whatever the boss was up to he clearly had no intention of confiding in her. She felt slighted, having always believed that he trusted her. Obviously she was wrong.

Finally she'd crawled out of bed at nine thirty, called SBA and told Alicia she had a migraine. Pulling a sickie was a minor act of rebellion; he probably wouldn't even notice. She made herself a coffee and sat on the sofa in her pyjamas, trawling online for jobs in the security sector. It was a thoroughly depressing exercise.

She was consoling herself with a long hot shower when she became aware of a knocking on the flat door. Neighbours and the postman were the only people who could get through the secure outer door and into the building. She decided to ignore it. It was probably the postman with a package for next door – they had a habit of shopping online and never being at home to receive their deliveries.

But the knocking persisted. In the end, wrapped in a towel, dripping wet and ready with an angry rebuff, she opened the door to Tom Rivlin.

'Oh, it's you.'

He smiled awkwardly. 'Your office said you were off sick, so I brought bagels.' He held up a paper bag.

'Oh.' Hair slicked back, red-faced from the shower, she must look a fright. She felt exposed and self-conscious. What the hell did he want?

'Can I come in?'

'Yeah.' She stepped back. He followed her into the hall; it was difficult to decide who was more embarrassed.

'Are you sick?'

'No, just pissed off with work.'

'Why?'

'Long story.'

'I'm a good listener.'

'Why don't you put the kettle on while I get dressed?'

Nicci retreated to the bedroom, dried herself off and put on some trackie bottoms and a T-shirt. By the time she emerged, Rivlin was toasting the bagels and making coffee.

He grinned. 'Did you get the flowers?'

'Yeah. Though I'm not sure why you sent them.'

'Bit OTT? I'm sorry.'

'I wasn't sure what you meant by them.'

'What do flowers usually mean?' He was standing with his hands on his hips, that cocky male stance. She wanted to be annoyed, not to have butterflies in her stomach. The possibility of touching him, of being touched by him, dominated her thoughts.

Rocking from foot to foot helped her release some of her tension. 'So what's the latest? Sadik Kemal's been released?'

'He was stonewalling. But the NCA has got some intel from Europol on the Turkish mafia and potential drug routes into the UK. Theory is, the Kemals might be expecting a delivery.

So the plan is to lull him into a false sense of security and keep him under tight surveillance.'

'Didn't they have him under surveillance on the day of the kidnap attempt?' Nicci had to struggle to keep the sarcasm out of her voice.

'Well, yeah, supposedly. But not a full team.'

'What does Stoneham think?'

'We're going with it. No choice really. Short of a statement from Karen Phelps saying he tried to kidnap her, we haven't got the evidence to hold him.'

'I haven't heard from her, if that's why you're here.'

Rivlin shook his head wearily. 'Is that what you think of me?' He was giving her that gorgeous abashed smile, which annoyed her even more.

'I don't want to be used, Tom. It was a one-night stand, I get that.'

'Is that what you want it to be?'

The question seemed to hang in the air between them.

She sighed. 'Look, I need to dry my hair and go show my face in the office before the new boss sacks me.'

Rivlin took a step towards her. 'I don't want to get you sacked. But I need an answer to one question before I go.'

'What?'

'Have I been reading you all wrong? Do you really not want this?'

Before she could say anything he put his arms round her and, drawing her gently and firmly towards him, leant forward and kissed her full on the mouth. The immediacy and intensity of his desire surged through her and took her breath away.

His body was pressing against hers and she knew there was only one response: she kissed him back hungrily. They stumbled towards the sofa, collapsing onto it, and as she ripped at the buttons of his shirt, then the buckle of his trouser belt, he got his answer.

55

When they left the Safe Deposit Centre Sullivan suggested that they walked. He led Kaz through the side streets of Knights-bridge – he seemed to know where he was going – until they emerged on the main road close to the Albert Memorial. Throughout the morning a leaden sky had been threatening rain, but as they crossed the road and wandered into Ken-sington Gardens shafts of sunshine started to break through. The leaves were already turning russet and falling. They headed up a meandering path towards the Serpentine.

Sullivan set the pace, a leisurely stroll. Kaz was thinking about the gun in her bag and wondering if he knew about it.

Finally he spoke. 'Well, I'm sure you have a lot of questions.'

Kaz chuckled. 'What is this? A security thing? Now we're outside you can talk?'

Her tone was combative but he didn't seem offended.

He simply smiled. 'We needed to deal with the box first. That confirmed for me that you have your brother's bona fides, and for you that I am indeed instructed by him.'

'Bona fides? Does getting the envelope from my sister count?'

'Yes.'

'How did you recognize me? From a photo?'

'I've seen you before.'

'When?'

'Shortly after you were released from prison, you came to the office to see Helen Warner.'

He'd worked with Helen! Kaz's brain ricocheted back to that first heady meeting with her former lawyer and lover. To be out, to be free, to be able to just go and call on Helen at work – she'd been walking on air that day. It really wasn't so long ago, but now it felt like another life.

'So you work for Crowley whatsit and Moore?' They were her brother's lawyers too.

'Crowley Sheridan Moore. I used to.'

'That's how Joey knew you?'

'I was in the tax department. Neville Moore, our managing partner, asked me to . . . er, well, to give your brother some advice of a general nature.'

'I can't believe Joey paid tax.'

'My job was advising clients on how to minimize their tax burden. Within the constraints of the law. However, we had a number of clients with more specialized needs.'

'You mean villains who needed money-laundering?'

'I saw the opportunity to set up on my own, managing assets for a small portfolio of individual clients. Neville was supportive of the idea. It helped him keep things above board.'

'Does your firm have a name?'

'No. I work from home. I only take clients through very specific personal recommendation.'

'Where's home?'

'South of Newmarket. We have a farm; my wife breeds horses.'

'How do you get paid?'

'Through a remuneration clause in the offshore trusts I set up and administer.'

'If you control it all, why not just take the lot?'

Sullivan laughed. His whole bearing changed and Kaz realized she was getting her first proper glimpse of the man she was dealing with. 'That's not what I do, Karen. Nor would it be in my best interest. I like my life. I do pretty well. I don't want the police knocking at my door – or anyone else, for that matter.'

'Okay, so where does that leave us?'

Sullivan stopped and turned to face her, his expression becoming sombre. 'This is the first time I've had a client die. But, given the nature of their . . . occupations, shall we say, it's a contingency that's been thought about. Obviously, Joey left no will as such. We certainly wouldn't want to get involved with probate. But he did express his wishes in a letter. You'll find a copy with the documents in your envelope.'

Kaz gave him a rueful smile. 'Doesn't sound very Joey. He thought about the future, we even talked about it. But getting him to stick to a plan? Nightmare.'

'He was clear about the support he wanted to give to his family.'

'So basically there's stuff out there and he's left it to us? Me, Natalie and Mum.'

'Indeed.'

'How much?'

'I can't give you a current valuation immediately. It'll take several days. But if you wish to retain my services—'

'Do I have a choice?'

'Undoubtedly you do.' He threw out his arms to encompass the leafy canopy above and around them, which was starting to turn copper and gold. The traffic's roar was muted to a hum. It didn't feel like the heart of a major city. 'I love it here. Walk a mile in any direction and you will find the rich, the seriously rich of every nation. Why do they come to London?

Because it's possibly the best place on earth to securely warehouse your assets, see them accrue in value and avoid tax. There's an industry of people out there who will help you.'

'What you saying? I walk into my local bank?'

'No, obviously not. But you do have a choice.'

She sighed. 'I need some time to get my head round all this.'

'Of course you do.' He nodded sagely. Then a thought occurred to him. 'Tell you what, let me show you one other thing, then I'll leave you in peace.'

'Okay. Whatever.'

Emerging from the gardens near Lancaster Gate, they picked up a cab on Bayswater Road and headed south. Now it was Kaz who remained silent and stared out of the window. She knew Joey had made money and not peanuts. That was why Paul Ackroyd had been so keen to get her onside. He wanted his cut. But what were they talking about here? The lawyer had said he would need several days to give her a valuation – that suggested serious money.

The taxi crossed the river at Wandsworth Bridge. Her gaze skated over the tiered facades of the swish new apartment blocks rising up beside the river, but she paid them little real attention until they turned into a side road and stopped at the entrance to one of these blocks. Next door was still a building site and flags flapped over the adjacent sales office.

Sullivan turned to her and smiled. 'Not superstitious, are you?'

'How do you mean?'

'You'll see.'

He led her through the foyer, gave the concierge, who appeared to recognize him, a nod, and they entered the lift. He pushed the button for the thirteenth floor and smirked.

As they alighted from the lift, he pulled a bunch of keys

from his bag. 'This one's currently on the rental market. Partly furnished. But it faces the river – the view's fantastic.'

Kaz stopped in her tracks and sighed. 'Hang on, I thought you were giving me time to think. I don't even know that I want to rent a place at the moment.'

Sullivan tilted his head and grinned at her. The starchy lawyer had morphed into something softer. 'Oh, no. You misunderstand. This is part of the portfolio. I was planning to rent it out, but I thought you might find it useful while you sort yourself out. It's yours. You own it.'

Kaz stared at him in disbelief. He slotted the key into the heavy double doors and opened them up. The security system bleeped. Stepping inside, he tapped in the code to disable it.

'Come and take a look.'

Kaz felt as though she should take her shoes off. Engineered oak flooring stretched away from her down the hall and into a double-height sitting room flanked on two sides with wall-to-ceiling plate glass. There was a wrap-around balcony, a high-gloss kitchen, a sweeping staircase leading to an upper floor. It was like something out of a design magazine and Kaz could imagine her brother here, choosing fixtures and fittings, like a kid in a toy shop. He loved the trappings of luxury and regarded it as payback, reparation for their shitty childhood. Other people lived like this, why not them? That had been Joey's line.

'This must've cost millions.'

The lawyer nodded. 'We bought off plan, paid three point two. Not bad.'

Having completed a circuit of the sitting room, Kaz slid open the balcony door and went out. The river snaked below her; turgid and brown, swollen by the recent rains, it surged under the low arches of the bridge before sweeping on eastwards.

The wind on her face felt refreshing. If only it could blow the chaos away. She was finding it hard to make sense of her feelings. In the last week she'd been bounced from terror, through shock and despair, to elation, without time to really process any of it. And gnawing away at her beneath the surface was death and loss: Joey gunned down in a London street, Helen's murder disguised as suicide. But she was alive and free, she had a gun in her bag, and now she had this. If nothing else, one thing was clear to her: the Kemals were going to rue the day they came after Kaz Phelps.

56

It was early afternoon by the time Nicci finally swanned into the office. Alicia greeted her with a smile.

'How you feeling now?'

'Oh, fine. Thanks. The doctor put me on this new medication. Works really fast. Few hours, the migraine's gone.'

Nicci was aware that she was giving way more explanation than necessary, but she felt like a guilty teenager who'd bunked off school to meet her boyfriend in the park. She was half in a dream full of flashbacks of the morning she'd spent with Tom Rivlin and it was still making her smile.

Settling her features in a serious, businesslike expression, she headed across the room to the investigations section. Pascale was typing away. There was no sign of Eddie.

'Busy?'

Pascale removed her earbuds and smiled. 'Yeah, Craig's asked me to do a brief—'

'Craig, eh?'

'He says to call him Craig. It's on that bloke whose wife you're supposed to be minding.'

'Qassim.'

'He wants a full in-depth background on him. How much time he's spent in the country, bank checks, the lot.'

Nicci frowned. 'Why?'

Pascale shrugged. 'I'm just glad to have something to do.'

Nicci wended her way back across the office. The cyber geeks were all at their desks. She smiled at Bharat, the departmental head, who was excited about the hieroglyphics on his screen. The conference room was empty and next to it the door to Simon Blake's office stood open. Craig Naylor was sitting behind the desk staring at his laptop.

Hovering in the doorway Nicci cleared her throat. He looked up, stroked his beard and smiled. 'Thought you were off sick?'

'Migraine. It's gone.'

He held out a hand, inviting her in. 'Stress. You've probably had a bit too much of that lately.'

She sat down, facing him across the desk. 'Where's Simon?'

'He's having a few days off. I told him to get out on the golf course. Forget about this place for a while.'

He was smiling benignly enough, but his manner didn't fool Nicci. Behind the chummy ex-cop facade there was something off-kilter about Naylor.

'So, are you going to sack me?'

Naylor gave a wry chuckle. 'Good God, Nic. Why on earth would I do that?'

He was presuming to call her Nic, as Blake did, which gave her another reason not to like him.

'Because there's clearly been some kind of takeover and no one's seen fit to tell me what's going on.'

'Well, you've been off sick.' He folded his arms. 'There's no great mystery. SBA has been going through a bad patch financially. A major investor pulled out and that created quite a few problems for Simon. I think you were aware of that.'

'Yeah. Sort of.'

When Naylor grinned, his beard seemed to bush out and he looked even more like a pirate. 'Y'know, I remember Blake when he was a commander – real copper's copper. I know he had his problems with the hats, but he had a lot of respect from everyone else in the job.'

'He earned it.'

'No question. But all this brown-nosing potential investors, it's taken its toll. Setting up a new business is stressful and it's hard to get the strategy right. That's why I'm here.'

'I thought you were the new head of security?'

'We're in the security business.'

'You mean you're the new boss? I'm not trying to be difficult here. I just want to know what's going on.'

'Fair enough. What do you want to ask?'

'First off, why have you got Pascale digging the dirt on Turki bin Qassim? He's a bodyguarding job.'

Naylor grinned and tilted his head. 'You're smart and ballsy, that's what Blake said. So let's cut to the chase.'

'I wish you would.'

'We've got new investors on board, but it's a crowded market. This business is only viable if we use all our potential resources.'

'Meaning what?'

'HNWIs come to us as clients, but they're also a valuable data resource. Security and investigations need to become an integrated operation.'

'What's that, translated into plain English? We're going to protect them and at the same time spy on them?'

'Yeah. Basically.'

'Isn't that illegal?'

'No. They're hiring us to guarantee their security. We need to know what we're dealing with. It's intel-gathering, that's all.'

'Until you sell it on.'

'Which we may or may not do.'

Nicci shook her head in disbelief. 'It's hardly ethical.'

'Ethics!' He laughed drily. 'I love that fucking word. Y'know I was a Federation rep for ten years, saw plenty of good officers – officers like you, Nic – get the chop for no good reason.'

'In my case there was a reason.'

He gave her a concerned look. 'Yeah, I heard about that and I'm sorry. Truly. But that doesn't alter the fact that the bloody government don't give a toss. Cut, cut, cut. They've made the job impossible and that's why I got out.'

'I wouldn't disagree. But what's that got to do with how SBA operates?'

'Everything. Globalization, mate. The world's changed. This country's changed. But I'm a pragmatist – you've got to be. Some filthy rich foreign fucker wants to get the drop on another filthy rich foreign fucker, so they can beat them to another dodgy deal – what do I care? It's no skin off my nose. And frankly, what do you care? I'll pass on a bit of intel, if it means I earn a bonus. And that bonus is going to pay to put my kids through uni so when they come out they can get a decent job without a mountain of fucking debt. Make sure me and mine survive – those are my ethics.'

His forehead had broken out in a sweat and he wiped a bubble of spit from his beard. They stared at each other for a moment. She noticed his eyes, glassy and hard.

He covered this with a sheepish grin. 'Sorry about the rant.'

Nicci shrugged. It was hard to judge exactly what she was dealing with here. Just another embittered ex-cop? There were plenty of those about. But was he still connected to Pudovkin?

He tapped his index finger on the desk. 'Look, Simon obviously rates you. All I want is for us to work together and get on.'

'Yeah, me too.'

He gave her a friendly nod. 'All right then? Glad we had this talk.'

'Yeah.' She got up.

'And call me Craig. Ex-job, we stick together, mate. Show these fuckers, eh?'

Nicci painted on a smile and started to head out.

'Oh yeah, I nearly forgot.'

She stopped in the doorway and turned back to face him.

'There's this ex-con, Karen Phelps? I've been told you know her.'

Taking her time to consider this, she betrayed no hint of surprise. 'Sort of. Why?'

'I've got a client who wants to track her down. Do you know where she is?'

Nicci pretended to think. 'No. Haven't seen her for ages. Sorry.'

'Perhaps you could do some digging for me? Nice big payday for us if you can ferret her out.'

He grinned, the beard bushed out again and it occurred to Nicci it was no coincidence that he looked like a pirate.

57

Returning to the hotel, Kaz had plenty to think about. Sullivan had given her the keys and alarm code to the apartment and he'd introduced her to the concierge. It all felt vaguely unreal. She had the envelope of documents from the safe deposit box tucked under her arm and an arrangement to call the lawyer once she'd read them.

Striding through the foyer, she headed straight for the lifts. She was distracted by her thoughts and so didn't hear the receptionist the first time.

'Mrs Ackroyd! Excuse me, Mrs Ackroyd!' It was the young man who'd checked her in.

Walking over to the desk, she gave him a smile. 'Sorry. I was miles away.'

'Your husband and son have arrived.'

'What?'

'They're waiting in the rooftop bar.'

Kaz felt the colour drain out of her cheeks. She glanced at the door; her first instinct was to run for it and lose herself in the crowds.

The receptionist grinned. He enjoyed being the bearer of good news. 'Your husband said he wanted to surprise you because he knew how desperate you were to be with Finlay on his birthday.'

'Finlay.' As she spoke her nephew's name the full horror of

the situation began to dawn on her. 'Have they been here long?'

'Half an hour.'

Paul – it must be Paul – had got Finlay. Did he have Natalie too? Would he hurt them? No, it was Kaz he wanted, not them. She was aware the receptionist was watching her.

'Do you have a safe? I've got some business documents here. Could you pop them in it for me?'

'Of course.'

Kaz handed the envelope over. The receptionist disappeared into the back office and returned with a numbered receipt.

Kaz thanked him and headed for the lifts. As she rode up to the rooftop bar her brain was in overdrive. She had a gun in her bag – if push came to shove she could protect her family. But that was a last resort. And Paul Ackroyd was no fool. He'd chosen to corner her in a public place.

The bar and terrace commanded a panoramic view of the East End skyline with the Olympic Stadium as its centrepiece. It was mid-afternoon so there was a smattering of late lunchers in the restaurant and people having tea or drinks in the bar.

Stepping out of the lift, Kaz saw them immediately. Paul, looking for all the world like an indulgent father, was out on the terrace, jiggling Finlay in his arms and showing him the view. Her sister was standing nearby with Darius.

Bloody Darius? Well, that answered one question. She'd been right to remain suspicious of him. For all his protestations, he'd been working for Paul all along.

It was Natalie who noticed her first and the anxious expression on her face turned to one of pure anger. She stomped over to meet Kaz and practically spat in her face.

'Now you fucking satisfied?'

'Okay, okay, we'll sort this out.'

Natalie's chin quivered; she was close to tears. Kaz reached out to comfort her but Natalie slapped her hand away.

Paul came strolling towards them; he was carrying her nephew. 'Well, if it isn't Mrs Ackroyd. You ran out on us without saying goodbye. Not very friendly of you, was it? And you stole Rafa's credit card.'

'This is between us, Paul. Leave them out of it.'

'Yeah well, I would've done if you'd've been a bit more cooperative. Luckily for me, my faithful bloodhound here tracked you down.'

Kaz shot a disdainful glance at Darius. 'Yeah, he's a useful bloke, isn't he?'

Paul grinned. 'He had the bright idea of following Glynis. She led him right to you and he's been on your tail ever since. He's only just got here.'

This meant he knew about Sullivan, he knew about the safe deposit box, he knew about the apartment; Kaz's heart sank. She snarled at him: 'Thought you were on my side.'

'Believe it or not, Kaz, I am.' The look was earnest. He was sweating. He must've run up the stairs while she was talking to the receptionist. His sombre eyes met hers. For an instant she got the impression he was pleading with her, willing her to believe him. But the bastard had suckered her.

'You two-faced tosser!'

'Now let's not get abusive. Don't want to upset this little fella, do we?' Paul handed the wriggling toddler back to his mother.

Natalie clutched Finlay to her and glared at Paul. 'You promised if I helped you do this then me and Finlay could go home. I wanna go home.'

'And I'm a man of my word, Nat. I think I've got your sister's attention. Think she realizes now that it's not too clever, running out on your friends.' He gave Kaz a sardonic smile.

Reining in her temper, she met his gaze. He was right about one thing: mouthing off would get her nowhere. It was a waste of energy. Maybe she'd been naive to think she could simply walk away and he'd let her go. Paul Ackroyd was as greedy as the next villain and totally convinced that whatever assets Joey had left belonged to him. Had he ever intended to share with her and Natalie? Kaz doubted it.

But before she'd done a bunk from the Ackroyds' lovely farmhouse Kaz had been hatching another plan. Now seemed like a good time to resurrect it and, with a little luck, it was possible she could turn the situation to her advantage.

Plonking down on the nearest sofa, she opened her arms. 'Look, this is really unnecessary. I was gonna get in touch.'

'I wish I could believe that.' Paul was looming over her, arms folded. He had the tight T-shirt, the sculpted pecs, the black pointed-toe cowboy boots that made him look every inch the screen gangster. In many ways he reminded her of Joey – the same confident swagger – but he wasn't nearly as smart. The outfit said it all: his weakness was his vanity. Kaz remembered their first romantic encounter. Back then he was a swaggering boy with a leather jacket and a motorbike. All the girls had fancied him, the boys too, and he'd basked in their adoration. Kaz was banking on the fact that underneath he hadn't changed that much.

So she dipped her head and hunched her shoulders. She rarely resorted to girly tricks but in the circumstances she judged it was worth a go.

Blinking several times to moisten her eyes she gazed up at him. 'You have to understand, babes, I've had a really shitty time.'

'Yeah, and who helped you?' He included Darius with a

glance. 'Who rescued you? Is it wrong to expect a bit of grati-
tude?'

'No.' She fluttered her eyelids like a chastened fawn. 'You
don't get it, do you?'

'Get what?'

'Seeing you again, happy, married. That was tough. I
needed to be on my own for a bit. Take some time to adjust.'

He unfolded his arms, put his hands on his hips and sighed.
She avoided his eye and stared demurely at the floor in the
hope that if she looked weak and pathetic enough, he'd buy it.

'Okay, I know it's been tough, but you didn't have to run
off. I thought we had a deal.' Now he sounded petulant.

Raising her eyes, Kaz gave him a simpering smile. 'Yeah, we
do. You were Joey's partner. You're entitled to fifty per cent, no
question.' Part of her didn't really expect him to fall for such a
blatant ploy. Then support came from an unexpected quarter.

Darius stepped forward. 'Fits with what she's been doing,
Paul. Just wandering around on her own all day.'

Kaz shot him a look; so he hadn't told Paul about the
lawyer and the places they'd been. Or maybe he hadn't had the
chance? What the hell was his game? Playing her and Paul off
against each other?

Paul scratched his chin; he looked unsure. 'You think she's
telling the truth then?'

'Yeah. I do.' Darius shoved his hands in his jeans pockets
and smiled.

Tears were welling up in Natalie's eyes. 'Give him the envelope, Kaz! Then we can all go home.'

Kaz sighed. 'He can have the envelope, if that's what he's
here for. It's in my room. It's got thirty grand in it, minus what
I've spent.'

Paul's gaze was flicking back and forth between the sisters.

It was becoming increasingly apparent to Kaz that he hadn't thought this through. He'd always been too impulsive and reactive in his thinking, rather than strategic. That's why, although he was older, he'd ended up working for Joey and not the other way round.

The fact she'd legged it had hacked him off and so he'd gone after Natalie. Threatening her and Finlay must've seemed like a good idea. But now he wasn't sure how to follow it through. Dealing with blokes was one thing – with them, violence was a straightforward transaction – but he lost the plot when it came to women. He always had. Kaz was tempted to feel sorry for him, but she didn't.

Getting up slowly and tilting her head coyly, she made sure she was still smaller than him. 'Can we have a word? In private.'

He gave her a curt nod, turned to Darius. 'Get the little lad an ice cream.'

Paul strode out on to the terrace, Kaz following in his wake. He turned to face her. 'You say you're jealous about me and Rafa, but what about this girl you was in love with?'

Kaz didn't miss a beat. 'I was in the nick. I couldn't have the man I wanted, the man I spent years inside dreaming about. I didn't want any other bloke, so it seemed like a good alternative.'

His face softened. 'Sorry, babes. I never realized.' This was proving much simpler than Kaz had imagined.

'Rafa's lovely. And Lacey's so sweet. But it was hard not to be jealous.' Kaz's eyes welled up and in a detached part of her brain she reflected that this must be what actors did: took a smidgen of an emotion that was genuine and inflated it.

'Is that why you called yourself Mrs Ackroyd?' A huskiness had crept into his voice and a hint of lust into his eye. Kaz watched the transformation with a certain fascination. He was such easy meat. Did he really think he was about to get his leg over, plus all Joey's cash?

She raised her gaze to meet his. 'Yeah, I suppose.'

He reached out and stroked her arm. She had the impression he was about to move in on her. He was on the hook. If she was going to reel him in, it was now or never.

She grabbed his hand. 'Can I tell you a terrible secret?'

'Course you can.' He cradled her palm. He was staring at her lips and her breasts.

'While I've been wandering around, I've been making a plan. I've decided to kill Sadik Kemal.'

This stopped Paul Ackroyd in his tracks. 'Fuck me, you serious?'

'I got no choice. Those bastards'll never give up. I'm gonna take him out.'

He shook his head in disbelief. 'Listen, you wanna go down that road, I got someone I can call. You don't have to—'

She looked up at him with all the flirty fervour she could muster. 'Thing is, babes, I want to do it myself. I have to. After what they done to me and my family.' She swallowed hard and, like magic, the tears came. 'After what they done to Mum. When I seen her in that hospital bed. Even with the drugs. Oh, Paul, the pain she's in! I wanna make that bastard pay. It's what Joey would've done.'

Letting go of her hand, he blinked at her several times, a mixture of incredulity and respect. 'How? I mean a bloke like that? He's a tough customer.'

She unzipped her shoulder bag and showed him the gun.

'Yeah, but he ain't bulletproof. I got it all worked out. But it's our secret. Promise me, babe!'

58

Nicci met Eddie Lunt in a branch of Pizza Express on Baker Street. He was demolishing a Romana with spicy beef and extra pepperoni. She ordered a coffee and watched him eat.

In between large mouthfuls he brought her up to speed. 'So Naylor says, "I want you to go round and see this bloke, pick up the gear." Took me ages to find it. Warehouse out beyond Heathrow.'

Eddie lifted up the hessian shopping bag at his feet. Nicci took it and peered inside. 'Listening devices? They're not very big.'

'GSM surveillance bugs. Plant them in the target area, voice-activated, they transmit back to a mobile phone. He told me to go and get them, then liaise with Bharat.'

Nicci shook her head wearily. 'How many in here?'

'Fifty. Second consignment to be picked up next week.'

'I can't believe Simon would ever agree to us carrying out blanket surveillance like this. It's a total betrayal of client trust.'

Eddie shrugged and wiped his mouth with a napkin. 'You tried calling him again?'

'He's not picking up.'

'How about going round to his place?'

She sighed. 'I've thought of that. But if he's not there, I don't want to upset Heather.'

Eddie took another bite of pizza, chewed it briefly and

swallowed it down. 'I've met some bent coppers in my time – no offence – but this Naylor, there's something more than dodgy about him.'

'I would agree with that.'

'So what d'you want to do?'

'Why are you asking me?'

''Cause as far as I'm concerned, you're my boss until Blake tells me otherwise.'

Nicci gazed at him. She found him a difficult bloke to fathom. Pascale – clever, hard-working, serious-minded – her loyalty to the shared values of the firm Nicci would've expected. Yet she'd shown herself more than willing to follow Naylor's instructions, slipping seamlessly over to the new regime. Whereas Eddie Lunt, a man whose moral compass Nicci would never have relied on, appeared to have the same instinctive response to the situation as her. It was unsettling.

Eddie prodded his side salad with a fork. 'The other interesting thing is that this warehouse I went to, sort of electrical wholesalers, the bloke I was told to ask for was Russian.'

Nicci shot him a worried glance. 'You sure?'

'Dmitri.' He shrugged. 'Not saying we should read anything into that, but . . .'

'Naylor says he's got a client who wants to locate Karen Phelps. Told me to find her.'

'Fuck a duck! That has to be Pudovkin.'

She nodded. 'Question is, who exactly is he as far as Naylor's concerned? Client? Boss? Maybe even our new investor? Who the hell knows?'

'You've got to find Blake.'

'No, Eddie. I need you to find him. Discreetly.' She got to her feet. 'I'm due at the Qassims'. In fact, I'm late. Naylor is expecting us to spy on them. I want to know why. What are we being set up to do? Is it a random trawl or something specific?'

He reached into the bag and brought out several of the bugs. 'You could take some of these.'

Nicci scowled at him. 'Use them, you mean?'

'I thought maybe I'd put one in Naylor's office? Play him at his own game.'

She grinned and took the bugs. 'Fuck it. Why not?'

59

Darius escorted Natalie and Finlay to Stratford station; he'd offered to take them all the way home, but she'd categorically refused. This followed a faintly farcical game of pass-the-parcel with ten thousand pounds.

They'd all accompanied Kaz to her room and she'd offered one of the unopened shrink-wrapped packets of cash to Paul Ackroyd. He'd told her to keep it. She'd insisted. She didn't want any more misunderstandings. In the end he split the packet open, divided it into three wedges, gave one to Natalie, one to Kaz and shoved the third in his jacket pocket. They were partners, he told them. And Kaz was right: no more misunderstandings.

While Darius took her sister to the station, Kaz suggested she and Paul return to the bar for a drink. She bought him a large vodka and Red Bull and herself a black coffee. It was time for the second phase of her plan, but, in reality, there was no plan. It was more of an improvisation. She was thinking on her feet and had to remind herself to take care. Paul was easy to sucker in one way, but he wasn't a complete fool. Maybe she needed to tone down the seduction a notch; she didn't want to overplay her hand, nor did she want to have to sleep with him.

As they settled on their bar stools she asked him to show her a picture of Lacey. He pulled out his phone and found a video clip of his little girl playing in the garden.

As he watched it, he became misty-eyed. 'Listen, babes, I wouldn't want Rafa to find out—'

Kaz put her hand on his arm. 'Paul, I totally get it. Your family means everything to you. And nothing's happened. So there's nothing to lie about.'

He looked faintly disappointed.

She gave him a wistful smile. 'In another life, eh? Maybe I really would've been Mrs Ackroyd.'

'Yeah.' He downed his vodka and ordered another.

Kaz put on a serious face. 'So let's talk business, eh? Here's what I know. You seen the envelope Joey left for Natalie – all it contained was cash.'

'He probably thought she couldn't cope with anything else. She's a bit flaky.'

'Yeah, well, she's done a lot of drugs. But remember you said to me that what I had to do was think. That I knew more than I realized. Turns out you was right.'

'You've remembered something about the offshore accounts?'

'Not yet. But I've remembered about the skunk factories.'

A glower of annoyance spread across his features. 'That crafty bastard! I knew he'd started growing skunk. That was my fucking idea, y'know! But I was stuck out in Ibiza.'

'Joey set up five factories. He took me to visit one, up off Seven Sisters Road.'

'Devious sod!'

Kaz grinned. 'That was Joey.'

'Five! How big?'

'Not sure. The one I saw was in an old clothing factory. Hundreds of plants.'

Paul knocked back his second large vodka. 'Now do you see why I'm so pissed off about all this? I was his partner and he shafted me.' He patted her hand. 'I know that's not your fault, babes.'

Kaz smiled sweetly. 'He was my brother. I feel responsible.'

'You don't have to.'

'I do. And I think by rights you should have them. I mean, what are me and Nat gonna do with them?'

'Who runs them now?'

'Joey had this old Vietnamese geezer called Quan. Him and his family did the actual growing. But when Joey got nicked and went to prison, things got a bit lairy. The Kemals moved in on them.'

'The Kemals? The lot that was after you?'

'I think it's all connected. North-east London is their turf, that's probably how they saw it. But then Joey sent Yevgeny to sort them out.'

'His Russian enforcer? Great big bastard, I remember him.'

'It was just before Joey died. Yev got rid of the Kemals, got the factories back, 'cause he told me. Then at Joey's funeral, he got whacked.'

'By the Kemals?'

'That's what the old bill reckons.'

Paul signalled the barman and ordered another drink. 'I don't know that I want to mix it with the likes of them.'

'I told you: you don't have to. I'm gonna deal with them.'

He gave her an amused but indulgent smile. 'Babes, be realistic. They whacked the Russian – what do you think they're gonna do to you?'

'They're only thugs, they're not invincible. They've had three goes at killing me and they haven't succeeded.'

'I admire your balls, but—'

'I want you to get in touch with them and offer to set me up.'

'What?'

'You tell 'em . . . you'll give them me in return for a large consignment of their best weed. And you want to see where it's grown. Quality control. You want to meet them at the place off Seven Sisters Road. You'll bring me along, do the swap there.'

Paul shook his head. 'That is never gonna work. Not in a million years.'

'It will, because they won't be expecting it.'

'You gonna turn up and shoot them?'

'Why not? I get rid of them, you get the factories.'

She watched him thinking about it. He was right, it was a completely mad idea. But would his greed outweigh his fear?

Reaching over, she laid a hand on his. 'Look, if you feel it's too risky, say no. You got a nice life.' She smiled sadly. 'A lovely family. Why stick your neck out? But I got nothing to lose, no one to go home to. So I'm going after the Kemals one way or another.'

She let her gaze drift off and out of the window. Giving the impression she was a lonely lost soul wasn't really that much of an act. He watched her for a moment.

Then he drained his glass and slapped it down on the bar. 'Fuck it!' He had three double vodkas inside him, fuelling his bravado. 'Let's do it! We're partners, right?'

Her gaze returned to his face. 'Yeah.' She lifted his hand to her lips and kissed it. 'Thanks, babe. I knew I could rely on you.'

60

Nicci was expecting to spend the remainder of her afternoon in the Qassims' kitchen and, if she got lucky and he was out, she planned to have a good snoop around the rest of the house. She wasn't lucky.

Within moments of her arrival, Turki bin Qassim appeared with a scowl on his face. 'You're late. I phoned your office and told them two o'clock.'

'Sorry, I didn't get the message.'

'I don't pay to be kept waiting. Nor does my wife.' He beckoned for her to follow him. 'Ayisha has been invited to a caviar tasting. My driver will take you. Make sure she's all right.'

He walked briskly from the kitchen through the hall and into the drawing room. The furniture was reproduction Louis Quinze and, sitting in a satin-backed armchair, Nicci finally got her first glimpse of the woman she'd been hired to protect. She wore a cream silk hijab, sat with her hands demurely folded in her lap and glanced up as her husband entered the room. Nicci did a double take. Had she been hired as a bodyguard or a babysitter?

Ayisha was beautiful in the manner of a startled fawn, but she was hardly more than a child. Nicci's best guess was sixteen. Wouldn't she have to be that for them to be legally married? Nicci wasn't sure. However, one thing soon became clear: this was no love match.

Turki pursed his lips in annoyance. 'This is Nicci, the body-guard. She will take you.'

His wife gave him a surly look and replied in Arabic.

'Speak English!' His tone suggested a man already at the end of his tether.

Nicci realized she'd inadvertently stepped into the middle of a ferocious battle of wills. Though Ayisha gave the initial impression of being a meek child bride, that was just a front.

She tossed her head, every inch the sulky teen. 'I don't want to go.'

'This is business. His wife has invited you. These are important people. You must go and be polite.'

'Caviar tastes like shit.'

'Don't eat it.'

'How will I be polite if I don't eat it?'

Turki shovelled his hands through his thick dark hair and growled in frustration. 'I'll take your phone away.'

Ayisha pulled a large iPhone 6 in a diamond-encrusted case from her pocket and held it out. 'Take it! I tell my father that you beat me.'

Turki spun on his heel and faced Nicci. 'You were a fucking cop. You make her go!'

Nicci stared at him in disbelief. 'Excuse me?'

Ignoring both women, he turned and stalked out of the room. Nicci looked at Ayisha, who gave her a guileless smile. 'So what are you? One of his whores?'

Nicci fixed her with a chilly stare. 'No. I've been employed to protect you.'

'My father is the Emir's third cousin, that's why he married me.'

'Not your stunning personality then.'

The girl sniggered. 'That's rude. I could have you sacked.'

'You'd be doing us both a favour.'

Ayisha got up from the chair. Small and delicate, the hijab was her only concession to tradition. The skinny jeans were Roberto Cavalli, the lacy tunic top was Oscar de la Renta, her tiny wrists and fingers were weighed down with jewellery.

She giggled again, a hollow, slightly desperate laugh, Nicci thought. 'Well, let's go and eat shitty caviar, shall we?'

The black Mercedes was waiting outside. Nicci held the back door open for her charge then got into the front seat next to the driver. It was a short journey from Mayfair to Holland Park and, apart from a small snarl-up of traffic in Notting Hill Gate, a smooth trip.

Lounging in the back seat, Ayisha didn't look up or out; she spent the entire time texting on her phone. Tapping away with both thumbs, grinning to herself as messages zapped back and forth, she seemed like any teenager in the globalized world. She had friends somewhere, though possibly not in London.

Nicci found herself wondering, for the millionth time, about her own daughter. What sort of teenager would Sophie have become? Would she too have been obsessed with gossiping on her phone? Would Nicci have got annoyed and chided her? Death had robbed her of all these experiences and possibilities. And when she thought about that too much the pain became physical.

The car drew up outside a huge porticoed mansion; it was the largest house on a street of outsized detached residences. Nicci got out of the Mercedes, opened the back door and waited.

Ayisha finally glanced up from her phone and Nicci was surprised to see a look of trepidation. 'I hate all this. I never know what to say to these women. They're all so old.'

'Tell your hostess she has a lovely home and you're really looking forward to trying the different sorts of caviar.'

The girl considered this. She was an odd combination of imperiousness and naivety. 'Won't she know that I'm lying?'

'People like to receive compliments. You're nice to them, they'll be nice back.'

'My mother says that to be a good wife you have to know how to lie.'

'There's a difference between lying and not telling people the whole truth if that would upset them.'

'Are you married?'

'Divorced.'

'So you are a whore?'

Nicci looked down at the teenager, hiding in the back of the car like a frightened rabbit. 'We look at these things differently over here, Ayisha.'

'Turki never takes me to meet his friends because they'll think I'm a stupid kid. But he makes me do stuff like this. Some Russian businessman he wants to impress.' The sourness and the sorrow in her tone made it hard for Nicci not to pity her.

She leant into the car and put her hand on the girl's shoulder. 'Listen to me, these things are never as bad as we imagine. Everyone gets nervous. You go in, you smile and you say nice things. About the house, about peoples' clothes. They'll like you and then Turki will be pleased, won't he?'

Ayisha nodded, though she still looked scared.

'Come on. It'll be okay and you'll have some funny stories to text to your friends.'

'I text my sister.'

'Your sister then. Look out for things to text her about.'

This did the trick. Ayisha emerged from the back of the car

and followed her bodyguard up the path to the massive front door. It opened magically before them without any need to ring the bell.

Nicci stood aside for her charge to enter. The hallway was huge, more of a foyer designed to impress than a domestic interior. The walls and floor were beige marble and led the eye back to a magnificent sweeping staircase with an ornate gold balustrade, which snaked round and up to the floor above. The finishing touch was an enormous crystal chandelier.

Ayisha – to her credit, Nicci thought – didn't seem that impressed. A butler dipped his head and held out his arm in welcome. But the hostess was already bearing down on them.

A foot taller than her young Qatari guest, with tumbling tresses of honey-blonde hair, she opened her arms. 'I am Galina. So delighted you could join us.'

Nicci was left on the doorstep watching Ayisha being borne away by the statuesque Russian.

Casting her eye around, she found the overall effect gaudy. The butler stared straight through her and walked away. A large minder was closing the front door.

He grinned at her and jabbed his finger. 'Hey, SBA, innit?' The accent was pure South London and he was six foot six of solid black muscle crammed into a tightly tailored suit. 'Ex-cop'd be my guess.'

Nicci smiled. 'Yeah. How d'you know?'

He stepped forward. 'You're looking at everything, checking it out. I was with 3 Para. Name's Jerome.'

He offered her his large meaty paw and they shook.

'Nicci. Pleased to meet you. How d'you know I work for SBA?'

'That Craig's a lucky bastard. Sweet deal.'

'You know Craig?'

'Oh yeah, we worked together. That fucking beard though!'

Nicci's gaze spun around. How could she have been so slow? It was obvious. 'You mean you work for Viktor Pudovkin? This is his house?'

Jerome grinned. 'Yeah, one of his houses. But probably his favourite. The boss is a real Londoner.'

61

During her time in the Met and subsequently, Nicci Armstrong had seen inside a fair number of London's classier addresses, but Viktor Pudovkin's Holland Park mansion was in a league of its own. It was a twenty-first-century urban palace, three floors of which were subterranean, set discreetly behind walls and trees in a landscaped garden. The opulence and scale of the place could only really be appreciated from within the electronically controlled perimeter. And like any traditional stately home, it comprised two worlds: upstairs and downstairs.

Jerome took Nicci down in the service lift to the underground bunker occupied by the staff. The kitchen was a hive of activity as two chefs from the fine food company who had been brought in to cater the caviar tasting laid out their wares.

He grinned at her. 'You like caviar?'

'Probably not.'

He helped himself to a plate from the counter. One of the chefs gave him a dirty look.

'You got a problem, mate?' In the modern below-stairs pecking order it wasn't the butler who ruled the roost, it was security, and Jerome was the man in charge.

He led Nicci down a corridor to his office suite. A bank of security monitors covered all entrances and exits to the mansion plus the main rooms. Nicci caught a glimpse of Ayisha, in the grand conservatory, chatting to another girl in a hijab; she'd found a friend.

Jerome offered Nicci the plate. 'Caspian Beluga. The boss has it flown in. You're supposed to eat it on its own, but most people can't hack it so we get these guys in to stick it on blinis.'

Nicci picked up one of the small squares loaded with dark beads. It smelt slightly fishy. She took a bite and ended up with a mouthful of popping bubbles. It wasn't as bad as she'd expected.

Still she wrinkled her nose. 'Bit too salty for me.'

The security man grinned. 'And that's the good stuff.'

'Quite an operation you got here.' Nicci was gazing at the computerized security system.

Jerome shrugged modestly. 'We got places all over the world, but this is our main base. The boss prefers London, so does the missus; kids go to school and nursery here.'

'Good bloke to work for?'

'Yeah, the wages and perks are good. He rewards loyalty.'

Nicci tilted her head; she didn't want her curiosity to be too obvious. 'I would've thought he'd want his security team to be Russian, though.'

Jerome chortled. 'Yeah, you'd think. Actually, it's the opposite.'

'Why?'

'You need a lesson in Russian politics to explain that fully.' He shook his head. 'Oligarchs and the Kremlin are pretty much in a head-to-head nowadays. Though the boss and Putin go way back. A few of the regime's opponents have been whacked in the UK and often it's their own Russian bodyguards who carry out the hit. The solution, if you're cautious like the boss, is to hire professionals with no connections to Moscow.'

'Makes sense. But didn't some gangster try and shoot your boss recently? He wasn't Russian.'

'You remind me of Craig – full of questions. Once a cop always a cop, eh?' Was that a warning shot across the bows? He was still smiling, so Nicci couldn't be sure.

'I like to understand what's going on. And I haven't been in security that long; I want to move up.'

'You got languages?'

'GCSE French.'

'That won't get you far. My Russian's not bad now. I done a couple of stints with the boss in Moscow. Arabic and Chinese – they're the other two, if you want to get on.'

'What was Moscow like?'

'Hard work. The whole place runs on bribes. From traffic cops up, you always got to be ready to slip them a note. And they blame everything on foreigners. Old ladies used to curse me in the street 'cause I'm black.'

'Doesn't sound much fun.'

'Why d'you think we got so many rich Russians living here?'

'I want to get on in this business. Only . . . y'know, you read stuff in the papers.' She didn't want to push too far in case he got suspicious. But she wasn't likely to chance upon a better opportunity to get the inside track on Viktor Pudovkin.

Jerome picked up one of the remaining blinis. 'Paper's all make it up as they go along.'

'Yeah, but I've heard stories too about what's expected. I did firearms training in the Met, but I've never shot anyone.'

'Close protection's not that different to being a cop. The job is to anticipate trouble and take evasive action. When those two assassins came after the boss, truth is on that day we failed. We found ourselves under attack, but we dealt with it – that's what we're trained for.'

'Did the police ever find out what it was about?'

Jerome shrugged. 'I never spoke to them.'

'They didn't question you?'

'Listen, Nicci, the cops stay out of our world. It's nothing to do with them. The boss talked to his contacts in the security service; one of the shooters was Russian, so somebody back there was probably behind the move. We'll be making our own inquiries.'

She painted on a smile. 'I guess I'm not used to this world. Spent my life chasing drug dealers.'

'I get it. You got scruples. And I'd rather have that on my team any day of the week.' He beamed at her, but it was clear the discussion was over. 'Tell you what, fancy a look round? This place is amazing. More modern art than the fucking Tate.'

'Is that allowed?'

'Yeah, if I say it is. Anyway, I got an ulterior motive.'

'Which is what?'

'Want you to put in a good word for me with Craigie. Never know when it might come in handy.'

Jerome proceeded to take her upstairs for a conducted tour of the ground floor. The drawing room was large, with comfortable white leather sofas and, as he explained, hung with the boss's unique collection of twentieth-century Russian painters. Nicci vaguely recognized two: Chagall and Kandinsky.

Over the fireplace in the library there was a sleek racehorse painted by George Stubbs; it matched the oak panelling and more traditional feel of the room. As she admired it, Jerome pressed his earpiece. Someone was talking to him. Excusing himself for a moment, he disappeared into the hall.

Finding herself alone in the room, Nicci was in a quandary. She was inside the Russian's house, fortress Pudovkin, and it was an opportunity she couldn't ignore. In her bag she had the voice-activated bugs that Eddie had given her. But the place was riddled with cameras; doing anything would be a hell of a risk. Reaching down, she carefully pulled out one of the tiny devices and cradled it in her palm. She knew she had only seconds to make up her mind. Would she ever have a better chance than this to gather some serious intel on the untouchable billionaire?

She scanned the room rapidly for the camera positions and, stepping out of what she judged to be their sightline, searched for a suitable place to hide the bug. There were plenty of bookshelves full of unopened books. She found an appropriate nook, clicked the device on and tucked it away. The place was probably swept regularly, but they might glean something before it was found. There was a leather wingback chair set beside the fire, so there was an outside chance Pudovkin might actually use the room.

Nicci rejoined the security man in the hall; he was issuing instructions to a subordinate. She gave him a smile and said she needed to go out and check on her driver. What she really wanted to do was call Eddie Lunt and see if he could pick up a signal from the bug.

The Mercedes was parked on the road behind several other luxury vehicles. There was a double yellow line, but no one seemed to be bothered by it. Walking along the pavement, she took out her phone, but before she could make the call it rang. The caller ID read withheld; she clicked the button to accept the call.

'Hello?'

'Hi, is that Nicci?' The voice was familiar, but she couldn't quite place it.

'Yeah, who's this?'

'Kaz, Kaz Phelps. I heard through Eddie that you wanted to talk to me. Sorry I didn't get back to you sooner.'

'My God! Are you okay?'

'Yeah, I'm fine. Listen, I can see you might be a bit pissed off with me, but I need a favour. I wondered if you'd meet me for a coffee.'

62

It took Paul Ackroyd a couple of days to make contact with the Kemals. Asil Kemal refused to speak on the phone and Paul ended up having to go and see him in his office over a kebab shop in Walthamstow. To say the Turks were wary was an understatement.

Asil fixed him with an icy glare. 'I don't know why you come to me.'

'Look, Mr Kemal, Joey Phelps shafted me good and proper and his sister's trying to do the same. Now, I'm not generally a vengeful bloke—'

Sadik, standing with his arms folded behind his brother, smirked. 'Everyone is vengeful, if only in their hearts.'

'I've known Kaz Phelps since she was a kid. I know what she's like. You want her and I can deliver her. At a price.'

'How d'you know we want her?' Asil shifted in his chair.

'C'mon, I keep my ear to the ground. You been asking around, you been looking all over for her.'

'And why should I trust you?'

'Call up Ilker in Basildon. He knows me, we've done business.'

The brothers exchanged glances. Paul knew full well that Asil Kemal wouldn't even have agreed to the meeting if his credentials hadn't already been thoroughly checked.

'Ilker says you are a good customer.'

He was buying cocaine from the local Turks in hundred grand tranches and distributing it around the bars and clubs of Essex, so he was more than that. But he merely inclined his head in polite acknowledgement.

Asil folded his hands in front of him. 'You want twenty high-quality cannabis plants and you want to choose them yourself. Why?'

'I have a private client. He's in the music business. Famous, in fact. Wants to grow his own. But he's very exacting. I can't afford to disappoint him.'

'How will you persuade Kaz Phelps to accompany you?'

'That's my problem.'

'You could just tell us where she is.'

'That bitch has caused me a lot of grief. Maybe I want to see the look on her face when she realizes what I've done.'

The brothers had a brief conversation in Turkish. Paul got the impression that Sadik was possibly more in favour of his proposition than Asil.

But what he'd said to them seemed to have done the trick. An appeal to their cruelty had been Kaz's idea and it looked as though she was on the money with that.

The older brother leant back in his chair and his cold, hooded eyes rested on Paul. Then, abruptly, the decision was made. The Turk held out his hand, they shook and Asil Kemal agreed to call the following day with a time and an address.

Driving out of town on the M11, Paul felt elated; he knew he was taking a considerable risk, but maybe his life had become too safe. He missed the buzz. He was a middle-ranking player and he did all right. A beautiful home in the country, a lovely family and, since Joey went to jail, he'd established a niche for himself.

The story about cannabis plants for the musician wasn't a

lie. He specialized in offering rich clients a personal service. The second-hand car dealership on the A127, set up twenty years ago by his dad, now did a good trade in four-by-fours and provided the perfect front for his other activities. The old bill didn't bother him, nor did the taxman. So why had he agreed to Kaz's crazy scheme?

Did she think he was a total moron? He may have got a bit pissed, but he could see exactly what she was doing. The bitch thought she could wind him round her little finger. She and Joey were peas in a pod, always had been, charming but arrogant. Their old man had been a total psycho, a cold-hearted killer, and they were just a more sophisticated version. Would she walk in there and shoot the Kemal brothers dead? It was entirely possible. She was a Phelps; she was mental enough to do it. On the other hand, Sadik could prove too fast for her.

As he pondered the possible outcomes, he was sure about one thing: whichever way it played out, Paul Ackroyd wouldn't be the loser. If it looked like the Kemals were going down, he'd weigh in on her side. He'd take the cannabis factories but more than that, she'd owe him big time, and he'd get to those offshore accounts.

However, if it looked like going the other way he wouldn't intervene. Sadik could have her. Getting onside with large-scale importers like the Kemals could open up all sorts of opportunities. In fact, the more he thought about it the more that began to seem like the safer and more profitable outcome for him.

He was under no illusions about what Kaz really thought of him. She'd run out on him as soon as she got the chance and he certainly didn't buy this hogwash about her being upset and jealous that he had a wife and kid. He still fancied her – who wouldn't? If anything, the last ten years had transformed her from a hot teenager into a real knockout. And the dyke thing added spice to the mix. He'd fuck her, no question. Rafa need never know. But trust her? No way.

She was a Phelps and they were all the same: manipulative, two-faced liars. The old man had shafted him, made sure he went to jail. He'd worked for the son and got shafted by him too. But those bastards were both dead. Now it was his time. Did that stupid bitch really think she could sucker him? She was about to discover her mistake. She was about to discover that it was him, Paul Ackroyd, and not her precious Joey who'd been the smart one all along.

63

They'd arranged to meet early on Sunday morning. Following Kaz's suggestion, Paul picked her up at Finsbury Park tube. He arrived in an old Range Rover with untraceable plates; Darius was riding shotgun and in the back was a pale, extremely young skinhead, who he introduced as Lee.

Darius offered Kaz the front seat and they headed north up Seven Sisters Road.

Turning his head, Paul gave her a wintry smile. 'Nervous?'

'Not particularly.'

'I only brought Darius and Lee. Didn't want the Kemals to get suspicious.'

'Sensible.' She was wearing figure-hugging jeans and a short biker-style leather jacket. Her hair had been trimmed to remove the strands singed in the fire and the tortoiseshell Ray-Bans were pushed up casually on top of her head. She carried no bag and Paul wondered where she'd stashed the gun. A jacket pocket, probably.

He'd put the address in his satnav and it led them to a side street round the back of Seven Sisters tube station. Kaz recognized the building; faced with crumbling yellow London brick, it gave the appearance of being deserted.

'Yeah, this is where I came with Joey.' She pointed. 'That's the door.'

Paul slotted the Range Rover into a parking space across

the road. Killing the engine, he took a breath. He'd had butterflies in his stomach ever since he woke up, though he didn't want the others to know that. He liked to think he was an adrenaline junkie but that wasn't really true. Kaz, in contrast, seemed unnaturally calm, which proved what he'd always thought: she was a psycho like her brother.

She gave him a cool smile. 'All right, mate? You look a bit pale.'

'I'm totally fine. Right, let's rock 'n' roll!'

They all climbed out of the Range Rover; a motley crew, Kaz reflected. Lee was a skinny kid with a glazed expression; he was definitely on something. But Darius was alert. Kaz wondered if she could rely on him. Probably not. Unless he thought it was to his advantage. She still couldn't make him out. He'd proved he wasn't particularly loyal to Paul. So why had he come and what the hell was his agenda?

Paul strode across the road towards the old clothing factory; his shoulders were hunched. Kaz got the impression he was bricking it. Gazing up at the sky, she saw a hint of blue breaking through the clouds. It was a mild enough day; people would soon be out in the London parks taking their Sunday-morning walks. A stroll to admire the autumn foliage, stopping off for a coffee and a bacon sandwich – that would be a pleasant way to spend the day. Would she ever have the chance to do that again?

The gamble she was about to take carried enormous risk. Sadik Kemal on his own was a pitiless killer – and he wouldn't be alone. There were too many ways this could go wrong, she was well aware of that. Did she have the ghost of a chance of getting out alive? She doubted it.

Paul pressed the button on the metal intercom beside the door. He shot Kaz a guilty look and painted on a smile. At least he was predictable. The look said he planned to double-cross her, but that was what she'd been expecting.

The door opened, wooden but backed with steel, and Kaz recognized Quan, the ageless Vietnamese plant expert who'd worked for her brother.

She grinned at him. 'Hello, Quan. How's tricks?'

Was he smiling back? It was hard to tell.

He extended his arm, inviting them in. 'Please.'

Kaz knew the route. A narrow stairway, a short corridor, then through several layers of black plastic sheeting into the growing space. They reached the vast room full of cannabis plants and filled with the hum from the low oscillating fans. Paul and his sidekicks gazed in amazement.

This was Joey's handiwork and she felt proud. 'Neat, eh?'

Paul simply nodded and Kaz got a whiff of the envy he must've felt towards her brother.

They followed Quan as he skirted around the edge of the room and the sea of plants, through more plastic sheeting and a doorway leading to the offices at the back.

Blocking their way were two large minders. The first one gestured for them to raise their arms. One by one they were patted down for hidden weapons. Paul shot Kaz an anxious glance, but they all passed muster.

As they continued down the corridor, he whispered in her ear: 'Where's the gun?'

She turned to look at him. 'Oh, I didn't bring it. Changed my mind.'

'What?'

'Well, you're gonna hand me over, aren't you? That's your plan.'

'No—'

'C'mon, don't lie to me as well. Let's just do it.'

She didn't wait for his reply but carried on down the corridor in Quan's wake. Paul was completely thrown. What the fuck was she playing at? How did she know? Instinct told him to turn tail and run, but Darius and Lee were behind him. He had no time to think, he had to go forward.

In the glass-panelled office at the end of the corridor, Asil Kemal was seated at the desk. Sadik stood beside him.

Kaz strolled in, hands in her pockets, a smile on her face. 'You nicked this place from my brother. We've come to take it back.'

Asil laced his fingers. 'You're not serious.'

'Never more so.'

Paul appeared in the doorway behind her. She could feel the nervous tension burning off him; he was desperate to complete the deal and get out.

He gave the Kemals a curt nod. 'I've fulfilled my part of the bargain. Now do I get my plants?'

Asil gave him a cursory glance, then signalled to one of the minders. 'He'll help you choose.'

Kaz turned to face her former lover. She could sense his confusion and panic, but it served him right.

The look she gave him was almost teasing. She feigned shock, but it was for the Turks' benefit. 'What? We were gonna take this place back, that was the plan – and now you're gonna let them kill me for a few cannabis plants?'

Paul was out of his depth, caught between Kaz and the Kemals. His plan had been to simply pick the winning side. But that wasn't simple at all.

He struggled to meet her eye. 'I'm a businessman, babe.'

'Oh, is that what you call it?'

Both Kemal brothers were smirking. They said something to each other in Turkish as Paul pushed past Lee and Darius and scurried off down the corridor to collect his blood money.

Kaz turned to Asil. 'Well, you never know who you can trust, do you?'

'You are one stupid bitch!' He was chuckling.

She shrugged. 'Looks a bit that way. Just out of interest, have you taken over the other four factories Joey set up?'

Asil glanced up at his brother. 'Can you believe this bitch?'

Sadik laughed. 'Too many questions. I soon shut her up.'

Kaz placed her hands on her hips. 'Oh come on, Asil. No one wants to think they've been beaten by a complete dip-shit. Have you got all five?'

'You stupid bitch, of course we have.'

'I thought you were smugglers. You sure you're smart enough to grow good skunk? I mean, I know you got Quan. But this takes a bit more brains than running a kebab shop.'

'Oh, I have plenty of brains.' Asil leant forward and fixed her with a steely glare. The cheek of this whore! She should know her place. His rage was rising. He wanted this matter settled. Only then would the shame be expunged. The memory of the shoot-out in the alley behind his office had haunted him ever since. She would feel his vengeance, then he'd be free.

But the bitch was standing there, smiling at him. Where was her fear?

Goaded by her insolence, he drummed his index finger on the desk. 'This is my territory. Every drug deal that goes down in North London is controlled by me. You and your stupid brother dare to think you can move in on my territory?'

'Yeah, but I still got Joey's Russians to back me up. Don't forget that.'

'You mean like that toy soldier he sent round?'

'Yevgeny Koshkin.'

'I don't know his fucking name. But I don't see him here troubling me no more, do you?'

'Was it you who had him shot then?'

'I deal with my enemies – and I dealt with him just as I'm going to deal with you.' He turned his head to his brother and growled something in Turkish. Sadik nodded and sniggered.

'Could you translate that into English so we can all understand.' Kaz tilted her head. 'By all, I'm including the old bill.'

Asil stared at her, then he rocked back in his chair and laughed. 'Nice try.'

Kaz started to unbutton the front of her shirt. 'No really, I'm not bluffing. Your meathead of a minder didn't have the balls to put his hand down my cleavage.' She revealed the tiny microphone taped to her sternum. 'They're clever, these little gizmos. You didn't seriously think I was going to walk in here with that tosser, Paul Ackroyd, and no backup?'

A life of caution had kept Asil Kemal out of jail, but a moment of fury had caused him to drop his guard. Realizing the horror of his mistake, he jumped to his feet. Sadik pulled out a gun and shouted instructions in Turkish. Then he pointed his gun straight at Kaz's head.

This had always been the danger: the gangster would simply react by shooting her, thinking he'd still have time to get away. Asil rushed out into the corridor; the two minders were already racing for the back door.

Kaz felt the thump of her heartbeat. All she could see was Sadik's angry face looming over her; he was cursing her in Turkish, spitting out the words. She didn't want this to be the image in her mind at the moment of her death so she closed her eyes. She thought of her sister and Finlay. At least now they'd be all right.

The explosion of the gunshot seemed to fill the tiny office.

Kaz's eyes flew open as someone was thrown back against her. It was Darius. He'd made a grab for the gun and Sadik had shot him in the leg. The Turk steadied his hand to take a second shot but there were shouts of 'Armed Police!' and a thundering of heavy boots fast approaching. Sadik Kemal changed his mind and ran.

Darius slumped on the floor. He'd been hit in the femoral artery and the blood was pumping out of him. Kaz ripped off her jacket and then her shirt. Winding the material into a twisted braid, she tied it round his thigh to create a tourniquet.

She pulled it tight and grasped his hand. 'Look at me, Darius! Look at me! Hang on in there, mate.' Only a week ago she'd said the exact same thing to the young curate; it felt spooky. Would he die too?

His eyelids drooped. She could hardly make out what he was saying. It sounded like 'Not Darius.'

64

Tom Rivlin clambered out of the back of the police surveillance van. He was finding it hard to contain his jubilation and he was desperate to call Nicci. She'd wanted to be there and he'd pleaded with the Met commander in charge of the operation to allow it. None of this would've been possible without her, he'd made that argument robustly. But he'd got short shrift; she was a civilian, a chis. It could compromise the security of the operation. Nicci understood.

She was waiting in a coffee shop near Finsbury Park tube. They'd commandeered the back room to put the wire on Karen Phelps. At that point it seemed sensible to have Nicci there to reassure Phelps and calm any nerves.

Rivlin scrolled his phone to find Nicci's number and she answered immediately.

'Tom, how did it go?'

'We got the bastards!'

'Brilliant! Is Karen all right?'

'Yeah. There was one casualty. The Kemals made a run for it and Sadik tried to shoot his way out, but an officer from SCO19 shot the pistol right out of his hand. Brilliant piece of marksmanship. It was textbook.'

'You saw it?'

'We got it all through the headcams. Kemal stood there like he couldn't believe it.'

343

'And what did you get on the wire?'

'Enough, I think. It's going straight to the CPS, but the charges will be serious. Both Kemal brothers will be going down for a very long time. We got enough to charge Paul Ackroyd too.'

'That'll please Stoneham. A bonus for her.'

'Yeah, but none of this would've been possible without you, Nic.'

'Karen came to me. I was just the conduit.'

'She came to you because she trusted you. She wouldn't have trusted us without you as a go-between.'

There was a silence on the other end of the line. Rivlin couldn't be sure – was she crying?

'You okay, Nic?'

'Yeah.'

'It's the stress. Listen, once I've finished up here, I'm coming to collect you. I'm going to buy you the best dinner in London. Michelin stars, the works.'

She chuckled. 'You'll need deep pockets for that. But do you know where Karen is now? I need to talk to her.'

'I'm not sure. I can probably find out.'

'Yeah, would you?'

'She's fine, Nic. You don't have to worry about her any more. The Kemals are under lock and key. She's earned herself enough brownie points with Stoneham; they won't revoke her licence. She's got her life back.'

'Yeah, well . . . There's something I need to tell her. I didn't want to mention it before.'

65

Kaz was put in the back of a police car for an initial debrief. Her jeans were covered in Darius's blood and she was shirtless, wearing only her leather jacket.

The Met officer who'd been appointed her handler got into the vehicle with her. DS Amy Raheem was small and delicate compared to Helen and Irina. But she had the air of a tough London kid and that was something Kaz could relate to.

Raheem smiled at her. 'You okay?'

'Anyone get away?'

'Nope. We arrested all of them.'

Kaz leant her head back against the seat and sighed. She was still wired but as the tension in her subsided, her limbs were becoming leaden. 'You're not gonna nick Darius as well, are you? He saved me.'

'He's gone to hospital. I'm not exactly sure of the situation there.'

Kaz read the evasion in her voice. 'What d'you mean? He's gonna be okay? He's not gonna die?'

'No, I don't think so.'

'Can I go and see him?'

'Listen, Karen, I'm being honest with you, I don't know . . .' Raheem hesitated and looked at Kaz. 'Oh, why the hell not? You're covered in blood, so let's say you need checking over too. A sensible precaution, I think. But don't do a runner on me, okay?'

'I haven't got the energy. I just wanna see that Darius is okay.'

Raheem made a phone call and, having obtained permission for Kaz to go for medical treatment, instructed the driver to take them to University College Hospital A&E on Euston Road. This was where Darius had gone.

Her warrant card got them through triage straight away and once a nurse had sponged the blood off Kaz, it turned out some of it was her own. She had a nasty gash on her hand. Most probably she'd cut it when Darius had knocked her backwards as he grappled with Sadik Kemal for possession of the gun.

Those few seconds when she'd closed her eyes, assuming she was going to die, then opened them again, meant Kaz hadn't seen exactly what Darius had done. But he'd been there for her, he hadn't run out on her with Paul. He was unarmed, as far as she knew, yet he'd tackled Kemal. And she was determined to make sure the police didn't get stupid and nick him.

When they first arrived, Raheem had made inquiries and discovered that Darius was in surgery – they'd have to wait. This was a relief to Kaz. She needed some time out, to give her body and brain time to settle.

Once her hand had been dressed, they found a quiet corner in the hospital cafe. Kaz must've dropped off. When she woke up she was lying on the leather banquette, her jacket draped over her; the cop had disappeared. Her brain felt groggy. She wasn't sure how long she'd been asleep. The stress had taken its toll. Getting up slowly, she peered around. Then she noticed Raheem near the cafe entrance. She was talking to someone, a woman, and there were a couple of uniforms there too.

Kaz had a feeling she'd seen the woman before. She moved her position to get a better look. Then she recognized her: it was the fat boss cop from Essex, DCI Cheryl Stoneham.

Stoneham and her sidekicks walked off and Raheem headed back in Kaz's direction. It was obvious from her expression that something was going on.

The cop painted on a smile but the tone was brisk. 'How you feeling? We need to go.'

'Not until I've seen Darius.'

'That's not going to be possible.'

'What's happened? Is he dead?'

'No, but . . .' Raheem hesitated. 'Look, you can't see him, okay.'

Kaz got to her feet. This was too much. 'Says who? DCI Fucking Stoneham? I don't believe this! You bastards are not gonna nick him! I told you, he saved my life.'

'I know. But it's complicated—'

'Like fuck!'

Anger gave her a surge of adrenaline and that produced energy. Kaz stormed out of the cafe and down the corridor in the direction Stoneham had taken.

Raheem had to trot to keep up. 'Karen, will you just let this go. It's not what you think.'

'If I have to search this whole fucking hospital, I'll find him!'

In the event, that wasn't necessary; instead she went to the enquiry desk and gave them Darius's name. Raheem was talking anxiously into her mobile – reporting to Stoneham, no doubt. Kaz left her to it and headed for the lifts.

The ward was on the fifth floor. Kaz strode past the bays until she caught sight of Stoneham standing at the end of a bed.

As she approached, the DCI turned, frowned and shook her head. 'Karen, you can't—'

Darius was lying there with a drip in his arm, still woozy from the anaesthetic. A young woman sat beside him, holding his hand.

Kaz glared at Stoneham. 'You lot, you're like fucking vultures. Can't you leave him alone? He saved my life.'

'I know that.'

Darius grinned weakly from the bed. 'And you saved mine, Kaz. I'd have bled to death if it hadn't been for you.'

'You came through for me, mate. I wasn't sure I could trust you. Turns out I was wrong.'

He gave her a sheepish grin. 'Yeah well, not entirely. This is gonna come as a bit of a shock, but my name's not Darius. I'm Danny.'

Not Darius.

'What d'you mean, you're Danny?'

'DC Danny Mullen. I'm an undercover police officer.'

Kaz stared at him in disbelief. They were all looking at her: him, Stoneham, the girl holding his hand.

She started to laugh. 'What the fuck? You're a fucking copper! Who was you after? Me?'

Raheem appeared. She gave Stoneham an apologetic look. 'Sorry, ma'am.'

The DCI sighed wearily. 'It can't be helped.' She turned to Kaz. 'He wasn't after you, Karen. Not at all. Danny went undercover six months ago to target Paul Ackroyd. Part of our operation to round up the Essex drug dealers who thought they could step into your brother's shoes.'

Kaz shook her head. The Kemals, Paul, she'd anticipated all the moves. But not this. 'I knew you never went to my school.'

He smiled. 'I wasn't doing too well until you came along.

Paul didn't trust me. But once I'd helped you, he changed his mind.'

'So you was using me? Maybe I should've let you bleed to death.'

'It was a fluid situation.' Stoneham sounded like most coppers: full of shit. 'I told him to keep an eye on you – and not just so we could use you; it was way more complicated than that. You were the victim. And the Kemals were extremely dangerous. It was precarious for both of you.'

Kaz jabbed a finger in Danny's direction, her initial disbelief turning to anger. 'Maybe you did put yourself on the line for me, but I'm no one's fucking victim, okay? You suckered me, you bastard. And don't tell me you was only doing your fucking job!'

Danny shrugged. 'I was only doing my job.'

It felt as if her legs had been kicked from under her. Kaz could feel the tears prickling the backs of her eyes, but she was damned if she'd let them see her cry. 'You bastards are all the same.' She glared at Raheem. 'I need to get out of here. And I don't need a fucking babysitter.'

DCI Stoneham moved towards her. 'Hang on, Karen, we've got something for you. Bit of quid pro quo.' She extracted a slip of paper from her bag and offered it to Kaz. 'It's Mika Koshkin's address. Irina is staying with him. You told Danny you wanted to find her.'

Kaz took the paper and glanced at it. If they expected a thank you they could fuck off.

Stoneham smiled. 'You're not Joey. I know that. You took a huge risk today. And we are grateful.'

'You think I'd've done it if I had a choice?'

'I don't know. But all you need to do now is keep in touch with the probation service and get on with your life.'

'You expect me to be grateful? You lot make me fucking laugh. All the resources you got and you still couldn't nick the Kemals. You needed me for that.'

The DCI gave her a rueful shrug. 'Evil triumphs unless good people are prepared to intervene. Whatever system we invent, in the end it's not enough on its own.'

'Sounds like pretentious bollocks to me, but I'll take your word for it.'

'Why don't you let DS Raheem take you home so you can have a shower and sort yourself out a bit?'

'Either I'm free to go or I'm not.'

'You're free to go.'

'Then I'll take myself home.' Kaz turned on her heel and walked away.

Raheem gave the DCI an enquiring look. Stoneham shook her head. 'Let her go for now.'

66

Standing on the pavement, watching the belching queue of cars and buses and vans choking Euston Road, Kaz felt a degree of relief. It wasn't so much the fact that Darius was a copper, it was that he'd suckered her. It seemed that most of the people she'd ever cared about in her life had fed her a pack of lies. Her brother, Helen Warner ... the grief she felt for them still ripped at her insides. But neither had managed to be straight with her.

For the moment she was glad to be alone. All she wanted was to disappear into the swarm of eight million Londoners. The largest city in Europe offered a nook or cranny to all comers, native or immigrant. A glittering cultural hub and a haven for dirty money, it was also the best place on the planet to get lost.

Now that she had access to her brother's money and the Kemals were off her back, maybe she could finally settle. But where? The luxury apartment at Battersea Reach was very grand but it felt like a temporary bolthole. She wasn't sure what she wanted to do or where she wanted to be. It would depend on Natalie. And it would also depend on Irina. The problem was, neither of them would even speak to her.

The phone in her pocket buzzed. It was Nicci, for the umpteenth time. Five missed calls.

Clicking the phone on, she held it to her ear. 'Did you know about fucking Darius?'

The rumble of traffic drowned out Nicci's reply. Plugging one ear with her finger, Kaz managed a brief conversation. Nicci sounded in a flap but there was nothing new in that. She'd come to the hospital and had been searching everywhere for Kaz. They made an arrangement to meet up in a Starbucks on Tottenham Court Road.

Kaz wasn't entirely sure what she felt about Nicci Armstrong. She could be prissy and judgemental, and although she wasn't a cop any longer she still behaved like one. But since her release from jail, Nicci had been the one person Kaz had been able to consistently rely on. She didn't do bullshit and she spoke her mind. Kaz hadn't always liked what she said. But she knew where she was with Nicci, which was more than she could say for anyone else, including her own sister.

As she entered the coffee shop, Kaz's heart sank. Nicci was standing in line at the counter with her cop mate, Rivlin. They were laughing about something and he had his hand on her arm. It struck Kaz as an intimate gesture. Was something going on between them? The notion that Nicci Armstrong might actually have relationships had never occurred to Kaz. She was still wondering when they noticed her.

Nicci came over immediately. She looked Kaz up and down, her eyes taking in the jeans, still caked in blood and smelling vaguely metallic. 'You okay?'

'Yeah. Did you know Darius was an undercover cop?'

'No. Not until Tom told me a minute ago. And he didn't know until this morning.'

'Am I supposed to believe that?'

'The way the system works, other officers are only told on a need-to-know basis. Stoneham was the DCI in charge. No one knew about him but her.'

Kaz considered this. 'You sure lover boy is telling you the truth?'

Nicci tilted her head and grinned. 'Yeah. And it's not just because he's great in bed that I believe him. I also know that's how undercover operations work. It's kept as tight as possible, it has to be.'

Kaz cracked a smile. 'Tell him I'll have a chocolate muffin and a double espresso. I'm starving.'

After Nicci had relayed the order to Rivlin they found a table towards the back of the shop.

Sitting down, the ex-cop interlaced her fingers and frowned. 'You've been through a lot today.'

'At least it's over. And the Kemals won't be out any time soon.'

'There's no easy way to say this, Karen. Maybe it isn't over.'

'What d'you mean?'

'When I told you before that you were wrong about Pudovkin and the problem was the Kemals, I think maybe it wasn't the whole story.'

'What, now you think Pudovkin was behind the shootings and the fire?'

Nicci sighed. 'No. That probably was all down to the Kemals. But I've since found out that someone else is on the hunt for you. And I'm guessing it's Pudovkin.'

Kaz inclined her head in Rivlin's direction. 'You told him?'

'We've discussed it. But it's the same problem as before: the police would need a shedload of evidence to move against someone like Pudovkin. And, within the framework of the law, it's very difficult to get proof.'

'Doesn't matter who he's had murdered, he's still fucking untouchable then.'

Nicci opened her palms. 'Let's not panic. All we know at the moment is that he *might*, emphasis on might, be looking for you.'

'Fuck me, Nicci. You know how this works. You'll know for certain when my dead body washes up downstream and gets found by some bloke walking his dog.'

'Yeah. But he's got to find you first.'

Kaz's brain was reeling. Some instinct, a sixth sense, had always told her that Pudovkin was the real danger, but Nicci had talked her out of it. The dream of settling evaporated. Nothing had changed; she was still on the run.

Nicci reached out and grabbed her hand. 'Listen, Karen. Behind all his money he's no better than the Kemals. He's just another gangster.'

'You've already said no one's about to arrest him, though.'

'Maybe not. But I'll tell you something: I've had it with all this.' There was no mistaking the bitterness in her voice.

'All what?'

'I may not be a police officer any more, but this is still my city. And it sticks in my throat that rich villains like him think they can come here and be above the law. It won't be easy, but somehow I'm going to find a way to get the evidence to take him down.'

'You serious?'

'I'll tell you how serious.' A glint came into Nicci's eye. 'I've been inside his house. Well, mansion. You should see it. And I've bugged one room already. I've got Eddie listening in.'

'Isn't that ever so slightly illegal?'

'I've come to the sad conclusion that sometimes the end does justify the means.'

Rivlin was starting to walk across the room towards them carrying a tray of drinks. Nicci shot a quick look in his direction. 'Tom doesn't know about any of this. So keep it to yourself, okay? I don't want to put him in an awkward position.'

Kaz scanned her. Something in Nicci Armstrong had indeed shifted. The toughness had always been there but, as she talked about the Russian, a steely look had come into her eye. Her anxiety and habitual confusion over whether she was doing the right thing had gone. She seemed calmer and happy, smiling at her lover and joking with him as he unloaded the tray.

Bugging Viktor Pudovkin's house? That sounded like the far side of crazy. Kaz wondered what else she had in mind. Setting up the Kemals was one thing, but Viktor Pudovkin wasn't some low-life drug smuggler with a gun. He had his own private army, for starters, plus a selection of influential people in his pocket. If he was looking for her, Kaz knew that the most sensible course would be to hide. Brave and bold as Nicci's approach sounded, it was also naive – and there was a good chance it would get them both killed.

67

Although she'd only met him a handful of times, Kaz knew Mika Koshkin was some sort of third cousin to Irina and a surly individual who'd worked for Yevgeny on what had appeared to be an ad hoc basis. He'd served a short stint in the Russian army but had gone AWOL when his unit hadn't been paid. Spare muscle when it was needed; he wasn't that bright and after a year in the country his English was still rudimentary. He also had a thing for Irina; she and Kaz had even joked about the way he would gaze at her like a drooling bulldog.

The address Kaz had received from Stoneham led her to a mansion block in Maida Vale. She rang the doorbell several times and got no answer. Finally she slipped into the building as another resident was coming out and made her way to the third floor. Then she simply hammered on the door until it opened.

The flat, puggish features glared at her. 'She don't wanna see you.'

'Come on, Mika. I ain't going away. I just wanna talk.'

In the hallway behind him, a female voice said something in Russian. With a shrug he let go of the door and allowed Kaz to enter.

Irina was standing in the doorway to the sitting room. With her hair raked back in a severe bun, her pale face was starkly beautiful.

She flapped a hand ineffectually at Kaz. 'Cops come here, ask stupid questions. I don't fucking know what's going on. I think maybe they deport me.'

Kaz followed her into the room. 'All the more reason why you need my help. 'Cause Mika, bless him, might be useful in a punch-up but he knows fuck all about anything else.'

An old sofa, covered in a tartan throw and littered with crumpled tissues, dominated the room. Curling her legs under her, Irina sank down in the middle of it like a broken bird settling on her nest. The room felt overheated and stale with the taint of nicotine and grief.

Kaz folded her arms. 'Is this what you been doing? Just sitting here.'

'What the fuck should I do?'

'Go back to your house.'

'Mika say not safe.'

'Irina, if the old bill can find you, anyone can. Anyway, the thugs that had Yevgeny shot have been arrested.'

'How you know this?'

'It happened this morning. I was there.'

The Russian stared at her and tears welled up in her eyes. Kaz walked over to the sofa, sat down and pulled Irina into her arms. She stroked the fair hair and kissed her forehead. 'Oh, babes. I know this is shit. But you gotta let me help you.'

'Yev, always so tough. I can't believe he dead. Why he dead? So not fair, Kaz. Yev, he a good man.'

'Both our brothers were the same. They chose the life for themselves. They knew the risks.'

'My mother want me to go home.'

'What d'you want?'

'I want Yev back. And Tolya.' Her head sank on Kaz's shoulder.

Small and muscle-bound, in a soiled vest, Mika was scowling at them from the doorway. He mumbled in Russian.

Kaz shot him a stony look. 'What's he saying?'

'He say is your fault my brother's dead.'

Kaz got up. In two strides she was in Mika's face. 'Don't piss me off, you little scrote. I'm here to help. You know how things work over here? How you get the coroner to release a body? How you arrange a funeral? I'm guessing not.'

Irina translated and there followed a rapid-fire exchange in Russian between her and Mika. Kaz read the escalating tension between them and the rising anger in his voice.

'What's he saying now?'

But Mika answered for himself, spitting the words in Kaz's face. 'You, queer bitch! You sick! No good! No fucking good for her! Yev knew this, he kill you!'

So that was his beef. He wanted someone to blame, someone to hate. She took a step back.

Irina was sobbing and Kaz could tell from her tone of voice that she was trying to placate him. She wondered idly if Yevgeny had been as homophobic as his cousin. Would he have been shocked and disgusted if he'd realized she was in love with his sister? The fact he'd never remotely suspected probably gave her the answer to that question.

Ignoring Mika, she calmly turned to face Irina. 'What do you think? Do you agree with him? 'Cause if you do, I'll walk away.'

Placing her palm over her mouth, Irina gulped down her tears. She couldn't speak.

'I'm in love with you, Irina. Is that sick? You tell me.'

Mika was talking again, short argumentative phrases, emphasized with a jab of the finger.

Kaz stood stock-still in the middle of the room and waited.

Irina looked up. 'You love me? Really?' She seemed puzzled.

'Yes, why the fuck d'you think I'm here?'

The Russian wiped the back of her hand across her tear-stained face. She'd been holed up in this crummy flat for nearly two weeks and the truth was she was frustrated and bored. It reminded her of Magnitogorsk and the life she'd escaped. Mika was like her mother, full of dire warnings and foreboding. But here, in England, they did things differently and it was definitely more fun. Kaz was more fun.

Irina frowned. 'Girl with girl. Is probably wrong. My mother, she would not like. Church say is a sin.'

'Okay.' Kaz nodded and turned to go.

'But I don't care.' A grin spread across Irina's face. 'No, I don't fucking care!'

She burst out laughing. Kaz joined in. Mika cursed them in Russian.

Kaz held out her hand. 'Good. So let's get out of this shithole. It stinks.'

68

Tom Rivlin was as good as his word. The restaurant had a Michelin star and a price tag to match. Looking up from her menu, Nicci smiled at him across the table. 'You eat out in places like this, people are going to think you're bent.'

'They can think what they like. We've done a good day's work. We deserve a treat.'

Nicci gazed around. There were as many waiters as diners but the atmosphere was relaxed. She reflected that this was what London offered now: the best of everything for those who could afford it.

Rivlin adjusted his cutlery and put on a serious face. 'So now, Ms Armstrong, we need to order. Then you and I need to have a talk.'

'That sounds ominous. Am I in trouble, officer?'

Ignoring the question, he beckoned the waiter. She ordered a complicated confection with quails' eggs followed by lamb. He chose some sort of pâté and beef.

The waiter topped up their glasses. The wine was red, a Margaux; it tasted rich and decadent to Nicci.

Rivlin raised his glass. 'Confusion to the enemy.'

'But who is the enemy?'

They chinked glasses and each took a sip of wine.

Rivlin placed his glass back on the table and turned the

stem. 'The thing is this: I've had a word with Stoneham and she agrees.'

'Agrees to what?'

'You should come back. You were medically discharged, so there'll be a lot of paperwork and the pension to sort out. But if you apply, she'll back your application.'

For a moment she simply stared at him. 'Me – become a police officer again?'

'Nic, if there's one thing I know about you it's that you've never really stopped being a police officer. You're the real deal. Anyone who knows the job can see that.'

'You saying I should apply to Essex?'

'Yeah. And with Stoneham's recommendation, they'll snap you up.'

'What, now? With all these cuts?'

'You're an experienced DS. You're value for money.'

She took a large swallow of wine. 'Tom, it's too late for all that. I appreciate what you're trying to do, but—'

'It's never too late. You suffered a terrible tragedy. You needed time out to recover.' Reaching across the table, he placed his hand over hers. 'It's time to get back in the saddle.'

'I'm not sure I'd even get through the medical panel.'

'The secret is, when the shrink asks you a question don't tell him to go fuck himself.'

She grinned. 'I can't say I haven't thought about getting back in.'

'Come and talk to Stoneham. She's riding high. She's just got a great result. And you were instrumental in making that happen. There'll never be a better time.'

Her bag was beside her chair, resting against the table leg. The phone inside buzzed.

She frowned. 'Sorry, I need to see who that is. I'm waiting for a call from Eddie.'

'It's Sunday evening and you're off duty.'

'He's doing a special job for me.' Lifting her bag from the floor, she extracted the phone.

'That's another reason for becoming a police officer again. You wouldn't have to work with sleazebags like him.'

Nicci checked the phone. She did indeed have a missed call from Eddie. 'He's not so bad.'

'I thought you said he's done time for phone hacking?'

'Can you excuse me a minute? I need to call him back.' She got up. Rivlin shrugged. He had to suppress his annoyance.

The foyer of the restaurant was busy and she looked in vain for a quiet corner. So she went outside, passing the gaggle of smokers in skimpy dresses and shirts, shivering in the autumn chill as they got their fix.

Pacing the pavement, she returned Eddie's call. He picked up straight away. 'All right, boss?'

'This had better be good.'

'Oh, it is. Pudovkin uses that room quite a lot. Especially in the evenings.'

'It's a sort of library.'

'Maybe he uses it to hide away from the wife and kids. Anyway, I got a voice clip to send you. I've edited it down.'

'Are we going to need a translator?'

'Not for this. They're speaking English. The interesting thing is who he's talking to.'

'You recognize the voice?'

'I think so. But let me send the clip.'

'Okay.' She ended the call and waited.

It was a side street in Belgravia, lamp-lit but sombre. The pavements were slick with rain from a recent shower and the damp breeze was raw enough to make her hug her arms round her body for warmth.

She wondered what the hell she was doing. A man, a gorgeous man she was rapidly falling for – smart, kind and undeniably sexy – was waiting for her in a posh restaurant. What's more, he was offering her a way back in to the only job she'd ever cared about. Yet she was out here, hanging around in the street, waiting to receive an illegally obtained audio file from premises she herself had bugged. Would Rivlin think she was fit to be a police officer if he knew about this?

The phone in her hand buzzed. She pressed play on the clip from Eddie and put the handset to her ear.

The sound quality was good, considering the size of the listening device she'd planted.

The first voice was definitely Pudovkin's; precise English but with an obvious Russian accent. '*I know from experience that most of them will try to launder funds through the Middle East. But then they will want to use it to buy property in London.*'

'*And that's where we'll nail 'em.*' The second voice was home-grown. It could be South London, so Nicci immediately thought of Jerome. '*The set-up we're putting in place, in six months we'll get access to all the key players.*' But the tone wasn't quite as deep as Jerome's. '*Then we follow the links in the chain. We'll have better quality intel than any of the security services, I guarantee it. Mass data harvesting – all they got is quantity.*'

The Russian chuckled. '*When you think of the billions they spend on the technology.*'

'*Without skilled interpretation, it's useless. And trust me, boss, the Kremlin will recognize the value of what we're offering them.*'

It was the *trust me, boss*. Recognition hit Nicci like a bombshell. The second voice belonged to her new colleague at SBA: Craig Naylor.

69

Eddie Lunt started his Monday morning early. He wanted to be sure he'd have the office to himself. Bugging colleagues was not a particularly ethical practice but he knew, from his time in the newspaper industry, that it wasn't that unusual. If the technology was there, people would use it. Hiroshima had proved that, and Eddie didn't believe human nature would change any time soon.

He chatted to the cleaners and once they'd clocked off, he got to work. Using some of the devices he'd collected on Naylor's instructions, he bugged the conference room, Blake's office, the coffee station and the toilets. He knew from experience that a surprising number of people thought that the safest place to have a confidential conversation was in the bog. He used Naylor's equipment because it was good quality, he had plenty of units and saw no reason to shell out for additional hardware. He didn't think the ex-cop would miss them.

Software was a different matter. Through a contact in the surveillance business, he'd obtained a specialized app that could manage input from up to fifty separate devices on one phone. He'd splashed out on a brand-new smartphone specifically for the purpose. Writing all this up on his expenses might be problematic, but he decided to worry about that later.

Once the job was complete he popped out to get a bacon sandwich and a paper. It was still only seven a.m. so he put his feet up. The bugs were voice-activated; now that everything was in place he'd get immediate notification of any conversations taking place in the SBA locations and also Viktor Pudovkin's library.

He'd taken the added precaution of running phone trackers, not just on Blake's phone but Nicci's too. Earlier the previous week she'd instructed him to find Blake; with the tracker's help, it had been a simple matter to establish that he was at home in Surrey. Eddie had driven down there on Friday, staked the place out and waited.

The house was detached, a family home with a large double garage, fairly close to the centre of Reigate. Eddie had spent most of the day parked up down the road. Finally, shortly after three, Heather Blake left in her hatchback to collect the boys from school.

This was the only window of opportunity Eddie was likely to get. Pulling into the drive, he'd parked and rung the doorbell. The boss answered. He didn't seem particularly surprised.

Blake was wearing an old rugby shirt and tracksuit pants. He looked pretty relaxed. Eddie was invited in and led to the kitchen, where Blake made him a cup of tea.

'How long you been out there?'

Eddie shrugged. 'Most of the day.'

'I noticed you about half eleven.'

'Nicci was quite particular. She said she didn't want to upset your wife.'

Blake gave him a rueful grin. 'So you're here at Nicci's behest?'

'She's worried, boss. We both are. Stuff's clearly going on.'

'You're a biscuit man, aren't you, Eddie?' Blake produced a tin from the cupboard. 'Few chocolate ones left, I think.'

'Cheers.' Eddie helped himself to two chocolate digestives.

Blake sat down at the long pine table and rested his elbows. 'Listen, mate. The situation is . . . well, fluid, at present.'

'You mean Naylor's trying to edge you out?'

'Look, I can't go into details. But I don't want you to worry about your jobs.'

'Nicci's worried about you as much as anything.'

He frowned. 'She's always been loyal, I know that.'

'You know Naylor used to work for Viktor Pudovkin?'

'The security industry's not that big.'

'And he's been asking us to do stuff—'

Blake folded his arms and smiled. There was a tension in him, even though he was trying to appear relaxed. 'Go with the flow, that would be my advice.'

Eddie had relayed this message to Nicci on the phone later the same day and her exasperation had been clear. 'What's that supposed to mean? Go with the flow?'

'Beats me, boss. I think he's planning his own exit strategy and leaving us to get on with it.'

'Excellent. So we're on our own.'

The notion that Nicci Armstrong regarded him as some sort of partner pleased Eddie. She'd always made it clear that she disapproved of him. But as they'd continued to work together, both had adapted. No one could accuse her of being nice to him, but that was probably a bridge too far for the ex-cop.

From eight thirty onwards the SBA employees started to drift in and settle at their desks. Eddie kept a surreptitious eye on his second phone and watched the surveillance app do its work.

At nine thirty Pascale took a call. Eddie earwigged; it was from Nicci. Although they'd never discussed it, after receiving

Blake's so-called advice, they'd both slipped into defence mode and avoided discussions on the phone. There was no way of telling whether or not they were being monitored, but it seemed an obvious precaution.

Eddie gave Pascale his pixie grin. 'What's she up to this morning then? Still in bed?' He knew from the tracker that she was already in another part of London.

Pascale gave him a baleful look. 'She's gone to see Samir Naseer.'

'Who?'

'He runs the cleaning contractors we use in a lot of the luxury blocks where we've got the security contract. A week or so ago there were complaints about Chelsea Wharf. Owner turned up, thought the place wasn't clean enough. Nicci had to go and sort it out.'

He nodded thoughtfully. 'Why's she letting you know?' The question was partly to Pascale but also partly to himself.

'She wanted me to make sure it was in the diary if Craig checked. Now he's boss, I suppose she wants him to know she's on the case.' Turning from her VDU she glared at Eddie. 'You could take a leaf out of her book instead of sitting there doing nothing.'

Getting up from his desk, he gave her an affable smile. 'How about I get you a nice cup of coffee?'

She was tapping away on her keyboard again and didn't look up. 'No milk or sugar.'

Wandering to the coffee station, Eddie took a covert glance at the tracker. Nicci was on the move but he could tell from the speed she must be on foot. The map located her close to the junction of Cheyne Walk and Lots Road. This made sense if the story about the cleaning contractor was true; she could be walking down to Chelsea Wharf. But would this really be her priority, or was it merely a cover for something else? Who was she meeting? Kaz Phelps maybe?

He pinged her a brief text: *Morning, boss. Any instructions?*

Pouring Pascale and himself a coffee, he waited for a reply. The door to Blake's office – if it could still be called his office – stood open. There was no sign of Craig Naylor. Nicci had agreed with Eddie that it was Naylor's voice on the audio clip. So if there was any remaining doubt that Naylor was still being employed by Viktor Pudovkin, that scuppered it.

Eddie let his eye travel around the office and he felt a sense of nostalgia. Simon Blake had brought him into SBA very shortly after he set up the company. He remembered Nicci's arrival and his struggle to make any headway with the chippy ex-cop. He'd seen the place grow. Personnel had gradually increased but the staff turnover wasn't huge. It was a pleasant place to work and people had tended to stay.

The problems SBA had suffered were, to Eddie's mind, largely external. In a competitive industry, the investors had not been patient. It took time to build a business but their only focus was a quick return – they called it shareholder value, he called it greed. If Simon Blake had lost heart and sold out to the highest bidder, and if that highest bidder had turned out to be a Russian billionaire, Eddie wasn't about to blame him for it. The final shape of the deal was probably still being negotiated, which would explain why Blake had gone to ground. In a few days, redundancy notices would be issued and they'd find out who was to go and who to stay. Eddie had seen it all before.

He delivered Pascale's coffee to her desk and got a curt thank you in return. Like many, she was dealing with the uncertainty and fear of losing her job by demonstrating how hard she could work. But that wasn't Eddie's way. He wasn't the type to tug his forelock to the bosses. He checked his phone again: still no reply to his text from Nicci.

Settling in his chair, he turned on the phone tracker. Blake was still at home. But the cursor marking Nicci's position on the map was teetering on the edge of the river. He zoomed in to get a more accurate picture. It suggested she was standing on the end of Chelsea Harbour Pier. He wondered what she was doing there. Catching a riverboat? Having a quiet think?

Then an odd thing happened: the signal flickered and disappeared. It could be a glitch in the system; these things weren't 100 per cent reliable. She could've decided at that moment to switch the phone off and remove the SIM. Or she could've thrown it in the river.

As Eddie tried to puzzle it out, a sense of deep foreboding slithered into his peripheral consciousness. Without warning or explanation, she'd vanished from the grid. Why? He could think of half a dozen plausible explanations. But he already knew none of them were true. Something had happened to the ex-cop and it wasn't good.

70

Kaz and Irina had paid a flying visit to Yevgeny's old house in Berkshire and collected three suitcases of clothes. It amused Kaz that, despite the circumstances, her girlfriend found it impossible to travel light. Thinking of Irina as her girlfriend, even if only in the privacy of her own mind, excited Kaz and lifted her spirits. It suggested a future and a permanence that she'd never really had in her life before. She could never have called Helen Warner her girlfriend. It had been made painfully clear to her that Helen didn't want that.

The house had obviously been searched by the police and it had an abandoned and desolate air. For Irina, it was full of painful remembrances. Clothes and personal items belonging to her brothers were still littered about. All this would need sorting out before the place could be sold. But Kaz put it on her mental list of things to do later. Now she had money and professionals she could hire to carry out these tasks for her, life was going to be so much more straightforward. She'd already acquired a car and a chauffeur to drive them wherever they needed to go. Money made a massive difference; anyone who denied that had never been without it.

They'd returned to London and the apartment at Battersea Reach; Irina loved the place on sight, as Kaz knew she would. She'd installed Irina in her own room, plus en suite. She didn't want to make any assumptions. If they slept together it had to be because Irina wanted it. Irina giggled with delight as soon as she saw the room and especially the walk-in closet, which could easily accommodate her heap of designer dresses.

When Kaz looked in on her the next morning the Russian was curled up in a nest of pillows, fast asleep. Once again Kaz found her pale beauty stirring; the temptation to reach out and stroke her hair was almost overwhelming. But she held back, reminding herself that Irina had been through the mill; the shock and grief of Yevgeny's murder had taken its toll. She was exhausted and, tiptoeing out, Kaz left her to sleep.

Jonathan Sullivan arrived, as arranged, at eleven on the dot. Kaz made him coffee. Like all the kitchen appliances, the coffee maker was built in and slotted back into place behind the pristine high-gloss facade. They sat down at the round glass dining table and waited. Kaz had sent the car to collect her sister and Glynis, but she had no idea whether they'd actually turn up.

At eleven thirty the concierge rang to say they'd arrived. Kaz went down to greet them. Natalie was busy strapping Finlay back in his buggy. It was Glynis who stepped forward to give Kaz a hug.

Natalie scanned the lobby. She was wearing a surly expression, tinged with the determination not to be impressed. Kaz concluded that she was feeling awkward about their last meeting.

Focusing on her nephew, Kaz squatted down beside the buggy and wiggled his pudgy fingers. 'All right, buster? Think it's about time you and me got to know each other.'

The boy grinned. His dimples, the piercing blue eyes – there was no mistaking whose genes he carried. But Kaz had resolved to forget about that. This was Finlay, he was his own little person and, if Kaz had anything to do with it, he would grow up in a totally different environment to the one that had shaped Joey.

Straightening up, she faced her sister. 'Listen, Nat, there's just one thing I wanna say. We've both had a shitty time since I can't remember when. But today that changes.'

'I told you before, I don't want Joey's money.'

'Well, let's go upstairs and talk about that.'

As they entered the huge open-plan living area of the apartment, Sullivan stood up. Kaz made the introductions and then watched the skill with which the lawyer made himself agreeable to her sister.

In the time that they'd sat waiting he'd explained to Kaz that Joey's estate, if it could be called that, had been left, through a complex network of untraceable offshore trusts, to both sisters. They would need to agree a course of action and act together.

Kaz made more coffee. She'd had the foresight to include juice for Finlay in the supermarket order that had been delivered that morning. Glynis took charge of the boy, wheeling him out onto the balcony in his buggy so the others could talk.

Natalie sat at the table, legs crossed, cradling her mug and with a sullen look on her face.

Sullivan propped his iPad up in the middle of the table so all three of them could see it. 'Your brother was a prudent investor—'

'He was a fucking drug dealer and a villain.' There was no mistaking the suppressed anger in Natalie's voice. 'And you can't tell me that the old bill aren't after his stash and won't start hounding us too if they think we've got money. I've got a son. I don't want him growing up like we did, knowing his family's dodgy and that everyone else thinks he's scum.'

Kaz reached across the table to her sister. 'Nor do I. But

listen to what he's got to say, Nat. That's all I ask.'

Natalie huffed and folded her arms.

Lounging in his chair, Sullivan gave her a solicitous look. 'I understand your feelings, Natalie.' He enjoyed the role of counsellor, Kaz had already figured that out. He was the wizard who could make it all happen, and that suited his vanity.

He stroked his chin. 'Y'know, my wife loves horses and the countryside. She also gets very emotional about climate change. We donate to all sorts of charities. But here's the thing: the global economy is neither fair nor just, and it's never likely to be. The rich get richer and the poor get screwed. Throughout history revolutions have come and gone. But in every single one, it's been the desire for power in specific individuals that has destroyed or undermined all attempts to promote the common good. Human nature is what it is. The ruthless win.'

It all sounded a bit pompous to Kaz, but he was an educated bloke. She could see why her brother had trusted him. He knew what he was talking about.

Natalie was scowling. 'I don't see what this has got to do with us. Or Joey.'

'It means that all we can do, all we can ever really do in the end, is protect our own. Okay, your brother was a drug dealer – and he happened to be very good at it. But the products he sold were arguably no more harmful, either to individuals or the planet, than many other things. He asserted his will through violence, which has always been the way of our species and continues to be. He wasn't a good man, but I don't judge him. That's not my job. The market is all about what works, and it works best when it self-regulates. Ethical judgements, like emotions, only get in the way of business.'

'Right, well, if I can even remember all that I'll tell it to the old bill when they come knocking, shall I?' Natalie's expression was sulky, like a kid at the back of the class, bored by the bullshit.

The lawyer's manner remained serene. 'My job – for which I am well paid, if you're wondering – is to ensure that doesn't happen.'

Kaz caught her sister's eye. 'Thing is, Nat, Joey's put us in a different league. We go away, start a new life somewhere—'

'What about Mum?'

'We'll take care of her.'

'I'm not living with her again.'

'You don't have to.'

Natalie heaved a sigh. 'Oh, I don't fucking know. All I want is for Finlay to have a better chance.'

'And he will. I told you when we was downstairs, today everything changes. Finlay can grow up strong and loved, go to a posh school, speak a couple of languages, have a totally different life.'

'You really believe that?'

Kaz met her gaze. 'I absolutely do.'

Sullivan tapped the iPad with his finger and the screen came to life. 'This is a conservative valuation of assets. The UK property portfolio has performed very well and currently stands at sixteen point two million. Offshore funds retained in cash stand at two point five. Equity investments and overseas commercial property, I estimate at around five. Total assets, twenty-three point seven. Even with your brother's difficulties, asset growth of the portfolio has been close to twenty per cent in the last year.'

Natalie's astonished look veered from the lawyer to her sister and back. 'Joey was worth twenty-three point seven million pounds? He was a fucking drug dealer.'

Sullivan smiled. 'I think, Natalie, it's more accurate to say he was a very innovative entrepreneur in recreational pharmaceuticals and an astute investor.'

She shook her head in disbelief. 'It's like we won the lottery. It's unreal.'

Kaz rocked back in her chair. She was equally astonished. She'd already realized it was a lot. But twenty-three point seven million? It was Monopoly money.

An inane grin spread over her features as she turned to her sister. 'It's real, babes. Believe it.'

71

When Tom Rivlin had crept out of Nicci's flat it had still been dark. He'd left her sleeping. The relationship – and it was definitely that – kept surprising him at every turn. As he got into his car to drive back to Essex he remembered his father's comments at his parents' thirtieth wedding anniversary bash. He'd thought at the time that the old fart was being soppy and sentimental. How could you know she was the one on the first date? But when Nicci Armstrong had walked into his office two weeks ago, something in Rivlin's universe had shifted.

She wasn't a girl that you'd fancy on sight, although she was undoubtedly beautiful. Maybe it was that she wasn't a girl, full stop. She was a woman, a fully fledged grown-up and, once you got beyond the tough carapace, endlessly intriguing and seductive.

A grey and overcast day was dawning as he drove across Hackney Marshes and he wondered if he was falling in love. It was an odd feeling: excitement and apprehension, the sensation of things speeding up, a tumble of emotions pitching you forward.

Back at the office, a mountain of paperwork awaited him. Case files on the Kemals had to go to the CPS. Stoneham was cracking the whip.

He texted Nicci at eleven but got no reply. She was probably busy. SBA was having problems and her boss, a former Met commander, was being difficult. In Rivlin's opinion, she should just hand in her notice. He'd put to her the proposition that she should rejoin the police, but he hadn't got a straight answer. All she'd said was she'd think about it.

In the course of the afternoon he sent two more texts. He phoned her around five o'clock but she didn't pick up. They'd talked about meeting up that evening for dinner. He phoned the SBA offices and spoke to an evasive receptionist who kept repeating what was obviously their standard mantra: she wasn't available but would call him back.

He worked until nearly seven then began calling her in earnest, both her mobile and the landline at her flat. Had she forgotten about their dinner date? She was probably out on a job and her phone battery had died, that was the most likely thing to have happened. Rivlin was a pretty level-headed bloke, he knew the mundane explanation for any mystery was usually the correct one. He also knew that Blake had got her doing bodyguarding work and that often involved antisocial hours.

By nine p.m. he was feeling annoyed. Was she trying to make some kind of point? He was assuming the attraction between them was mutual, but perhaps he was being arrogant. Did she think it was all moving too fast? Was this an attempt to cool things off? If it was, then he'd prefer her to be honest with him and tell him to his face. He hated relationship games and had assumed, up until now, that this simply wasn't Nicci's style.

Looking for an outlet for his fretful energy he went for a run. It was dark and drizzling but he hammered out a fast ten kilometres in under forty minutes. Back at his flat he showered, made himself beans on toast and called her again. There was still no answer. Women didn't treat him like this. Did she think he was some sap she could pick up and then drop when it suited her? At half past eleven he decided to drive to London and tell her exactly that.

By the time he got there, the flats were mostly in darkness. He pressed several entryphone buttons at once to blag his way into the building, then banged on her door. His insistent pounding brought the next-door neighbour out into the hall. She was wearing pyjamas and a belligerent look. Rivlin was polite and apologetic, but the only information he could glean was that she hadn't seen or heard Nicci and didn't think she was home.

The rebuffed lover was rapidly morphing into the suspicious cop. Where the hell was Nicci? If she'd been planning to go away overnight, surely she would've mentioned it? Could there have been some sort of family emergency? He racked his brains to remember where her parents lived. That was the explanation he settled on. An accident, maybe a sudden illness? He had no idea about her parents' state of health.

As a police officer, he had the means to track people down, though to use such resources for personal purposes was a disciplinary offence. It was after midnight and he told himself he needed to be patient and wait until the morning. If she still hadn't surfaced, he'd go to Stoneham and ask permission to trace her parents.

Stepping out onto Newington Green where his car was parked on a double yellow line, Rivlin became aware of a figure in the shadows.

A short, fat barrel of a man moved out into the light. 'You Rivlin?'

'Yeah. Who are you?'

'Eddie Lunt. I work for Nicci.'

'What you doing here?'

'Waiting to see if she comes home.'

'Why?'

'I'm worried about her.'

The two men stared at one another. Rivlin scanned the pixie features and the neat sculpted beard. Nicci had talked about Eddie and her annoyance at having to work with him. He looked cold and damp. 'How long have you been here?'

'Couple of hours. Saw you go in. Wondered if it was you. She went off the grid this morning. I been trying to track her down ever since.'

'What was she supposed to be doing today?'

'She said she was going to meet this cleaning contractor who does some work for us. But I went round to his place and he denies all knowledge.'

'Do you think he was lying?'

'Why would he? I thought maybe she had a meet with someone and was using the cleaning bloke as a cover. That's why I'm here, figured in the end she'd come home.'

'Meeting someone? Like who?'

Eddie shrugged.

The cop fixed him with a direct look. 'And why would she need a cover?'

'Y'know, office politics. Can get a bit complicated.'

Rivlin smiled. Nicci was right about her sidekick, he had the evasive manner of someone who sailed pretty close to the wind.

'I know she was worried that Viktor Pudovkin was looking for Karen Phelps. Is that what we're talking about here?'

'Probably.' Eddie scratched his beard. Rivlin wasn't sure who he thought he was protecting.

'Have you talked to Phelps?'

'No. Don't know where to find her.'

The cop grinned. 'I do.'

72

The money did the trick, as Kaz had always suspected it would. Her sister's amazement rapidly turned into compliance. When someone tells you that you've inherited a fortune, that from now on everything is going to be different, it's pretty hard to say no, I don't want it. And Sullivan was able to calm Natalie's fears about the police.

Assets deemed to be the proceeds of crime were recovered, he explained, but usually only in circumstances where people were being flash or stupid. Money-laundering was a specialized financial service that the City of London offered to a global clientele. Regulation was light and easy enough to circumvent. Once you stepped up into the multimillion pound league you were a high net worth individual and a potential investor. The police only had the resources to chase the most blatant offenders and, provided you behaved with discretion, it was in no one's interest to dob you in.

The lawyer's advice was to relocate abroad for the time being. Natalie said she needed to think about this. But for Kaz it was a no-brainer. Her fantasy was a villa beside a beach, somewhere she could paint and where she and Irina could live happily and quietly together, away from the threat of both the law and Pudovkin.

This was the dream that she had tried so hard to get Joey to sign up to. Why act stupidly and risk prison when you had enough squirrelled away to keep you in comfort for the rest of your days? She'd have to find a way to get the probation service onside until her licence expired. But Sullivan suggested that this could be achieved by finding a suitable course of study to apply for. She'd already been online and discovered an interesting history of art course in Barcelona.

All of this had left Kaz fired-up and hopeful. There were a few details to be ironed out. Ellie was obviously a problem. Once she'd recovered, where would she live and who would take care of her? But like everything else, Kaz reasoned, money would help find a solution. Glynis was resolute in not wanting to be involved in the family move. She'd be happy to come and visit, she said, but she liked her life just the way it was. She wasn't that keen on *abroad*.

After they'd all gone, Kaz remained buoyed by the lawyer's confidence. Once you'd made your money, it seemed, going straight and legit was really not a problem. All fortunes throughout history were based on some kind of villainy – that was another of Sullivan's inspiring fables. If only her brother could've seen things this way, he'd probably still be alive.

Kaz got out her iPad and was soon scrolling the Net and familiarizing herself with the Spanish property market. Mainland or the islands? Mallorca appealed to her. By the time Irina finally emerged from her room, in a silk dressing gown, Kaz was checking out beachfront villas.

Irina gave her a sultry smile. 'Your family visit. Is nice. I hear. I don't want to disturb.'

'You should've come down and said hello.' She turned the iPad towards Irina. 'Come and look. Wha'd'you think?'

The Russian peered at the screen. 'For holiday?'

'To live. For us to live.'

Irina huffed. 'No way! I live in London. Best place in the world. You had seen Magnitogorsk you know this.'

'Yeah, but this is so beautiful and peaceful. You could walk on the beach every day.'

'And who would be your friends? You have this place. Why you want some white-painted – ' she screwed up her nose in disgust – 'peasant house.'

'I can't stay here, babes.'

'Why not?'

'Oh, too many hassles.'

'Which hassle?'

Kaz sighed. This was not the reaction she'd expected. But then she hadn't really considered what Irina's point of view might be.

Irina's lovely features had taken on a mulish expression. 'Which hassle? The cops? You pay. They go away.'

'That's not so easy here, babes.'

'Is easy. Cops like money, same as everyone else.'

'Thing is, there may be other people after me.'

'Who?'

'I don't want you to worry about all this.'

'But you want me live in peasant house. Who?'

Irina was standing over her, hands on hips, like some pissed-off Valkyrie. Kaz was at a loss. She wanted Irina to be impressed by her at the very least. And maybe one day to love her. This didn't look promising.

The Russian folded her arms. Her frustration at her limited command of English was fuelling her anger. She heaved a sigh. 'Okay. I talk to some people. Friends of Yev. No need to run.'

'I'm not running.'

Irina flicked her hand at the screen in disdain. 'You want live here?'

'Why not?'

The Russian simply shook her head. Her disgust was all too apparent. She walked over to the kitchen. 'You got coffee?'

Kaz got up. 'I'll make some for you.'

'I make it.' The tone was combative. 'Machine?'

Kaz pointed to the wall unit. Irina pulled out the coffee maker. She was mumbling to herself in Russian. Standing beside the table, Kaz felt like a fool. This was their first row; she didn't want it to be their last.

'Look, I'm sorry. I shouldn't have assumed—'

Irina glared at her. There was obviously a lot more she wanted to say but couldn't articulate in English. 'I lose my brothers. So much I cry. I stay here. London.'

'Okay.'

'Who after you?'

With her dreams rapidly dissolving, Kaz saw no point in continuing to be evasive. 'Viktor Pudovkin.'

Irina stared at her, then burst out laughing. 'No! Is fixed. After Joey die, Yev, he talked to Pudovkin. All is good.'

'How d'you know this?'

'Yev say. He don't want no more trouble. He went to Pudovkin and he fix.'

'Yeah, but since then—'

'Okay, I talk to Galina.'

'Who?'

'She wife of Viktor. She good friend.'

'You know Pudovkin's wife?'

'Well, she friend of Alexei.'

'Who's Alexei?'

Irina lifted the small, brimming espresso cup from under the nozzle of the coffee maker. She took a thoughtful sip. 'I stupid. I stay with Mika. Stupid! I was scared.'

'That's understandable.'

'Should've left Mika, gone to Alexei.'

'Well, you're with me now, babes.'

Irina gave her a cursory glance. 'I go see Alexei. He good friend Galina. He fix.'

'I'll come with you.'

'No.' There was an abruptness in Irina's tone. Then she seemed to recollect herself and gave Kaz a seductive smile. 'Just me. Is better.'

An hour later Irina sashayed out of the apartment to the waiting car. It was painfully obvious to Kaz that she'd dressed to impress. The teasing neckline, the killer heels, her blonde hair carefully washed and styled to look sexy. She was undeniably gorgeous. Irina was on some kind of mission but was it on Kaz's behalf or did she have an agenda of her own? The latter seemed more probable. And who was Alexei?

Kaz sat staring out of the window as the weak October sun gradually sank over the rooftops of West London. She'd gone from exuberance to wretchedness in the course of a day. She longed to take the money and run, to escape the hassle forever, to be free. But one name kept coming up.

After Joey was gunned down, she had wondered at the ease with which Yevgeny Koshkin had negotiated a truce with her brother's target. How had he done it? A serious attempt had been made on Pudovkin's life and Tolya Koshkin had been part of it. So what could Yev have possibly said to square things with the billionaire spook? Whatever his ploy, Irina was convinced it had succeeded.

Now she'd come up with some kind of plan that she was either unable or unwilling to explain. She claimed to know Pudovkin's wife – how?

Pudovkin was a nexus for the various Russian factions in

London. They all knew him or knew of him and whatever their loyalties no one dared ignore him. So perhaps it wasn't so surprising.

Whatever the plan was, it relied on this friend, Alexei. But who the hell was he – and was he more than a friend?

Kaz churned these questions over in her mind as darkness fell. She tried to phone Irina only once. The call went immediately to voicemail. Kaz didn't leave a message. She had no idea what to say.

To pass the time, she rang her sister. Natalie was still guarded, but it allowed Kaz the illusion that there was at least one person out there who actually cared about her. They chatted about Finlay. Kaz learnt that he was big for his age; the midwife who'd delivered him had commented on the size of his hands. He'd probably grow to be over six foot, Natalie had been told. Neither of them compared him to Joey, although that thought must've been in both their minds.

Kaz ended the call thinking that perhaps she'd be better off in her villa by the sea with her little nephew and Natalie, if her sister could be persuaded to join her. And if Irina didn't sell her down the river to Viktor Pudovkin in the meantime.

For several hours Kaz stared at the television screen, waiting and hoping that Irina would come home. But it wasn't home, it was simply a way station for both of them and as luxurious and impersonal as any five-star hotel. She'd come back eventually for her precious clothes, that was the only thing Kaz could be sure of.

Whether from exhaustion or the disappointments of the day, she finally fell asleep on the sofa. She was woken by a harsh electronic buzz. It took her several seconds to realize it was the doorbell. She jumped up. Irina had come back.

Running to the door, her stockinged feet skated on the polished wooden floor. She didn't bother with the spy hole but opened the door with a relieved smile.

But the smile faded when she found herself facing DI Tom Rivlin. He greeted her with a pugnacious look. Lurking behind him with a foolish grin was Eddie Lunt.

73

'Do you know what the fucking time is?' Kaz didn't exactly invite them in but allowed Rivlin and his unlikely sidekick to follow her into the apartment.

'It's a bit of an emergency, Karen.' Rivlin's eyes were everywhere. 'You've fallen on your feet then.'

'It belongs to a friend. She's Russian. How d'you find me, anyway?'

'We were very grateful for your assistance with the Kemals and the Met have been keeping a protective eye on you.' In fact, he'd got the address from Raheem. Rivlin's phone call had woken her up, which she wasn't too happy about.

'Well, what d'you want?'

'We're looking for Nicci. We thought you might've seen her.'

'Not since Sunday. With you, in that coffee shop.'

Eddie stepped forward. 'Thing is, Kaz, she's gone off the grid and we're really worried. We thought she might've had a meet with you but didn't want anyone else to know.'

'I ain't lying, Eddie. I haven't seen her.'

'Text? Phone call? Has she tried to contact you?' Rivlin's face was pale and drawn. Kaz remembered the intimacy between him and Nicci. His anxiety was obvious. This was personal, he wasn't just being a cop.

'No, I'm sorry. Have you checked her flat? Y'know, she

sometimes gets a bit upset with stuff. Has too much to drink and crashes out.'

'I've been to the flat, but not inside.'

'She could be in there, sleeping it off.'

'I don't know anyone who's got a key.' The cop turned hopefully to Eddie. 'Would anyone at your place?'

Eddie was shifting from foot to foot and he folded his arms over his ample paunch. 'Thing is . . .' He sighed and shot a look at Rivlin. 'She's gonna kill me for telling you this . . .'

'Then you should definitely tell me.'

'It's a bit complicated.'

Kaz and Rivlin were both staring at him. He took a breath. 'She planted some bugs in Pudovkin's house. She went there on a bodyguarding job. The opportunity presented itself.'

'Why would she target him?' The cop glared at Kaz. 'You know anything about this? Is it because of your friend who was murdered? The MP? What was her name?'

'Helen Warner.' Kaz met his eye. She had a sinking feeling. Here he was again, the fucking billionaire spook. 'Okay, look, on Sunday, while you was getting the coffees, she told me about the bugs. She said she was going to get the evidence to take Pudovkin down.'

Rivlin shook his head in disbelief. 'What? Did neither of you tell her how mad this is, not to mention illegal?'

Kaz didn't reply. Of course she knew how mad it was. She'd simply hoped that Nicci would come to her senses and realize it too.

Eddie gave a wry grin. 'She's not an easy woman to argue with, mate. What complicates the issue is that we suspect SBA has been taken over by a bloke who works for Pudovkin.'

'Why?'

'That's what Nicci wanted to know.'

Rivlin pulled out a chair from the dining table and slumped down on it. 'I don't believe what I'm hearing here.' He shot an irate glance at Eddie. 'Are you telling me the whole story? 'Cause if you're not, you'd better do it right now.'

Eddie pulled out a chair and sat down beside him. 'Well, I was tracking her phone. A precaution. In case she needed backup.'

'And what kind of fucking backup were you going to provide?' Rivlin was struggling to keep his temper.

'She said she was meeting this cleaning contractor.' He glanced up at Kaz. 'I thought that was a cover and she was probably meeting you. She was on Chelsea Harbour Pier when the signal disappeared.'

Kaz shrugged. She appeared calm but her brain had started to seethe with thoughts of Pudovkin. 'She dumped it. She wanted to be sure no one could follow her.'

Rivlin was chewing his thumbnail. 'What time?'

'About ten o'clock this morning.'

The cop checked his watch. 'You mean yesterday morning. So we're talking nearly sixteen hours ago.'

'Where did she go then? To Pudovkin's?' A battle was going on in Kaz's mind. This wasn't her concern, she wasn't responsible for Nicci. If she'd been crazy enough to go after Pudovkin on her own – but at the same time just the thought of that bastard enraged Kaz. He'd had Helen killed to protect Robert Hollister and he'd had Joey shot in the street; the rich murdering scumbag thought he was untouchable. Only Nicci had the balls to consider challenging that assumption.

Eddie shook his head wearily. 'She didn't go to the cleaning contractor, 'cause I talked to him.'

'What if he was lying?' Rivlin rapped the table with his finger.

'That don't make sense. She tells the office that's where she's going, then she dumps the phone 'cause she don't want to be followed.'

Kaz joined the two men at the table. 'It makes sense, Eddie. If she was off to meet this bloke but then she realizes she's being followed. And chucking a phone – she wouldn't do that unless she was really worried.'

Rivlin leant forward. 'What did she want with the cleaning contractor? Information?'

'Access? Cleaners go everywhere. No one takes any notice of them.'

Eddie frowned. 'Well, she was worried that the bug we'd planted wouldn't get us that far. We needed more.' A sorrowful look came into his eye. 'I did check about midday, and the one she put in Pudovkin's library had gone dead.'

'You think it's been discovered?'

Eddie couldn't meet Kaz's eye. 'Probably. To tell the truth, that's when I started to get really worried.'

Kaz took a deep breath. The connection between her and Nicci Armstrong was something she couldn't explain, either to these two, or to herself. But if Pudovkin had got hold of Nicci, that really was the last straw. She felt a cold rage seeping into her veins.

But her voice was deceptively calm. 'We need to find her.'

74

The small industrial unit – offices, storage and garaging for a fleet of vans – from which Samir Naseer ran his cleaning firm, was on a trading estate in Acton. They started early, well before dawn, and Naseer used that quiet time to catch up on his accounts. It was a competitive business so to keep costs down he ran most of the back office functions himself. It meant working ridiculous hours, but it was worth it. The company specialized in the high-end luxury residential sector and made a healthy profit.

Naseer was alone in the office and didn't expect any callers at five a.m. so the hammering on the door surprised him. When he saw Eddie Lunt, the suspicious bod who'd been snooping round earlier, he felt a mixture of anxiety and irritation.

He got up slowly from his desk and took his time opening the door. But there were two other people with Lunt, a tall bloke and a woman.

The bloke came through the door first and he shoved a warrant card in Samir's face. 'I'm DI Rivlin, Mr Naseer. And I've got a few questions for you and not much time. So, you need to tell me the truth. Got that?'

Naseer held out his palms in a placatory gesture. 'I am always happy to help the police, Inspector.'

'Glad to hear it. Nicci Armstrong? Did she come to see you yesterday?'

Naseer shot a glance in Eddie Lunt's direction. But Rivlin stepped forward. 'Don't look at him. I'm not interested in anything you might have said earlier. Just tell the truth to me now.'

'I promised her my discretion.' Naseer's brow furrowed. 'She's a lovely lady. I don't want to let her down or get her in trouble.'

'I assure you that you're not. So she came to see you? When?'

The little cleaning contractor sighed and shrugged. 'Yesterday morning. Eleven o'clock, I think. But she didn't come here. I met her at Chelsea Wharf, where we service some apartments. She helped me before. She understands the difficulties of this business. So obviously I was anxious to cooperate.'

'Cooperate with what?' Rivlin had his arms folded and was flanked by Eddie and Kaz. There was a tension rippling through all three; they knew what they were about to hear was unlikely to be good news.

Naseer blinked behind his rimless glasses; to him they seemed intimidating and the last thing he wanted was trouble with the police.

Adjusting the glasses, he took a breath. 'We share a client in Holland Park. Well, not a regular client. We specialize in removing stains from Persian rugs. He called us in for that. Ms Armstrong – well, her firm, SBA – has been hired to review his security. It turns out there were some issues around entry codes and I had to admit that I did still have an entry code on file for those particular premises. You have to understand, Inspector, I didn't realize I'd done anything wrong. Most of my clients aren't quite so fastidious. They don't want to have to bother letting cleaners in and out, and they trust us.'

'Let me understand you correctly, Mr Naseer. You had these entry codes and you gave them to Nicci?'

'I was anxious not to lose any future business and Ms Armstrong said that if I no longer had the codes then the client need never know. I gave her the codes then erased them from my database. I was grateful.'

'And who owns these premises?' Rivlin asked the question although they all felt the answer screaming them in the face.

'A Russian gentleman: Mr Pudovkin.'

Kaz had to smile to herself. The skill with which Nicci had blagged the security codes to Pudovkin's house out of the unsuspecting cleaning contractor put her in the same league as a top-flight fraudster. But cops often made the best villains.

Rivlin's tight, angry face obviously frightened Naseer.

'Will I need to come to the police station and make a statement?'

'Not at present, Mr Naseer. We'll be in touch if we need anything further from you.' Rivlin turned on his heel, conscious only of the need to get out of there. Then he recollected himself and paused: 'Oh, and thank you for your help.'

Rivlin, Kaz and Eddie reconvened on the pavement outside. It was still dark. Naseer's cleaners were loading supplies into their vans.

Rivlin stared at his watch; he was holding it together – just. 'If she got an entry code at eleven . . . maybe she went in some time in the afternoon. That's, I dunno—' He rubbed his face, willing himself to focus.

Kaz did the maths for him. 'Over twelve hours ago. Which means, yeah, they've probably got her.'

75

She was about the last person Simon Blake would've expected to find on his doorstep at seven o'clock in the morning. But when he opened the door he found Kaz Phelps glaring at him.

There was no preamble. 'We need you to help us find Nicci.'

Eddie Lunt was hovering behind her; he'd driven them down from London. Blake had little option but to invite them in. His wife was getting the boys up and the dog was still dozing in her basket.

He led them into the kitchen, but only so Heather and his sons wouldn't hear their conversation. 'Right, now one of you two jokers can tell me what's going on.'

Eddie could see he wasn't best pleased. 'I'm sorry, boss, but—'

Kaz didn't let him finish. 'Whatever you're playing at with Pudovkin and your fucking firm, you need to sort this out.'

'Really?' Blake gave her a disdainful look. 'And what concern is this of yours?'

'Nicci decided to target Pudovkin, put him under surveillance. 'Cause none of the rest of you useless cops and ex-cops have got the balls. We think she went into his place in Holland Park, probably sometime yesterday afternoon. No one's seen her since.'

Blake huffed, shot a glance at Eddie. 'Are you sure of your facts here?'

Eddie nodded. 'Yeah. Once we realized the firm had been taken over and that you was stepping back—'

'Who told you it had been taken over?' The anger in Blake's voice was palpable.

'You said go with the flow.'

'Did you and Nicci really think I would sell the company to a man like Pudovkin?'

'Naylor's Pudovkin's man, we knew that.'

Blake shook his head. 'How could Nicci be so stupid?'

Eddie gave him a surly look. 'With all due respect, maybe you should've trusted us a bit more.'

'That wasn't possible.' Standing in his pyjamas and bathrobe, Blake was looking shell-shocked.

Kaz stepped forward. 'We haven't got time for this. If that bastard's had Nicci murdered, it's on your head, Blake.'

Heather walked into the room in time to hear this. She stared at her husband. 'What's going on, Simon?'

He heaved another heavy sigh. He'd known for some time that he was playing a dangerous game, but what he hadn't factored in was Nicci. 'Okay, let's not jump to conclusions. All we know is that she's disappeared, right?'

'Getting on for maybe fourteen hours ago.' Kaz was in his face, she wasn't letting him off the hook. 'So what you gonna do?'

The rage pulsing off Kaz forced him to take a step back. 'I can see you're upset, Karen. But this isn't helpful.'

'You don't even know how to sort this out, do you?' She made no attempt to hide her scorn.

He glanced at his wife. She gave him a distraught look. 'Simon?'

But Blake turned to face Kaz, his voice cracking. 'You're not the only one here who cares about Nicci Armstrong.'

76

He knew he should speak to someone in the Met and wondered about asking Raheem to help him. But going through
the correct procedures would simply take too long. Even if he
only managed to fire a warning shot across their bows, it might
be enough. So, standing on the porticoed doorstep of the
Holland Park mansion, Tom Rivlin took a deep breath and
rang the doorbell.

He had his warrant card ready and showed it to the maid
who answered the door. She invited him in and asked him to
wait in the hall. The palatial surroundings exuded power and
privilege; the idea was to awe the visitor into submission. But
Rivlin was too keyed up. He scanned the place with a dispas-
sionate eye, focusing on the cameras and noting that, if Nicci
had been here, there would be evidence.

After several minutes a large black guy with an easy smile
appeared. The suit accentuated his physique and the perfect
shine on the shoes suggested he was ex-military.

He grinned and held out his hand to shake. 'Jerome Todd.
I'm head of security. Can I help you?'

Rivlin ignored the proffered hand and held up his warrant
card. 'DI Rivlin. I'm here to see Mr Pudovkin.'

'It's a bit early, Inspector. Do you have an appointment?'

'I don't need an appointment. Could you tell Mr Pudovkin
I'm here.'

'I can give you the contact details for Mr Pudovkin's lawyers and you can make an appointment.'

Rivlin eyeballed the security guard. They were a similar height, but Jerome was around twenty kilograms heavier and it was all muscle.

The cop smiled. 'Here's the thing, Mr Todd. You can fob me off now and I will come back with a warrant to search these premises and a vanload of armed officers from SCO19. I don't think your boss will appreciate that when the matter could be resolved now with a simple conversation.'

'You'll have to have that conversation with me, Inspector. Mr Pudovkin left very early for a business lunch in Dubai.'

The security guard's cold eyes bored into him and Rivlin got the distinct impression he was enjoying the game.

The cop shrugged. 'I have no way of knowing whether you're telling the truth.'

Jerome grinned. 'No. You don't. So why don't you say your piece, mate, and we'll take it from there.'

'Do you know Nicci Armstrong? She's a private investigator working for Simon Blake Associates.'

'Yeah, Nicci. Cute. I thought she was a bodyguard. Least, that's what she said she was doing when she came here.'

The sarcasm in his tone annoyed Rivlin, as did the blatant implication that Nicci had lied to conceal an ulterior motive.

'I understand her job includes both security and investigations.'

Jerome chuckled. 'Well, it's a tough business. Full of ex-cops trying to make themselves a rep, maybe cutting a few corners to get ahead. She a special friend of yours?'

The security guard's attempts to needle him had the effect of crystallizing Rivlin's anger. He was used to dealing with sleazebags like this and the training kicked in.

'When did you last see her?'

'Only met her the once. And you know what I thought? I wouldn't mind giving her one myself.'

'She's missing. You know anything about that?'

'Why would I?' Amusement danced in his eyes.

Rivlin leant forward. 'You kill many ragheads, Jerome? When you were out there in Helmand or whatever hell-hole they sent you to. 'Cause here's the thing you need to understand: you're not in bandit country any more. You harm one hair on her head and we will come for you.'

The security guard chuckled again. 'Yeah, right. Look around you, copper. This ain't your manor. You got no jurisdiction here.'

'Your boss is not above the law. And think about this: when pressure gets put on him, you think he'll have any loyalty to you? I'm not naive, I know how money works and the influence it buys. But if he wants to stay in London and needs to placate the authorities, he'll need a fall guy. Wonder who that'll be?'

Jerome dismissed this with a snicker and a shake of the head. 'You don't know shit 'bout how this world works, mate.'

'Don't I? 'Cause I'm one of the little guys, one of the plebs? But so are you, mate. So are you. Don't be a sucker. Think about what I've said.'

Producing a business card from his pocket, Rivlin tucked it under the lapel of Jerome's slick suit. 'My number.' And turning on his heel, he headed for the door.

77

Kaz and Eddie drove back to London largely in silence. They had the frustration of rush-hour traffic to contend with and by the time they arrived at SBA's offices, Blake was already there. He'd taken the train.

Feeling frazzled from lack of sleep, Kaz was in no mood to be patient. Blake had assured them, before they left Reigate, that he'd make some calls. She saw him through the glass wall of the conference room and, ignoring the receptionist's protestations, she barged straight in.

Blake had removed his jacket and was standing, hands on hips, addressing a thin, balding man with vulpine features.

Kaz glared at them both. 'Who's he?'

Blake sighed. 'Colin, meet Karen Phelps. Here in her capacity as . . . what? Nicci's friend?'

McCain gave her a disdainful look. 'The gangster's sister? Jesus wept!'

'And who the fuck are you, Colin?' Kaz folded her arms and stood her ground. Encouraged by her brazen contempt, Eddie sidled into the room in her wake.

'This is Eddie Lunt – he works for me.'

Colin McCain nodded and raised his eyebrows. 'Well, your friend has certainly created an awkward situation for us.'

His calm, slightly bored tone infuriated Kaz. 'Really? And who the fuck is *us*?'

Blake and McCain exchanged looks, but it was Eddie who answered. 'MI5, right?'

Blake sighed, slipping his hands into his trouser pockets. 'Listen, you two, locating Nicci is our absolute priority. And that's what we're trying to do.'

'Our absolute priority? You part of the spook brigade too?'

Blake met her eye. 'No.'

'How about this for an idea then?' There was no mistaking the vitriol in Kaz's voice. 'Go round to Pudovkin's house and kick the fucking door down.'

McCain opened his palms. 'If I thought that would achieve the objective—'

He didn't have a chance to finish. There was a small commotion in the reception area, with Alicia trying desperately to assert her authority, then Tom Rivlin swung open the plate-glass door. He, too, had a look of cold fury on his face. Kaz had never thought she'd be glad to see a cop, but she was.

Rivlin scanned the room. 'Who's McCain?'

'That would be me.' The MI5 officer puffed out his cheeks. This was a grade-A balls-up and he blamed Blake for not keeping his people under proper control.

The cop pulled out his warrant card. 'I'm DI Rivlin, Essex Police. I've just been to see the Commander of SCD7. She assures me you're going to sort this out. I assured her that if you don't, and if any harm comes to Nicci, I'm going to the press.'

McCain didn't look like he was about to placate the officer, so Blake stepped forward and offered his hand to Rivlin. 'I'm Simon Blake. You need to understand, Nicci's safety matters to me, to us, more than anything. We've already got the matter in hand.'

'In hand? How? There's good evidence to suggest that Nicci's been kidnapped—'

McCain held up his palm. 'Look, Rivlin, don't come in here and try to play the righteous policeman. She's a private citizen who's gone blundering into an ongoing security operation and, in doing so, has probably broken the law. This isn't our fault.'

Rivlin turned on Blake. 'And whose fault is it then? How was she to know?'

'Me.' Blake looked him in the eye. 'I take full responsibility. Okay?'

McCain's phone buzzed. Giving them all a sour look, he answered it. 'Yes. Right-oh.' He strode out of the room to continue the conversation.

Blake ran his fingers over his close-cropped scalp. He was sweating. Rivlin and Phelps were both glaring at him. Eddie Lunt was perched on the end of the conference table, watching everyone with tense concern.

Blake took a breath and scanned all three. 'Look, I admit I should've taken Nicci into my confidence. You too, Eddie. Then this would never have happened. But Thames House were insistent. And I suppose I underestimated her.'

'Is she gonna be all right?' Kaz fixed him with a steely look. ''Cause you know full well it was Pudovkin who had Helen Warner murdered.'

'Yes. I know that. In fact, it's part of the reason I agreed to this in the first place.'

'Agreed to what exactly?' Rivlin moved in on him, staring him down.

Blake shook his head wearily as he sank into a chair; everything seemed to be spiralling out of his control and the possibility he could've caused Nicci Armstrong's death was ripping him apart.

He focused on Kaz. 'You know that Nicci and I did our level best to connect Robert Hollister and Viktor Pudovkin with Helen Warner's murder. I practically bankrupted this firm in the process.'

'Yeah, and what Nicci told me was that you was warned off!'

'The Met didn't have the evidence to make a criminal case. But no one gave up. You think that the notion that a foreign national probably had a British Member of Parliament murdered here in London doesn't concern the powers that be? And that's before we even get on to the reasons why he did it.'

Rivlin pitched in. 'What are you saying? There's an ongoing security operation targeting Viktor Pudovkin?'

'Yes.'

'How did you get involved with it?'

Blake shrugged. 'Colin McCain asked me to help. He and I go way back.'

Rivlin gave a bitter shake of the head. 'Why the hell didn't you trust Nicci with this? Don't you and she go way back too?'

'I wanted to. Thames House thought it was too risky.' He glanced at Kaz. 'It was when your brother tried to shoot Pudovkin that the whole thing kicked up a gear.'

'Whatever the fuck you lot think, I didn't ask him to do that.'

Blake sighed. 'The point is, Pudovkin somehow got it into his head that it was a professional hit commissioned by Moscow.'

Kaz chuckled. 'My brother was a lot of things, but I don't see him working for Putin.'

'Might not have been true, but Pudovkin believed it and he was desperate.'

Kaz walked over to the window; she needed time to process this. It was all starting to make sense. Could this be the story Yevgeny had sold Pudovkin? To stop him coming after them and to protect her?

Eddie Lunt folded his arms. 'Well, I listened to the surveillance material between Pudovkin and Naylor. Sounds like SBA is being turned into a front to gather intel.'

Blake nodded. 'That's about the size of it. Pudovkin was on the lookout for a company he could buy out and use. He got nudged in our direction.'

Rivlin was still looming over him. 'What sort of intel?'

'London has more Russian agents today than during the Cold War. But what they're mainly interested in is what their own citizens are up to – all these Russians who are living the high life over here. So Pudovkin came up with the idea of going into competition with his old comrades in the FSB and gathering better information than them on corrupt Russian officials and businessmen and their money-laundering scams. Then he could send it all back home as a gift for Putin.'

Eddie grinned. 'He thought the Kremlin had tried to top him and this is his way of getting them back onside.'

'The operation was to run initially for up to a year.'

'And what do you get out of it? A golden handshake from the government?' Rivlin eyeballed Blake.

'There's obviously a compensation package.'

Rivlin jerked a thumb in Eddie's direction. 'Were any of your employees going to get a share of that?'

Kaz moved back across the room to face the ex-cop. 'Why the hell didn't you tell Nicci?'

'Yeah, I should have. But it was early days. We were only just starting to—'

Eddie was gazing through the glass wall into the reception area, so he saw Naylor first. He spun round to Blake. 'Shit, boss, it's Naylor! I'd forgotten about him.'

But before Blake could respond, Naylor was opening the door. 'Morning, one and all.' The beard bounced, revealing his piratical sneer.

Blake inhaled. 'What did he say?'

'He's being very cagey. Could be they've got her. Could be she's already dead. I didn't want to spook him.'

Rivlin glared at the new arrival. 'Who you talking about?'

'Jerome. He's Pudovkin's gorilla.'

Eddie was watching them with a puzzled frown.

Naylor jabbed a finger at him. 'Yeah, Eddie. Thanks to you and your fucking inquisitive mate, my cover is probably blown. Nearly two years I've been working on Pudovkin, gaining his confidence. I'd only just dangled the bait under his nose.'

'You mean the security job? That Qatari bloke? Turki what's-his-face?'

'Turki bin Qassim. His old man's one of the biggest money-launderers in the Middle East. Handles more looted Russian cash than anyone else. Putin's being such a lairy bastard lately, it was our chance to get the drop on Moscow. But that's all down the fucking toilet now!'

'Sorry.'

'Why couldn't you bloody well do what you were told?' He caught Kaz's eye. 'I'm guessing you're Karen Phelps.'

She nodded.

Naylor gave a wry smile. 'I asked Nic about you. She denied all knowledge, trying to protect you. So I guess she qualifies as a good mate.'

'Yeah. She does.'

He plonked down in a chair and folded his arms. 'Got more balls than anyone I've ever worked with. Hope you lot fucking deserve her.'

78

When Colin McCain finally returned to the conference room it was close to eleven o'clock. Blake had ordered in coffees and pastries, which hadn't been touched, although Eddie had eyed them briefly.

McCain positioned himself at the head of the table and addressed no one in particular. 'Well, here's the situation: Pudovkin won't take any of our calls.'

Rivlin was fidgeting; he could hardly contain his anxiety. 'Is he even at home?'

'Oh yes. Apparently it's his wife's birthday. I persuaded the director to try, which is the equivalent of us begging. That's why it's taken so long. But he's old school KGB, a real canny bastard. He knows when he's got the power. Maybe he had the whole thing sussed all along. So, Craig, we're pulling you out. As of now you're on leave. Shave off the beard, hop on a plane somewhere.'

Kaz put her hands on her hips. 'What about Nicci?'

'We're still talking to the FSB, trying some back channels. But I don't think they've got any pull with Pudovkin.' He sighed. 'And she may already be dead.'

Rivlin seemed about to explode. 'I should've never listened to you. This is a waste of time.'

McCain shrugged. 'If you go back to your colleagues in the Met, you may persuade them to go storming into Pudovkin's mansion. But my guess is they'll refer it up to the Commissioner first. And where's the evidence she's even there? There is none. The Commissioner won't want to deal with the fallout.'

The cop slammed the table with his fist. 'Are we so fucking scared of a Russian billionaire?'

'She's dead, Rivlin.'

'You gutless bunch of—'

'Hang on, mate.' Naylor was lounging at the table. He picked up his vibrating phone and tapped the screen. 'Bingo! A text from Jerome. I thought I'd managed to rattle his cage.'

Blake was standing behind him. 'Read it out!'

'*Package delivered. Basement garage.*'

Rivlin beat everyone else to the door, but Kaz was only a step behind him. They ran across the reception area to the lifts. He slapped the call button with his palm. In the moments it took the lift to arrive, Blake and Eddie caught up with them.

They all piled into the lift. The descent to the basement took less than a minute and a half. No one spoke but Kaz was convinced she could hear her own heart thumping.

The lift doors opened onto a low-ceilinged parking garage, raw concrete walls and a taint of exhaust fumes. Most of the bays were full. Around thirty vehicles were positioned in neat double rows, nose to nose or nose to boot, with an access way looping around them.

Blake took charge. 'Spread out and look!'

Kaz turned to her left and ran along the row of cars, looking in between, under, behind. Reaching the end of the row, she spun round. Then she saw it. Dumped in a corner, a long plastic bundle, the size and shape of a body.

She heard herself scream. 'Over here!'

As she approached, she could see that the bundle was made up of tightly wound, heavy-duty packing tape. It formed a transparent plastic sarcophagus moulded to follow the contours of a human cadaver. She lurched against the wall for support; it was Nicci's mummified corpse.

Feeling the bile rise in her gullet, Kaz had to swallow hard to stop herself puking. Then she heard a sound. A low moan. And it was coming from the bundle.

Stumbling forward, she fell to her knees. Two short drinking straws protruded from the tightly wrapped head.

Rivlin came up behind her. She could hear him panting.

Clawing at the tape, Kaz half turned. 'She's alive! She's alive! We need something to cut!'

He seemed frozen, but only for a second. He shouted to Blake and Eddie. 'A knife – get a fucking knife!'

Eddie Lunt produced a Swiss army knife from his pocket and tossed it to Rivlin, who pulled open the penknife blade. Kneeling beside Kaz, he began to saw away at the thick plastic packing tape that encased the head. As each strand was released she pulled it back to unwind it. They worked quickly and efficiently together.

Nicci was groaning. The plastic was stripped away from her face to reveal a piece of duct tape stuck over each eye. Released from the binding, her parched, cracked lips opened and she gasped for breath.

Kneeling behind her and supporting her, Rivlin eased her into a sitting position as she gulped for air. 'Slowly, Nic. Deep breaths.'

Kaz carefully peeled back the duct tape over each eye. 'It's okay, babes. You're gonna be okay.'

Nicci gave an involuntary shudder as her eyes flew open. She blinked several times, then stared up blindly in wild, black terror.

Rivlin cradled her. 'It's okay, Nic. You're safe now. You're safe.'

With a steady hand, Kaz drew the straws from each blood-caked nostril. Nicci yowled in pain, a feral wail that was barely human. Rivlin gently rocked her. 'It's okay, it's okay.' Tears were streaming down his face.

Blake had his phone in his hand and a look of total shock on his face as he called an ambulance.

Eddie patted his arm. 'I'm gonna get some water. I'll be back.'

With Rivlin behind Nicci, holding her in his arms and strok-ing her hair, Kaz began to cut and hack her way through the plastic coils still imprisoning her torso and legs. Blake crouched beside her, ripping off each strand as Kaz cut through it.

Nicci was only wearing a bra and pants and the bindings had left deep welts in her flesh. Rivlin slipped off his jacket and wrapped it around her.

Returning with a bottle of water, Eddie handed it to Rivlin. Naylor and McCain were right behind him. They stared in disbelief.

Naylor punched his palm with his own fist. 'That fucking bastard's laughing at us.'

As Rivlin fed her the water, Nicci spluttered and choked in her desperation to guzzle it down. He stroked her face. 'Easy. Not too much at once.'

Finally Kaz hacked through the last piece of tape round her feet and Nicci was released from her plastic shroud. Kaz rocked back on her heels; freeing her friend had taken the best part of ten minutes.

With a keening sob, Nicci rolled over onto her side and drew her knees up to her chest in a foetal hug. Then she urinated, warm piss puddling out around her on the rough concrete.

79

Kaz lost track of time as she walked. From SBA's offices, along Cheapside, she wound her way down through the City to the river. She felt frozen and numb and, having lost a night's sleep, totally enervated, but moving, putting one foot in front of the other, seemed to help.

When the paramedics had arrived they'd given Nicci oxygen, wrapped her in a silver space blanket and whisked her away to the A&E at the Royal London. She was in deep shock and remained unable to speak. A bruised puncture mark in her neck suggested she'd been injected to knock her out. She was probably still suffering from the effects of the drug.

Rivlin went with her in the ambulance. Blake waited for the police and took steps to preserve the scene of the crime, although there was considerable doubt as to what follow-up there would be to any investigation.

Eddie offered to drive Kaz home, but she declined. What had been done to Nicci was a warning, a statement, in case there was any doubt, of what happened to those who crossed Viktor Pudovkin. Kaz felt sick, not with fear but with rage. And there was nowhere for that feeling to go. So she walked.

Having crossed the river at Southwark Bridge, she took the riverside walk along the South Bank. The tide was high, the choppy waters slapping up against the embankment wall. But Kaz remained oblivious to everything outside her own seething brain. Should she go to the airport, get on a plane, now, tonight? Yes, she should have the sense to do what Nicci hadn't done. She should run.

As she passed Westminster Bridge and the back of St Thomas' Hospital it started to rain, a sudden torrential downpour. In moments she was drenched. Hair plastered to her face, she kept on walking. When she reached Vauxhall Cross, and realized that the brutal post-modernist monstrosity looming over her was the headquarters of MI6, she thought of McCain. She hadn't understood all the ins and outs of the supposed security operation that, with Blake's help, he'd been trying to run against Pudovkin. But one thing was clear: it had been about as effective as a fleabite on an elephant.

Continuing down Nine Elms Lane past the hulk of the old power station, new luxury blocks sprouting around it, she began to feel energized. She'd walked through her exhaustion and onto a calmer plateau. Her anger had risen up from her gut and now it was singing in her ears. In her mind, thoughts were less chaotic and random. Her whole body seemed lighter.

The rain had eased to a fine drizzle; she was wet but quite warm as she walked through Battersea. She wondered what she should do next. Was there any need to panic? What had happened to Nicci was pretty shocking. But it was designed to terrorize and subdue, and she refused to be intimidated.

Reaching the apartment block, she greeted the concierge almost cheerfully.

He smiled. 'The Russian lady didn't have her key. I let her in, I hope that's okay.'

Irina. She'd totally forgotten about Irina.

As she unlocked the door and walked into the apartment she called out, 'Irina!'

The Russian appeared in a bathrobe with her hair wrapped in a towel. 'Where the fuck you been? We need get ready.'

'Get ready for what?'

'I say you before. Alexei help us. He get for us invite to party.'

'I don't think I'm quite in the mood for a party, babes.'

'Is birthday of Galina.'

Kaz was peeling off her sodden jacket; this stopped her in her tracks. 'Pudovkin's wife?'

'Yes, sure, his wife.' Kaz's obtuseness was irritating to Irina. 'I say you before, we go and she make things right. No have to run. No peasant house in Spain.' Irina beamed in the expectation of praise.

But Kaz couldn't even manage a smile. She strode into the kitchen, took a mug from the drainer and filled it with water from the tap. Was this a trap or a random coincidence? It was impossible to tell.

Irina pursued her. 'Kaz! I fucking do this for you!'

Drinking down the water, Kaz became aware of her heart pounding in her chest.

Irina stood in front of her, looking petulant. 'I fix for you, babes.'

Kaz stared at her so-called girlfriend. Had she been suckered? Was Irina working for Pudovkin? But why would she? She'd been hiding out with Mika until Kaz rescued her, and she had every reason to hate Pudovkin – her brother Tolya had also been gunned down by his goons.

'I fix. Like I promise.'

'Yeah, I heard you.' Kaz put the empty mug down on the counter with a snap.

Her head was full once again of Nicci, alive but embalmed in a plastic shroud, fighting for every breath through two tiny straws. Then she thought of Helen, her bloated corpse washed up like a sack of rubbish. And her brother Joey, her beautiful but crazy brother, shot dead in a London street.

The colour had drained from her cheeks, but she turned to Irina and painted on a smile. 'Okay, fuck it! We're going to a party!'

80

Alexei was older than Kaz had imagined. Close to forty, with a receding hairline, he had an air of solidity and reliability about him, which was probably what appealed to Irina. He picked them up in a vintage Jaguar XJS; it was a dirty bronze colour with white leather upholstery. In a dinner jacket and a dicky bow, he looked every inch the English gentleman, apart from the Russian accent.

Kaz and Irina had been through the whole of the latter's wardrobe to find something suitable for Kaz to wear. Irina favoured a slinky dress and made Kaz try several on. But Kaz settled on sparkly leggings, a silk tunic top and black patent boots. There was no way she was wearing heels. If she needed to, she wanted to be able to run.

As they pulled up outside the Holland Park mansion, Kaz thought about Joey. The street outside Pudovkin's house was the spot where her brother and Tolya had died. But on this damp October evening it was full of minders armed with umbrellas and a roster of drivers to valet-park guests' cars for them.

Following Irina and Alexei up the steps and through the front door into the palatial hall, Kaz was surprised at how calm she felt. There were waiters with trays of champagne to greet them and a stream of overdressed, over-exuberant partygoers preceding them in a slow procession through several rooms to the huge drawing room at the back of the house.

The babble of conversation, in English and Russian, swirled around Kaz. Irina was holding Alexei's hand and chatting animatedly to him in their own language. Kaz felt like a gooseberry; her fantasy of a life with Irina was, she realized, just that.

The only girl and the youngest in the family, Irina had grown up petted and protected by her brothers. She was flirtatious with everyone, that was her nature. But she was also a user.

Kaz knew her declaration of love to the Russian had been foolish. And was it even true? She'd wanted to rescue Irina, certainly. But was that necessarily the same thing as being in love? Since Helen Warner's death she'd felt so lonely. And when she'd lost Joey, too, a chasm had opened up in her life. She stood alone on a precipice. Ordinary happiness felt out of reach. Had the pain of too much loss simply left her coldhearted? She wondered about that.

In the drawing room, Galina Pudovkin was holding court. Guests were queuing to wish her a happy birthday. The gifts and cards she received were handed over to her assistant, who piled them on a table. As they waited their turn, Kaz speculated on what you could possibly give a billionaire's wife for her birthday. Alexei was carrying a small gift-wrapped box. Perhaps it was the thought that counted.

They moved into pole position and Alexei stepped forward to air-kiss their hostess. The process struck Kaz as something akin to meeting royalty. Smiles, some chat in Russian, Irina was introduced and embraced.

Then Alexei drew Kaz forward. 'And this is our good friend, Karen.'

Kaz beamed. 'Happy birthday.'

Galina's eyes flickered briefly over her. If she had any clue at all as to who Kaz was, she gave no hint of it. She tossed her silky mane and her smile was toothy and wide. 'I love London so much. New English friends are always welcome.' And that was it, audience over; they moved on.

In the adjoining dining room a huge buffet had been laid out. Chefs were serving guests and plates were piled high. Kaz soon got fed up with trailing around after Irina and Alexei. Any pretence that Galina would be asked to intercede with her husband on Kaz's behalf seemed to have been abandoned. As they made for the food, Kaz hung back and, letting them go, drifted off into the crowd.

Why had she even agreed to come? She wasn't sure she knew any more. To please Irina? To get a closer look at the man who'd created such mayhem in her life? Maybe to finish the job her brother had started?

As she wandered among some of the richest people in London, she felt oddly serene. The fact she could walk in here undetected showed there was a chink in the impenetrable armour of wealth in which a man like Pudovkin encased himself. You couldn't exactly frisk all your VIP mates at the door, it would be rude. So if they were HNWIs like you, courtesy obliged you to trust them.

At a rough estimate Kaz reckoned there were about a hundred guests milling around; designer frocks and ostentatious jewellery abounded. They were served by an army of waiters and kept safe by a dozen men in dark suits with earpieces. She strolled through several rooms on the lookout for Pudovkin himself. Having been introduced to him once by Yevgeny, she wondered if he would recognize her. There didn't appear to be any sign of him, although his two children were dashing around and playing tag with some playmates of their own age.

An obese, rather drunken Russian was eyeing her lasciviously. When he started to follow her, Kaz returned to the dining room to get some food. The aromas wafting up from the tables reminded her that she hadn't eaten for quite a while. The delicate flavour combinations and artistry of the offerings were designed to excite even the most jaded palate. Kaz couldn't put a name to half the items on her plate, but she tucked in with relish.

As she ate, she continued to scan the room. That was when she saw him. Robert Hollister was standing in the doorway to the drawing room and staring straight at her. Their eyes met and for a full fifteen seconds he held her gaze. The expression of surprise on his face turned to disgust and fury as he glared at the slag who'd ruined his life. Then he turned and grabbed the sleeve of one of the security men standing nearby.

The security man was a large black guy. He bent his head to listen to Hollister, who gestured in Kaz's direction. Dumping her plate on the nearest table, Kaz didn't hang around to see more. She slipped seamlessly through the throng and out into a corridor. Waylaying a passing waiter, she asked where the toilets were. He pointed up a flight of stairs. She ran up them two at a time, turned into the upstairs hallway and waited a moment. Cautiously peering back round the corner, she glanced down the staircase. The security man and Hollister were below, searching.

Ducking back, she continued down the hall until she came to a door with a printed notice in Cyrillic script tacked to it; she assumed this was the toilet. She opened the door and found herself in a small but luxurious bathroom. It had another door, which led to what looked like a guest bedroom.

Having locked both doors, she dropped her diamanté clutch bag on the floor and pulled off her tunic top. Taped to the small of her back, with its muzzle tucked into the waistband of her leggings, was the Sig P220 she'd retrieved from the safe deposit box. She'd brought this as a precaution. Having seen what Pudovkin's thugs had done to Nicci, she didn't fancy getting caught by them.

Ripping off the tape, she removed the gun and suppressor, clicked the magazine release, checked the cartridges were loaded and snapped the magazine back into the heel of the pistol. She put her tunic on again, screwed the suppressor on to the barrel, slipped the gun into her clutch bag and tucked it under her arm.

She could hear approaching footfalls in the hall. Unlocking the bathroom door, she went through into the guest bedroom, locked the connecting door behind her and waited. The door to the bathroom opened and then shut again. The footfalls retreated.

Counting in her head calmed the butterflies in her stomach and gave her focus. When she got to two hundred she opened the bedroom door and stepped out into the hall. The last person she'd expected to see at the party was Robert Fucking Hollister. Surely he'd been arrested. Maybe he was out on bail. Still, seeing him there, socializing with these rich tossers and acting as though it was business as usual, incensed her deeply.

Her pulse racing, mainly from anger, she strode down the hall, hoping to find another way out. Turning a corner she saw them before they noticed her. Pudovkin – she was sure it was him – was standing in an open doorway.

In front of him was an agitated Hollister. 'We had a deal, Viktor.'

'Calm down, my friend.' The Russian patted his shoulder. 'If you are right, Jerome will find her and sort it out.'

'I know I'm—'

'Yeah, actually he is.'

Both men spun round at the sound of her voice. Kaz was holding the Sig at arm's length, grasping it lightly with both hands and pointing it straight at them.

She walked slowly towards them. 'What's in there?'

A sardonic smile curled Pudovkin's lip. 'My study.'

'Go in. Slowly!'

Hollister looked petrified as Kaz came right up to him and held the gun to his head. 'You too.'

Pudovkin moved into the room and Kaz shoved Hollister after him. It was furnished in the style of an executive office suite with a large glass desk, several computers and a lot of leather and chrome.

She nudged the door closed with her foot. 'Put your hands behind your heads.'

Hollister complied immediately. He was shaking.

The Russian took his time. 'Have you thought this through, Karen? This room is of course covered by CCTV cameras, so within about two, three minutes at most, there'll be an armed response.'

It was a ridiculous question. Of course she hadn't thought it through. It was an impulsive gut reaction and, even though she was pressing the muzzle of the gun into Hollister's temple, she was already regretting it. 'How come you've invited this paedo to your party?'

'Why wouldn't I? All the charges against Robert have been dropped.'

Kaz dragged Hollister by his collar until she'd positioned herself, back to the wall and facing the door. She had no choice now but to play the scene out. In a couple of minutes she'd probably be dead. But there was a part of her that didn't care. With any luck, she'd have the satisfaction of taking this scumbag with her. That would be something at least, some payback for Helen.

The sweat was pouring off him. 'Don't shoot me, I'm begging you. I didn't have Helen killed. He did.'

Pudovkin chuckled. 'I think we would agree on one thing, Karen: he is a gutless individual.'

'And you're not? You just have others do your dirty work.' It was surprising to her how very calm she felt.

'Now, yes. But I spent many years in the field before perestroika. Anyone can kill in anger, but to look into someone's eyes and execute them in cold blood, that's a talent. Could you do it?'

'My brother could. I'm not like him, though. I may be a killer, but I'm not a murderer.'

'That's an interesting distinction.' The Russian seemed to be musing on this notion. Or was he merely waiting? They both knew the clock was ticking.

And all her senses were heightened. Her eyes darted about, noticing everything: the warm pool of light from the desk lamp, the texture of the paint on the Picasso hanging on the wall. Time stretched and she realized how fluid it was, not absolute at all. Did everyone's life end like this, with a burst of feelings and impressions?

It was all over in less than a minute. The door inched open, then was flung back. Jerome stood there brandishing a gun.

'Shoot them both!' Pudovkin barked his order.

As Jerome fired, Kaz propelled Hollister forward to shield herself. Jerome's first two shots struck the politician in the chest and neck. In the same instant the Sig's double action pumped two bullets into Jerome's gut. Raising and steadying her arm, Kaz's third shot struck him in the centre of the forehead. He went down with a heavy thud.

Flinging Hollister's inert body aside she swung round towards Pudovkin. As soon as the shooting started he'd gone for the filing cabinet drawer behind him. Hauling it open, he pulled out a gun.

His arm came up to shoot but she jumped sideways as they both fired. His bullet whizzed past her head, hers tore into his shoulder and he was thrown backwards to the floor.

Taking two strides forward, she stood over him. Clutching his shoulder, he uttered a curse in Russian.

Then he looked up at her. 'You stupid bitch, you'll never get out of here.'

Her nerve endings were singing. The serenity she felt was blissful. It was the thrill of still being alive. Would he beg? She doubted it, although she could smell his fear.

'Maybe I do have the talent. Let's see, shall we?'

Her dark eyes locked onto his and pointing the pistol at his forehead she squeezed the trigger and fired. Blood sprayed up and out in a fine mist.

Wiping her face with her sleeve she glanced around and took stock. Hollister was dead, his sightless eyes staring at the ceiling. Jerome's corpse blocked the doorway. Stepping over it, she peered out. The hall was empty. Music drifted upwards from the famous string quartet playing in the drawing room below. Sliding the gun into her bag, she tucked the bag under her arm and walked away.

EPILOGUE

DI Tom Rivlin met Kaz Phelps at the main entrance. Both felt awkward; he offered her his hand.

She shook it. 'How's she doing?'

'Good, I think. She's hyper-vigilant. Gets really bad nightmares. But the trauma specialist thinks she's doing well.'

Nicci Armstrong had been diagnosed with post-traumatic stress disorder and admitted to the Nightingale in Marylebone, a private acute mental health hospital; Simon Blake was picking up the bill.

'You sure it's okay for me to visit?'

The cop nodded. 'Absolutely. I told her you were coming. She was really pleased.'

'You're sticking around then?'

He gave her a side-eyed glance. 'Why wouldn't I stick around?'

'She deserves something good in her life. Don't fuck her over, will you?'

'My boss, DCI Stoneham, said a similar thing.'

'At least we agree on that.'

They walked through the foyer and down several corridors.

Rivlin finally broke the silence. 'You seen the news? Pudovkin got his comeuppance.'

Kaz frowned. 'Yeah, what happened there? You know anything about it?'

'It happened at his wife's birthday party. Quite a shoot-out. Pudovkin was killed, plus one of his bodyguards – a Brit – and Robert Hollister, the politician.'

'Blimey! Do the police know who did it?'

'The Met's inquiries are ongoing, as they say. But according to Blake, the security service reckons Moscow decided he'd got too big for his boots and the FSB whacked him.'

Kaz allowed herself a small smile. 'Hard to feel sorry.'

'For him, I agree. But there were two other victims, both British citizens. So there'll be a robust response. Not that it'll get very far. You can pretty much guarantee that the killers caught the next plane home. And, as with the Litvinenko case, even if we can name them, the Russians will never agree to their extradition.'

'What will happen then?'

'Bit of diplomatic posturing. It's infuriating, but there's not much else we can do. What you won't have read about in the news is that a few days ago, another body turned up.'

'Who?' Kaz tried not to look surprised.

'Bloke called Ahmad Karim. Lebanese. Found him on the rocks at Beachy Head. But it wasn't a suicide.'

'How do they know?'

'He was missing his fingernails. He was also an MI6 asset. McCain and Naylor used him to hook Pudovkin into their intel-gathering scheme. I got this from Blake, in confidence.'

'Then why you telling me?'

Rivlin raked a hand through his hair and sighed. 'Oh, I don't know. 'Cause what happened to Nicci was their fault? And 'cause, frankly, the whole thing pisses me off.' There was no mistaking the bitterness in his tone. 'Ex-cops turned spooks? There's no justification for it. It's all a political fucking power game.'

'So who killed this bloke?'

'FSB probably. The theory is, that's how they figured out what Pudovkin was up to and that's what led to the birthday party shoot-out.'

Kaz Phelps gave him a ghostly smile. 'Makes sense, I suppose.'

They'd reached the door to Nicci's private room. Rivlin tapped softly and opened it.

Nicci was sitting, feet tucked under, in a large armchair listening to music. As the door opened she started, but she soon relaxed as she recognized them and held out her hand to Kaz. 'Hey, come in.' She pulled out the earbuds.

Rivlin smiled. 'I'll leave you two to chat.' He disappeared.

'You look better than I expected.' Kaz drew up a chair.

Nicci chuckled. 'Yeah, not bad for a mummified corpse.'

'I'm surprised you can even talk about it.'

'Therapy. We talk about everything here. Yak, yak, yak – it's knackering. But, hey, I'm glad you came. I wanted to say thanks.'

Kaz shrugged.

'If it hadn't been for you and Eddie—'

'I think you should cut Eddie some slack. He's not a bad bloke.'

'I realize that.' She pointed to the enormous bouquet of flowers on the chest of drawers. 'That's from him. But then, he'll know a bloke who could do him a deal.'

They both laughed.

'It's the way the world goes round, Nicci.'

'Yeah. You could be right. You heard about Pudovkin?'

'Bit of a turn-up.'

Nicci met Kaz's gaze directly. 'Certainly is. What do you make of it?'

'Cops seem to think he upset the Kremlin. Who knows?'

'Yeah. Blake came to see me. Told me the ins and outs. Sounds complicated.'

'Yeah.'

Nicci's eyes rested on her friend and, not for the first time, she wondered. 'Hollister was shot too. Apparently the CPS had decided there wasn't enough evidence to bring a case against him for what he did to Helen Warner.'

'Really? Scumbags always get away with it, don't they?'

'Not this time.' Nicci stared at her hard, the way a cop scrutinizes a suspect; she'd had plenty of practice. But Kaz didn't waiver, she simply stared back and smiled. 'No, not this time.'

The two women sat facing each other for a moment. Nicci Armstrong reflected that she'd never really been able to fathom what Karen Phelps was thinking. She remained a closed book. But did that really matter?

She smiled. 'I'm hoping, once they sign me off here, to rejoin the police service.'

'Probably safer.'

'Yeah, I'm going to stick within the law from now on. What about you?'

'I'm going to live with my sister. She's got a little boy now. And I'm going back to studying art. Abroad maybe, if I can get permission from the probation service.'

'Maybe one day you can send me one of your pictures.'

Kaz smiled but her dark eyes remained inscrutable. 'Yeah, maybe I will.'

ACKNOWLEDGEMENTS

This is my third novel and completes a trilogy which began with *The Informant*. Once again I have relied on the generosity and expertise of various people. My good friend GC remains indispensable. Stuart McCall, a former police officer, was patient and thorough in his explanation of the world of cyber-crime. Former Chief Superintendent Graham Bartlett has been an invaluable resource both in terms of providing information and of critiquing the final manuscript.

The team at Pan Macmillan have continued to give me sterling support. I have relied, once again, on the excellent advice and guidance of my editor, Trisha Jackson, assisted by Phoebe Taylor. James Annal produced a great cover, Emma Bravo led a first-rate marketing campaign, while Stuart Dwyer and his sales team got the books out there and on the shelves. Laura Carr and Anne O'Brien were meticulous copy-editors. They have taught me a good deal about grammar and syntax. But the mistakes and quirks remain my responsibility alone.

My agent, Jane Gregory, backed by an able team, is both a counsellor and a champion. Last but not least my two first readers, Sue Kenyon and Jenny Kenyon, continue to challenge and support me and bring me cups of tea. Thanks to all of you.

THE INFORMANT
by Susan Wilkins

Corrupt cops. Ruthless criminals. Obsessive love.

As a drug-fuelled teenage tearaway, Kaz Phelps took the rap for her little brother, Joey, over a bungled armed robbery, and went to jail.

Six years later she's released on licence. Clean and sober, and driven by a secret passion for her lawyer, Helen, Kaz wants to escape the violence and abuse of her Essex gangster family.

Joey is a charming, calculating and cold psychopath. He worships the ground his sister walks on and he's desperate to get her back in the family firm. But all Kaz wants is a fresh start and to put the past behind her.

When Joey murders an undercover cop, DS Nicci Armstrong is determined to put him behind bars. What she doesn't realize is that their efforts are being sabotaged by one of their own.

The final test for Kaz comes when her cousin, Sean, gets out of jail. A vicious, old-school thug, he wants to put the girl back in her place. But can Kaz face him down and get her life back?

THE MOURNER
by Susan Wilkins

A murder dressed up as suicide. Corruption that goes to the heart of government. Ex-con and ex-cop unite in a dangerous quest to discover the truth. What they expose proves what both have always known: villainy is rife on both sides of the law.

Kaz

Living anonymously under the witness protection scheme to escape her brother and her criminal past, Kaz Phelps is striving to achieve the freedom she craves. Her ex-lover and ex-lawyer, Helen Warner, is now a rising star in parliament, but it seems she's made enemies on her way up that have no regard for the law.

Joey

Banged up and brooding, Joey Phelps faces thirty years behind bars. He's got cash and connections on the outside, and he's plotting revenge. He wants to find the person he's closest to – and the one who betrayed him.

Nicci

Ousted from the police and paralysed by a tragic and personal loss, Nicci Armstrong is in danger of going under. But maybe a job with an ex-colleague will help her to put her life back on track?

If you enjoyed *The Killer*,
read on for an extract from
the first book in the trilogy,
The Informant

PROLOGUE

Seeing them go, that's what really did it for Joey. The moment of death, if he could just glimpse it. But the eyes had to be open; he liked it best when the pupils were wide with terror. Then, one click, the screen went blank. They were gone and that vacant stare shot through him like two hundred and fifty volts. Better than crack, better than charlie, way better than shagging. It was the ultimate hit. It was the power. Game over, you'd won. They were meat, you were the butcher.

Joey stood over Marlow, nerve ends zinging, his cock stirring in anticipation. Marlow fingered his broken nose, blood dripped onto the concrete floor. Joey unclenched his fist, rubbed his knuckles. He was in no hurry. He enjoyed a bit of foreplay.

'So you gonna tell me the truth now?'

Marlow looked up at him, trying to gauge his mood. He had to make his next words count.

'Seriously Joe, what is this about? Someone's got their wires crossed here.'

Joey smiled. He seemed relaxed, unconcerned even.

'You reckon?'

Built like a bruiser, face like an angel, Joey Phelps had charm to spare. Even as a small boy he had drawn people to him; those hypnotic baby-blue eyes under thick sandy lashes, his quirky smile. Joey reached into his jeans pocket, pulled out a neat wedge of folded tissues, squatted down beside Marlow.

SUSAN WILKINS

'Here. Clean yourself up.'

Marlow took the tissues warily, wincing as he pressed them to his nose.

Straightening up, Joey thrust both hands in his pockets and took a leisurely turn about the lock-up. The night air seeping under the door was chilly and dank. He gazed up at the vaulted arch of the ceiling, row upon row of blackened bricks, laid maybe a hundred and fifty years before to carry the railway from the smoke to the suburbs. Joey peered around; he knew he could take his time, savour his power.

'Look at this place. You ever think about the blokes that built the railways?'

The remark hung in the air. Marlow glanced from Joey to Ashley. Ashley, as usual, was waiting on Joey's next move. He was picking his teeth. He'd seen some actor do this in a clip from an old film he'd streamed, thought it looked cool.

'All them millions of bricks to lay. Now *that* was grafting.'

Marlow eased himself up into a sitting position and rested his back against the wall. He could feel the dampness through his shirt; icy cold, it seeped through his flesh, chilling him to the heart. He knew that Joey was toying with him. He'd suspected for almost a week now that his cover had been blown. But when Joey and Ashley had called for him that evening, full of laddish high spirits, his fears had been allayed. They'd been clubbing, done a couple of lines, had a few beers. They were going on to a party, some soap actress Joey had been shagging. Then Joey announced he needed to make a quick stop.

Marlow cursed his own stupidity, he really should've guessed. He was twenty-nine years old, he had parents, retired now to Swanage, two older sisters. How would they cope with all this? Should he cry? Should he beg? He sucked in a few deep breaths to calm himself; exhaust fumes from the nearby main road, rancid fat from the kebab shop on the corner. The smells of London were suddenly all there, flooding his senses in both reality and in memory. And he was sure of one thing: he didn't want to die.

'Listen Joe, I dunno what lying bastard's been telling tales about me, but—'

The silver toecap of Joey's handmade boot caught him squarely in the temple. His head jarred with the impact and ricocheted back against the wall. Joey gazed at him calmly.

'The Net's a wonderful thing, innit? I got a couple of illegals who're dead clever with all that. Hack into anything. They hacked into your file ... Detective Sergeant. A Commissioner's commendation. Ash was impressed. Weren't you Ash?'

Ashley, intent on quarrying with his toothpick, simply nodded. Dazed from the blow, Marlow lurched forward and vomited on the floor. Joey watched, a smile of amusement and expectation spreading across his face, as if he were waiting for the punchline to a joke.

'You ain't gonna deny it then?'

Marlow wiped a shaky hand across his mouth, raised his head slowly. His gaze was watery but unflinching.

'You're a psycho Phelps. A real nut-job.'

'Yeah?' Joey laughed. 'Hear that Ash? I'm a nut-job.'

Ashley slipped the toothpick in his pocket, glanced at Joey, the blue eyes shining iridescent, sweat beading on his upper lip. Joey smiled.

'Nah mate, you're the sucker here. No one plays me.'

Ashley pulled a pair of vinyl gloves from the back pocket of his jeans and calmly drew them on. Now it was really going to kick off. Joey selected a tyre iron from the tools on the workbench, weighed it in his hand. Marlow swallowed hard, glanced at the door and the tantalizing chink of neon beyond; it was worth a shot.

As Marlow scrabbled to his feet Joey slammed the tyre iron down on top of his skull, cracking it open. He lifted the iron and blood gushed up over splintered bone and the ruptured pearlescent membrane of the cerebral cortex. Joey seized Marlow's jaw, twisted the face round to look right at him – the eyelids drooped. Marlow had already slipped into unconsciousness. Joey shook him with frustration. He wanted to see, but it was too late. Shoving him away Joey took another couple of swings. Ashley watched in annoyance. He was going to have to clean this lot up. He huffed.

'Yeah all right. I think that's done the trick.'

Joey paused and turned. Ashley caught a look of feral rage and quickly stepped back. Joey's breathing was fast and shallow. His heart thumped. He closed his eyes. Ashley had seen this enough times before, yet still he never knew how to react. He focused on the blood puddling out round the lumps and bumps in the concrete.

'I'll get them bin bags out the car, shall I?'

Joey ignored him, the tyre iron clattering to the floor. He let his arms hang loose. He inhaled slowly. His shoulders sagged as the tension in his muscles slackened. Ashley stood rooted to the spot; he wasn't going to risk the noise of the door. After a couple of moments Joey opened his eyes. Ashley held his breath then Joey grinned broadly.

'Fuck me, what a blast!'

Ashley's nerves evaporated. He grinned too and laughed. 'Yeah! Wow!'

Joey filled his lungs, hooted with joy. 'Fucking bastards! They think they can get me. Send all the fucking shit-eating filth you like. I'm Joey Fucking Phelps. And you'll *never* get me!'

1

A pair of brown eyes stared directly at Kaz. Not solid brown, more muddy spiked with flecks of amber. The look itself was harder to read; some anger, resentment certainly, but behind that a void, a hollow of despair.

Kaz returned the look with her own searching gaze. Then she selected a pencil from the battered tin box, a 2B, she always started with a 2B. Opening the sketchbook to a fresh page she rapidly plotted out the main features. The eyes first. Her hand moved across the sheet of one-twenty gram cartridge with practised assurance. Her own eyes darted from the face in front of her down to the drawing and back again.

Yasmin's brow furrowed.

'Dunno why you don't just take a picture.'

'This is better. You see more.'

The contours of the head, the nose, the planes of the cheek were quickly taking shape. Kaz paused and forced herself to look harder. She was missing something. Was it in the angle of the chin? Somewhere deep in the gene pool below the whores and the drug mules, the servants and slaves, there lurked a Nubian princess, mistress of all she surveyed. And that pride was still there in the tilt of Yasmin's battered jaw. Kaz smiled to herself, adjusted the line.

A key clanked in the lock and the cell door swung open. A

prison officer stood there. It was Fat Pat. A short bundle of venom, she'd always had it in for Kaz.

'You ready then Phelps?'

Kaz closed the sketchbook and slipped it with the tin of pencils into the plastic carrier at her feet. She stood up and smiled awkwardly at Yasmin. Yasmin rose stiffly and opened her arms.

'Be lucky babe . . .'

Kaz stepped into the hug.

'You be out yourself soon.'

'Yeah and he be there waiting for me. Nah, I'm better off where I am. Least I got no broken bones.'

Fat Pat marched Kaz down the corridor. Being escorted was an all too familiar routine: walk in front, wait, the body odour and rasping Lycra as Pat waddled along behind. Kaz stopped at the door to the block and stood aside for Pat to unlock it. She towered over Pat by at least five inches. At first the daily sessions in the gym had been an outlet for her pent-up rage. Later it had become part of her discipline, the way forward, the way out. At twenty-five she was certainly the fittest she'd ever been; more importantly she was four years clean and sober. And she planned to stay that way.

Pat glared up at her. Kaz returned the look with a steady gaze.

'Y'know Phelps, you may fool the shrinks, your offender manager and the parole board. But you don't fool me. You're pure evil. Clever, I'll give you that. But underneath it all, evil.'

'Well you know better than any of them, don't you Pat? All them smarmy gits with degrees that get paid shedloads more than you.'

Kaz could see Pat rising to the bait, she always did. Her neck flushed, her cheeks reddened.

'The Lord will smite thee Phelps! He will cast down the ungodly into the pit of hell!'

'What's that bit in the Bible, Pat? Something about more joy in heaven over one sinner that repents? You should check it out.'

Pat's eyes glistened with hate.

'You'll be back on crack in a week. You won't be able to help yourself.'

Kaz smiled equably. Through the door her freedom was waiting. She felt almost high, suffused with the natural joy of being alive. She took a deep breath and wished she could hold on to this precious feeling, this golden moment. For she knew one thing for certain: it wouldn't last. Once she stepped outside there would be no respite, it would all begin again.